STEEL

FIRE & STEEL

KING'S BANE

C. R. MAY

COPYRIGHT

This novel is a work of fiction. The names, characters and incidents portrayed in it, while at times based on real figures, are purely the work of the author's imagination.
It is sold subject to the condition that it shall not by way of trade or otherwise, be lent, resold, hired out, or otherwise circulated without the writer's prior consent, electronically or in any form of binding or cover other than the form in which it is published and without a similar condition including this condition being imposed on the subsequent purchaser. Replication or distribution of any part is strictly prohibited without the written permission of the copyright holder.

Copyright © 2016 C. R. May
All rights reserved.

ISBN-10: 1519600496
ISBN-13: 978-1519600493

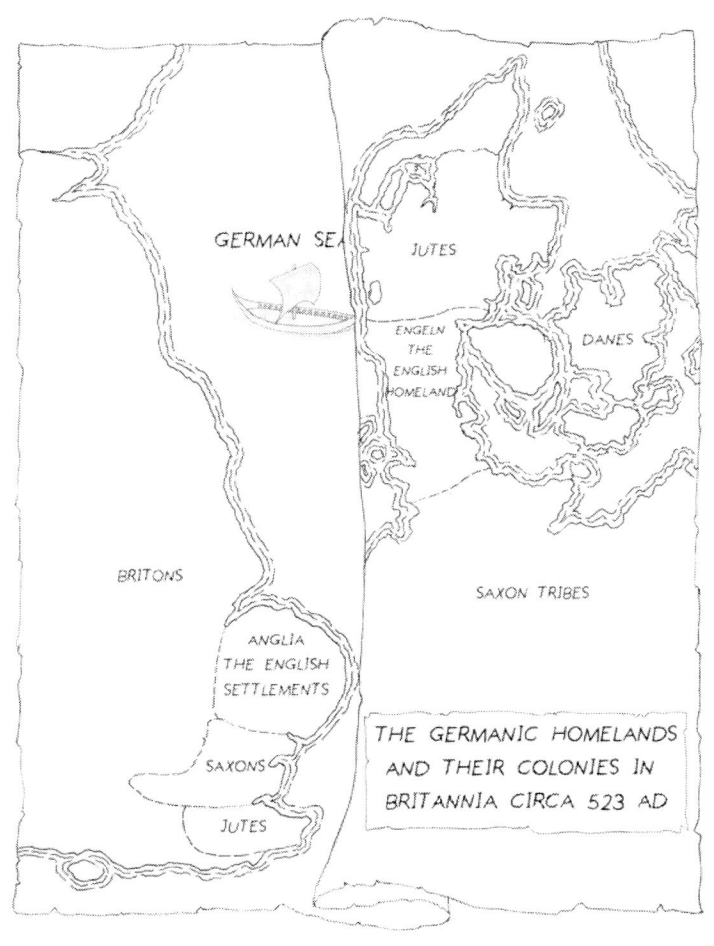

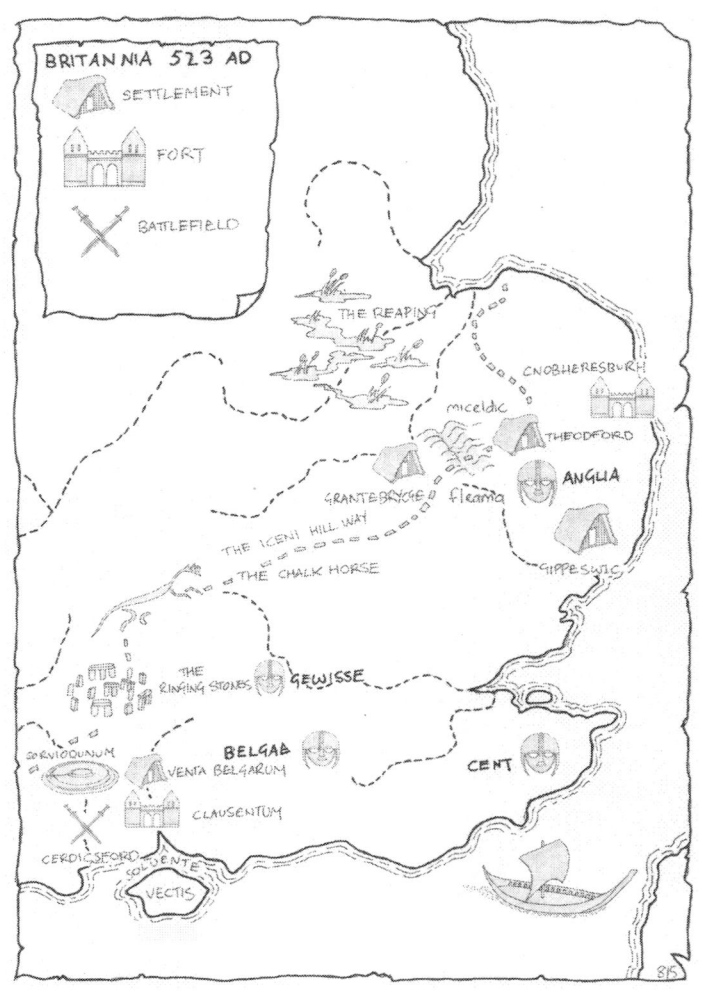

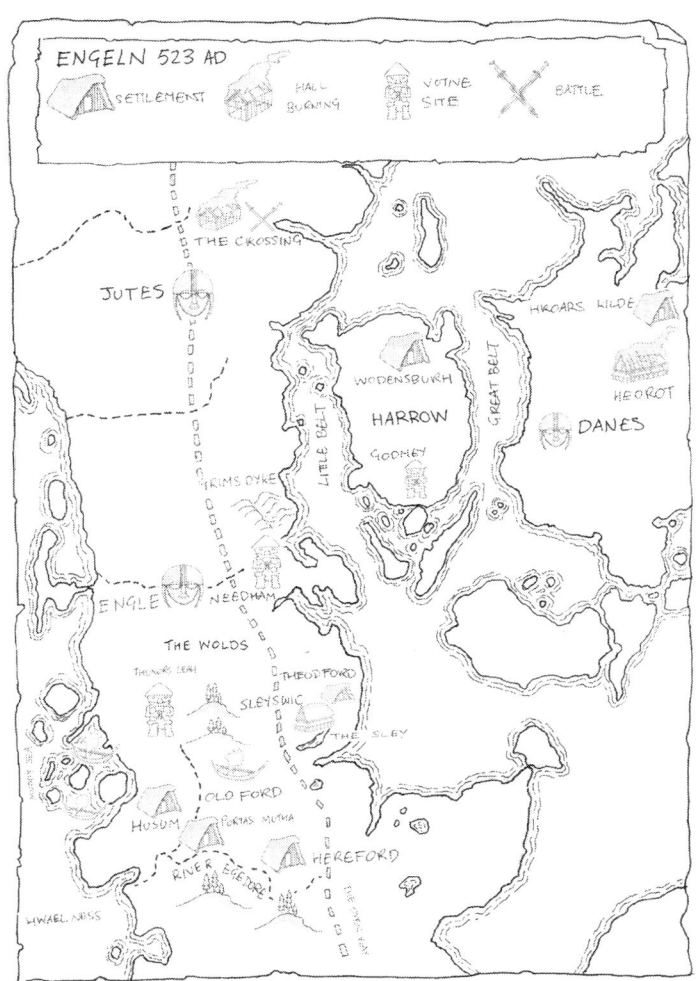

GLOSSARY

Duguth—Doughty men, veteran fighters.

Ealdorman—A provincial governor.

Eorle—A hero.

Fiend—The enemy.

Folctoga—A leader in war, the ancient English equivalent to a General or Field Marshal.

Gesithas—The king's closest companions, a bodyguard.

Guda—A male priest/holy man.

Scegth—A light warship.

Scop—A poet/word smith, usually itinerant.

Snaca—Snake, a larger warship, forerunner of the later Viking period dragon ship, the 'Drakkar'.

Thegn—A nobleman with military obligations.

Wælcyrge—Valkyrie.

Wicingas—Vikings.

*Hroþwulf ond Hroðgar heoldon lengest
sibbe ætsomne suhtorfædran,
siþþan hy forwræcon wicinga cynn
ond Ingeldes ord forbigdan,
forheowan æt Heorote Heaðobeardna þrym.*

*Hrothwulf and Hrothgar held the longest
peace together, uncle and nephew,
since they repulsed the viking kin
hewn at Heorot Heathobeards army and Ingeld
to the spear-point made bow.*

Widsith

PROLOGUE

The island of Harrow, Engeln.
Five miles north of Godmey,
AD523: Hærfestmonth.

'Death haunts us,' the rider murmured as he gained the boundary ditch. The horse blew out after the mad dash down from the hills, the wet slap of its lips loud in the desolation.

His eyes scanned the settlement as the others moved into a skirmish line. In the muted light of the early dawn, the hamlet looked like the others. Doors hung crazily from twisted hinges, the stout door posts among the only timbers to survive the hunger of the flames that had followed. The remains of the buildings themselves were little more than a latticework of charred beams nestling in a pale grey mush, ash soup made by the steady drizzle that gusted across from the Belt in ribbons. Wulf clicked his tongue and his mount walked on. Godwin spoke. '*They* deserve a warrior's burial.'

The eorle saw the pair for the first time and nodded. The corpses of a boy and his dog lay where they had fallen, hacked into meat, but the boy still gripped his spear and the dog's lips were drawn into a snarl of defiance. There was a place for the boy in Valhall, he agreed. The dog? He doubted that the Allfather had as much need. 'We will cover him with a boat near the shore and enclose it in clay when we return from avenging him. He had the body of a child, but the heart of a man.'

His *duguth* gave a mirthless laugh and the pair exchanged a look. They had seen the flames that night, the killers must be near. This dawn, iron grey and grim, was very likely to be their last.

Wulf twisted in his saddle and ran his eye across the twenty warriors who made up his hearth troop. Few would wilfully spend the night on the wastes of Troll Heath, a place inhabited by spirits and the dæmons of Hel. But the heights were centrally placed, the view commanding, and something drastic needed to be done to halt the attacks. They had been rewarded near the dawn as the first petals of flame flickered into life, and they had sent a fire arrow arcing in the direction for the other war-bands to follow. The need for concealment thankfully over, they had lit their brands and tumbled down from the hills, only to find that their enemy had eluded them once again.

Wulf looked at the grim faced warriors with pride. They were a tough bunch, but they would need to be if they did overtake the raiders. They would be outnumbered at least two or three to one if help failed to arrive in time.

Eanmer called, his voice monotone. 'They are over here, lord. It looks like all of them.'

With a heavy heart, Wulf dismounted and led his mount across.

Eanmer hurdled a low wattle fence and yelled as he

swung his spear in great circles. A murder of crows cawed into the air, and the eorle's heart sank a little further.

The men and boys lay in a bloody pile. Their hands bound, each had been hewn, once, twice, at the rear of the skull. Wulf picked at his beard as his eyes took in the scene. At least it had been quick. The younger women and older girls were laid out singly. Most were naked, at least from the waist down, the bloody smears marking their thighs telling the tale of their final humiliation.

Godric was there again. 'It doesn't make sense, lord. These are young and healthy. They would fetch good money in the markets at Nyen, or down in Frankland.'

The eorle pursed his lips and glared. 'No, it doesn't. Let's find the men who did this and ask them why.'

The trail was easy to follow. Although the fiend were on foot the rains had left the grass slick, and the passage of so many heavily armed men had cut a swathe that ran, spear straight, towards the nearby coastline. A small brook cut the track and Wulf led the riders down into its rubble strewn course and up the opposite bank. The land rose gently as it approached the coast, and Wulf spurred his mount on. There was no guard posted on the ridge line ahead, they may already be too late. Cresting the rise, he reined in as his men fanned out to either side.

A dragon ship lay with its wide belly on the stony strand, its prow snarling defiance at the spirits of Harrow, the holy island. Banners bearing the white hart of Daneland and what looked like a monster's claw snapped at its masthead. The wind carried the rhythmic chanting of the crew as they shouldered the hull and began to heave it into the surf.

At his shoulder, Godwin spoke again. 'Still no sign of captives.'

Wulf nodded that he understood the importance of the

words, without shifting his gaze from the men below them. This was no opportunist raid, out to plunder what they could and be away. The Danes were making a point and that was far more dangerous. He tightened the strap of his helm. 'I will ride down there and issue the challenge. Get the men into a shield wall and wait until I return.'

Wulf unstrapped his shield, slipping a hand into its grip as the first cries of recognition carried up to them from the beach. Rolling his shoulders, he hefted his spear and urged the horse on. The sun had risen now, and the drizzle fell away as the clouds parted to paint the waves with its pale light.

Wulf looked across as the horse picked its way down the stony path, tallying the numbers they were to face. The fiends were rushing to form their shield hedge at his approach, and the eorle gave an ironic chuckle as he left the path and began to cross the narrow beach.

A full keel and more, upwards of eighty warriors. It's to be four to one then. It must be my lucky day.

The Danes brought their shields together with a crash as their jarl strode proud of the line. Wulf put spurs to his mount and accelerated as a cry of defiance rolled across the strand towards him. The horse broke into a canter and Wulf pulled at its reins as he guided it directly at the enemy leader. A watercourse snaked across the sand there, its edge forming a small lip before the Danish position, and Wulf tightened his grip as he waited for the perfect moment to halt the steed's mad dash. The horse clattered into the channel in an explosion of spray, and Wulf waited until it was through before sawing at the reins, bringing it up only feet from the immobile Dane. As his horse reared and stamped the sand to dust, he pointed accusingly with his spear and called out his challenge.

'I am Wulf Wonreding, a thegn of the English.

All men who seek knowledge, as men should, know of my deeds and those of my clan.

Tell me, raider, your name, unless shame forbids it.

Who creeps into my lord's country like a fox in the night, staining Harrow with the blood of king Eomær people?'

The leader of the Danes raised his chin proudly, and Wulf was surprised to hear the higher tones of a youth reply from behind the silvered faceplate.

'My name is Hrothmund Hrothgarson, an ætheling in your tongue.

I have heard men speak of your clan, and your challenge was bold and well-made.

For that reason, I will allow you to leave our land with your life.

Go to King Eomær. Tell him that this island of Fyn belongs to King Hrothgar.

Withdraw his interlopers to the mainland, or there will be war between us.'

Wulf let out an involuntary gasp at the revelation that the Danes were claiming the island as their own, and he shook his spear as he replied angrily.

'Even a skull of ash wood knows whose land this is; your ship still bears its beast head. I have no need to travel anywhere. I carry my king's reply to your over-proud boast in my scabbard.'

The line of foemen broke into grins at his impotence, and mocking laughter followed as a Dane hawked and spat into the sand.

Seething with rage at his humiliation, Wulf wheeled his horse and cantered back towards the men lining the horizon as jeers hung in the crisp air.

As the horse regained the crest, he leapt down and drove it to the rear with an angry slap of its rump. Godwin caught his eye and indicated to the west with a jerk of his head. Wulf chewed his lip as he scanned the horizon, desperately seeking a sign that help would reach them soon. Four to one was just too great a number, even with men of this quality. The duguth came to his aid. 'There, just emerging from the tree line,' he swept his finger through to the north and pointed again, 'and alongside the stand of alder, following the course of the brook.'

He concentrated his gaze on the dark line marking the edge of the wood, and he had them. Points of light danced in the gloom and suddenly a knot of horsemen burst forth, the weak morning sunlight flickering from mail and helm. In the clear, Wulf grinned as he watched the warriors toss their brands aside and come on at a gallop.

Switching his gaze, he could see that the other group were further away. All depended on delaying the Danes for long enough to enable his countrymen to come up. Within a heartbeat, his hopes were dashed again as his duguth spat a curse.

Wulf looked and saw that Godwin was staring sullenly at the beach. Following his gaze, he saw that Hrothmund had drawn his men back into a defensive arc about the prow of their ship as others manhandled the vessel into the swell. A glance back down the reverse slope told the eorle that the nearest riders were approaching the brook. They were a mile distant, almost within hailing distance, but he could not wait. He turned back to his men, and the smiles of deliverance faded from their faces as their leader launched into a battle speech.

'They flee from us, we few; but we will not let them slink away while our dead lie unavenged, our king insulted.' Wulf raised his weapon and stalked the line, striking each man's spear with his own as he passed. 'They think that we grow weak, they covet that which the gods gave us long ago.' He grinned as he hefted his shield and rolled his shoulders once again, warming blood and muscles for the work to come. 'We will show them that they are mistaken.' He flicked a look beyond the nearest man's shoulder and saw that the first riders were through the watercourse and climbing the nearside bank. 'We must hold them here. We go down fast and hit them hard. By the time they have recovered, our friends will be up with us, and we will crush their proud necks.'

Pacing before them, Wulf held each man with a stare as he barked out a question. 'Who is your king?'

The shield wall raised their spears and cried out in reply. 'Eomær!'

His entire body quickening with the power of the moment, Wulf turned and planted his feet on the sod of his ancestors. Below him, the Danish drakkar was beginning to lift as the waters of the Belt flowed back beneath its keel. There was no time for the full barritus, the war cry of the North that would draw the Allfather and his battle maidens to the clash; he would miss his prey. One last shout would have to do.

Wulf Wonreding beat his spear against the rim of his shield and began to chant the age-old battle cry of the English.

'Out! Out! Out!'

The men of his war-band raised their shields before them, and the cry rolled down from the ridge as a full-throated roar. As the Danes in the surf stole nervous glances their way English steel hissed from scabbards, and spears became a hedge as Wulf moved forward and broke into a run.

1

Gwened,
Bro Gwereg,
Summer AD523

Eofer crossed his legs before him and wriggled his shoulders further into the coils of rope, sighing with pleasure at the warmth of the sun on his face. Closing his eyes against the glare, he felt the corners of his mouth curling into a smile as Osbeorn paced the deck like an expectant father.

'Where is he? How long can it take?'

Eofer chuckled to himself as he pictured the dockside in his mind. Squat buildings of dark grey stone backed a landing made of the same grim material, the whole liberally scattered with nets and woven pots, the everyday tools of the fishermen who had made the port their home. In the middle distance the walls and massive towers of the fortress that the Romans had called Benetis jutted above the tree line, and Eofer imagined the dark stones glowering over the town that had grown up in its shadow. At the far end of the quay, a large trader rode the flood tide, the portly lines and workaday air at odds with the sleek warships that had journeyed down from the North.

They had wended their way through the maze of islands and shoals the previous day to reach this place, following the withies that marked the channel to the anchorage where a small river emptied into the bay. The port reeve had immediately despatched a rider to hurry the few miles to this town of Gwened to report their arrival, unbelievers being unwelcome in the Christian settlement. Within the hour he had returned with the news that the British lord and his men would sail with them on the morning tide, and the English war-band had settled in for a night of freshly cooked food and dark Welsh ale.

The land that bordered the bay was already a swatch of green despite the earliness of the year, lush with beech, oak and birch. Overhead, the skies echoed to the trill of swallows, the red throated birds darting and slashing as they fed on the wing. Their pearl-like bellies would not be seen in the skies above the northern homelands for another month, and the English wondered at their appearance. It was the first time that any of them had driven their ships so far south. The Romans had called the land Armorica but, as in the north, people were on the move. Britons in their thousands had left the shores of Britannia to settle here, transplanting the names of their homeland, Cornouaille, Domnonia, until men began to call the whole peninsula Bro Gwereg, the land of Gwereg. Now one wished to return, and he was willing to pay good silver to do so.

Osbeorn cupped his hands as the boy reappeared, and his voice boomed across the anchorage. 'Come on, Oswin, they will be here soon!'

Eofer abandoned his reverie and reluctantly opened his eyes. Glancing across to the dockside, he watched as the boy struggled along with the wicker basket. Almost as large as the youth himself, the wickerwork completely obscured the boy's view ahead, and the thegn called across to Porta to go to the aid of his fellow as a vision of their breakfast ending up back in the water came to his mind.

The lad scurried off, and soon they were tucking into a meal of hot sardines and fresh white bread. They had arrived back not a moment too soon, as the sound of hoofbeats carried across from the roadway that led inland. Warriors were arriving there and, dismounting, they formed in twin ranks as a knot of riders in gleaming mail emerged from the shadows.

Hemming rolled a ball of phlegm around the roof of his mouth with his tongue and sent it spinning over the side. 'Here's our man.'

Eofer gripped the wale and hauled himself to his feet, brushing the dust from the seat of his trews as heads turned towards the dockside and the troops there stabbed the sky with their spears, roaring their acclaim. 'Good, let's get going,' he murmured. 'I don't like sailing in another man's ship, even if that man is my father.'

Above the spear points, the golden draco battle flag of the house of Uther shone as it broke free of the enclosing buildings and the sea breeze teased it out. The men of the flotilla exchanged smiles as they compared it to their standards. The white dragon war flag of the English curled from each masthead in the little group; the men were happy at the coincidence, it was a good omen.

A quick glance up at the weather vane, high up in the mast top, confirmed that the wind still blew steadily from the south. Sæward began to organise the crew as the British warriors funnelled down to the mole and began to follow their lord onto the nearest ship.

Hemming turned back to Eofer and spoke again as the big ship master ordered the spar run up the mast and oars were fitted to thole-pins. 'What do you know about these Britons, lord?'

Eofer pulled a face, 'Cerdic and Cynric?' He shrugged and shot his duguth a grin. 'They pay well!'

They shared a laugh as the British warriors hopped from ship to ship, filling each in turn as the crews prepared to cast off. Eofer continued as the first of the dark-haired warriors began to climb aboard the *Sæ Wulf*. 'Cerdic and Cynric, father and son. Cerdic strong-arm is the son of the old champion of the Belgae, Elesius, who in turn was the son of one of the warlord Arthur's close companions, Osla big knife.'

Hemming looked at him quizzically. 'Osla? Unusual name for a Briton.'

Eofer snorted. 'That's because he wasn't.' He repeated the nickname. 'Big knife?'

Hemming's expression softened, and he nodded that he understood. 'Big knife, a Seax. So, he was a Saxon then?'

Eofer nodded. Although the short, stabbing, seax was a common weapon among the armies in the North, the sword length bent-backed blade was more characteristic of the warriors who belonged to the Saxon tribes. 'When Arthur died, Cerdic's faction lost the power struggle, and he had to flee abroad with his son. Now that he has had time to rebuild his strength, he has hired us to carry his army across the sea and add a touch of steel to his homecoming.' The English thegn lowered his voice as the British leader leapt the final obstacle and landed amidships. 'Let's hope that he has not underestimated the level of support waiting for him at home. Three keels is hardly what you would call an invasion fleet!'

Eofer watched as Sæward took the draco from Cerdic's banner man and threaded it to a halyard. Within moments, the golden dragon was rising to the mast top in a series of short, jerky movements. Cerdic's men let out a cheer as the golden dragon took the wind and pointed its tail to the north. Eofer painted his features with a smile and went to greet his paymaster as the last of his warriors tumbled down into the hull.

'Welcome aboard the *Sæ Wulf*, lord,' he said. 'I am Eofer king's bane. Are you set?'

The Briton returned his smile, and Eofer felt the charisma of the man wash over him. A head taller than the men of his guard, the lighter skin tone and flaxen hair of the British leader served to reinforce the fact that his ancestry lay further north and west of the land he now called home.

The Briton ran his eyes over the Englishman and nodded, obviously satisfied with his choice. 'As set as I will ever be, Eofer,' he answered. Cerdic glanced up at the draco as it stretched out to the north, before returning his gaze. 'It seems that my banner is as impatient to be home as I am.' He turned and called his companion forward, and Eofer recognised the younger man for who he was before the introduction. 'This is Cynric,' Cerdic beamed proudly, 'my son.'

Cynric came forward and Eofer was pleased to see that the boy had inherited his father's easy manner as well as his physical features as he welcomed him aboard. Cynric flashed him a smile in return. 'King's bane,' he said. 'We were introduced by a travelling bard to the tale of the fight in Swede Land where you earned your name. We are pleased to have your sword with us on our little adventure.'

As Eofer inclined his head in thanks, Cerdic indicated Sæward with a jerk of his head. 'Your senior helmsman?' Eofer called his duguth across and the magister nodded to a thick set man who had hovered to one side as they spoke. 'This is Anwyl, my ship master.' The sailor ducked his head in acknowledgement as his master continued. 'I hope that you don't mind, but I would like him to guide you through my home waters. No man knows them as well as he, and if we let the tides sweep us into the waters we call the Soluente, we could be in big trouble.' He smiled again. 'The tides and currents are treacherous there, and I would feel rather foolish stranded on a sandbank as my enemies came to finish me off!'

As Sæward led Anwyl aft, the last of the British warriors came aboard. Eofer and Cerdic exchanged a look as they settled themselves into the area that had been prepared for them. 'That's it,' Cerdic smiled as the last of his men stacked their shields and spears amidships. 'I am keen to be away while this wind holds. If you leave now, we should exit the bay before the tide turns.'

Bassa and Beornwulf, the youth who formed the permanent crew on Eofer's own ship, *Fælcen,* were within earshot and a quick nod from their eorle sent them scurrying ashore to release the bowline from the mooring post there. The action was mirrored on the other two English ships as the crews came alive and moved to their stations. As the boys leapt back aboard and the ships moved away from the land, the crews waited patiently until there was enough sea room to slip the oars into thole-pins. Sæward caught his eye as the ships slid apart, and Eofer nodded. Filling his lungs with the cool morning air, the ship master cried out time as the rowers curled their backs and the oars swept the surface. Slowly the *Sæ Wulf* gathered way as the men settled into their rhythm and the other ships took station to either side.

Eofer cast a look back at the shore as the vessel gathered speed. A cloud of gulls dipped in their wake as the ships pulled clear of the land, the dark headed birds searching out the fish guts and smaller fry that they associated with men and ships. On land, the white line of grins split the faces of several fishermen as one of their number chased a shrieking woman around a pile of woven fish traps. It was not quite the rapturous send-off he had imagined that Cerdic strong-arm, the saviour of Belgic Britain, would have had. But then the Welsh were Christians, and it did sometimes seem that the religion frowned upon unnecessary displays of emotion. Eofer's hand moved instinctively to his sword hilt as he contemplated the summer ahead. One way or another, he doubted that the blade would sleep in its scabbard until the harvest was gathered safely in.

THE WAVES SLAPPED NOISILY against the hulls of the ships as they wallowed in the swell, and the last of the ropes that bound them together were lashed down. Low to the south, the moon was full, and ships and sea alike were bathed in a silver sheen. As the temperature began to tumble and the men huddled into their cloaks and waited for their food, Cerdic made his way aft. Eofer had watched the British magister as the ships had cut their way north across a sea as green as any meadow. Alone among his men, the man had barely cast a look towards the ragged coast of Bro Gwereg as it slipped astern, the ramparts of dark rock that turned their face to the sea seemingly holding little attachment to his affections. To a man, the Britons had cut their hair short, immediately marking them apart from the Englishmen who surrounded them. Although their garments were of the best quality, they were noticeably less flamboyant than those of their hosts—the muted browns, greens, and blues brightened only by the red cloak that hung at every man's shoulder and the enamelled broach that held it in place. Their leader was dressed in similar fashion to his men, and Cerdic flashed

Eofer a smile as he gained the steering platform and hopped up at his side.

'We are making good progress,' he said. 'This time tomorrow, we shall be ashore?'

It was more a question than a statement of fact, and Cerdic glanced towards Anwyl seeking confirmation. His ship master nodded in agreement. 'If this wind blows steadily, we should drift down on Afen mouth around dusk, lord,' the man replied.

'Let us hope that the Durotrige and our new Jutish friends are safely at their ale before we appear then.'

Cerdic noticed the look of surprise that flashed across Eofer's face at the remark, and the magister moved to allay his concerns. 'The Durotrige live to the west of my people, the Belgae.' He paused and smiled again. 'The Jutes I think are more familiar to you than they are to me, it's one of the reasons that led me to recruit Engles for this journey. Perhaps we can share what knowledge we possess of our common foe?' Thrush Hemming, Eofer's *weorthman*, his leading warrior, approached them with platters of bread and cheese. Handing one each to the British leader and his own eorle, he dipped his head before returning to his companions. It had been a long day, and both men tore hungrily at the bread as Cerdic continued between mouthfuls. 'As I mentioned this morning, I already know something of the exploits of Eofer king's bane and his war-band. Even in these troubled times, campaigns, and battles that claim the lives of two kings are rare events.' Cerdic glanced across as he broke the corner from a heel of cheese. 'Did they die well?'

Eofer shrugged. 'Ongentheow, the king of the Swedes, died the death of a hero. My kinsman Hythcyn, the Geat usurper, failed to attain those heights.'

The British leader nodded, thoughtfully. 'How we face

death is important, it is the final capitulum in our life story.' The eorle gave him a blank look, and Cerdic looked surprised. 'Capitulum, it's a Roman term for the division of a book?' Eofer continued to stare at the Briton, who finally realised his error. 'I am sorry,' he said awkwardly, 'I assumed that you would know the Latin tongue. I know that many æthelings do.'

Eofer pursed his lips. 'Knowledge, considered appropriate for our princes, is not necessarily imparted to the sons of ealdormen.'

Cerdic grimaced. 'It was stupid of me,' he said. 'Please accept my heartfelt apologies.' He rallied with a smile. 'Let's make sure that our final capitulum lies many years in the future. Tell me,' he added, 'since I clearly know only enough of the customs of the North to enable me to offend good men. What do you know of me and the situation in my part of Britannia?'

Eofer dipped his head, acknowledging the British leader's apology, and cleared his throat to speak. 'You are the grandson of Uther Pendragon's hearth warrior, Osla big knife, a Saxon, and the son of Arthur's duguth, Elesius.' It was Cerdic's turn to give a blank look, and the men shared a laugh as the tables were turned. Eofer flushed, the haughtiness driven from him as he explained. 'A duguth is an English term for a senior man in his lord's hearth troop, a doughty warrior. Younger warriors in the war-band are just known as youths until they have proven their worth and reached sixteen winters.'

Cerdic nodded with a twinkle in his eye, and Eofer felt himself warm to the Briton as he took up the tale. 'When Arthur died, the people split into two factions. Those who wished to work towards a future that included all the people on the island of Britannia—Saxon, Engle, and Briton, under one leader, and one God—lost the ensuing war against those who wished to return to the old ways. Those that prevailed in the islands before the coming of Rome. Their leader is a man called Natan, and they call themselves the combrogi, which just means the people in our tongue. They call everywhere by the old names,' he gave a chuckle, 'and nobody knows where they are any longer. This Natan styles himself a chieftain in the old way, even the centre of the civitas at Venta Belgarum is now known as Cair Guinntguic.' He gave a low sigh. 'Order within the civitas is breaking down, it is coming under attack from all sides. The people are in despair and I have been recalled from Bro Gwereg to lead the fightback. Already my supporters have stopped calling the great hill fort at Sorbiodunum, Cair Caradog, and driven away Natan's supporters there.'

Eofer looked up and nodded his thanks as Hemming handed the pair cups of ale. As Cerdic drank, he cut in. 'So we are to get you and your men through to the army in Sorbiodunum?'

Cerdic winced. 'Essentially yes, but there is a complication.'

Eofer tried hard to hide his amusement. There was always a complication when silver needed to be paid to hire swords and ships. The Briton pretended not to notice and pressed on.

'Natan has settled Jutes in the forts that surround the Soluente. Clausentum, Portus Adurni and Carys on the island we call Vectis. Their ships have closed the entrance to the great bay there, we shall have to beach our ships further west and follow the River Afen to the hill fort. My friends cannot abandon the fortress and come to our aid, or it will fall to the combrogi. It's the obvious route for us to take. If our presence is discovered, I expect to have to fight my way through.'

2

Eofer watched as the rowers swept the sea with gentle strokes, keeping station below the wall of rock as the sun slowly sank in the west. Ahead of them, across a sea turned bronze by the dying sun, lay the great island that Cerdic had called Vectis. A quick glance towards Sæward told the eorle that his steer man shared his anxiety. To be caught, wallowing beneath great white cliffs as dusk came on, was the stuff of nightmares. Anwyl stood at the stern post as he studied the movement of the sea with a look of grim determination, as aware as any that the lives of his magister and every man aboard the three English ships depended on his good judgement.

A quick glance to the west and the Briton reached down and tossed another handful of bladder wrack into the current, and men chewed their lips as the tension mounted. The seaweed spun through the air to land an oar's length from the hull, and the man smiled and turned as the air-filled sacs that lined the fronds floated on the surface and edged the plant eastwards. The tide had finally turned, and the relief among Engle and Briton alike was palpable.

The sun was now a pyre resting on the sea, the sheer cliffs aflame as Eofer gave the order to pull past the headland and into the bay. He looked across. 'Do we cut across the bight or hug the coastline?'

Anwyl exchanged a look with Cerdic, who gave an almost imperceptible nod. 'Keep inshore. We still have a way to go before we enter Afen mouth. Even with the glow of the sun at our backs, we may be seen from the shore or the clifftop on Vectis. If we remain in the shadow of the land, we may yet pull through.'

It was Eofer's turn to exchange a look of concern with his steer man. The nervousness of the Britons was obvious. Maybe, Eofer thought wryly, he should have asked for payment in gold.

As the *Sæ Wulf* cleared the headland, a small bay opened up to landward. The other English ships tucked in their wake as the current began to carry them across its face. Masts had been stepped, sails furled and stowed long before, and the three ships hugged the beach as the long low silhouettes blended into the shadows. Ahead of them, a series of sea stacks marched into the bay, grim and forbidding, a line of misshapen teeth jutting into their path. Far away on the opposite side of the bay matching stacks, their western edges licked orange by the last of the day's dying light, came off the island of Vectis. Eofer shivered, as he imagined the tiny force sliding into the maw of a monster. High above, gulls wheeled, the white of their wings points of light, squawking and cawing as they circled their roosts.

Pulling past the stacks, the land fell away, and Sæward hauled on the big steering paddle as he edged closer to the land. Anwyl hurried across and Eofer noted again the anxiety in his voice. 'You will have to stand out from the land here. There is an inlet up ahead that contains the port of Bol, the main trading place for the Durotrige. The twin spits of land that straddle the entrance are guarded day and night, we *will* be challenged.'

Oswin, Eofer's youth, chose the moment to utter a verse, and his lord winced at both the message and the timing.

> 'Then over sea-road exiles arrived.
> Bold spear-men, ignorant of their fate…'

Eofer cast an anxious look at Cerdic to gauge his reaction to the doom-laden words, and his lip curled into a grimace as the Briton's face paled. 'Oswin fancies himself as a scop,' he explained apologetically, 'although so far, the evidence of his words and timing say otherwise. I owe a debt to his father, but the way he fights, I am hoping that an ash shaft will settle the account before too long.'

Cerdic recovered quickly, and he smiled reassuringly as he sought to make light of the awkward air that had settled over the ship. He raised his voice a notch, speaking clearly so that all of his men could hear their leader's confidence. 'It's of no account, your patience with the boy speaks well of your character. You forget that we are Christian men, Eofer. The lord decides the number of our days, not the words of beardless boys.'

The eorle smiled his thanks at the Briton's handling of the situation and shot the boy a withering stare before raising his eyes to take in the bay that was opening up before them.

The distance could not have been much more than a couple of miles, three at most. On the far side the land was heavily wooded, and they would be swallowed by the gloom. Before they could reach cover though they would have to cross the stretch where the cliffs petered out and the sunlight still shone brightly. They would be visible for miles around, three dark forms attempting to move with stealth. Even the Jutes could not be that blind, he mused. 'It can't be more than a few miles to this Afen mouth,' he said. 'We still have enough sea room to steer inshore and hug the shadows. Isn't it worth the risk?'

Cerdic had moved aft to support his shipmaster, and he shook his head. 'Bol is their main port Eofer, it is heavily guarded. There are always manned ships at the entrance to the pool during the hours of daylight. It would be madness to take the risk when we are so close to our destination.'

Eofer sucked his teeth as he thought but, in truth, the final decision was not his to make. He turned to Sæward. 'Take the straightest line across the bay.' Hopping down from the steering platform, he spoke to his men as Sæward moved to the stern post and passed the information to the following ships. 'We need to clip this bay, lads. The quicker we can do it, the safer we will be.'

As the crew bent to their oars, Eofer joined Cerdic at the stern as he scanned the surface of the inlet. Within moments the great curved stem post of the *Sæ Wulf* had emerged into the full glare of the dying sun, and the rowers redoubled their efforts as they attempted to reach the shadowy shoreline undetected. Eofer watched with mounting disquiet as the silvered wakes of the three ships reflected the last rays of the sun as it lanced across the bay. As he feared, a call came from the man in the bows before they were even halfway to safety.

'Two sail in the east!'

All eyes turned towards a hook of land curving into the bay in the distance. There, between the shingle headland and the great hump of Vectis opposite, two sails had appeared, shining in the light like new nail heads on a wall.

Eofer looked on as Cerdic glanced anxiously towards his ship master. 'Will we make the Afen?'

Anwyl shook his head, his expression grim. 'They are already closer to the bay there, and they have the wind at their backs. Despite the tidal flow, they should make it long before we do, lord.'

Sæward cut in. '*If* they know we are heading there.' They all turned his way and he shrugged. 'Unless they know who these ships carry we could be anyone, we have no flags flying, not even sails set.' He scratched at his beard as he thought. 'If we have been betrayed there would be more than a brace of sail heading in this direction, we could be those Durotrige guard ships you mentioned for all they know.'

Cerdic beamed. 'He's right, we are still in their waters. The Afen forms the border between our civitas, they would be encroaching on our territory.' He turned to Anwyl. 'Keep the shingle banks between us, and you can warn them off. We outnumber them, and I doubt that Jutes will be able to tell one group of Britons from another.'

Anwyl nodded as Cerdic plucked at Eofer's sleeve. 'Come, lets prepare for the worst. If it does come to a fight, we will need a quick and decisive victory before the light goes completely. We cannot let them take news of our arrival back to the mainland if they discover our true identity.'

As the pair moved into the waist of the ship, Eofer stole a glance to the east. The ships were closer now, and he could see that, although they were clearly ships of the North, they were smaller and therefore less heavily manned. They were obviously guard ships come to sniff at these warships that had appeared out of the setting sun. A robust response from the heavily armed men aboard the three English ships should see them off. Between them, he could see the area that Cerdic had called the shingle banks. The surface grew choppier there as the current plucked at the underwater ridge, and his spirits rose. No shipmaster in his right mind would hazard his ship in such a place in fading light, and he settled in among the British warriors as Anwyl hailed them.

'Why are you in Durotrige waters, pagan?'

The answering voice drifted back across the waves, the accent confirming that these men were the new Jutish settlers. 'It is our duty to safeguard the coast, Christ man.'

The man was about to continue, but Anwyl cut him short with a snarl. 'Wrong, pagan. Your duty is to safeguard the coast of Belgica. Scamper back to your Belgic bitch, puppy. Before we decide to redden the boards of your ships with your blood and add them to our fleet.'

Cerdic's spearmen rose from the thwarts and glared across the waves, and Eofer chuckled to himself as he recognised the Jutish leader backtrack as he attempted to retreat without losing face.

'Keep to your side of the border or there will be a heavy price to pay, *wealas*,' he spat, and Eofer snorted as he saw the men surrounding him stiffen at the word. It was the term that all northern folk used for foreigners and carried more than a hint of scorn. Anwyl held a steady course as the Jutes sheered off and spilled the wind from their sails. Moving with the current but against the easterly wind now, they watched with relief as the oars slid proud of the Jutish hulls and began to stroke their way back to their waters.

Cerdic flashed his helmsman a smile as the warriors exchanged grins around him. 'Expertly handled, old friend. But remind me never to let you handle any negotiations that might call for more subtle diplomatic skills,' he laughed.

The bay ended abruptly as the coastline turned back on itself. Ahead, a hazy white line marked the point where yet another sandy spit ran parallel to the sea. Cerdic clapped Eofer on the shoulder as Sæward hauled at the steer board and headed in. 'Afen mouth,' he smiled. 'We have survived the sea crossing and the portents of Oswin's poetry at least.'

'THAT WILL HAVE TO DO,' Eofer said. 'We can't haul them any further in.'

The three ships were tied up stem to stern in a side channel of the Afen, as far from the main watercourse as possible. With their masts shipped their profile was as low as it could be, but not for the first time Eofer wished that he had his ship, *Fælcen*, with them. The graceful sweep of the stem and stern of the snaca still stood proud of the banks of rushes and eelgrass that covered the salt marsh on the Belgic side of the bay; but time snapped at their heels like a hungry wolf. Every moment spent at the ships ate into the hours of darkness, and they had upward of thirty miles to cover before they reached the safety of the hill fort at Sorbiodunum. The snake ships carried forty rowers apiece and, although they were as sleek and deadly as their namesake, the long hulls had been needed to transport the British magister and his large warband across the sea. Eofer's own ship, *Fælcen*, was of a type that the English called a scegth, and he missed her keenly. Half the size of the big snacas and drawing barely a hand's breadth of water, the little ship at twenty oars a side was ideal for raiding far into the river systems of Britannia, Gaul and Frisia. Eofer reflected ruefully that he would have been able to complete the journey to Sorbiodunum in a few hours if she were here.

Sæward read his thoughts and made a suggestion as the warriors formed into a column on the higher ground. 'We could load them with stones, lord. Let them settle deeper.'

Eofer shook his head. 'We haven't the time, we need to be

away. Besides,' he continued as he glanced about them, 'can you see any?'

The ship master's teeth showed white in the moonlight as he ran his gaze across the banks of thick glutinous mud that surrounded them. 'No, lord,' he admitted with a snort, 'not to hand.'

Eofer leaned in and dropped his voice to a murmur. 'If this goes badly, we may need to get away quickly. We have no idea how much support this Cerdic has, it may even be a trap. I will leave Edwin, Bassa and Beornwulf with you, that will give you enough spears to take care of any curious locals. Anything more organised, and you will have to fire the ships and follow on. If we are not back by the evening of the second day, take the *Sæ Wulf*, and we will meet at Cnobheresburg. You will still have to fire the other ships,' he shrugged, 'but that can't be helped. I will have to pay compensation to the owners, but that's the chance we all take when we sail in these waters.'

Sæward nodded grimly, and they clasped forearms without another word. Movement from the bank caught the ship master's eye, and he glanced across as a figure hurried across to them.

'My father wishes to know if there is a problem?'

Eofer changed his mood quickly and smiled brightly as he shook his head. 'No Cynric, I am coming now. We have done the best we can to hide the ships.'

The British warriors had taken up the vanguard of the column as agreed, with Cerdic and his son safely ensconced halfway along the steel-clad line. The remaining English duguth of Eofer's hearth troop, Hemming, Imma Gold, Osbeorn and Octa were stood waiting for their eorle to lead them forward, with the youth standing tall behind their shields as they covered the rear. Beyond them, the crews of the other English ships formed into their divisions and waited impatiently for the off.

Imma, the flaxen hair that had lent him his name shining brightly from beneath the plates of his helm, winked mischievously as Eofer gained the column and the eorle let out a snort. The big man would be itching for a fight, he knew. Whether Cerdic and Cynric felt the same way, he had his doubts.

Cerdic looked back, and Eofer raised his arm to confirm that all were set. As the golden draco banner of the house of Uther was raised again over British soil, and the breeze whispered across the salt marsh to unfurl its long tail, the column hefted their shields and took their first paces towards the distant hill fort.

The moon was climbing higher as the night wore on, its silver glow slanting down to light the waters of the Afen as the column trudged warily along its eastern bank. The river divided to either side of a large island, and the burnt out remains of a small settlement there told of the conflict that was ongoing as the rival tribes wrestled for control of the area. The valley sides steepened as they moved steadily inland, and the wild wood that capped the pass closed in on them a little more with every mile trod. Soon the road was hard-pressed by trees on the eastern side and the meandering waters of the river to the west. Although the roadway itself was wide and well constructed, a sombre air of abandonment hung over the vale and the warriors. Briton and Engle, alike, gripped their weapons a little tighter as they searched the gloom for any sign of opposition.

As the first grey light lit the eastern sky and the moon paled above them, the men watched as a herd of deer emerged from the tree line on the far side of the vale. Led by a large hart, the heavy fronds of its antlers spearing the air as it rolled its neck and snorted defiance, the females watched impassively as the armed group ghosted through their domain. A light mist had risen to fill the hollows with a milky wisp, tendrils snaking down to the river as the light began to chase the shadows away.

Suddenly, the hart snapped its head to the north, and the hinds that had grouped in his wake skittered nervously. Eofer shared a look of concern with Thrush Hemming, who marched at his side, and soon their fears were confirmed as the shadowy figure of a British scout came rushing back along the road towards the column. Within moments the man was reporting to the British magister, and they watched as Cynric left his father's side and trotted back along the column towards them, concern writ large on his features. As the Belgic warriors instinctively began to check their equipment and grip their shields a little tighter, Cynric reached the English eorle.

'You had better come up, Eofer,' he panted. 'There is an army blocking our path.'

3

Eofer strode purposefully forward as the men of his troop rechecked buckles and fastenings. Untying the peace bands from his sword, Blood-Worm, he greeted Cerdic with a smile. 'We have company, I understand. What do we know?'

The British leader was nodding earnestly as the scout completed his report on the armed force that had appeared ahead, and Eofer felt a kick of optimism as he watched a smile spread slowly across Cerdic's face. Finally, he clapped the man on the shoulder and turned to the eorle.

'It's a small force, most likely the men from the fort at Clausentum. Here,' he said, smoothing a patch of earth with his foot, 'this is what I believe the situation to be.'

Eofer watched as Cerdic hastily sketched out a map of the area with the point of his spear.

'This is the valley of the Afen, and we are here.' He stabbed out to the left and right of the line in the soil. 'These are the two great woodlands that border it, and here is where we left the ships at the coast. This bay,' he said, stretching to score a great oval, 'leads up from the Soluente, almost as far as the capitol at Venta. Clausentum at the head of the bay guards the mouth of the River Icene, and the roadway that lead directly to it. There is another good road that skirts the woodland and leads directly to the ford up ahead, where they have set up their line of defence.' He looked up and flashed a smile. 'It is known locally as Cerdicsford, after the victor in a battle that was fought there a decade or so ago. It's my guess that our Jutish friends from last night reported our presence to their masters at the fort, and they in turn realised that your ships very likely carried me and Cynric.' He raised a brow in question. 'What would you have done in their place?'

Eofer replied straight away. 'Send word to the main army at Venta and then rush across and try to delay you here until they come up and finish you off.'

Cerdic nodded. 'It's the obvious thing to do, the only thing really,' he agreed. 'I can't fault their bravery. Their cause may be misguided, but they have my respect.'

Eofer interrupted. 'If you know this fort, you should know how many men usually garrison it.'

'Cedwyn just confirmed that we are facing a hundred or so, that would be the full compliment, so with my two hundred, plus the hundred and...' Cerdic let the sentence hang in the air and wrinkled his brow.

'One hundred and twenty-five, without the four left at the ships,' Eofer answered.

'So, we have the advantage in numbers and quality. But,' Cerdic added with a grimace, 'it is an excellent defensive position. I should know,' he snorted, 'I defended it in the previous battle. There is a pinch point there, where the woods come almost down to the river. It cannot be outflanked from the west because a smaller river joins the Afen at that point. So, you would need to cross the Afen, then this other river, the Nootr, and recross the Afen to get to grips with the enemy.' Cerdic shook his head. 'Even if we attempted it, it would take time, and time is something we don't have. There could be a thousand warriors riding here as we speak, only God knows how close they are. We must punch through these men blocking our path, or we shall be overwhelmed.'

Eofer sucked at his teeth as he thought, before an idea came to him. 'There are a hundred men blocking our route ahead, and these men came from the fort at Clausentum?'

Cerdic nodded.

Eofer asked another question. 'Tell me again how these men got here so quickly.'

The British leader looked uncomprehending for a moment, before a smile lit his face. 'Do it for me,' he said excitedly. 'Quickly!'

EOFER CROUCHED in the shadows and ran his eyes across the scene before him. Hemming stood at his shoulder as the pair noted the number and position of the guards. The sweet smell of horse came to them as the animals grazed contentedly on the lush summer grasses that grew at the roadside, despite the noise of fighting that carried up from the vale beyond the tree line. The woodland bowed to the north there, and the road fell away before it turned the corner and was lost from sight. The lads of Eofer's youth were fighting there alongside the other English crews and Cerdic's Britons, and he sent a plea to the gods to watch over them until he could enter the fray.

Hemming turned his head and murmured to the eorle. 'I can't see any more than those four, lord.'

Eofer gave a small nod of agreement. 'No, neither can I Thrush. Let's get on with it.'

He estimated that the four young Britons who had been left to tend the horses were about ten or eleven winters. Their boyish excitement, as they peered in the direction of the fighting, told the experienced English warriors that here were four lads who had yet to endure the special terror that accompanied the push of shields. A terror that could twist the guts, and liquefy the innards as ably as any spear thrust. He would let them live if he could.

He drew his sword with a flourish and glanced at the men of his duguth. 'Fierce faces lads. Let them go unless they resist. They can do us little harm.'

Eofer stalked from cover and glowered beneath the boar brow rim of his helm as he led the four warriors towards the backs of the gesticulating boys. Caught up in their excitement, the Britons were unaware of the danger until Eofer bellowed out as he closed on the group.

'Go!'

The boys spun around and Eofer almost laughed as he saw the excited smiles drain from their faces as their jaws gaped and a look of horror came over them. The largest of the boys was the first to recover, and he began to lower his spear. The other boys looked to him, and Eofer knew that he had found the leader of the group. The delay had allowed him to close, and he brought Blood-Worm across with a contemptuous sweep. As the spear shaft was sent spinning from the boy's hands, he reversed the blade and struck him on the side of his head with the flat of the blade.

'This is your last chance, boy. Go, now.'

Despite the unlikelihood that any of the lads spoke Eofer's tongue, the instruction should have been obvious enough to even the dimmest of them. He jerked his head to the east to make it as clear as he could and barked out again.

'RUN!'

The spell that had held them in place finally broke, and the Britons dropped their weapons and fled. Imma and Octa had already moved across to cut the ropes that the riders had used to hobble their mounts before they left for the valley. Eofer and Hemming sheathed their swords and drew their knives as they moved across to help.

Hemming looked across to the east and shook his head. 'Should have killed them, lord. When we had the chance.'

Eofer looked and saw that the Britons had run as far as the crest of the nearest rise, and he frowned. If more riders arrived from that direction, they would be well-placed to help them with directions and the latest news.

'It's too late now. Anyway,' he spat, 'we will be long gone by the time that their main army arrives.'

The horses were ready, and they chose the largest animals with the finest saddles and most ornate bridles, knowing from experience that these would belong to the most important warriors among the British force. Like their owners, these horses too would be the pick of the herds and the other animals would instinctively follow their lead.

Eofer and Hemming guided their mounts towards the sound of fighting as Imma led Osbeorn and Octa to the rear of the herd. Eofer twisted in the saddle as he checked that the three were in position and, as Imma raised his arm to signal that they were set, the thegn dug in his heels and whooped for joy. The great war horse bounded forward, and within a heartbeat, the roadway reverberated to the thunder of hooves as the herd gathered speed and dipped towards the valley floor.

Eofer tugged at his reins as the power of his own great mount threatened to outpace the following horses, and he reached across himself to draw Blood-Worm with a flourish. He sensed Thrush Hemming draw level on his own war horse, and Eofer risked a look as they rounded the wooded outlier and the valley floor came into view. His duguth was crouched low over the neck of his mount, his sword swinging in wide arcs above him as the horse put back its ears and charged on. Clear of the trees, the roadway curved to the left and then straightened as it hugged the tree line and swept down to the crossing place, half a mile ahead.

The sun had fully cleared the hills to the east, the slanting light driving a great shadow before them like an angry cloud. Eofer glanced up as the harsh note of a war horn cut the air, watching as a gap opened up between the rival forces as Cerdic's men withdrew to safety. A moment later, the first of the enemy warriors became aware of the headlong charge that was bearing down upon their flank.

Faces turned their way, and he was taken aback as the nearest members of the enemy formation stabbed the air in triumph, mouths voicing silent cries of joy, beckoning the wall of death onward. With a jolt, Eofer realised that the hard-pressed men from Clausentum must be thinking that the mounted column that had burst from the eastern woodland were their saviours—the warriors that would be hastening to their aid from the garrison at Venta Belgarum. With Cerdic's men apparently withdrawing in disarray before them, the men were intent on celebrating their heroic stand against the odds and anticipating the reunion to come as the pretender and his force was ridden into the dust.

Unable to believe his good fortune, Eofer spurred his mount on, desperate to reach the disordered ranks before they realised their mistake. As the road straightened out and dipped down to the crossing, the first signs of alarm could be seen ahead as men began to notice that this relieving force carried very few riders. The first spear points were pointed in their direction as men finally woke up to the danger bearing down upon them, and men hastily scrambled to swing their battle line around to face the new threat.

It would be too late, Eofer knew, as the road bottomed out

and his horse began to charge across the flood plain. A heartbeat later he was among them, and he brought Blood-Worm crashing down onto the helmeted head of the nearest Briton. A crimson arc misted the air as the blade bit through metal, bone, and brain. Eofer was already bringing the weapon back across, hacking down to the opposite flank as the horse forced its way deeper into the enemy ranks. A mighty crash to his rear told the eorle that the riderless horses had acted as he had hoped, blindly following the big stallion that was carrying him further in to the mayhem, as a flicker of silver to his right told him that Hemming had forced his way to his side.

A spear point glanced from his mail shirt, and Eofer instinctively twisted his torso to send the leaf-shaped blade sliding harmlessly across the face of his chest. He glared down at the man who had made the thrust and watched him take a pace backwards as he hacked down to shatter the shaft. Eofer drew back his arm, readying the sword thrust that was to follow, but his intended victim disappeared quickly as the rampaging horses created chaos among the British warriors, and he was swept away. The horses swirled around him, the dun coloured sea driving the enemy before them in an irresistible tide to fetch them up against the riverbank like bloody wrack. Lifting his gaze, Eofer could see that men there were already starting to abandon their weapons, leaping into the waters of the Afen in a desperate attempt to survive the slaughter.

Their work was done, and Eofer exchanged a look of joy with his weorthman as the herd milled about them.

Hemming laughed. 'That worked well!'

Eofer shot him a triumphant grin. 'Did you blood your sword, Thrush?'

The duguth held up his reddened blade with a look of delight, and his eorle smiled and nodded at the sight.

From their left, the warriors of Cerdic and Cynric were streaming back across the meadow as they fell on what remained of their enemy with relish, hacking into the flank of the panicked warriors as they attempted to regroup with their backs to the Afen. A quick reckoning told Eofer that about a third of the men who had rushed across from Clausentum in the night to block their path had fallen in their attack—a few to the swords of Hemming and Eofer himself, but most beneath the hooves of the stampeding horses. Many of the dead lay broken by the impact of the charging animals, the arms, and legs that lay in grotesque patterns about them telling the tale of the shattered bones within. One warrior lay on his back, his face a bloody cup, the result of a stamp from one of the hooves of the war horses that had carried him here. A momentary image of a goblet of red wine came into Eofer's mind, and he turned away and forced his mind to other things.

A voice cried his name from the tangle of bodies that lay scattered about the floodplain, and Eofer looked across to see that Osbeorn and Imma Gold were frantically beckoning him across. As a stab of apprehension flared within him, he exchanged a look with Hemming and hurried over. The body of a horse lay on its side, the left foot of its rider still held fast in its stirrup, and Eofer realised immediately that it could only belong to Octa. Hopping across the scattered dead, he rounded the rump of the horse as Osbeorn and Imma heaved against the back of the animal. To his relief, Octa was still alive and conscious, and his duguth forced an ironic grin as his lord came up. 'I picked the wrong horse, lord,' he gasped through bloodied teeth, 'the stirrups were made for a dwarf. I tried to jump clear, but my foot was jammed tight!' Hemming was already using his knife to hack away at the earth beneath his friend's trapped leg, and Eofer saw that they would soon have him free. Glancing across to ensure that no enemies were close by, he saw for the first time the shaft of a heavy spear protruding from the horse's chest. Little remained to be seen of the stout weapon, and Eofer was in little doubt that the force of the onrushing horse had driven it deep, dividing its great heart, killing it instantly.

Hemming scooped out the last of the soil and scampered around to grip Octa by the shoulder.

'Ready? After three!'

Octa's eyes went wide, and he grunted with pain as Osbeorn and Imma put their shoulders to the horse and Hemming pulled their friend free.

Eofer cursed as the degree of damage the tumble had caused his duguth became clear. 'A dislocation! Shit!' he exclaimed. 'You won't be going far with that, Oct.'

The surviving enemy troops were pinned safely against the riverbank and the immediate danger had receded, but they all knew that Octa could not be moved in his present condition, the pain would be unbearable and probably fatal. It would be an ignominious death for a warrior of his standing, and Eofer was not surprised when the man spoke up. 'Hand me my sword. Leave me here, lord.'

He opened his mouth to protest, but the words caught in his throat as he realised the futility of them.

'You have to leave before this Nathan arrives with his army. Prop me up and ride away.' Octa's fatalistic smile turned into a wince as another wave of pain shot through his body. 'Think of me sinking Woden's mead when you are next sleeping under a bush in the drizzle.'

A small knot of Nathan's men, no more than a dozen, had become cut off from the main force in the chaos. Spearmen had rounded them up nearby, and they watched fearfully, already guessing their fate. If the barbarian had to leave one of his number here as they rode away, he could not leave them alive to overwhelm the wounded man. They could be dead in moments.

Cerdic came up and Eofer hauled himself to his feet and forced a smile as the British leader clasped him in delight. As the magister took a step back, Eofer recognised the light of victory that shone in the Briton's eyes. It had been in his own before he had recognised Octa's boot.

'That was well done, Eofer,' he said. 'The enemy swept away and a supply of horses to boot!'

A group of warriors hovered nearby headed by the magister's son, and Cerdic was again the leader as the smile fell away. He indicated the horses with a flick of his head. 'Get going, ride like the wind.'

Cynric gave a curt nod and led the men across to the milling animals. Cerdic watched as they mounted up and hauled their heads to the north.

'It is little more than five or six miles from here to Sorbiodunum. As soon they are aware of our presence here, my friends will escort us safely home. I will not abandon my men and ride to safety, even with our destination so close. If the army from Venta do catch us between here and the fortress, Cynric will take my place at the head of the Christian forces.'

Cerdic's face took on a more sombre hue as he glanced at Octa and back to the eorle. 'That's a bad twist. Is the leg fully out of joint?'

Eofer gave a slight nod.

'It's a fortune of war,' the Briton said sadly. 'I am afraid that we can't wait.'

'The matter has already been discussed. Octa will remain here and die, sword in hand. I will join him in Valhall when the wyrd sisters decide the time has come to snip my life thread.'

'Maybe,' Cerdic mused sceptically as he fingered the cross that hung at his neck, 'maybe not. I respect the right of any man to choose his God, but I will pray for his soul along with those of my men who died here today when we are safely in Sorbiodunum.' He shrugged as he raised a brow at the Englishman. 'Unless you feel that it will offend your gods. I am confident that you will agree that it shan't do any harm.'

The sounds of fighting tapered away from the riverside, as the British and English warriors pulled back and awaited instructions from their leaders. Every man knew that they were still far from safety. To continue fighting against a beaten enemy only invited unnecessary casualties among their number, and ate into the time they needed to gain the refuge of the hill fort that was their goal.

Cerdic left Eofer with a pat of encouragement and stalked across, pushing his way to the front. As his men nervously looked on, their leader addressed the remaining knot of survivors, the closest of which stood little more than a spear's length away.

'Quickly throw your weapons into the Afen. Follow in their wake and you will live. Any man still standing on this side of the river will be killed when I reach my horse.' Cerdic spun on his heel, and his men parted gratefully as he retreated out of danger. Within moments, the first of the enemy had turned and slithered down the bank to splash into the shallows. As all opposition crumbled and the men seized the unexpected opportunity to survive the rout, the last of them tossed their spears aside and struck out for the opposite bank.

Their departure could be only moments away, and Eofer knew that the time to deal with the captives had arrived. Octa shuddered, a savage pain shooting through his body as Hemming and Imma began to prop him upright against the broad back of his fallen mount. Eofer led Osbeorn across to the sullen group. As he drew a breath to give the order to begin the slaughter, a voice cried out from the rear of the terror-stricken prisoners.

'I can fix that.'

As Cerdic's men drew their swords and prepared to strike, the voice called again in desperation.

'I said that I can fix your man's leg.'

Eofer hesitated and searched the group with his eyes. The voice came again, and he realised for the first time that it carried the higher pitch of a young woman.

'If you spare these men, I can have your man on a horse before the rest leave.'

Eofer eagerly grasped the chance to save his friend. 'Come out, quickly. You have until Cerdic returns, or you die along with the others.'

The body of Britons parted to allow a girl of about fourteen winters to make her way through. Clad in the russet colours typical of the lower sort, the young woman had brightened her appearance by attaching the long swarthy feathers of a hawk to her chestnut coloured hair. It lent her a wild appearance, and Eofer saw that her expression was resolute despite the nearness of death.

She drew up before him and held his gaze despite the difference in height, and a hint of steel came into her voice. 'They leave first,' she said.

Anger flared within him as he realised that he was in no position to bargain. The girl was Octa's only hope, and she knew it.

He looked across to the men guarding the prisoners and snapped out an order. 'Let them go.' As the men hesitated, unsure if they should follow the orders of a barbarian, he shouted angrily. 'I said let them go. NOW!'

As Cerdic's men lowered their spears, the prisoners exchanged a look of disbelief at their fortune before they turned and pelted for the cover of the trees.

Eofer gripped the girl roughly by the sleeve and shoved her across. 'Get it done, quickly,' he snarled, 'or a spear in the guts will seem like a merciful death.'

Two of the Britons, an older man and what looked to be his son, had hung back from the fleeing captives and the girl shouted across to them as she crossed to where Octa lay. 'Lose yourself in the greenwood. Go!' The younger man plucked at his father's sleeve, and the pair threw the girl a final look before reluctantly melting into the shadows.

'Lay him on his back,' she said to Hemming as she came up, 'and give him something to bite down upon.'

As Hemming cut a length from Octa's belt and jammed it between his teeth, the girl knelt and worked her fingers into Octa's groin. His eyes widened again as the pain redoubled, and the girl nodded to herself. 'Hold his shoulders still,' she ordered gleefully, 'this is going to very painful.' Taking hold of his foot, she gingerly eased her own into the duguth's groin and exchanged a look with Hemming. The Englishman understood and lent his weight onto his friend's shoulders as the Briton heaved and gave the leg a sharp twist. Octa's eyes bulged as the leg jumped back into place with a dull click, and a moment later he spat out the leather and gasped with surprise. 'The pain's gone!'

Broad grins spread around the group as the realisation that Octa's journey to Woden's high gabled hall had been postponed.

'He will need the leg splinted for a while, a spear will be ideal,' she said, 'nice and straight.'

Eofer placed a hand onto her shoulder and gave it a squeeze in gratitude. He indicated the tree line with a jerk of his head as he slipped a gold ring from his finger and handed it to the wide-eyed young woman. 'You have my thanks. Go and join your friends, before the warriors return from the riverside.'

To the thegn's astonishment, the girl handed back the ring. 'I have no need for gold. For payment, I only ask that you take me with you, lord,' she pleaded. 'I can use a bow, and I know something of what you call leechcræft. Your man will need help with the pain for the next few weeks until any muscle tears heal.' Despite her earlier steeliness, the girl's lip began to tremble, and she lowered her voice in a plaintive cry. 'Please, lord.'

Eofer was taken aback, but a quick glance at his men confirmed the acceptance in their eyes. He gave a curt nod, his thoughts already returning to the need to be away from this place. 'Retrieve your bow stave and travel with Octa. We will speak later.'

Mocking shouts carried across from the riverbank as the last of the enemy splashed across the river. His own duguth and youth back at his side, Eofer watched as Cerdic crossed to the horses and, back to his jovial self, shot him a grin. 'Three to a horse, Eofer! Not quite the triumphant procession that I envisaged when we set out!'

Eofer turned to the English as they checked their weapons, gently stroking sharpening stones along their blades as they teased out a nick, restoring the edge after the fighting. 'Well, you all heard the man. Let's get to this Sorbiodunum before the avenging horde arrives.'

4

The road crested a small rise before slanting away into a wide vale as their goal came into sight. The sun chose that moment to break through the pillowy clouds to the east, and a shaft of golden light played on the great grassy banks of Sorbiodunum.

Even at a distance, the hill fort was impressive, and Eofer studied the defences with the practised eye of an attacker. Perched atop an isolated hill, a deep ditch was backed by a high bank that angled back to follow the contours of the hill itself. The raking light revealed that the outer bank was backed up by an inner ring that contained the town itself. A pale line capped this bank, indicating where the main defences were built. A wall of stone rose to the height of a ship's mast, above which a palisade of stout timber encircled the whole. Points of light glinted there as the sun reflected from the helms and spear blades of the defenders lining the walkway. What appeared to be the only entrance was guarded by a gatehouse atop its own small hill before the high stone walls of the main gateway itself, the great archway visible even from distance. The sun was hot now, and a thin skein of woodsmoke lay across the roofs of the town in the sultry air as the inhabitants prepared the first food of the day.

The riders exchanged broad smiles as their destination hove into view, and Eofer snorted again at the rag-tag appearance of Cerdic's great relieving army. Most of the English horsemen had been able to mix in duguth with the smaller forms of their youth. But the Britons had been less fortunate, and Eofer's mouth creased into a smile as he watched them now, bouncing along three-up on the backs of the labouring horses as they rode down into the vale.

A host of crows rose noisily into the air and passed them heading south as a lone shepherd, a timeless silhouette against the skyline, rested against his crook and held out a calming hand to the black and white dogs at his side. Movement from the town drew his eye back to the fortress as a dark line of horses left the great archway and snaked past the gatehouse. Clear of the town, they broke into a gallop, and they could see that each rider led a pair of spare mounts. Cerdic rode nearby, and he edged his mount across as the end of their journey together approached. A quick glance to the east told them that the expected cloud of enemy horsemen had yet to appear, and the leaders exchanged a smile. Natan had missed his best chance to end the war in a morning.

'Are you accompanying us into the fortress?'

Eofer pursed his lips. 'I need to return to the ships. Is there a different road that will take us back?'

Cerdic shook his head sadly. 'I am afraid that the men you left there are already dead, my friend. If the Jutes did alert Natan's forces to our presence, as seems likely, I am certain that they would have returned to Afen mouth in force to deal with the ships at first light. Trapped in the lagoon…' He hesitated and grimaced. 'I am sorry.'

Eofer persisted. 'Are there no other roads south?'

'Only paths through the woodlands that we passed through during the night. Very few men live in the wilderness, and most of the trackways that do exist, do so merely for hunters and wolf heads.' He nodded across to the British girl who was busily massaging feeling back into Octa's groin, much to the amusement of those around them. 'You can ask your new companion, they meander all over. The bay where you left your ships will be seething with our enemies, long before you can regain it.' He leaned across as the riders from the hill fort crossed the wide vale under a shroud of dust. 'Fight for me, Eofer. I pay well for men with verve and intelligence, men such as yourself. Believe me,' he chuckled, 'I have fought with many men during my time on God's Earth, and they are qualities that are seldom found together within the same man.'

Eofer snorted. 'Fight a war against my gods? My ancestors await me in Valhall. A simple fight is one thing, a religious war quite another. I will not jeopardise that long-awaited reunion for silver.'

'You misunderstand this war, my friend,' Cerdic replied. 'Which God a man turns to for succour is the least part of it. Many of the men who fight for our cause still follow the old gods of Albion, they have always held sway among the country folk.' He fingered the cross at his neck as he spoke. 'God understands and loves them still. In time, they flock to his light like moths to the flame of truth, and he will rejoice in it. God has sent me a vision, Eofer, a vision of the future. Nathan and his followers want to return the land to a mystical past, a land of druids and magic, but those days can never return. A spark has been lit today, the first kindling of a flame that will sweep the land of Britannia. These fields around you now are the crucible from which armies will go forth to unite the various civitates and chiefdoms, it will be one kingdom under one God, indivisible and strong.' Eofer watched as Cerdic's eyes shone with the fervour of his vision. 'The process has already begun. Our cousins the Atrebates to the north have added their spears to ours. Beyond them their friends the Saxons of the Gewisse control the River Thamesis and the lands thereabouts.' He turned his charismatic smile on Eofer, and the Englishman felt the power of the moment. 'Wouldn't you like to play a part in the birth of a great nation, Eofer, to help inscribe the very first capitulum of its story? Think on it,' he urged. 'If your people who have settled the old lands of the Iceni joined with the Gewisse, this nation would already stretch from the shores of the German Sea to the Soluente.'

Eofer snorted. 'You forget that I am a lowly thegn, the leader of a war-band. My king still lives in our homeland across the German Sea, the new settlements are just that, lands that owe my king allegiance. I have no power there.'

Cerdic chuckled. 'I think that you underestimate your influence, all men of worth have heard the tale of Eofer king's bane. Tell your prince of my plans here and remember,' he said, 'there is always a place for you among us.' The Briton laid a hand on Eofer's sleeve and fixed him with his gaze. 'I offer you good land and honour, king's bane. Dark soil in which to sink your roots. Settle your family here among us and I will make you one of my most powerful lords.'

Horns sang in the near distance, and the pair looked up to see that the horsemen from Sorbiodunum had gained the ridge. They were only a mile or so away, hurrying on beneath their long-tailed banners of scarlet and gold. As Cerdic put the spur to his horse and galloped forward to meet them, Hemming caught Eofer's eye, and he saw the excitement written there. Both men knew that the Briton was offering them all that they craved in life. Eofer allowed his eyes to run across the wide vale before them, and he breathed in the scent of the wildflowers that lay scattered about as his mind began to construct his new hall. He would journey home for the harvest and make his plans. Come the spring he would be a lord of the Belgae.

THE RETURNING sun was little more than a blush on the distant trees as the English riders rode out from the shadow of the great fortress. Thundering beneath the gatehouse, they slanted across the scarp and turned the heads of their mounts to the north.

Deadbeat after two days at sea followed by a night march and battle, Cerdic's Britons and Eofer's English alike had stayed at the celebrations that marked the return of the exiles no longer than good manners required. Shown to a guest hall nearby, they had quickly settled down, and soon the space had echoed to the sound of sleeping men.

Eofer had delighted the Briton by accepting his offer of lordship, promising to return in the spring to swear his allegiance. To his surprise, Cerdic had laughed when Eofer had asked him for the best route to take, now that their ships were gone, and they were about to traverse an unfamiliar country. The Briton had explained that Sorbiodunum lay at the southern end of the age-old road known as the Iceni Hill Way, that wove its way to the north-east and ended at the new English settlement of Theodford itself, his destination. The route that the English knew as the Great South Road could not have been more fortuitous, and the eorle wondered that the hand of Woden lay on this gods luck.

Cerdic had supplied the Engle with fresh mounts and remounts for their homeward journey as compensation for the loss of their ships, and the common folk stopped their work and watched in awe as hundreds of horses swept past the dew covered fields.

Clear of Sorbiodunum, the road climbed steadily until it broke free of the woodlands, out on to a wide grassy plain. Dwynwyn, Octa's saviour, had kept to her word, and the duguth was already out of his splint and moving freely once the mash of herbs and seeds that the girl had concocted had dulled his pain. The Englishmen had found the girl's name almost unpronounceable, and it had quickly become obvious to Eofer that if she were to remain with his troop she would need to change her name, quickly. She, in her turn, had disliked the sound of the English names suggested by the men. Finally, they had settled upon the Engle name of the bird whose feathers she wore so proudly in her hair— Spearhafoc, the Sparrow hawk.

They had only spoken briefly the night before, but Eofer recalled that she had promised him that he would be passing through a landscape unlike any other the following day. He still knew little about the latest member of his hearth troop and, intrigued, passed word back through the column that she ride forward to join him at its head. She came up as the sun finally broke through to bathe the downland in its golden light, and Eofer ran his eyes across a vista of hills that rolled away to the east and west. The Afen, the river that they had followed from the coast, ran nearby within its deeply incised valley. Eofer idly wondered how long it would take the water that burbled across the rocks there to pass the site of the battle of the previous day, and the burnt out hulks of his ships at its mouth. A carpet of hair grass stretched up to a stand of juniper, crowning a knoll like a young lad's unruly mop. Tall stalks of meadow brome, the sunlight playing from the purple ears as they swayed gently in the breeze, reminded him of the sea that he loved so much, and he felt a pang of regret as he was reminded of Sæward and the lads. Had they saved themselves? It would be some time until he found out for sure.

A polite cough brought his mind back from its meanderings, and he saw that Spearhafoc was at his side. He was pleased to see that she rode well and, in her muted clothing of greens and browns, polished bow stave and full quiver, she certainly looked the part of a woodsman. He turned to her and smiled. 'This is a beautiful place, is this the landscape you promised me?'

Her mouth turned up into a knowing smile and her face lit up in expectation. 'No,' she replied, 'trust me, you will remember this day for the rest of your life, lord.'

'Well,' he said as the horses walked on, 'perhaps you can tell me a little about yourself while I await this great thing? You can begin by telling me how you learned to speak our tongue so well.'

'In a way,' she began, 'it's the reason I am here with you now. The men who were waiting for me at the tree line after the battle were my father and brother. They were the only ones who meant anything to me there, the only ones I was desperate to save. But I preferred not to return with them.'

Eofer took a swig from his water skin and handed it across. The day was warming up nicely and promised to become hot. Talking was thirsty work. She took a sip and smiled her thanks as she handed it back and explained.

'My family live within the great forest that you passed. We hunt there and trade the skins and meat in the towns and villages near the coast for fish, milk, cheese, bread,' she rattled off, 'the usual stuff. When Nathan took over, he settled Jutes from Cent near the coast and across the water on Ictis. You might know it as Vectis,' she added as an afterthought. 'The Saxons have all but taken over the lands of the Regni, our neighbours to the east,' she explained, 'and Aelle's son,

Cissa, was forever raiding the borderlands. The Jutes hate the Saxons, and they were settled there to keep them at bay.'

Eofer chuckled. 'The Jutes hate everyone, especially the English.'

She widened her eyes in surprise and he explained. 'The Jutish homeland lies to the north of my own, across the German Sea in Engeln. We have had many dealings with them over the years,' he said with a wolfish smile. 'They are our favourite prey.'

A butterfly, its golden brown wings flicking erratically, settled on the ear of his horse and the beast flicked its head in irritation until it fluttered way. They shared a chuckle at the sight before she continued with her story.

'My father was keen to make friends among the Jutes, they bought a lot of our meat and pelts, and he described them as the future. One of them took a shine to me, and my father promised me to him when I reached my fourteenth year. Until then, I had to learn their words so that I could take my place among them when the time came.'

'And when was that?'

'At the end of summer, lord, after the harvest.'

'So you ran away to join the barbarians.'

She grimaced. 'I never saw myself as what you call a *wyf*, sitting at a loom and sweeping out the hut every day. My mother is a healer, respected for her craft. I learned to hunt from my father and the secrets of healing men and animals from my mother. They are rare gifts for a girl born in the backwoods and I wanted to be able to use them, so when I saw the chance I ran away with you, lord.'

He nodded, thoughtfully. Woden, the Allfather, was the god of healing, and he roared through the sky at the head of the wild hunt every Jule eve. If the Allfather had sent this girl to aid him, it could prove to be a powerful gift.

'I have seen your skill at leechcræft,' he said, nodding towards the bow that bounced at the horse's flank, 'but I have yet to see you loose an arrow.'

She shot him a look and unhooked the stave from the saddle horn without a word. Bracing it against her hip, she forced the bow into shape and hooked the bowstring to the nocks. Scanning the grassland to the east, she nocked an arrow and sighted high. A soft grunt escaped her lips as the arrow was released, and Eofer watched in bemusement as the shaft sailed into the empty sky.

'You can hit the sky!' he exclaimed sarcastically, 'very impressive.'

Spearhafoc was already fitting another shaft to the string as Eofer glanced across his shoulder at the men following on. To a man, they were raising their heads to follow the flight of the missile, and the thegn hoped that the girl was not about to make a fool of herself. Looking back, he saw that the shaft had reached the top of its arc as the head tipped down towards the earth. The arrow plummeted vertically into a thicker growth of sedge, and immediately the air was filled with movement as a covey of quail exploded from cover. A shaft sped from Spearhafoc's bow, and then another as the birds wheeled and climbed in all directions. Eofer watched as the first took a hen bird, its brown and tan plumage perfectly matched to its surroundings, full in the chest. As the body of the bird was punched back by the force of the blow, the second arrow plucked another from the air and sent it spinning away into the undergrowth. The quail had scattered now, and Eofer watched as Spearhafoc nocked a final arrow, quartering the sky for what must be her final victim. One terror-stricken bird, its plumage a burnt orange as it caught the rays of the sun, had flown directly towards the men. Eofer looked on in admiration as the girl hooked her foot into the bridle, leaning back until she was almost horizontal to the saddle. A sighting glance along her chest confirmed her aim, and the arrow was away. The men of the column held their breath as the shaft and its target converged until, with a dip of its wing, the quail flashed past the arrow and made its escape.

At his side the girl spat a curse as the bird lost height and sheared off into a gully, and Eofer for the first time realised that the column had come to a halt as they watched her demonstration. The spell broken, the men whooped and bawled their delight, and Eofer turned to the girl and added his praise to her efforts.

'That was fine shooting,' he laughed. 'Was *that* the thing of wonder that you promised to show me this day?'

Spearhafoc was the centre of attention for perhaps the first time in her life, and she flushed with pride as she pointed to the road ahead.

'No, lord,' she giggled self-consciously. 'That awaits you just beyond that rise.'

5

Crossing the stone bridge, Eofer had split the party into two and hobbled the horses. He would lead the first of the men forward along what was clearly a sacred way that curved towards the great megalith, dominating the skyline to the west. Despite the sanctity of the site and the eagerness of the men to visit its heart, he had been forced to post guards on their mounts. Ahead, in the near distance, the road ran below another of the hill forts that the old people had spread liberally across their land, and although Cerdic had assured them that the walls were held by men loyal to the house of Uther, it paid to take precautions. Hundreds of war horses would be enough to tempt any man, but the sight of three score English spears formed up in battle array should be enough to dissuade all but the most determined attackers, he had reasoned.

The processional route ran from the place where the Afen took a great bow to the west, following the contours of the land as it arced uphill to the great monument. It was a plain that had clearly been one of the main centres of gods worship ever since men had walked the soil of Middle-earth. Scores of barrows littered the landscape, singly and in groups, testament to the age-old connection here between men and their gods.

Hemming walked at his side as Spearhafoc led them on, the young girl clearly fighting against the urge to move ahead faster as they travelled between the standing stones that marked the path.

Spearhafoc spoke, and the pride that she felt for the landscape shone through her words. 'Have you anything to compare in your homeland, lord? My ancestors built everything that you see here with their bare hands.'

Eofer glanced at her and shook his head. 'You are mistaken. Woden placed these stones here. He used spells and the great strength of his son Thunor to shape and move them into place at the beginning of time.'

The Briton looked doubtful, but decided that her desire to remain within the group far outweighed any feelings of pride. There was a Jutish loom waiting for her in the south, and she decided to discover more about the beliefs of the big northerners and see how closely they tied in to those of her people.

'Did Woden create everything, lord?'

'No, he was the son of a god and a giant.'

'So what came before?'

He looked down and, recognising that the Briton seemed to be genuinely interested in the ways of his people, decided to describe how the world had begun. The sun was hot now, and a light breeze pushed downy clouds away to the northeast as he loosened his shirt and instinctively fingered his hammer pendant. A warrior life had led him to be as fatalistic as any man, but it paid to ward off malevolent spirits, especially in such a place as this.

'At the beginning there was a great void, a place of silence and darkness. To the south lay the realm of fire and to the north, a world of ice. Where the cold air met the warm, the icy mist was warmed and droplets of water appeared. From these the giant, Tuisto, was born. His son, Mannus, coupled with a giantess who bore him Woden. Woden killed Tuisto and created the Earth from his body.'

She pulled a wry smile. 'You are not much of a storyteller, lord, but I get the idea.'

Eofer exchanged a look with Hemming, and the men laughed.

'No,' he admitted, 'storytelling has never been one of my great strengths.' He enjoyed her company, and Eofer flashed her a smile as he finally resolved the question that he had turned over in his mind over the course of the last day. 'As I have decided to admit you to my hearth troop, I will introduce you to a guda, one of our priests, when we reach Theodford. He can guide you in our ways.'

Spearhafoc's face lit up at the revelation, and she uttered her thanks as a life spent teasing wool and stirring great cauldrons of pottage receded into the shadows. The sacred way turned sharply south and conversation trailed away as Eofer saw that the monolith was near. Seen up close, the great stones glowered over the surrounding countryside, and Spearhafoc lowered her voice as she spoke again.

'They are called the ringing stones, lord,' she explained. 'I will show you why when we reach them.'

A single stone stood upright in the centre of the way, and the warriors removed their weapons before passing through a bank and ditch into the interior that contained the structures themselves. The men gathered around and listened to the Briton as she explained. 'The final part of the causeway leads directly down to the heart of the ringing stones themselves. Belanus, The Shining One, rises on the summer solstice directly in line with the solitary stone that we passed, and the light floods down to fill the cup made by the central ring. The outer circle that surrounds them, the ringing stones themselves, represent the circle of life. At midwinter the sun sets directly in line with the sacred way and the energy captured and held within the circle at midsummer drains away, returning to Belanus, restoring the god's strength for the coming year and completing the circle.' She crossed to the nearest of the upright columns and fished out a small iron rod that hung at her neck. 'Listen carefully,' she said as she leaned closer to the stone. Spearhafoc rapped the surface with the pendant, and a high-pitched ringing sound carried to the awestruck men. She ushered in one of the warriors and handed him the pendant. 'Let's see who has the gift among us.'

The men shuffled their feet nervously, exchanging sheepish looks, until Imma Gold shook his head and threw a look of pity around the assembled warriors. 'I will go first. Wyrd decides the days left to you, not god stones.'

They strained their ears as the duguth took the pendant and gave the column a sharp tap, but no sound came. Imma shrugged and shot them a grin. 'I'm not spooky. Who's next?'

One by one the men came forward, and the reluctance to volunteer receded as it became plain that none of the men possessed what the girl had called 'the gift'. Finally, only Eofer remained and, confident now that he would not cause the stone to ring, the eorle took the iron shank and struck the upright squarely.

EOFER GLANCED BACK across his shoulder and cried out to his banner man as the dyke came into view. 'Keep that *herebeacn* high Hræfen. I have ridden far too far to end the journey impaled on the point of an English spear.'

Back in familiar territory, the men of the eorle's war-band exchanged smiles and happy banter as they grew nearer to the great earthwork of *fleama,* its high ramparts bringing back memories of distant Sorbiodunum to the travel-weary column. As faces began to appear along the palisade that ran the length of the dyke and the great wooden doors were hauled inward in welcome, Eofer's mind ran back through the journey they had just undertaken. It had taken them three days to wend their way along the great chalk spine that carried the ancient path called the Iceni Hill Way, and he chuckled at the memory of the first night. They had pitched up at another of the hill forts that seemed to litter the countryside in the southern part of the island as the sun sat low on the horizon. The bright glow in the west had hidden their identity for long enough to enable them to enter the fort before the small force there could close the gates to them, and they had spent a safe and comfortable night among the party of Saxons who had been tasked with defending the outpost by their Atrebatic overlords. Eofer snorted with amusement as he recalled the wariness of the garrison that evening as the Engles cavorted around them. They had had the look, as Hemming had described them full of beery cheer, *'of mice caught by a party of cats',* knowing that at any moment the captors could tire of the game and the claws would slide from their sheaths. Eager to have them on their way, the Saxons had promised to show the English the great white horse that had been carved into the hillside below the camp as it caught the dawn sunlight. Despite their doubts, the figure had proven to be a thing of wonder.

The vistas from the highest points of the chalky hills had been impressive, and Eofer had come to realise that he must be among the very first of the English to see so deeply into the heart of the new lands. If he had harboured any doubts before, he was certain now that this island of rolling hills and trackless woodlands held the future for his people.

The thegn responsible for the men at the portal came forward as the horsemen approached, and Eofer flashed a grin and called a greeting as the tall Englishman before him removed his helm and cradled it in his arm. 'Long shanca,' he laughed. 'Did they send your ugly face here to scare the Wealas away?' Eofer slipped from his saddle, walking to greet his old friend with a smile. They shared an embrace, and he saw that the men lining the palisade were grinning happily as they parted.

'Eadweard long shanca,' he laughed, 'the terror of the Britons. Who did you upset to get sent here?'

Eadweard had fought in the war where Eofer had killed the Swedish king, Ongentheow, earning the nickname king's bane. It was the same campaign that had resulted in Eofer's father-in-law taking the Geatish king helm. To his surprise, his friend's expression became sombre.

'A lot has happened since you sailed south in the spring, Eofer. The British have been raiding all along the frontier. They have burned Grantebrycge and harried almost as far as Theodford itself.' As Eofer's mouth fell open in shock, Eadweard indicated the earthwork with a jerk of his head. 'I am holding a forward position here at the fleama ditch while practically the rest of the able-bodied men available in Anglia are busy building what men are already calling the *miceldic*, the great ditch, six miles further up the way.'

Eofer squinted across to the west. There, a half dozen miles away, the sunlight sparkled on the nearest reaches of the great waste of the Reaping. A home to trolls, sprites, marsh goblins and the barbarous Britons known as the Gyrwe, it was the perfect place to anchor a defensive ditch. But the eorle found that the need irked him like an ill-fitting shirt, and his promise to Cerdic began to tug at his conscience.

A gleam entered Eadweard's eye as he looked across to the great column of horses and men that filled the Great South Road. 'Your men look like they could use a drink or two. They will be pleased to discover that we have just been supplied. Come,' he said, clapping Eofer on the shoulder, 'I will slaughter an ox, and we will mark your safe return with a feast. It will give my lads a break from peering down the road looking for British war-bands.'

Eofer accepted gratefully, and soon the meadow in the lee of the earthwork rang with the sound of men glad to be home. As the great carcass of an ox sizzled and spat above the flames, Eadweard sank another horn of ale and shook his head sadly. 'It's no good, king's bane, the time is coming when we need to decide whether we are to live in the old country or the new. We have too few warriors to defend our lands here *and* guard the homeland. The German Sea is too broad to enable one to come to the aid of the other if they come under attack.' He pointed to the edge of the great woodlands that lay to the east. 'On the other side of that, the Wulfings are settling the coastal heathland between the Gipping and the Aeldu and threatening to push both northwards and south towards Gippeswic itself. Even the Wealas are becoming over bold.' He spat in disgust. 'I never thought that such a time would come, but unless King Eomær sends more warriors here…' He paused and held the eorle with his gaze to add emphasis to his words. 'I am not the only one thinking of returning to my lands at home, Eofer, rather than skulk behind earthen walls. If that's the only choice available to us, Anglia will have to be abandoned.'

. . .

THE SEA SPRAY hung in the air as the bows rose again, a thousand droplets shimmering like pearls in the morning light. Eofer braced himself, his back resting in the curve of the stern, thrilling to the sight of the little ship as she breasted another wave before switching his gaze outboard to take in the remainder of the English fleet. Twenty ships this year would make the journey back to the motherland of the English, each ship with its cargo of warriors—hardened fighters who were desperately needed to defend the new lands. Eofer's mind drifted back across the events of the previous week.

The summer was drawing on, the harvest in full swing, as they had rowed the *Fælcen* into mid-stream and put the walls of Theodford behind them. It would still be another month or so before the apples were ripe enough to pick, and he would be home long before then, ready to help gather in his crop from the orchard that stood beside the brook. Other than the Briton, Eofer had been the only one among them who had caused the great stones to ring, and Spearhafoc had stuck to his side, doe-eyed with wonder. It had been, she had assured him, a sign from the gods of the old people that the Englishman had a great part to play in the future of the island. Eofer had assumed at first that they were confirming his decision to join Cerdic's quest to unite the Britons. But the meeting with Eadweard had confirmed to him, that it had been the Allfather and his son who had constructed the great monument, after all. He was sure now that his wyrd was to help settle his people in the new lands, even if that meant abandoning the motherland itself. Tiring of Spearhafoc's adulation, Eofer had packed the girl off to the ealdorman's guda to help her learn the ways of the gods. At first, he had thought to leave without her. But she had proven to be a popular addition to the hearth troop, and her prowess with the bow had saved her from that fate.

No word had reached the ealdorman at the town of the fate of Sæward and his youth, and Eofer had begun to reluctantly accept that they were lost. The shipowners had been delighted to accept war horses as compensation for their lost vessels, while the men who had manned them had been sent on their way with purses groaning with silver and great tales to recount. It was treasure well spent, Eofer knew. Men would flock to his banner if he ever called again.

The snake ships of the homeward-bound fleet had trickled away singly and in pairs from the western settlements as the leaves began to lose their summer sheen. Deep laden after the raiding season, the larger ships were forced to take the waters of the River Udsos north through the wild lands of the Reaping, before sailing around the great sweep of the Anglian coast and steering a course for the south. Of a shallower draft, the *Fælcen* had followed the same river eastwards towards its headwaters, before taking the River Wahenhe directly to the East Coast. The river spilled out into the great bay that sheltered beneath the walls of the old Roman fort the English called Cnobheresburg, and it was here that the fleet had assembled for the crossing to Engeln.

The sun was lower in the southern sky, the slanting light painting the crests of the waves the colour of silver as the long days of summer drained away. Eofer thought back on the conversations that he had had within the settlement at Theodford and later, when they had called at the burh of Bunoncgahaye. Sited on higher land where the Wahenhe took a great bow to the north, Bonna, the thegn who had lent his name to the fortress at the neck of the peninsula, had worried the eorle with tales of encroaching Wulfings, Saxons and even Swæfe.

It had added to the general feeling of unease that he had sensed among the beleaguered settlers, and as the water meadows and woodlands of the interior had drawn back to become the salt marsh and reed beds of the coastal strip, it had strengthened his resolve to press his father, an ealdorman and trusted retainer, to bring the matter to the king's urgent attention when next they met. He had seen the interior of Britannia, and he was sure now in his mind that the future of a vibrant and proud people such as the English lay there. It would be madness to let their hold on such a land slip away without a fight.

Sæward's cry brought the eorle's thoughts back to the present as he pointed away to the south and exchanged a grin with his lord. A longship, the wolf's head pennant of the Wulfings flying proudly from its mast top, had chosen prudence over duty and was edging further inshore as the English fleet bore down upon it, their dragon banners teased out to the east in a cat's paw of wind. Eofer had found the duguth safely ensconced within the stone walls of Cnobheresburg and, even though it had not entered their heads to send word of their return onward to Theodford, all had been quickly forgotten as the steersman and his youth told the tale of their escape and heard the story of the fighting at Cerdicsford for the first time.

As the ships of the fleet came abreast the estuary of the Gipping, they turned together and put their prows to the sea. Eofer took a last look at the low dark hills that backed the shoreline there and smiled with satisfaction. It had been a good year. He had prospered and enhanced his reputation; soon he would be riding the path that led to his hall. Already he could picture Astrid at the door, little Weohstan running to greet his father. A quick trip across the cold waters of the German Sea and he would be there. The army of his kinsman, King Hygelac, was raiding in the lands of the Franks and

Frisians opposite and Eofer toyed with the idea of seeking them out en-route but discounted it. The season was well advanced, and the best pickings would already be safely stowed in Geatish hulls. It had been the talk of Anglia and many men had left to try their sword arm, despite the actions of the Britons on the frontier.

The sun shone steadily, the light airs matched his mood, and he relaxed as the *Fælcen* ploughed the sail road. The Allfather had flicked back the curtain that hid the future from the eyes of men, offering him a glimpse of the path ahead for his people and the part he must play in it. The weather was perfect for the crossing, a lazy passage, and he would be home before the new moon waned.

6

The thegn scanned the horizon and chewed his lip. It didn't look good. It didn't look good at all.

Sæward wiped his hands on the seat of his trews and took a firmer grip on the steer bord. 'Look at it move.'

Away to the south, a boiling rampart of darkness was bearing down on the ships of the English fleet, and the pair watched as the steersmen instinctively hauled at their own big blades and fanned out. They would need all the sea room they could get, and soon. The storm was little more than a mile or so distant now, moving quickly, the leading edge pulsing as lightning bolts flickered with silent menace.

The sea was already coming alive and the *Fælcen* began to saw as white caps showed alongside, creamy waves slapping against the strakes of the sleek longship as they shot by.

The men exchanged a look, Sæward spoke; 'Half way?'

Eofer risked a glance to the south and was horrified to discover that the storm front had already gobbled up half the distance to them. He shook his head, crying out against the force of the freshening wind as he began to make his way down the ship. 'A third, any more, and we will be lucky if we only lose the sail. If the mast goes over the side…'

The crew had gathered amidships, and they wrenched their faces away from the wall of death as their eorle approached.

He would need the strongest, most experienced men at the oars if they were to ride this one out. Eofer snapped out his orders. 'Duguth, you row. Lash oars to thole-pins and keep us from broaching.' He turned to the expectant faces of the younger warriors. 'Youth, you bail.'

Rounding on the two dark-haired lads, he stabbed out a finger. 'Crawa, Hræfen, lower the spar two-thirds and square it off. Reef the sail to a third, then I want you to stand by the sheets. Keep your eyes on the sail. If it looks like it is about to blow out, forget pulling the pins, just use your knife to cut them.' He flashed them a smile of encouragement. 'Better to go two sheets to the wind than swim home.'

The twins gave a nervous laugh and scampered off to their task as Eofer cast a look of longing at the twin wash strakes lying snugly on the cross trees amidships. Fixed along the wale they were used to raise the freeboard in heavy seas but, casting a look beyond the sweep of the stern, Eofer could see that it was already too late to peg them into place. The storm was upon them.

The crew looked up as a dark hand reached out to smother the sun and a spray of raindrops, as large and heavy as peas, swept across to freckle the deck.

Eofer hurried back to the steering platform, ready to throw his weight alongside the steersman. A last glance outboard, and he gasped at the terrible beauty as the English ships, islands of colour and life in a vista of purple and black, were swallowed by the monster.

In the blink of an eye, the *Fælcen* was engulfed. Wind

and wave searched out the smallest chink in their defences and found one as the power of the first roller nudged the stern aside. It was only a fraction, but it was enough, and the following wave smashed into the tall stern post like a shield strike, the ship recoiling from the blow and offering up a glimpse of her flank to the onrushing madness. As the *Fælcen* began to broach, Eofer threw himself bodily into Sæward and desperately added his weight to the push. Both men grimaced with effort and fear as they stared down at the shredded waves that threatened to swamp them. The steerbord sheer strake was kissing the sea, they were a heartbeat from the end as she began to respond and drag herself back to an even keel.

Before the ship could right herself the next wave shovelled the stern, thrusting it skyward as the bows disappeared in a mantle of spray, but she was a well-found ship, and she lived up to her name, lithe, fearless; a hunter. Rising again from the swell, she shook the water from her timbers and forged ahead. As the great hooked beak of the prow crept around, Eofer scanned the deck and the breath caught in his throat as he saw that the boy, Hræfen, was missing from his place at the steer bord side. As his eyes moved out to search the wind-torn surface of the sea for any sign of the lad, the arm of Imma Gold reached out from his place at the benches and casually plucked a dark mass from the waters, depositing it in the scuppers like a bundle of sodden rags. The big warrior bent to his oar, the eorle watching with pride as the bundle came back to life and the boy dragged himself across to his station by the steer bord sheet. Kissing the lashing that had saved his life, Hræfen resumed his watch on the tortured sail.

Up for'ard, Eofer saw that Spearhafoc had taken up a position in the bows. Balanced perfectly, she was a young woman of many talents, and he was pleased with the qualities that she had added to his war-band. Cocky, deadly with the bow, the youth had soaked up the teachings of the guda in Theodford like parched soil after a summer storm.

The tawny feathers of the hen Sparrowhawk corkscrewed from her hair as the gale snatched away her invocation to Ran, mother of the waves, Spae-Wife of the sea god Gymir. Bracing herself in the very upturn of the prow as her daughters hurtled past only feet away, Eofer saw silver flash as an offering to the goddess, and he smiled as he lipread the last words of an invocation:

...the stormy breast-driven wave;
With red stain running out of Ran's white mouth.

The gale set up an unearthly howl in the rigging, fire bolts danced at the masthead but, with the ship running steadily before the gale, Eofer knew that the worst moments were already behind them. Clinker built in good English oak from the Wolds near his hall, the hull flexed and sang as the little scegth was driven before the white caps like the pure-blood she was.

He relaxed his grip on the steer bord and let Sæward run her on. They shared a look, and each man knew just how close they had come to joining the legions of those lost at sea, spending an eternity in Gymir's wet-cold hall.

Sæward leaned across, and they shared a laugh as the steersman cried above the noise. 'That was fun. Shall we do it again?'

EOFER CUPPED his hand and cocked his head as he strained to hear. Still, the wind snatched the words away and hurled them to the east. The worst of the storm had left them as quickly as it had arrived, but the sky remained a broth of purple and black, almost as if it had been bruised by the violence that had gone before, the sea choppy. Visibility was still poor, and he had sent the nimblest of the youth up the mast to see if any other English ships were within sight as the yard was hauled and the sail shaken out.

He cast a questioning look at Sæward, but the big steersman only shrugged, laughter dancing in his eyes. Eofer sighed and hopped from the steering platform, tossing a remark to the rows of smiling faces as he picked his way through a tangle of limbs.

'If you want something done well...' he threw out as he skipped from thwart to thwart. A chorus erupted from the upturned faces, and the eorle joined in the laughter that followed as the answer to his question came back in a yell. *'Do it yourself!'*

Reaching the mast, he gripped the lower peg and scurried aloft. Away from the shelter of the deck, the wind redoubled and Eofer clung on tightly as he climbed. The sail was as full as a fat man's shirt, the shroud lines sang and, at the masthead, the white dragon pennant writhed then snapped taut with each new gust.

The boy, Bassa, looked fearful as he came up alongside him, but Eofer shot him a grin and a heartening wink. Clear of the sail, he rested his arm on top of the spar and called above the last of the gale. 'What?'

Bassa hugged the mast and pointed away to the east. 'There are many ships over there, sailing north.'

Eofer blinked to clear his vision as the *Fælcen* crested a wave, searching hard. The horizon was blanketed in mist and spray, but he saw nothing in the moments before the ship lowered her prow and descended into the next trough. 'You are certain?'

Bassa gave a firm nod. 'Yes, lord, it looked like two groups. A larger group chasing a smaller one.'

The *Fælcen* lifted her bows, hauling herself up the side of the next grey wall, and Eofer squinted into the gloom again. Still nothing. If they *were* his countrymen, they were not where he had expected them to be, and he hesitated to approach a lee shore in this weather. Only the gods could know just how far the storm had carried them, and the coast of Frisland could not be far off in the murk. The eorle had a vision of the islands and sandbars that girdled the coast there, and shuddered. 'How many?'

The boy threw him a cheeky smile. 'I have young eyes, lord. I am not a wizard!'

Eofer suppressed a smile and stared at the lad. Admonished, the boy cleared his throat as the smirk dissolved and fell away. 'Half a dozen or so in the lead group, maybe a score or more in the chasing pack. I can't say any closer than that. I only got a quick glimpse before it all closed in again.' He looked away momentarily as the wind snatched the breath from him. Taking a gulp of air, he turned back. 'There's another thing, lord.'

Eofer shifted his weight as he awaited the revelation. The masthead was not the most comfortable place to be at the best of times, and this was far from that. 'Well, if you don't tell me quickly,' he cried as the wind snatched at his words, 'you will be beating me back to the deck, head first!'

Bassa paled, all the cheekiness of earlier driven from him. 'I couldn't make out the flags, but it looked like the ships at the rear carried crosses at the masthead.'

Eofer let out a sigh. 'Franks? Could they be chasing our ships?' He wiped the sleeve of his shirt across his face in a vain attempt at clearing away some of the salty spray that still fogged the air, and stared back to the east. Still nothing. Looking back, he opened his mouth to question the youth again, but Bassa's face was deadpan. 'I am convinced, lord.'

Eofer smiled at the boy's confidence and clapped him on the shoulder. Bassa's eorle was Eofer, king's bane. Men across the northern world knew the tale of his great deed. It took nerve to stand your ground against a man of reputation. 'Very well, hawk eye, we shall go and have a look. Call down to one of the men below as soon as they reappear.' He smiled again. 'It's unseemly for an eorle to scamper around at the beck and call of a youth!'

Eofer let himself slide back down to the deck, throwing a few words to the expectant faces as he returned to the steering platform. The wind was blowing steadily from the south-west. They would soon close with the ships and discover the identity of the mysterious flotilla. 'It looks like the Franks may be hunting some of our ships. Get the baling finished and ready yourselves for a fight, just to be certain.'

Eofer hopped up onto the steering platform and opened his mouth to speak, but snorted as he saw that Sæward already had the handle of the steer bord hauled hard into his chest. The stern post began to swing to the north as the ship responded, and, as if to light a beacon at their destination, a dagger of golden light stabbed down from a break in the clouds.

The storm was lessening with every passing moment as its front rolled away to the north-east, and soon Beornwulf was hurrying back to his lord with the latest report from the masthead. The young warrior, his face flushed with obvious disappointment, waited for his eorle to look his way and gave his report. 'Bassa can see them clearly now. Twenty-five ships are pursuing four large warships. The main group is definitely Frankish, but those in front are not our ships, lord. They fly the white boar at their masthead.'

Eofer exchanged a look of surprise with his steersman.

'Geats? I thought that they would be back in their forests by now.'

Sæward gave voice to his thoughts. 'Either the Christians have caught a few stragglers or King Hygelac's raid has met with a disaster.'

Both men shared a look of concern. The Geat king was Eofer's kinsman, the grandfather of his son. He had led a great host into the lands of the Frisians and Salian Franks early that summer, burning and plundering the rich lands at will. Merchants from the South had lived well on the English coast of Britannia that year, as thegns and warriors alike plied them with ale to hear the latest news of the fighting there. Many English ships had slipped from the mouths of the eastern rivers, the Udsos, the Blithe, looking for opportunities to flex their sword arm and earn renown, and the weakness that had resulted in Anglia had encouraged the Britons in their attacks around Grantebrycge. It was always thus, Eofer sighed, but he had to admit that he had been as culpable as any that summer. It seemed that every man on the *Fælcen* had a friend or kinsman there.

Sæward spoke again. 'Shall I come about, lord? We want to avoid blundering into the middle of a sea fight alone.'

Eofer scanned the sky and pulled at his beard as he thought. The sky away to the south was clearing to a softer blue, marbled white, but the clouds were still moving on at a pace.

He shook his head. 'We have the weather with us. Take us closer and stand-off when their hulls appear above the horizon.' He sniffed, and a smile curled at the corners of his mouth. 'I have an idea that may save these Geats from spending the rest of their days being buggered in a monastery.'

Eofer left the steering platform and made his way back

along the thwarts between the rowers. Unlike the larger ships, the small scegth were not flush decked, and any trip made fore or aft on the vessel involved negotiating either a series of hurdles or becoming an expert at keeping your footing. Eofer insisted that all of his men use the latter method. It was the best teacher of the art of balance and poise that he knew, invaluable in a fight. Reaching the mast, he threw an arm around it and called out to the leader of the small knot of bowmen. 'Grimma!'

Grimma and his men had taken passage on the *Fælcen* at Cnobheresburg, just before they had left the fortress for home. Not having the agility of a scegthman, he drew amused smiles from the men of Eofer's hearth troop as he swung a leg and vaulted each thwart in turn to reach their eorle. 'Lord?'

'Who is your worst bowman?'

Indignant, Grimma pulled himself upright. 'I don't have bad bowmen, lord.'

Eofer chuckled. 'No, of course, I will put the question another way. Which of you three has the weakest draw?'

The bowman gasped and began to splutter a reply before Eofer cut him short. 'There is a reason I am asking. It's important.'

Grimma was clearly wrestling with his conscience, as both bowmen were within hearing distance. He leaned in with a compromise solution. Lowering his voice to a whisper, he indicated the bows with a jerk of his head. 'The lassie is good with a bow, lord. She is not as strong as the lads here, but she is as accurate as any.'

EOFER WATCHED the bronze plate of the weather vane as the cockscomb straightened and snaked towards the Frankish ships. The sealskin tassels told the steersman the moment that the wind shifted, but today it blew steadily. In truth, it was unnecessary. The final blows from the storm were whipping the waves into white caps, long tendrils of spindrift echoing the actions of their man-made brethren above. Spearhafoc turned her head to him, twin fingers curled around the bowstring, a shaft nocked. 'I think that I can reach them from here.'

He nodded as her companions craned to watch the strike. 'Try to hit the steersman,' he smiled. 'It always gets their attention.'

She rolled her eyes at her eorle, and her fellow hearth warriors laughed as she offered him the bow. Eofer laughed along with the others, but he felt that he was beginning to get the measure of the girl now. She would strain every sinew of her body to hit the man now that the challenge had been made. The leading ships were well within the range of Grimma and his bowmen, and the *Fælcen* banked to bæcbord as Sæward put the helm about to run parallel with their foe.

They had arrived not a moment too soon. The Frankish ships, although heavy and unwieldy, had weathered the storm well, their bulk lending them a stability that was denied the sleeker longships of their Geatish prey. Eofer had seen immediately that the Frankish commander meant to trap the Geats in a bay a little further along the coast. Standing off from the nearby string of islands, he had cleverly bided his time as he patiently waited for the wind and tide to dash his enemy against the shore. Denied sea room, the Geats were unable to use their sails to tack so close to a lee shore, and the oarsmen were clearly tiring fast. A long low promontory, little more than a sandy bar, stood proud of the coastline a mile ahead, a dirty white fringe marking the breakers that pummelled the shore there. Ribs and masts littered the strand like the sun bleached bone-cages of sea monsters. The Geats were rowing to their doom, and they would know it.

Eofer stood back and gave Spearhafoc room as she raised the bow and drew the bowstring to her cheek. Glancing across to Grimma, he recognised the look of approval on the experienced bowman's face as the young woman calmed her breathing, bringing it into harmony with the rise and fall of the ship. Spearhafoc's eyes flitted between her target and the coil and curl of spume as the wind teased it from the wave crests, and her body relaxed as she made the final adjustments to her posture. Suddenly, she released with a grunt, and the heads of the men turned together to follow the flight of the arrow. The missile sped away, its slender shaft aimed far to the rear of the Frankish ship, but as the men watched in eager anticipation the gusting wind slowly pushed its head around to the east.

Eofer was amused to see that hundreds of Franks were mirroring their actions, their hands shading their eyes as they followed the flight of the dart. The point dipped as the shaft sped towards its target, now obvious to all as the steersman on the leading Frankish ship, and they held a collective breath as they began to realise just how good the shot was. Driven on by the powerful following wind, the arrow bore down to flash between the steersman and the heavy stern post just feet to his rear. It had been a remarkable shot, and the men of the troop whooped with joy at the skill of their new friend.

Eofer joined the laughter and turned to congratulate the woman, but stopped as he saw her spit in disgust and nock another shaft. As Spearhafoc drew the bow and sighted, he called for quiet, and a hush descended on the men as they waited for the next arrow to fly. A gull seemed to appear from nowhere, and the men laughed nervously as it hung suspended in the line of sight. But Spearhavoc's concentration was absolute and the moment that the bird sailed upwards with a harsh parting cry, the arrow sped away.

Eofer looked back across to the Franks and saw that men were attempting to attract the attention of the steersman to the threat, but the man, his eyes fixed on the Geat ships ahead, seemed oblivious. The wind had increased again, and the arrow was already into its final death dive as Eofer looked back at the target. Shifting his gaze to the Frank, Eofer gripped the wale in excitement and waited for the dart to arrive. Across the waves men were pointing to the sky and calling out a warning but, just as the steersman seemed to become aware of the approaching danger, the arrow flashed down to take him in the neck.

The men on the *Fælcen* yelled in triumph as the Frank clutched at the shaft, staggering to one side before falling forward and becoming hidden from view by the curve of the hull. As the men of the troop cheered and called, their eorle nodded to Grimma and within moments the three bowmen had nocked and loosed. The arrows flew true and spattered the steering platform of the disabled ship as the Franks desperately attempted to bring her head back on course. It was enough and, driven to steerbord by the wind and the running seas, the leading ship swung out of line and smashed into the vessel to landward. Suddenly, the lee shore beckoned the ships of the Frankish fleet. The English watched joyfully as the pursuit, seemingly so unstoppable only moments before, descended into chaos as hulls collided and yards fouled, bringing masts and rigging crashing down onto the decks below.

As the larger part of the fleet sought to extricate themselves from the crush, a ship pointed her bows seaward and oars slipped proud of the hull to stroke the sea as the outraged Franks attempted to overtake their tormentor. It was now that the foresight of their thegn became apparent to the troop as the unwieldy ship, wide of beam and heavy with men and equipment, struggled to make headway against the choppy swell. A volley of arrows arced into the air and sped towards the men of the *Fælcen* but, loosed into the teeth of the wind storm, they quickly faltered and put their heads into the sea.

Waves slapped the hull, splashing inboard as Sæward pushed away the handle of the steering board and shook the scegth free of the coast. The lithe, leaf shaped hull of the English ship skimmed the surface and sped away from its pursuer as Bassa and Beornwulf hauled on the braces, resetting the yard to capture the wind. The *Fælcen* put the coastline and its mayhem astern, as the men of the troop jeered and called at the pathetic efforts of the Frankish bowmen to reach them with their shafts.

To the north, the Geat ships had grasped their lifeline and were rowing with all the vigour of the saved to escape the trap, their long oars glistening as they rose and fell like the wings of a mighty bird. Eofer exchanged a smile with Spearhafoc.

'Let's go and see who we have delivered them from fate. Big ships like those are bound to carry a lot of ale!'

7

The sun was a memory when the time came to touch brand to kindling. A moon, full and bright in the southern sky, glossed the cap of the pyre as it reflected from the steel of mail shirts, helms, and swords.

Ringed by flames, the bier had drained the last reserves of strength from the exhausted Geats but no man, with wound or without, had shirked the duty as they had scoured the strand and stripped the ships for fuel.

Heardred said his piece and thrust the first torch into the base of the shield ringed pile. Soaked with fats and oils from the stores aboard the ships, the flames flickered and grew as the Geat leader withdrew into the shadows and dozens of brands arced across to join his own. Drawing aside, the warriors exposed the flames to the full force of the onshore breeze, and the smouldering stack transformed itself into a roaring, living thing. As the flames sawed and rose higher with each gust, Heardred Hygelacson turned and led his men away.

A voice rose into the night air from the watching English, and the Geats stopped almost to a man and glared.

'The fire crackled.
The wind blew.
The Geats went to Valhall with the smoke…'

Eofer whirled around and spat through gritted teeth. 'Oswin, not now! They think that you are making fun of them.' His mind raced, and he could see the rest of his troop wincing and shifting uncomfortably. Looking at the faces of the Geats, only the fact that they owed their lives to the men before them and their state of weariness was keeping the stern faced men from drawing their weapons. An idea came to him, and he grabbed at it. 'Get yourself down to the dunes and relieve Porta. Tell Rand that Cæd will relieve him soon.' He jerked his head and Oswin hurried off, the look on his eorle's face alone being enough to tell him that speed was important. As the tension of the moment drained away and the warriors of both nations began to disperse, Heardred crossed the beach. 'Who was that, kinsman?'

Eofer pulled a pained expression. 'Oswin word-poor, one of my youth.'

To Eofer's relief, the Geat laughed. 'Word-poor, I'll say! I thought that it was another example of your unfathomable English humour.'

Relieved that no offence had been taken at such an emotionally charged moment, Eofer added with a chuckle. 'We called him Oswin dire-poet when he first began to spout a verse or two. At least he is improving!'

They shared a laugh and Heardred indicated the rapidly receding figure with his head. 'Any good?'

Eofer shook his head. 'Spear fodder,' he sniffed. 'I owe his father, but the truth is the lad seems to be as thick as a horse's prick.'

They laughed again, and the Geat held the Englishman by

the shoulders and fixed him with his gaze. In the gloom, the Geatish warriors exchanged tired smiles as they gathered with their friends and cleared a space on the strand. Their lord was laughing. The world was righting itself after the chaos, and they could begin to look to the future.

'Eofer, I am in your debt once again. I never thought that I would laugh again after this day.'

The Engle nodded in the direction of a nearby tree stump, bone pale in the moonlight, its bole worn smooth by countless tides. Too large and twisted for the pyre, it had escaped the axes of the tired men. 'Are you up to telling the tale?'

Heardred stifled a yawn but nodded. The left side of his face was encrusted with dried blood, and his shield arm had warded so many blows that there was barely a paler patch among the angry purple bruises. But, the Geat knew that the story of that day had to be told. 'I need to unburden myself,' he said, placing a hand on Eofer's shoulder as they made their way across, 'and I can think of no better victim than my childhood friend—the husband of my only sister.'

Thrush Hemming appeared from the gloom and handed each man a horn of ale, melting away with a nod and a grin.

Heardred took a pull and indicated the receding figure with his horn. 'Why Thrush?'

Eofer circled his face with his hand. 'The freckles, he looks like the bird.'

Both men lowered themselves onto the stump with a sigh. It had been a hard day for them both.

Clear of the spit, the Geat drakkar had hoisted their sails instantly, leaving the Frankish ships floundering on the coast. The big sheets had billowed, and the sleek warships had shot free from the trap. The *Fælcen* had skimmed the waves as Sæward brought her within hailing distance, and Eofer had been surprised and delighted to recognise the grinning face of his kinsman as the Geat crew called and cheered. Relieved of the need to row, the exhausted men had still found the strength to acclaim their rescuers, and the scegth had passed through the dragon ships accompanied by the rhythmic beat of ash spears on linden boards.

Eofer drank again and was the first to break the silence. 'This was the perfect place to beach the ships. Have you used it before?'

Heardred swallowed noisily and cast his eyes about the island. The moon was edging above the dunes to the south, painting the narrow strand with its milky light and turning the sea beyond, calm now after the fury of the storm, into beaten silver. He shook his head. 'My cousin told me it was here. He uses it on his forays across to Britannia.'

Eofer remembered the Geat champion and threw his friend a sidelong glance. If the king had fallen in battle, the man would be a rival for the vacant kingship. 'Did he escape?'

Heardred shook his head. 'He was never there. He was sent with gifts to assure the Saxons of our friendship in case they felt threatened by the raid on their border. He was to join up later if he could, but he had to escort the Danish warloca, Unferth, to the midsummer *blot* at the Irminsul first.' Eofer looked surprised, and the ætheling shrugged. 'It would seem that the Allfather still has plans for my kinsman.'

Eofer realised the importance of the revelation immediately. If the war god *was* scheming, Heardred could be sailing home to his death. He placed a hand on Heardred's arm and gave him an earnest stare. Despite the dangers, kin were kin.

'You have my sword if you ask, or a haven at my hall.' He gave the Geat what he hoped was a reassuring grin. 'If old one-eye comes calling, I'll spit in it!'

Heardred smirked. 'I will face my wyrd. If Beowulf has

beaten me home, I doubt that he will take the king-helm even if it is offered. We talked about this when we were exiles together in Swede Land, and he promised me his support.' He paused and nodded. 'I know that as exiles it was an easy declaration to make, but I know my cousin as well as any man. He may be a famous monster killer, but he harbours no ambition to take on the responsibilities of kingship, the lack of freedom would drive him mad.'

Eofer was unconvinced. 'Words are a fine thing, but once that kingly grim-helm is brought out any man would be tempted. If he feels that it is the Allfather's will…'

The eorle let the statement hang in the air, but Heardred shook his head and smiled. 'If it's Woden's will, I have done enough to sup in his hall. I will join my father at his ale bench and await the end of days.'

'You are convinced that Hygelac is dead, then? He may have escaped.'

Heardred pulled a wry smile. 'Unless his body can make its way home alone,' he snorted, 'about as sure as I could ever be. The Franks were taunting us with my father's head impaled on the end of a spear for most of the chase!'

The Geat glanced at his ale as he swilled it around before sinking the dregs in one. Eofer pointed to his drinking vessel and Thrush Hemming, attentive as ever, loped across with a full barrel as his eorle attempted to move the subject on to happier days.

'Tell me about the raid. We were still in Anglia when you landed among the Hetware, and all seemed well. Thereafter, we were in the south and news was sparse.'

Hemming refilled the horns and placed the barrel at their feet. Heardred shot him a smile of thanks as he began to tell the story of Hygelac's Raid.

'They were completely unprepared for us at first. We hit

the northern coast and defeated the local forces before splitting the army. We moved south, skirting the Ælmere while the ships, under half crews, shadowed us. The Frisian king, Ida, never concentrated his forces but just committed them piecemeal, so we just swept them aside.' He took a long draught from his horn and grinned. 'It couldn't have been easier. Once we put the inland sea behind us, we fortified a base at a place called Dorestada and used it to raid further south. The great River Rin flows there as it approaches its estuary on the German Sea. Using it we could raid with our ships deep into Frankland, that and the other rivers there, the Woh, Masa, Sceald.' He shrugged. 'It was perfect. The countryside was rich and fairly groaning with food. We spent the best part of the summer there and never saw so much as a hostile cow, never mind an enemy spear.'

Eofer shook his head in wonder. The southerners had a reputation for easy living among the people of the North, but he knew from his experience in Britannia that the people were tough, good spearmen. Their leaders, however, were callow fools, always putting personal gain before the good of their folk. It appeared that the same had happened to the Franks. Maybe it was the Christ god, he reflected. Wherever he was worshipped, the poor grew poorer and the rich, richer still. Eofer came back as his kinsman concluded his tale.

'The days started to shorten and men wanted away with their spoils. With every day's passing, you could sense the feeling grow a little more. Eventually, Hygelac decided that the raid was over. I took the fleet down the Rin and the king was to follow on with the men who remained with him.' Heardred glanced up and pulled a weary smile. 'We knew that we were taking a chance, dividing the army, but the ships were overloaded as it was. It was late in summer and the river was at its lowest ebb, it would only take a few ships to get stranded in a shallow and block the channel, and we would all have been in a vulnerable position.' He shrugged. 'Maybe they were watching us, but I think that it was just *wyrd*—the way that it is. After a summer of gods-luck, ours gave out at the moment of most danger. My father and his men were obviously overtaken by an army from the south, and the next thing that I know, the estuary of the Sceald is spewing forth dragon ships and galleys. Heavily laden on a lee coastline with a rising swell, short of men...' He shrugged again. 'I don't need to tell you what it was like. Only the full onset of the storm, and superior seamanship, saved those that managed to get away.'

A HAND gently shook his shoulder. Eofer forced his lids apart and sighed wearily as he attempted to focus on the figure crouched over him. Imma Gold was there; the big duguth's teeth flashed red in the firelight. 'The Golden Mares are back in the east, lord, Treachery snapping at their heels.'

Eofer took the cup. Sipping, he fought against the desire to retch. Against his will, he screwed up his face as he forced out what would have to pass for a witty reply. He didn't feel very witty, but it was expected. 'Ask Shining Mane to pull the sun in a circle for a while. Maybe the wolf will get dizzy.'

Imma chuckled dutifully, his golden hair falling to frame his face as he looked down at the suffering form of his eorle. Eofer took another sip and rolled from his cloak. Ambling over to the surf, he relieved himself with a sigh. There was something deeply satisfying about the sound of water meeting water.

The English were a solid block a little along the beach, and Eofer took up a brand from the watch fire and crossed to the place where he knew that Heardred lay rolled in his cloak and wondered. His kinsman had woken yesterday as an ætheling, does he do so this day as a king? He nudged Heardred with his foot rather than lean over him with the flame, aware that a dozen pairs of eyes were fixed on him in the darkness. They at least regarded their lord as the rightful king of Geatland, and the Engle knew that a sudden move could well prove to be his last, kin or no.

Eofer knelt at his cousin's side and nudged his shoulder with the cup. 'Brother, the dawn is near.'

Heardred nodded without opening his eyes, and a hand reached out from his cloak. Taking the cup, he took a sip, inhaled deeply and rolled from his bedding. The Geats rose from the ground with a clatter of arms as the first lightening showed in the east. Heardred jerked his head towards the dark outlines of his ships, dispatching men hither and yon as they prepared to depart. Eofer watched in admiration as the weary and battle-worn *here,* the raiding army of the previous day, was replaced by a purposeful brotherhood of warriors.

The anchorage had been well-chosen. Steeply sloping, the ships could be drawn up to the shore with little danger of stranding by the outgoing tide, and already men were back aboard preparing the vessels for sea. As others carefully raked through the remains of the bale-fire, sifting the ashes of their companions and placing them carefully into earthenware containers for the journey home to kith and kin, Eofer caught up with Heardred as the Geat shed his grimy clothing and shot him a look. 'Coming in?'

Eofer grinned and began to strip off as Rannulf, Heardred's own weorthman, replaced his lord's soiled clothing with clean items from the ship. The sky was lightening in furrows, bands of washed out lilac in a rinse of grey, with just the solid point of light that was the morning star remaining to shine like a distant beacon. They would soon be away. The ætheling ducked beneath the surface and emerged a moment later, shaking his hair to spray his friend with a laugh. The years rolled away and with them the responsibilities of their adult life, with just the nagging concern that all naked men feel when standing chest deep in murky water to spoil the moment. The shallows were unexpectedly warm, and both men felt quickly reinvigorated as the cares of the previous day sloughed off them with the grime.

Eofer looked at Heardred earnestly as the Geat sipped seawater and worked the brine around his teeth with a finger. 'The offer of my sword still holds, kinsman, Blood-Worm is yours. My father would supply an army to bolster your claim, you only need to say the word.'

Heardred squirted the contents of his mouth. 'I know, brother. Don't think that I am ungrateful, or that your friendship will ever be forgotten. But my uncle, Hythcyn, was put on the throne by a Bronding army and look how that turned out; war, *wræcscip,* and the death of kings.' He shook his head. 'You think that Woden deserted my father to put Beowulf on the gift-stool of the Geats, and you may be right. But he is not the only god who schemes on Middle-earth.'

Heardred turned and waded ashore. As both men dressed, the last of their warriors were clambering aboard the ships and preparing to haul the anchors. Away to the south, the twin figures of Finn and Æsc had left their vantage point and were hurrying back along the beach. As the last of the Geats returned to the ships, carrying the vessels containing the still warm ashes of their dead reverently before them, the friends embraced and Heardred flashed a grin. 'Even if Beowulf *is* Woden's favourite, I have the support of old red beard.' He winked as he turned to go and threw a parting comment. 'Who else but Thunor could send a storm to drive my kinsman from the gods-know where in my moment of greatest need.' He laughed as he recalled the events of the previous day. 'A tiny ship emerges from a wall as black as jet, and a girl and three bowmen drive off the fiend and rescue us from being driven ashore.' Heardred fixed the eorle with a steady look. 'If that's not the work of the thunderer, I don't know what is.'

8

A whoop of joy cut the air, and the group laughed as the lad put spur to horse and cantered across the neck of land. One by one his friends followed suit, and Eofer exchanged an almost paternal look of amusement with the men of his duguth.

They had arrived back at the great promontory that the English called Strand the previous evening. Peeling off from the Geatish fleet as they passed the welcome sight of Hwælness, Eofer had edged into the treacherous bay of the Husem. As the wind had risen to whip the shallows into froth, Eofer had kept the withies hard against his steerbord side as he ran the scegth through the maze of channels and creeks, running the *Fælcen* ashore as a pale, lowering Sun, threw long shadows to the east.

The ships of the returning fleet had dribbled home in ones and twos over the course of the previous day. Battered by the storm, the snaca and their crews had all but given up the little warship for lost, and Eofer and his crew had basked in the joyful acclamation of their countrymen as they swept through the anchorage.

Thrush Hemming tapped the barrel and passed around the cups as they rode. Charging each in turn, they waited until the horses set foot on the mainland and their eorle made the cry.

'*Wæs Hæl!*'

The duguth raised their cups and thundered out the reply.

'*Drinc Hæl!*'

The men laughed and drained their cups, tossing them aside as Hemming passed the barrel around. It was a tradition among them that they greet their land with the pledge on their return. This year it was heartfelt. They had had the ear of the gods at the spring sacrifice, and all the troop had returned to the motherland as the world turned slowly from green to russet and the harvest was stacked—despite the best efforts of the Jutes and Britons to whittle their number.

Salt marsh fringed the dune speckled shoreline, and the men exchanged a look as a flight of cranes, the grey mass of adults punctuated by the yellowish brown of that summer's brood, passed over the windblown acres of needlemarsh and cordgrass. Soon the birds would leave for the South as men hunkered down to see out the dark days of winter and made their plans for the spring.

Lines of smoke curled from the roofs of Husem to be snatched away by the autumn blow. The town that bore the name of the great bay nestled in the middle distance, whitewashed walls and darker thatch clustered behind its rickety jetties and boathouses, but their destination lay further inland.

Sheep gave way to cattle and the first villages appeared as the land rose slowly towards the distant solidity of the Wolds, now a darker smudge on the skyline.

A small knoll stood hard on to the roadway, its rough grasses sawing as the wind began to freshen, and Eofer edged his mount aside and walked it to the crest. Clouds the colour of lead were gathering in the west as the next storm front approached, and the eorle took in the vista as the world slowly turned grey.

'Are we going to push on or wait this out, lord? We could be cosy inside Eappa's hall before she hits.'

Eofer glanced across at Hemming, who had appeared at his side, and grinned. Tall and powerfully built, his weorthman instinctively returned the smile and raised his brow as he awaited his lord's decision.

The eorle turned the head of his mount back to the waiting group, casting a final look at the waters of the Husem as the horse picked its way down from the rise. The surface was growing darker by the moment as the clouds rushed in to extinguish the sun, the boats outside the town frantic at their moorings. He called across to the others. 'We will eat now while it is dry and then push on.' He shrugged. 'It is only a little rain. How bad can it be?'

UBBA SILK-BEARD finally gave up on using his fingernail and plucked a straw from the roof thatch. Working it between his teeth, he smiled in triumph as he finally worried the strand of pork free. Across the hall, a woman's cry was cut short as one of the men backhanded her and frogmarched her across to the table. As the raider splayed her legs with a kick, his jarl watched absent-mindedly as he hoisted her skirts and began to tug at his belt.

A crash came from the bower, and Ubba smiled again as he recognised the familiar sound made by silver falling on wooden boards. Haldor poked his head around the doorway and grinned. 'Found it!'

Free now of his tormentor, Ubba took another bite of the pork leg. 'You would think that at least one woman would hide her treasure somewhere other than the roof of her bedchamber.'

Haldor snorted and disappeared back into the shadows. The Dane took a last look around the hall and ducked back outside. The wind had continued to grow in strength as they had ransacked the place. Skeletal shadows swept this way and that against a sky the colour of iron as each gust shook the treetops. Darkness was almost upon them, and Ubba rested his back against the barn as he reflected with satisfaction on the course of his latest foray.

Rounding Fyn, the great island that the English called Harrow, his ship had taken the fjord up to the Jutish town known as The Crossing. Arrangements had been set in place there with the local jarl, like most in those parts no friend of the English, to exchange the chest of silver lashed securely amidships for horses and supplies. The remaining crew would double back and proscribe a great sweep, back around Daneland, meeting with their jarl at the next full moon near the remains of a hall that they had burned the previous year, a few miles to the east of the English settlement of Suthworthig. That would give them a full two weeks to burn and plunder the length of Engeln, time enough to humiliate King Eomær and bring honour and renown to his king, Hrothgar. The corners of the jarl's mouth turned up in a smile as he thought of the reputation that the attack would bring him among his peers. The rafters of Heorot would think that the Grendel had returned from the mere to shake their joints once again, as Ubba's Raid was acclaimed and toasted from the mead benches.

Haldor reappeared and walked across to his jarl as the men packed the silver into the panniers that flanked the remounts. He glanced up at the sky as he came and frowned. 'Are we staying here tonight, lord? This looks like it's getting worse; not the sort of night to be caught in the open.'

Ubba raised his eyes and squinted away to the west. The sun was down, but the full darkness of the night was still some way off. Haldor was right, it was a good hall. If it had been a little further from the road it would have been the perfect hideaway, but it stood hard on, and there was no telling who might arrive in the dark hours. The English were hunting them now and, stung by the audacity of their raid, he doubted that they would rest night or day while they remained at large. He shook his head. 'No, we will follow the valley down to that hall we saw beyond the watercourse. It's just that bit further from the road, and we will be able to see any riders approach from a good distance away.'

Disappointed, Haldor glanced up as a powerful gust brought a shoal of leaves sweeping across the paddock. 'I doubt that there will be any war-bands out in this, lord.' He grabbed at his groin and leered. 'This one is pretty. Even the maidservant is worthy of a tup.'

Ubba shook his head as he confirmed his decision. 'No, we move,' he snapped. 'Tell the men to kill the bitches and come outside.' The Dane swung himself up into the saddle and hauled at his reins, guiding his mount back towards the nearby track as he threw a last instruction over his shoulder. 'Haldor…'

The warrior paused and turned. 'Yes, lord?'

'Tell them to fetch brands from the hearth to light the way, but don't fire the hall. We want to avoid discovering an English shield wall barring our path in the morning.'

THE RIDERS SWEPT along the track as the wind roared through the canopy overhead, sending a blizzard of leaves, twigs and smaller branches cascading all around. They pushed on, the spectral light from the brands that each man held aloft marking their progress through the absolute darkness that surrounded them.

Eofer snatched at his reins and guided his mount around another fallen bough as he reflected on the homecoming that Thunor had provided for them. It was, after all, about as bad as it could be, and he gave a grim smile as he thought of the thunder god. Perhaps he had been listening when he made his comment to Thrush back at the knoll, or maybe he was too far away, shepherding Heardred safely home. His sacred grove was not far from Eofer's own hall, he would leave an offering if they all made it safely through.

The roadway spilled out into a glade and the eorle came to a halt and waited for the others to come up. High above, the moon reappeared to bathe the clearing in its watery light before the next storm cloud, its edges rimmed with silver, moved across to veil it once more. Brands hissed and snaked as the rain and wind found them, and Eofer let out a laugh as he saw the excitement writ large on their faces. Soon they were a mob of horsemen, their mounts kicking up muddy clods as they circled, and Eofer cried out above the wind as he did a quick headcount.

'This must be what it is like to ride the wild hunt with the Allfather.' He shot his weorthman a grin. 'Still wish you were cosy, Thrush?'

A line split Hemming's beard as he beamed in return, his eyes wide with the joy of the moment as he shook his head and the war-band jeered. It was little wonder that Woden chose to ride on nights like this, and Eofer yelled again as a powerful gust carried a heavy crack to their ears from the darkness beyond the circle of light.

'If it gets much worse, we will break our journey at

Penda's hall.' A quick glance at the moon told the eorle that the night was already well advanced, he doubted that they would reach home before daybreak, and he recognised that it was the sensible thing to do. They had been away as soon as the spring rites had been performed at Eostre, another morning would make little difference. Besides, he reflected with a smile, his father's weorthman always kept a supply of mead for guests, and it *had* been a long ride. Somewhere in the dark, an almighty crash told them that a great tree had succumbed to the blow. Eofer cursed. If large trees were beginning to topple, they would need to slow their pace even more. The ride *had* become much worse—Penda's hall really was the sensible choice. He grinned again at the childlike excitement on the faces ringing their lord. 'All set?'

Torches were thrust into the air and, as the gale reached down to pluck at the flames, the troop filed behind their leader with a throaty roar and spurred their mounts.

BRECC TAPPED GENTLY on the door to the bower and flicked up the wooden latch. Entering softly, he paused for a heartbeat to allow his eyes to become accustomed to the gloom. To his disappointment, the boy was sleeping beside his mother, he may need to quieten him if he awoke. Crossing to the settle, he bent over the sleeping figures and hesitated, unsure how to wake his owner. Realising that physical contact was improper, he took hold of the coverlet and gave it a sharp tug. As the woman stirred, he moved back into the pale rectangle of light cast by the doorway to enable her to recognise him for who he was. She saw him and came instantly awake. 'Brecc? What is it?'

The *thræl* moved forward and, dropping to his knee, lowered his gaze in supplication. 'There are lights moving through the Weald lady. Horsemen are on the road, they must be past the brook by now.'

She nodded that she understood. The wind outside was roaring, buffeting the stout walls of the hall with every gust. Only the mad or those intent on harm would be foolish enough to venture out on such a night. Spear-Danes had been raiding on Harrow all summer and there had been rumours that, emboldened by their successes, they had begun to turn their attentions to the settlements on the mainland itself. Her brother-in-law had fallen on one such raid, and she steeled herself as she prepared to exact some small measure of revenge before she too fell. The boy awoke and rubbed his eyes. 'What is it, mother?'

She reached inside her night clothes and freed a key from the ring that hung there. 'Go to the coffer and bring two *gar*, quickly now.'

She hesitated and looked back at Brecc. Slaves were forbidden to touch weapons, but he looked like a man who had known spear-play in the past. He had been faultlessly loyal all summer, she would take a chance. 'Weohstan...' The lad turned his head as he fumbled with the lock. 'Fetch three spears.'

Astrid looked back at her thræl and saw the gratitude on his face. There was no malice in his expression, and she relaxed slightly; she knew that she had not misjudged the man. Weohstan hurried back, the bare soles of his feet slapping on the cold wooden boards. Cradling three of the heavy thrusting spears, he handed them around. Taking down two shields from the wall to the rear of the bed, she handed one to Brecc as she hefted her own.

'Weohstan, fetch your shield.' A knot of emotion gripped her chest, and she smiled at the look of pride that illuminated his round face. The blond hair that framed his features were a legacy from her kin, but the steely gaze belonged to his father. She set her face and gripped her gar. 'Tonight we must all be men.'

Astrid led them out, past the high table, and down the length of the hall. The benches, the scene of so much merriment and laughter when the men were home, hugged the bare walls. Bereft of their shields and weapons, the bare plaster and posts looked skeletal in the flickering light from the hearth; a body without a soul.

Reaching the door, she paused and turned. Her *thyften* had accompanied her from her father's hall in Geatland on her marriage, and the old maid hung back in the shadows with a face as pale as the moon. Astrid smiled reassuringly and indicated the door to her bower with a flick of her head. 'Editha, if this is a hall burning, make your way to Ealdorman Wonred's hall and tell him what has happened here. He will protect you until the master returns.' The handmaid made to protest, but Astrid cut her short. 'It is not the duty of women to fight,' she pulled a wry smile, 'unless you are the daughter of a king.' She smiled again, more warmly this time, as the memories of their years together flooded back. The old girl had wet nursed her through her first year and attended her through the highs and lows of her life. If her wyrd was to die here, there was no reason why they should die together. As the thyften bustled off, Astrid's expression hardened once again, and she turned to her son. 'Weohstan...' The boy looked up, his expression resolute. 'You will lead us and make the challenge.' His face softened in gratitude for a heartbeat, before the iron will that she knew so well reasserted itself. 'Remember the words that your father taught you. You are the son of an eorle, the grandson of a battle king.'

She saw that Brecc had lit a brand from the hearth as he

passed, and she acknowledged his foresight with a nod. Slipping the heavy wooden bar from the door, she pulled it inwards.

Outside the wind still howled in the treetops, but the clouds had been chased away to the east and the open space that lay between the buildings was bathed a pewter grey.

Weohstan led them through, and mother and son took up position to bar entry to the riders as their thræl fixed the torch into a bracket. The horsemen, war grim in their polished helms, were approaching the paddock beneath a scroll of flame, the light gleaming from steel and gold as the men came on.

Astrid took her place at her son's right hand as Brecc moved to the left, and together the trio planted their feet foursquare as the war-band thundered into the yard. As the wind captured the flames and drove them eastwards, an involuntary gasp escaped Astrid's lips as she recognised the men for who they were. As she lowered her shield, the riders drew up in a line facing the hall, and Weohstan strode proud of the group. Clashing his spear shaft three times against the rim of his own little shield, the boy cried his challenge.

'I am Weohstan, son of Eofer king's bane, Hygelac's kin.

Rider, tell me now your lineage, and whether your intentions are base or honourable.

If you seek shelter from the storm, you will have it.

If you carry a hatred for my clan in your heart, you will find that we are no strangers to battle play.

I will not avoid it. Even if I knew myself doomed, I was not born a coward.

It is better to fight, than be burnt inside by men with hate in their hearts.'

Eofer grasped his helm and lifted it clear of his head, pride at his son's bearing and demeanour shining in his eyes.

As her eorle swung himself down to gather the boy in his arms, Spearhafoc slipped an arrow from her quiver and Oswin shot forward with a yelp as he received a sharp jab in the buttock. 'That's *wordcræft,* word-poor.'

The men of Eofer's hearth troop shared a laugh, all the discomforts of the journey home forgotten as they reached their goal.

'Four winters old,' she continued as they began to haul themselves, saddle weary, from their mounts, 'and already an eorle.'

9

The riders dug in their heels and took the grindle at a canter. That was the last of the drainage ditches that tapered down to the western bay, and the group settled into a trot as the lowering sun turned the water there to amber. Soon they would be back at Wonred's hunting lodge, and Eofer smiled to himself as he watched his father take the obstruction with the ease of a man far younger in winters.

The old man was a *folctoga* now, one of the king's leading advisers in the witan, the wise, a commander of armies. Never one to covet the kingship of his people, the man had risen as high as his ambition had ever stretched. The day that the norns had woven their threads to send Hygelac of Geatland into exile three winters previously had been the spark that propelled his old friend to the position that he now occupied. Seizing the opportunity to place an ally on the throne of the Danes' northern neighbours, King Eomær had supported his cause with an English ship-army commanded by the ealdorman. The *sciphere* had fallen on Geatland the following spring, only to discover that Hygelac's brother, King Hythcyn, was raiding in Swede Land. Following hard on their heels, the English had crushed the army of the Brondings and run Hythcyn's army to ground at a place called Ravenswood. Attacking in the dawn, they had surprised a Swedish relief force commanded by their king, Ongentheow, and in the heavy fighting Ongentheow had fallen to English might. Eofer had dealt Ongentheow, the old battle boar, his death blow. It had been the act that had earned the young Engle the title king's bane and the elevation of his father, Wonred, to the coveted position of one of the folctoga of the English.

Eofer rode at his father's side, their breath pluming as the chill of the evening descended. Away to the west the salt marshes were beginning to haze as a mist, sparkling like steel in the raking light, rose to veil the shallows.

It had been a good day. Dozens of birds, Mallard, Teal, Pochard, bounced against the flanks of the horses as they moved and the pair, father and son, each proudly carried his gyrfalcon atop his fist as he rode. Hooded now the birds, magnificent in their silvery plumage, were both from the same brood. A gift to each man from a grateful Hygelac, the birds were almost as large as the eagles that hunted the grasslands, and both men carried their charges with ill-concealed pride.

Eofer felt his father to be content for the first time since he had returned, and he took the opportunity to broach the thorny subject of his brother's disappearance. 'Is there still no word of Wulf's fate?'

Eofer noticed an involuntary grimace cross his father's face at the mention of his youngest son, but he was kin to Eofer, too; he had a right to ask. Wonred ran his free hand through the remains of his hair and sighed. The long locks of his youth were in the past. Eofer remembered the day when he had laughed along with his brother, as the old man had finally given up on the straggly mop and appeared in the hall shorn like a spring lamb. That too had been a good day, and he felt a pang as the face of his brother faded from his mind. Wonred shook his head. 'Nothing—not a peep.'

Eofer spat. 'I need to know the name of the fiend who overcame him if I am to exact a blood-price'

The old man shook his head, and Eofer noticed that he fingered the hilt of his sword as he replied.

'I have let it be known that I will pay for that information, but nothing has come back to me yet. All I know is what I told you the day you came to my hall.' He turned his face to his son, and Eofer was pleased to see a smile form on his father's features. 'He died well, Eofer, sword swinging against his king's enemies. The war-band that reached the cliffs above the fight saw Wulf lead the men of his troop against the *wicingas*. They cut their way through to the dragon ship, and Wulf managed to get aboard before the ship floated free of the strand and carried them out to sea. The sun had risen by then to shine directly in the faces of Coelfrith and his men, and the last that they could see was the dawn light glinting on sword play as blades rose and fell, and the seamen rowed for deeper water.' Wonred made a fist and reached across to thump his son on the shoulder. 'Rest easy, lad. All men know that the king's bane will take vengeance on his brother's slayer.'

Ahead of them the path curved around the settlement of Framasham, its longhouses radiating away from the open space at the centre in the manner of the westerners. Unlike the halls found throughout the higher Wolds and eastern parts of Engeln, those of the low-lying lands of the polder incorporated a space for their livestock within the body of the hall. The animals wintered within these byres or were gathered in the area at the heart of the settlement known as the common, where they could be safeguarded against the depredations of wolves or men during the warmer months of the year. As the sky hardened to a blackish-blue in the east, the last of the cattle were being driven between the boundary posts towards their winter lodgings as Eofer spoke again. 'At least Heardred seems safely established as king in Geatland, despite the wishes of his mother, I hear.'

Wonred threw him a look. 'Women's ambitions don't always match those of their menfolk. Hygd had just lost Hygelac and other kinsmen including her brother to the fighting in Frisland.' He shrugged. 'No woman wants to outlive their family; kings tend to live short and violent lives here in the North.' Leaning in towards his son, Wonred glanced behind to ensure that there were no riders within earshot before he shared the most dramatic news of all. 'Hygelac's death was the work of the Allfather.'

Eofer looked at his father in shock as the fear that he had shared on the beach with Heardred was confirmed. 'You know this?'

Wonred nodded. 'He told me himself, the winter he was a wræcca and his brother Hythcyn ruled. Woden came to his hall many winters ago and made a pact with the old fool. He was to ensure that his foster, Beowulf, became the Geatish champion and the king-helm would be his.' He sniffed as if the following statement was self-evident. 'The gods are powerful, but fickle all the same, Woden most of all. Show them respect, but place your trust in your sword arm, Eofer. They delight in chaos.'

Eofer knew that the moment had arrived to broach what he knew would be a difficult subject with his father. He looked across and held the old man's gaze. 'The Allfather has spoken to me also, father.'

Wonred looked aghast, and Eofer could not help but give a short snort of amusement, despite the gravity of the moment. 'Don't worry,' he smiled reassuringly, 'the Wanderer has not called at *my* hall!' The ealdorman's face remained a mask of concern, and Eofer continued quickly. 'Certain things occurred in Britannia this summer that could only be the will of the god. Trust me father,' he pleaded, 'soon the Allfather will send a sign and I ask for your support in the witan when that time comes.'

They passed the place where the cattle had crossed the track, hoof prints and sludgy pats of dung marking their passage, and swung to the east. The land rose slowly here and, rounding a spur, the twin storeys of the hunting lodge itself came into view beneath its hood of thatch. The horses plodded on as thoughts turned to good food, good ale and the companionship of the hearth. Suddenly, their warm feelings were interrupted by the blast of a horn and, following the sound, the men watched as the guards on the palisade pointed their spears. A shape detached itself from the shadow of the paling, cantering down the track towards them, the horn blast and the quality of the man's mount and clothing marking him out as a messenger of the king.

Eofer and Wonred exchanged a glance and reined in as the rider drew closer. Curbing his mount, the exhausted messenger nodded in recognition and flipped up the cover on a large leather cylinder and fumbled inside. Every man present knew what the tube contained, and the war-sword, its tip symbolically charred and blackened by fire, emerged into the light to be greeted by grins of delight. The royal messenger gripped the small wooden sword and handed it to the folctoga who rolled it between his finger and thumb as he read the battle runes inscribed upon its blade. He looked back to the man. 'When are we to assemble?'

'At Winterfylleth, lord, the first full moon of winter. There is to be a symbel of all the leading men.' The man dipped back into the container and withdrew another war-sword. Leaning across, he again gripped the blade in both fists and held it forward. 'I have a summons for Eorle Eofer also. King Eomær orders that he take ship to Sleyswic by way of the carrying place. He expects that you will be with him within the month.'

'Drizzle.'

Eofer looked at Imma Gold. 'Drizzle?'

The duguth wiped the flat of his hand down his face and shook the drops free from his beard like a big shaggy dog. 'Yes, drizzle. What a fitting word that is for this miserable shit.' They both squinted up into the murk, and laughter rolled around the ship as a voice came from the youth manning the oars. 'If it's a good word, it's not one of Oswin's!'

The pair snorted, and the eorle looked beyond the hooked prow that had given the *Fælcen* its name. Ahead, the River Trene took a turn to the left and disappeared in the washed out greyness of late autumn, the steady rainfall making a pock-marked road that led into the heart of the kingdom. Even though they had erected an awning amidship, most of the men not pulling the oars had given up all hope of remaining dry. After enduring days of non-stop drizzle, they had surrendered the space to keep their battle gear from the elements, as all good warriors should.

The weather had clamped down almost as soon as the royal messenger had left his father's lodge. Gathering his hearth troop about him, Eofer had sent word to the boat sheds at Strand that he would be making one final journey in the scegth that year.

The *Fælcen* had been re-rigged and provisioned when

they had arrived the following day. Sæward had Edwin and his lads work through the long night to re-caulk any leaky seams, and the ship had slipped free of the jetty almost unnoticed by a port already dozing in its winter slumber.

Fresh from their time on shore, the youths had bent their backs to the oars, and the ship had kept pace with the pale shimmer that marked the progress of the sun as it rolled along the southern horizon. That had all changed the moment that the scegth had nosed out from the shelter of the great promontory of Hwælness. The prevailing winds were now against them, and the ship master had given the shoals around the Ness a wide berth as he had tacked the ship well out to sea before coming about. With the wind now blowing steadily from astern, the *Fælcen* had bounded forward, sweeping into the estuary of the River Egedore as the sky had changed from slate to jet. Now, with the town of Portasmutha behind them, it was a steady row of two days to the carrying place, a further day of manhandling the scegth across the portage to the Sley and the king's hall that stood near its shore.

The river rolled by and the men of the duguth clustered on the steering platform. A grebe, the elegance of its long white neck and tufted cap at odds with the bleak dreariness of its surroundings, disappeared beneath the surface with a splash.

Octa broke the silence. 'Do you have any idea why the king wanted us to come by ship, lord? It would have been quicker and easier to ride.'

'And drier,' Beorn put in. 'We could have broken the journey at Coelfrith's hall and still been at Sleyswic within two days.'

Eofer shrugged. 'You were there when I received the war-sword. The messenger said, come this way—so here we are.'

A mournful lowing came from the mist shrouded bank, and the group looked across as the disembodied head and shoulders of a lone cow appeared to hover there, its jaws sliding sideways as it chewed on a ball of cud.

> 'King's bane passed me in his war glory.
> Eofer and I, both floating…'

The men of the duguth winced as the words reached them on the steering platform, and the twins, Hræfen and Crawa, reached forward from their thwart to strike the boy about the head. Eofer and Thrush Hemming exchanged a look as it became plain that word-poor would not retaliate to the blows.

'This is becoming serious, Eofer,' the weorthman said. 'We could have a death on our hands soon.'

The mood among the men now matched the weather, as Osbeorn asked a question of his eorle. 'Just how much do you owe his father, lord?'

Eofer still watched the youth as he rowed, head down and sullen. Hemming was right, the boy would never make a warrior, but if he refused to stand up to intimidation he would never live long enough to become a scop, either. 'He died at Ravenswood, helping to shield my brother from King Ongentheow's attack as he lay wounded at his feet.'

There were nods of agreement. A debt was owed to the man, but that was not going to be repaid by allowing his son to be harried to his death. Octa shrugged. 'I will give him some of my time, teach him to fight.'

Eofer looked at his duguth in gratitude and his man returned a wicked grin.

'Don't thank me lord, he certainly won't. I will teach him how to fight, but he might wish that he *was* dead by the end.'

. . .

It was late in the short northern day when Sæward worked the steer bord and brought the *Fælcen* prow-first into the slipway. Two boys, dressed identically in trews and shirts made from tough blue sailcloth, leapt up at their approach and disappeared into a hall that stood surrounded by workshops and barns. As Eofer stepped ashore, a tall figure emerged from the building and came across.

'Welcome to Old Ford, my name is Eadmund. Of course, it's not really a ford,' he smiled, 'but it is old, and it sounds better than 'The Ford'. Lends it a touch of loftiness, don't you think, lord?'

Eofer cast his eyes around the riverside. Like most boatyards he had ever visited, this was far from 'lofty'. The *Fælcen* was the only ship of any size to be seen, but the evidence of the summer trade lay scattered all around. Mounds of ballast lay where they had been discarded by the traders who had used the portage before, the roughly hewn rocks mouldering under a blanket of moss. Across the way, the big kettles that were used to boil the pitch and tar lay cold and unattended. But the evidence of their use lay spattered all about, and several frames for transporting the ships overland lined the track.

'You'll be wanting to cross to the Sley?'

Eofer fetched inside his cloak, and a smile of satisfaction slowly illuminated Eadmund's features as the war-sword emerged.

'At last, lord. The bastard Danes need to remember what English steel tastes like.' Eadmund moved closer and lowered his voice as though he was imparting a great secret as the men of Eofer's troop tumbled from the ship and shouldered her onto the slipway. 'A war-band burned halls within the Wolds here, not a month ago.' He hawked and spat at the memory. 'They tried to come here, down The Oxen Way, but the king himself led his hearth troop against them and chased them south.' He paused and spat again as if the very idea was unthinkable. 'Danes on The Oxen Way!'

Eofer looked across as his troop shouldered their belongings. 'Can we make a start today? The king expects us to make haste.'

Eadmund grimaced. 'A dart of a ship like yours, we could have taken most of the way east by way of yonder brook.' He indicated a side channel with a nod of his head. 'It'll be full of rushes and pondweed at the moment, they will need clearing, so she'll have to go overland like a fat bellied trader.' The porter's lips set in an apologetic line. 'Even that is not as easy as it should be. If it were earlier in the year, lord, I could have had you on your way as soon as the ballast was out of your ship, but this time of year…' He tugged at his ear as he cast a look towards the lowering sun. 'The men are spread all over, and so are the oxen. We never usually see a ship between Hærfestmonth and Eostre.'

Eofer pulled a face. 'I need to be with the king as soon as possible. My men are not above hauling their ship. Do we really need oxen?'

The man nodded gravely. 'Dangerous work, lord. I dare say that King Eomær would not thank me for using his warriors as beasts of burden.'

Eofer spun the tiny sword and looked expectantly at the porter.

Eadmund chuckled. 'Spend the night in my hall, lord, while I gather the men and oxen. We will have your ship in its cradle and ready to move at first light. You shall come before the king by nightfall.'

. . .

MUTTERED COMMENTS PASSED between the workmen, and a rumble of laughter ran along the line. Eofer and Thrush Hemming crossed the open space before Eadmund's hall and hailed the man. Casting a look across his shoulder as he emerged, the porter nodded in recognition before chivvying the men back to work.

'You will have to forgive them, we don't see many shield maidens here, lord,' he explained as he indicated the tree line with a jerk of his head, 'mostly merchants and the like.'

The pair glanced across and snorted as they saw the cause of the men's amusement. A line of backs presented themselves, silvered arcs playing on the bracken before them. On the extreme right of the line, a small figure squatted in her customary position.

'Spearhafoc used to just mix in among the boys when she pissed,' Hemming explained, 'until a few of the lads started to become a bit careless with their aim. A few sharp twists from the girl soon put paid to that little game,' he added with a chuckle, 'but you can never be too careful!'

The trio walked down to the *Fælcen* as Eadmund's men guided the team of oxen into position at the head of the ship and tightened their harnesses. The scegth nestled in a cradle made from tough English oak, ready for its overland journey. Thick layers of sheepskin padded out the spaces between the cradle and the hull of the ship, protecting and cushioning the finely worked strakes from damage as it was hauled down the eastern slope of the Wolds.

Other men were doubling a rope of horsehair, weft with whale skin to increase its strength, around the upright of the stern post. Walking the rope forward they began to run it through the heavy iron eyelets that lined the flanks of the beasts as Shining Mane pulled the sun clear of the horizon in a splash of pink.

The porter paused and pulled a pained expression. 'I couldn't round up all the men I would have liked, lord. With all the raids and the like, quite a few have returned to their home villages for the winter. Safety in numbers, I guess, you can hardly blame them. I wondered if I could use a few of your youths?'

Eofer nodded. 'We'll all pitch in, Eadmund. I told you last night, none of us are above a little hard work. There are no friendly porters to help us when we are deep inside British lands.'

Eadmund shook his head. 'I only need a few extra hands, lord. Most of the pulling will be done by the oxen and their drivers. There are a few areas where we need to use rollers where the portage crosses uneven ground and that needs the hands of men, willing or unwilling. No,' he added with a smile, 'your youth will be more than enough. With your reduced numbers, I will have enough horses in the corral for yourself and the men of your duguth to ride to Sleyswic. It will save you a day that way and, as you say, a war-sword demands haste.'

Eofer could sense the smile forming on Thrush Hemming's face as he realised that a day of toil and mud looked about to be replaced by a short ride and a day supping the king's ale. He nodded. 'It's a good plan. I will leave my ship master, Sæward, to keep an eye on things. Saddle up the horses, and we will leave straight away.'

Eadmund chuckled and looked across to the corral, where his sons were busy saddling a group of horses. 'Already being seen to, lord.'

The trio moved towards the prow, and Eadmund ran his fingers along the carvings that decorated the sheer strake of the little warship as they walked. Freshly repainted back at Strand, red falcons soared and plummeted on a field of blue, and Eofer watched the experienced porter's obvious approval with pride.

'She's a real beauty, lord,' he finally breathed, turning to flash a smile. 'A bit better than we are used to seeing up here, coasters and the odd fat bellied *cnar*. How far do you take her?'

'She'll sail anywhere,' Eofer answered proudly, 'but we mostly spend our summers in Britannia. She barely draws half a foot of water, ideal for moving along the rivers, deep into the heart of the place.'

A heavy thunk told them that the youth had arrived and were loading their belongings back on board as the rising sun raked the clearing with its light. A cry came from the leading handler, and Eadmund acknowledged him with a wave. 'First light, lord,' he smiled. 'We are ready, as promised.'

EOFER CURBED his mount at the brow of the rise and gazed back at the valley floor. The men of his duguth, elated to a man to be spared the heavy work, beamed as they circled him on their mounts. The spear blade shape of the *Fælcen* was edging forward as the ox team, already growing indistinct beneath a vaporous brume, dug in and huckled forward.

Beyond them, the Trene meandered away to become lost in the trees of the uplands that the English called the Wolds. Raising his gaze, the eorle looked out across the lowlands of the polder to the German Sea beyond. The rains had lifted there now, and the wetlands sparkled like a jewel in the pale light of the early morning. A voice came at his shoulder. 'It's a beautiful land, Eofer,' Imma Gold said. 'Worth fighting for.'

10

Osbeorn balled a fist and pushed it into his chest, lifting a cheek and forcing out a fart as the belch cut the air. 'Two birds in a bush.' He sniffed and threw them a grin. 'It must be your lucky day. The guard was right, this is good ale!'

Eofer shook his head in mock despair as the men of his duguth laughed into their cups.

'Good bread and cheese, too,' Osbeorn added as Imma refilled the cups from the jug, 'pass it over.' He jerked his head towards a further bowl, 'and the pickled onions.'

Thrush Hemming pushed the bowl through the ale slops and raised a sarcastic brow. 'No pickled eggs this time, lord?'

Osbeorn belched and sniffed again. 'Good idea, shove them across.'

They were sat in a hall given over to public drinking. Most of the larger settlements in Engeln had at least one such place that offered lodgings, food, and ale to travellers who were without kinfolk in that place to provide shelter. Sleyswic, situated where the portage deposited its charges into the great waterway of the Sley and near the north-south route known as The Oxen Way, had at least a score of these 'ale hus'. Judging by the number of men in the place, Eofer came to the conclusion that the ale hus' of Sleyswic numbered more than just travellers among their customers.

Arriving at the gates of the king's tun near the waterfront, the guards had politely but firmly told the eorle that the king was yet to rise and that nobody was to enter or leave the fortress until he appeared. It was little more than a distance of ten miles from the place where they had left the ship to the hall, and they had reached the town before the sun was a hand's breadth above the eastern horizon. Stabling the horses, the friendly guards had promised to report their arrival to the king's hall reeve and pointed them towards the squat building on the waterfront.

The Barley Mow seemed to be a popular call for the workers making their way to the nearby quayside. A stone-lined hearth had been constructed against one of the outside walls of the place, and an armful of logs were blazing away merrily. Smog rose to collect among the rafters, before drifting out through a smoke hole in the gable. Ena, the buxom ale wife, bustled across to stoke the flames, and Eofer and his men laughed as the conversations tailed away as she bent low and swayed rhythmically in time with every poke. Osbeorn raised a cheek and squeezed out another. 'By the way that she is moving that poker, she knows exactly what effect she is having here!' They all laughed at his observation as the woman straightened and moved back towards the kitchen at the rear. She threw them a look and wrinkled her nose as she passed by their table, and the group set their faces into masks of innocence as they pointed out the culprit. Osbeorn threw her a wink, 'cracking eggs, Ena!' The men of the troop roared as Ena shook her head, muttering a goodnatured curse on warriors in general as she favoured a regular with a smile.

Imma Gold sank another cup, pushed back his chair and whistled contentedly. 'This is the only way to start the day,' he sighed. 'Isn't life so much easier without the children.' They all smiled again as they imagined the youth sweating the ship across the portage. 'They should be just about up with those horrible ridges we passed earlier.' He upended his empty cup with a crash. 'More ale anyone?' Twisting on his stool, he drew a breath to summon Ena but let it out in a long sigh of disappointment instead. 'Sorry lads. My fault for tempting wyrd.'

Eofer followed his gaze across to the doorway. Framed in the rectangle of light, the guard from earlier was searching the tables of the gloomy room. Spotting them near the hearth, he ducked inside and made his way across. He threw them an apologetic look. 'Sorry to drag you away, lord. The king's up and about, and your arrival has been reported to him. He will receive you right away.'

EOFER STUDIED the king's tun as he approached at the head of his men. The outer defences consisted of a wide, steep sided ditch that funnelled traffic between the enclosing outer walls of the compound. The bottom twenty feet or so of these walls had been faced with irregular creamy coloured stone to counter the use of fire by any attackers. Above this, a palisade of smooth timber shielded the guards on the inner walkway from the elements and any hostile action. A robust timber gatehouse capped the portal, above which flew an enormous red flag adorned with the white dragon of the English. The full light of day was on the land now, revealing a sky of the darkest cobalt. To the north the last of the storm clouds, shredded and torn by the anger of the wind, hurried away towards the waters of the Belt.

Folk were already arriving at the outer gate as traders and their customers queued patiently for admittance to the compound within. 'You picked the wrong day to arrive, lord,' the guard explained as they walked. 'Wodensdæg is market day in Sleyswic, people come from all over.'

The guards manning the gateway nodded them through and ushered the multitude to one side as Eofer and his men approached. Raised eyebrows and haughty looks followed them from the more patient queuers, but nothing was said as they passed beneath the shadow of the gatehouse and spilled out into the compound beyond. Up ahead, the burh of King Eomær perched upon its knoll. The inner defences, stone faced and palisaded, mirrored those of the larger compound that surrounded it with, silhouetted against the skyline, the massive timbered hall of the king. Shining in its lime washed splendour beneath a mantle of golden thatch, the hall dominated the town and the dark waters of the Sley beyond from behind its ring of brightly coloured war flags.

Despite the early hour, dozens of stallholders had already set up, and the sellers of foods and ale were doing a roaring trade. A smith had erected a small forge, and the dark red flames had become a warm place to gather as folk met old friends and exchanged their news. An escaped piglet zigzagged, squealing, through the crowd as it made a desperate bid to escape its fate. The warriors laughed at the comical efforts of the sausage maker and his assistant to overtake the beast, before it could make the gate. Eofer wondered at the absurdity of the crowd, yelling the pig on as they munched happily on one of its littermates.

The track rose towards the gatehouse, and soon they were being nodded through. The warriors here, Eofer noticed, were older and generally larger than those in the outer compound. The quality of their mail and weapons marked the men as *gesithas*, the men of the king's personal hearth troop. Chosen from among the bravest and hardiest of the duguth, these were the king's close companions, the men who ate, drank and slept in his hall and formed his personal bodyguard in battle. Broad chested and full bearded to a man, the gesithas were not to be lightly crossed.

A gnarled old veteran detached himself from the shadow of the hall and made his way down to them as they reached the staircase. 'Eofer king's bane, my name is Ælfhelm, I am the new reeve here. Welcome back to *Eorthdraca.*' The reeve indicated that they follow him towards the great double doors that led into the magnificent structure that was Earthdragon, the hall of the king, as they began to remove their weapons. 'Did you bring your scegth? *Fælcen* is it?' Eofer nodded and shot the reeve a grin. 'We left our youth manhandling her across the carrying place and rode here at first light.' Ælfhelm chuckled. 'You'll have been spending some time in the Barley Mow then. Great tits that Ena, and a dab hand with the poker!' They all shared an easy laugh as they mounted the steps. 'What happened to the old reeve, Æscwine?' Eofer asked. Ælfhelm smiled genially. 'He is still here, you will meet him inside. He still has duties to perform, but he finds it difficult to hear what is being said most of the time.' He shrugged and leaned across. 'Between you and me he is as deaf as that post, but the king still accords him honour for the service that he has given to his family. He fought alongside King Eomær's grandfather, you know, Offa the Great.'

The twin gilt doors of Eorthdraca loomed above them, and Eofer studied the designs as the reeve announced their arrival by crashing down on the wooden boards with the heel of his staff. Chased into their faces were momentous events in the making of the English nation. The bairn, Sceaf son of Woden, pitching up on the shore of the Beltic Sea to found the tribe. The warrior king, Wihtlæg, crushing Amleth and his Jutes. Offa's defeat of the Myrging champion at Monster Gate and his son, Engeltheow's war of conquest that followed. His father had fought in the war as a youth, and he had grown up listening, spellbound, as the warriors recalled the fighting.

The great doors were drawn inward, and the group composed themselves as their shadows cut the plane of light that appeared on the hall floor. Ælfhelm took a step inside the hall, and Eofer and his men held their position at the threshold as the reeve's deep voice boomed into the void.

'Eofer Wonreding has answered the war-sword's call, lord.'

As his eyes became accustomed to the gloomy interior, Eofer noticed two warriors were stood, their crossed spears barring entrance to the party, just ahead of the reeve. Ælfhelm gave them a curt nod, responding to an unseen signal, and the men stood to one side as the retainer moved forward. Eofer followed and the familiar smell of the hall, wood smoke, ale, leather and men, engulfed him. It was a good smell, a homely smell, and Eofer and the men of his hearth troop took in the features of the king's hall as they paced the oaken boards of Eorthdraca in the reeve's wake. Twin columns marched ahead, their great girth cunningly chased as dragons and men fought duels that spiralled up to the great hammer beams of the roof above. Picked out in gold and red, the death struggles appeared to writhe and flail in the reflected light of the hearth that flamed between them.

The eorle's eyes were drawn beyond the stout figure of Ælfhelm to the dais that stood at the head of the hall and the figure upon it. King Eomær sat on his gift stool, resplendent in a pool of light lancing in from a side wind hole high in the eaves. The king was dressed in a knee-length tunic and hose of the purest white, cuffed and hemmed in gold, which gleamed like a star amid the deep shadows of early morning. Eofer, despite the solemnity of the occasion, stifled a snort as a piece of advice which his father had given him years ago popped into his consciousness like a bat in the night. *'If you want to impress Eofer, dress in the lightest colour clothing that you can. It shows that you don't have to scrabble about in muck and shit all day like other folk!'* The king's garb was completed by a cloak of the deepest blue, edged gold, pinned at the shoulder by a delicately worked gold and garnet encrusted square headed brooch. King Eomær's ancestral battle sword, *Stedefæst*, hung at the king's side as twin spearmen, gesithas dressed for war, flanked their lord. The pale light of the northern morning shone dully on the wall to the King's rear, where the great war flag of the English hung proudly. His battle shield, its red leather facing studded with golden dragons, ravens, and the eye of Woden, stood to one side alongside the silvery gleam of the king's ringed byrnie and helm.

Ælfhelm drew to one side as the procession came within twenty paces of the king, and the hubbub that had greeted their arrival from the benches stilled as Eofer and the men of his troop knelt and lowered their gaze. Eofer gripped the war sword and held it forward to show that he had answered its call.

King Eomær spoke. 'Welcome to Eorthdraca, Eofer king's bane. Approach me, speak with your king.'

Eofer rose and walked forward, and the king motioned that he remain on his feet with a smile. Closer now, Eofer was gratified to see that the trials of the kingdom over the past few years had not had any discernible effect on the appearance of his lord. Tall and stockily built, Eomær shared the handsome features of his clan. Square of jaw, a smattering of freckles lay upon a face that was more round than oval, open and welcoming beneath a crop of hair the colour of summer hay.

The king took the war-sword and motioned to a retainer who hurried forward with two golden cups. 'Drink with me, Eofer,' the king said, smiling again as he tapped Eofer's cup with a dull metallic chink. 'Did you have a good journey?'

'Wet, lord,' he replied with a snort. 'If it had rained much harder, we could have sailed here across the Wolds and saved a day.'

The king laughed easily. 'You have heard about the symbol?' Eofer said that he had, and the king continued cryptically. 'That is one of the reasons for it.' The king shook his head dismissively as he saw the eorle's incomprehension. 'All will be revealed in good time. The symbol is to take place next week at the Winterfylleth, but before that, there is a man who I would like you to meet. I will replace those nags that Eadmund loaned you at the Old Ford with a fine war horse, and we will ride to meet him after we have eaten.'

THE HORSES PICKED their way south, the sun, low in the sky, a blinding orb of white as it crept slowly along a ridge of darkened trees. 'Perhaps we should have left earlier,' the king quipped as he lowered his eyes against the glare.

'Have we far to travel, lord?' Eofer said.

King Eomær shook his head. 'Only a short distance. You will have to forgive the discomfort, but it will be worth your while.'

They had left Eorthdraca as soon as the horses had been saddled and made ready for the journey. King Eomær had donned his war gear as his gesithas had armed, and within the hour the party had joined The Oxen Way and turned south. Eofer, to his surprise and delight, had been asked to ride at the head of the column with the king and, despite the pride he felt, the eorle could not but help but wonder who they were travelling to meet. The men of Eofer's hearth troop had been shown honour by being asked to ride immediately to the rear of the pair. It was an unusual display of trust and regard for the king, to let an armed group come between himself and his gesithas. Eofer had chuckled as he compared the looks of pride that shone from the faces of his war-band, and contrasted them with the glum looks of the king's men, sensing their discomfort in every movement.

At the end of the armed group, barely visible as an occasionally glimpsed nodding head, Osbeorn brought up the rear of the column. Identified as the source of the miasma that had followed the group like a faithful wet dog, the king had banished the duguth there for fouling the air in the king's hall. Eofer could not help but notice that Osbeorn's standing had immediately risen among the king's men; Ena's eggs were evidently popular, even if the consequences were less so.

As the sun approached its high point, the outriders that had ridden ahead of the column took a track that led away to the east. Soon they were among a press of oak and elm, the ancient woodland that had witnessed the arrival of Woden and his war-band when the earth was young and the land had first been settled by Ingvæone folk. The wind sighed through the treetops as the party wend its way through a steady rain of crisp russet leaves that banked against the sides of the path and collected in the hollows. Fording a brook, King Eomær led the column out onto the side of a grassy ridge. Below them lay a sheltered valley. At its head stood a fine hunting lodge that looked out across the fields to the iron grey waters of Suthworthig Bay beyond.

A hawk hung in the air as it quartered the ground, and the pair watched it with admiration. The king spoke, excitement dancing in his eyes. 'A kestrel!' He turned his head to Eofer. 'Which hawk do you use to hunt?'

'My father and I were gifted gyrfalcons by our kinsman, king Hygelac, for our support during his exile.'

Eomær nodded, clearly impressed. 'Fine birds, it was a noble gift, manfully earned. You brought honour on me and the English folk by your actions in Geatland and Swede Land that summer and reputation for yourself,' the king said. 'I have heard accounts of your actions there and elsewhere, and you show promise, Eofer. But before you can be held to be an eorle by your king, you need to prove your worth and loyalty consistently.' Eomær fixed him with a hard stare. 'Have you decided to accept Cerdic's offer, or remain with your people in these difficult times?'

The blood drained from Eofer's face as he stammered a reply. 'My future and that of my people are irrevocably bound, lord.'

The king flicked Eofer a look of amusement. 'You are wondering how I knew?' he said. 'The truth is that I only had my suspicions until your expression gave you away. Leaders of armies can never have enough men of worth in their ranks, Eofer,' he added with a self-satisfied smirk. 'It was natural for a warlord in Cerdic's position to attempt to enlist your help against his enemies. You need to be fox-cunning to wear the king helm and stay alive for as long as I have!' The humour quickly faded from the king's face to be replaced by the stone-hard countenance of a leader of men. 'I am your natural lord and I have a task for you, Eofer,' he said. 'Complete it well, and you will rise even higher in the estimation of your king and people.' The king guided his mount along a badger run that angled off across the face of the valley side, changing the subject to put his thegn at ease as the tail of the column and its shamefaced outrider emerged from the tree line. 'Hygelac died like a king in Frankland, as did the men who accompanied him, I hear. Valhall will have had a riotous night welcoming all the new arrivals!' He glanced across as the horses walked on. 'Have you heard from King Heardred?'

'Not since he sent word that he had taken the gift stool of the Geats.'

A shadow fell across them, and Eofer glanced up to see that they had reached the outer compound that guarded the lodge. The ditch and mound that encircled the buildings were sharp edged, as yet unworn by the passage of time. Glancing up at the great timbers that formed the palisade above, Eofer could see that the wood had been recently felled. The defences were new additions, and he sighed inwardly as he realised that the waters of the bay opposite, so long an English lake, were slipping from their control.

The king led them through the gatehouse and dismounted as a groom rushed across to lead the horse away. Eomær indicated that Eofer step to one side as the other riders entered the stockade. 'King Heardred's position is secure. I have sent word to his neighbours that he is a friend of the English and promised him our help once again while he replaces the losses they incurred in the South.' Eofer made to thank the king, but he held up a hand and cut him short, his face suddenly fixed into a scowl. 'That is not why we are here today. The Danes have violated our land and people, and I will take a blood price for their arrogance.' He took the eorle by the arm and fixed him with a stare. 'Your brother, Wulf, lives. He is a captive in Dane Land and you, Eofer, will be the very point of our avenging spear.'

11

The giant warrior and the men of his war band knelt at the approach of the king. King Eomær indicated that they rise and turned to Eofer. 'Eofer Wonreding, king's bane, this is the champion of the Heathobeards, Starkad Storvirkson.' Starkad smiled in greeting, but the gesture carried little warmth. Despite the magnificence of the king, the sheer size and reputation of the great warrior of the War-Beards dominated the room.

Eofer studied the man as the king indicated that they remove themselves to the upper floor, where the more detailed discussions between them would take place. Starkad, he decided, combined the build of a bull with the mien of a wolf. Clad in a web of mail—close-fitting and glittering, where it reflected the flaming hearth—the War-Beard's most notable feature apart from his size was the three angry welts that scored his face. The result, stories told, of a fistfight with a bear. Starkad's left eye had been destroyed by a great swipe of the beast's paw, and the white orb that remained added to the menace that emanated from the man.

King Eomær led the pair to a stairway that climbed to the

upper story as the warriors, English and Heathobeard settled at the benches. Eofer glared at Starkad as they approached the staircase, and the War-Beard paused to allow the Engle to follow his king. Again the humourless smile flashed across the man's face, and Eofer found himself hoping that whatever the cause for his presence here, wyrd would never force them to become shield brothers.

The stairway emptied onto a wide, sunlit room that encircled the upper floor of the lodge. The wall spaces between the uprights of the building had been left open to the air from waist height to the thatch above, flooding the space with light. Food and drink had been provided at one end of the balcony, and king Eomær indicated to the servants there that they should leave with a flick of his head.

The king rested his hands on a sill and looked out down the wide valley with a sigh. 'This was a fine lodge,' he said, sweeping the area to the front with an arm. 'Game would be driven towards us here on this platform, and we could take them as they ran by.' He turned back and smiled ruefully. 'I had it built when my father, King Engeltheow, grew too old to hunt from horseback.' He gave a sad shrug. 'We think that we have recovered from the sword strike that came from nowhere, the spear that came beneath the shield. We forget them, but they never forget us. All the old wounds come back to torment our bodies when the vigour of youth wanes.'

The king's humour came back with a rush as he threw off the feeling of melancholy and smiled. 'Starkad, you have welcome news for my eorle.'

The cold smile returned, and the War-Beard nodded. 'Eofer, I am certain that your lord has broken the happy news of your brother's survival. I can tell you that he is being kept by the Danes at Hleidra. I was there only last month, and saw him with my own eyes.'

Eofer beamed, as the news that the king had passed to him in the courtyard was confirmed. 'You have my thanks, Starkad, my family are in your debt.' His eyes narrowed with suspicion as he looked from the Heathobeard to his king and back again. 'Forgive me, but the scops who tell of the deeds of the only Starkad Storvirkson known to me, have always failed to mention that he travels the northern lands bringing good cheer to grieving families. What is the real reason for your journey to my lord's land?'

Eomær and Starkad exchanged a look, before both men threw back their heads and laughed. As was right, the king spoke first. 'That was well said. You are your father's son, Eofer. King Ingeld has sent Starkad to me with the offer of an alliance against our common enemy, the Danes.' He took up a cup from the trestle and sipped from the mead within. 'It seems that the efforts that King Hrothgar has made to cultivate their friendship have come to nought.' He looked back to the War-Beard. 'Starkad, will you explain the weft and weave of the Danish scheming to my thegn?'

Starkad dipped his head. 'Hrothgar has been trying to placate his neighbours to the south with gold and peace-weaving. Ever since the death of the fell troll that plagued Heorot they have been rebuilding their strength, and now they are over-proud once more. Now that any threat from the Geats has been removed by the Franks and Frisians,' he shrugged and took a mouthful of ale as the king supplied the end to the sentence. 'They are free to raid the lands that they have always coveted, our lands being chief among them.'

Eofer looked back to Starkad. 'If the Danes are your enemies, why were you there so recently?'

Starkad chuckled and Eofer saw a degree of respect begin to tint his attitude towards him. 'You are right to be wary,' the giant smiled. 'My king is no friend of the English. You may or may not know, Eofer king's bane, but I am not a Heathobeard by birth. My people are the Eisti, who lie on the eastern shores of the sea that you call the Beltic. I was shipwrecked as a young man and entered the service of King Ingeld's father, King Froda. Early in his reign, Hrothgar attacked and killed my king whilst I was leading a raid on the lands of the Wulfings. His son, Ingeld took the king helm, but we could never avenge our lord's death.' He coloured with the admission, but set his face as he forced down the sense of shame. 'Last summer, Hrothgar sent word that he desired old enmities be forgotten between us. He sent my king a magnificent longship filled with treasure, gold rings, cunningly worked sword blades and mail byrnies, along with the offer of the hand of his only daughter, Freawaru, as a peaceweaver. Against my advice, the king accepted and led a party to Heorot to collect his bride. While we were there, I saw your brother and heard the tale of the brave attack he led against Prince Hrothmund and his vikings on Harrow.'

Eofer exchanged a sidelong look with his lord, and King Eomær recognised the eorle's mistrust. 'You are right to be wary,' he said, 'but there is more.'

Starkad brightened and a look of satisfaction returned to his face. 'During the feasting at Heorot, a young Dane was boasting of his father's war-luck. He brandished a blade that I recognised at once as the ancestral sword that had belonged to my friend, Withergeld, long ago. He had fought at the front when King Froda had died. All who escaped the reddened maw of the wolf and raven that day called him a hero. Withergeld's son, Brand, was with our party and I drew his attention to the blade.' Starkad drew himself up proudly as he described the result of his goading. 'Brand acted with honour. He challenged the Dane to holmgang before the assembly. Despite the efforts of Hrothgar and his cwen, Wealhtheow, the withies were set outside and Brand took blood-price, slaying his father's killer.' The War-Beard threw them a wolfish smile. 'Blood had been spilt and old wounds reopened. The betrothal was rejected. King Ingeld returned the woman to her parents, and we left for home.'

Starkad reached for a cup of ale with an air of triumph, and Eofer wondered at the man's disloyalty. It was plain that he had looked for a reason to disrupt the betrothal despite the wishes of his king and lord. A warrior's first duty was to the man who had received his oath, any personal ambition or feelings were irrelevant. He exchanged a look with his king that confirmed that both Englishmen were in agreement; this Starkad Storvirkson was about as trustworthy as a sack of adders.

Despite the mutually felt distrust, the king moved to allay his fears. 'I have heard this tale from other sources, but the detail about your brother, Wulf, is new to me. I would pay red gold for his return, but it is the opinion of King Ingeld—and I agree—that my offer would be rejected. It would also let the Danes know that we were aware that he had survived the fight, and that would make your attack less likely to succeed.'

Eofer's heart raced as the reason for his summons by warsword became clear.

Starkad nodded as he confirmed the king's statement. 'As King Eomær says, the Danes are not looking for ransom.' He fixed Eofer with a stare. 'Your brother is to be sacrificed at the winter solstice.'

THE LAST OF the warriors filed into the hall as the setting sun painted the town beyond the palisade a fiery red. The men exchanged glances as Ælfhelm, the reeve of Eorthdraca, drew the great doors together with a resounding boom. They had gathered and watched as the king and his guda had sacrificed a war stallion to Ing in the shadow of the hall, seeking his guidance in the deliberations to come. Each man there knew that, in the flames of the evening sky, the god had provided them with his answer.

Eofer, and the men of his hearth troop, had been shown great honour by the king. He smiled to himself in satisfaction as he recognised the whispered comments and envious looks of the other thegns present, as they took their place at the lower benches. Eofer looked across to his father and felt a surge of pride. Sat among his fellow folctoga and men of the wise, only feet away from King Eomær himself, Wonred had reached the pinnacle of his ambition. Eofer caught his eye and threw him a wink, chuckling to himself as his father beamed in return.

The last of the evening light was fading from the wind holes high in the side wall of Eorthdraca, casting the roof beams and the space between into alternating furrows of blood and soil. Ing was guiding his people to war and, as the hubbub subsided, the last of the thræls set the torches into the great iron stands and hurried away.

A voice boomed from the top table, filling the hall, and Eofer saw that the old reeve, Æscwine, had the duties within the hall that evening. He recognised the king's hand in it and found that he approved of his choice. The old man deserved the honour after a lifetime of devotion to his clan.

The sound of wood scraping on wood echoed around the walls as the warriors rose to welcome their lord's lady. Cwen Eahlswith entered the hall from a rear door, carrying the great drinking horn of the symbel before her. Throwing the hall a radiant smile, she moved to the king and passed the great horn across. Longer than a man's arm, the symbel horn was said to have been wrenched from an aurochs by Woden himself after a hunt long ago. Gilt figures of men and beasts encircled the mouthpiece and, curling up from its base, a silver terminal ended in the great sweep of a raven's beak, Woden's bird. King Eomær took the horn with a gracious nod to his cwen and sank the first mouthful of the specially brewed beer contained within. Stronger than ale and mead, the brew was infused with herbs known only to Osgar, the king's leading guda. The beer was an important part of the ritual, helping the men, king, and warriors alike, to enter the state that they called *giddig*, the swirling feeling when Woden came among them and the god entered their minds. The warriors remained silent as the cwen moved along the top table, passing the horn from folctoga to folctoga and conversing easily with each man.

Soon, Eahlswith stood before Eofer's bench companions, and she smiled warmly and wished them well as they sipped from the horn. As she moved through the great space, the men were free to take their seats once again and the real drinking of the evening could begin. Eofer charged the cups of each of his duguth and solemnly raised his own.

'Here's to our success…'

The warriors raised their cups in reply, and they came together with a clatter as they made the pledge and roared the retort.

'Wæs Hæl! *Drinc Hæl!*'

Imma Gold shook his head in appreciation and looked at his cup. 'Symbel beer,' he breathed, 'the drink of the gods.'

They all shared a laugh as they began to relax and enjoy the evening. All the men now knew the reason for the journey to the hunting lodge in the isolated valley, and they were eager to take the war to the Danes. Each man there had known their eorle's brother for a decade or more, and the men of the brothers' troop had fought side by side in shield walls in Swede Land and Britannia. They knew now that their shield-brothers were dead to a man. But they had died with honour, sword or spear in hand, and they were feasting with their ancestors in an even greater hall as they themselves sat at their beer. Soon, they knew, they would sail the whale-road, free Wulf and wreak bloody vengeance.

The hall was now abuzz as the cwen paused at the top table to kiss her lord before departing the gathering. The skylights were now solid squares of jet as the men set to their beer and the first dancers strode into the space before the king and took up their stance. Each youth carried a gar in each hand, the heavy thrusting spears of the English shield wall. Clad only in a belt of exquisite workmanship, the dancers crouched beneath the helms that symbolised membership of the wolf brotherhood. Binding friend and fiend among the warriors of the northern lands, the helms terminated in a pair of opposing raven heads that curled above the dome to form a crest. Every thegn had danced the dance of the wolf warrior at his initiation into the cult, and he carried a representation of the wolf dancers on a plate above the left eye of his battle helm. It served to identify the warrior elite on the battlefield. Although no quarter would be expected or given among opposing members of the brotherhood, they would seek to ensure that their opponent died sword in hand, and gain entry to Valhall.

As the youths danced, thrusting their gar in time to a steady drumbeat, Osgar reappeared with his underlings bearing sheaths of barley, feeding them into the braziers that were scattered about the hall. A weave of wildflowers and secret things known only to men of their craft, the sheaths represented the founder of the English people, Sceaf himself. It was the first indication to the warriors present that this symbol was to be much more than a call to arms, and the king watched from his gift stool as his men exchanged questioning looks. Soon the air was thick with the sweet smell drifting across from the fires as Æscwine came forward to strike the boards with the hall staff.

A veil of smoke moved to engulf the men at the top table and, as it cleared, the now giddy warriors in the hall saw that their king had been transfigured into Woden himself. The god sat on the king's gift stool, his great spear Shaker held in his right hand and a hart topped whetstone grasped in his left. A grim-helm of silvered plates enclosed the god's face and head, the left eye alone glowing a dull hoop of red in the reflected light of the hearth.

Æscwine crashed the staff and spoke again. 'The Allfather has been invoked, not as you imagined, to guide our arms against the Dane. King Eomær and the men of his witan have discussed the depredations, both here in Engeln and overseas in Anglia, but cannot agree on the solution.' He paused and seemed to compose himself before continuing. 'The matter is simply this. We are agreed that the point has been reached where we must decide whether the future of the English folk lies on this side of the sea or in the new settlements in Britannia. Our enemies here grow stronger and covet our ancestral lands. The Danes push us from the east and the Jutes from the north. We can recall the warriors from Anglia and smite these foes as we have always done in former days, or we can move to the new lands, but the king fears that we cannot do both. The floor is open. Speak now before the Allfather, whose wisdom will guide us in our search.'

A hush descended on Eorthdraca as, even in their giddiness, the thegns, and the men of their hearth troop sat stunned by the enormity of the choice that lay before them. Even the scops, the guardians of the folk memory of the people, agreed that the English had inhabited these lands since the days of

Sceaf. Their barrows littered the land, the very soil was made from the dust of their ancestors. A thegn got to his feet and addressed his god. 'Allfather, we cannot leave. You know these lands to be English lands.' He looked about the hall and his mouth curled into a smile. 'The men I see before me fear no man, Dane nor…' he paused and sneered as a rumble of agreement rolled around the hall, 'Jute.' He looked back to the figure on the gift stool and drew himself to his full height. 'Advise our witan, lord, to bring the men home. Let us sweep these Danes back into the lakes and pine forests of Scandia, from which they crawled.' The thegn regained his bench, and the hall resounded with the thunder made by stamping feet and pummelled tables.

As the noise resounded within the ancient walls, Eofer's mind began to drift. Whether it was the effects of the sacred smoke, or the presence of the Allfather, he could not say. But to his astonishment, he found that he was back on the windy ridge above the great white horse carving of the Atrebates. A brace of ravens rode the updraft, spiralling aloft as the woods and hills of Britannia melted into the distance. Suddenly, the sharp note of iron striking stone sounded clearly in his mind, and he snorted in recognition of the moment. The message was clear, and Eofer found that he was climbing to his feet.

The noise drained away like ale from an upturned barrel, and Eofer's heart quickened as the hall fell silent. He faced his god and the words spilt easily. 'You know as well as I, lord,' he began, 'that the quality of the new land is matched only by the cowardice of its leaders and the indolence of its inhabitants. The lands of Britannia are old lands, dotted with wondrous works of the old people, the work of giants. I travelled the width of the island this summer past and I saw with my own eyes roads and buildings of stone standing abandoned, fields and woods groaning with barley and game. It is a land ripe for a vigorous people, a people accustomed to toil and victory in battle play. A people who will oust the Christ and return the land to the old gods, the real gods—the only gods.' Eofer swept the silent hall with his gaze, before steeling his nerve to look directly into the glowing eye of Woden. 'Allfather, guide our people westward. Let us replace the weeds with a hardier seed. Let us grow strong there together, gods and folk.'

12

The *Fælcen* slid easily through the narrow waters known as the throat. Passing the town of Theodford, the people's ford, with gentle strokes of the oars, its wharfs and jetties squatted in the wan autumn light as they struck out for the mouth itself. Here the Sley took its final turn to the east, widening out into a broad bay before the enclosing arms of land moved back in. Free of the constriction and the trees that had hemmed them in, Eofer looked on as the crew cast hopeful glances at the dragon pennant that capped the mast. Within moments, they were rewarded as the first breath of wind that day snatched at the banner, unfurling it with a crack and sending it snaking away to the north. Their lord answered their hopes as he called down the ship with a smile. 'Ship oars. Bassa and Beornwulf—hoist the yard. And shake out the sail—let's make some real headway.'

The vessel came alive as the crew moved to unship oars from thole-pins and the spar was hauled up the mast. As the crew swung the oars inboard and stacked them on the cross trees amidships, the sail filled with a sigh as the *Fælcen* took a breath and bounded forward on the swell. Eofer flicked a look at Sæward, chuckling inwardly as he recognised the joy on his friend's features as the big oar began to bite the waters and the ship became a hunter once more.

The eorle turned to the south and noted the position of the sun. Placing his hand sidelong on the horizon, he counted to three as he moved it up to the pale ball.

Sæward spoke. 'Are we putting in at the burh, lord?'

Eofer shook his head. 'No, I want us to stay as far from folk as I can. Besides,' he said, glancing up at the flag, 'the wind is perfect. Let's make the most of it while we have it. We will make the Bight by nightfall and be at Needham first thing.' Eofer instinctively glanced down at the hatch cover where the collection of swords, spearheads, and helms had been stowed for their one-way trip. 'We'll shoot the Little Belt tomorrow if it holds and swing east to pitch our final camp on the northern coast of Harrow.'

A skein of geese flew low across the bows and, skimming the surface, beat their way to the south. Overhead, gulls came in ones and twos, their harsh cries cutting the air as they looked to scavenge any morsels that might find their way overboard. Eofer crossed to the steersman and leaned close. As a duguth, he knew the reason for the journey and could be relied on to guard that knowledge closely. The others had yet to earn that trust, and youthful bluster had cost more than one seasoned warrior his life. 'Starkad said that the Heathobeards will launch their attack one week after Winterfylleth. That leaves us little enough time to dally.' He shrugged. 'Only the gods know who will win the battle, but I do know that the Danes will react with speed and vigour, despite the lateness of the year.'

Sæward sucked at his teeth as he looked down the ship.

Octa was in a huddle with Oswin word-poor, his arm stabbing out an imaginary dagger as the duguth made good on the promise he had made to his lord. Spearhafoc sat with her back to the mast as she examined the fletching on an arrow. 'How many do you think we will lose?'

Eofer shrugged again. 'That depends on how much Woden likes our gifts.' The steersman gave his eorle a pensive look, and Eofer cocked his head in question.

Sæward tapped the steer bord of the ship lovingly and checked that nobody was within earshot. 'If the old girl here is making a one-way trip, what happens if the Danes have taken all the horses from this stud and ridden south on them to confront the War-Beards?' He sniffed and wiped his nose on the cuff of his sleeve, almost as if his body was disowning the thought, lest he be thought a nithing for harbouring a doubt at his lord's plan. 'It would make sense.'

Eofer shook his head. 'The horses there are Hrothgar's finest hunting mounts. They are not trained for war, he has other horses for that duty. Believe me,' he said, 'the king of Danes would not let anyone use his prize hunters to attack a spear-hedge. But, if he has, then we shall form our own shield-burh and die like men.'

THE SHIP SHUDDERED as they emerged from the shelter of the land, and headed out across the Bight. But the wind was astern, and the little scegth drove ahead, her tall bow sending back a shower of salty spray over man and thwarts alike. Eofer looked across to the west. The sun had left Middle-earth, the last echoes of its light shading the skyline against the dark, hard edge of the distant Wolds as a voice cut the gloom. 'I hope that they don't forget to light the beacon, lord.'

Eofer clapped Thrush Hemming on the shoulder and indicated the distant shoreline with a raise of his chin. A needle of flame had appeared, growing by the moment, and Eofer imagined the men toiling there to feed its hunger. He glanced back at Sæward to make sure that he had seen the marker, but the big steersman wrinkled his brow and shot him a look of pity. Eofer snorted. His old friend was an experienced seaman who knew the waters that girded Engeln as well as any man alive. Beacon or no beacon, he would have laid odds that the man could have delivered them safely to their destination through the darkest of nights.

Within the hour the waters of the Bight were behind them, and Sæward ordered Bassa and Beornwulf to strike the sail and take the way off the ship. Outside the orbit of light thrown out by the beacon, the land ahead stood out as a dense black against the star speckled sky above. A foamy iridescence lit the bow wave as the crew retrieved the oars from the cross trees once more and slipped them proud of the hull.

The moon was little more than a waxing crescent now, and Eofer's mind drifted away to the south. The War-Beards would be gathered near their ships as they awaited the horses to draw the sun back into the sky to herald tomorrow's attack. King Ingeld would be feasting his ealdorlings and thegns on the strand as each man pledged his life for the glory and reputation of his lord. Some men would be spending their last moments with women and children before they sailed away to meet their wyrd. Others would come back a hero. As of tonight, only the norns would know which was which.

A challenge came from the shoreline ahead, and Eofer exchanged a smile with Hemming as he recognised the anxiety that laced the voice. Ships rarely travelled at night, and then only if the need was great and the moon full or gibbous. The guard and his mates would have settled themselves in as cosily as they could, ready to see out a long night of boredom laced with apprehension. Eofer had stood watch in hostile lands, and he knew the fears of the lone guard, but this was far worse. Were night-walkers watching them from beyond the circle of light thrown out by their signal fire? The mire at Needham lay only a few miles inland, a place of *dæmons* and *wicces*. This could be a ship of the dead sent by Hel, the half decayed hag of the underworld.

The thegn thought for a moment to stay silent and prolong the men's suspense, but decided better of it. Spooked men were apt to throw sharp objects first and ask questions later. He cupped his hands and cried out across the frigid waters. 'My name is Eofer king's bane. These are the men of my hearth troop, we are journeying to Needham. The white dragon flies at my masthead, you will see it when we come into the light of your beacon.'

As they watched, a troop of warriors, armed and shield bearing, appeared from the gloom and hastened to the first man's side. Bowmen arrived, fanning out to either side as they raised their war bows, nocked, and sighted along arrow shafts.

Thrush Hemming sniffed in the blackness. 'Jumpy lot.'

The *Fælcen* was soon within the arc of yellow light thrown out by the pyre, and a small group clattered down a flight of wooden steps to the waterside as the ship entered the calmer waters of Needham Sound. As Sæward edged the scegth nearer the bank, the first warrior turned and raised his spear to the men above in a sign that all was well. Leaving his companions, he trotted down the remaining steps and threw them a smile. 'Welcome to Needham, lord. Sorry about the edginess to our welcome, but the Danes have been raiding up and down the coast all year.' He spat.

'Bastards, they'll get what's coming to them.' A rumble of voices from the *Fælcen* told the guard that he was not alone in his wish.

Eofer narrowed his eyes and peered into the glare as he suddenly realised that he recognised the man. 'You were with us in Geatland,' he said. The guard drew himself up and grinned in surprise. 'I was, lord!' Eofer clicked his fingers as he thought. Suddenly, he had it. 'Your name is Ecgfrith. You fought with Coelnoth's men.' The warrior beamed with pride, amazed that such an exalted figure would recall his face. 'I did, lord! I still bore the others here with the tale of your father's champion, that big Swæffe bastard.'

Eofer grinned at the memory. 'Wulfstan.'

Ecgfrith's eyes widened in surprise, and he leaned closer after glancing back at his companions, who were still lining the lip of the bank. 'Don't tell them that, lord,' he said, lowering his voice. 'I have been calling him Wulfsige for years. They already pour scorn on my tale, and doubt that I was even there!' He straightened again. 'Will you be sharing our fire tonight, lord? We've good ale and our own freshly smoked fish.'

Eofer shook his head. 'Not tonight, Ecgfrith, we have to be out on the fen by dawn.'

The guard suppressed a shudder, but kept his opinion to himself as he pointed along the waterway with the shaft of his spear. 'Needham is still a few miles ahead, but the sound should be navigable with this amount of moonlight.' They both glanced instinctively at the sky above them and the sliver of moon that lay to the south. The pillowy clouds of the day had moved away, and the stars shone bright. 'Once you are past the first mile or so, it is arrow straight. Rune-carved columns mark the entrance to the river that leads up to the mire, you can't miss it.'

Eofer nodded his thanks and rested his foot on the wale as he turned to the rowers. 'Let's get going.'

The youth pushed forward on their oars and watched Sæward for the signal. Raising his arm, he hesitated for a heartbeat and let it drop. The blades dipped as one, stroking the scegth forward with barely a ripple to mark the surface.

Eofer turned to the bank as the ship moved back into the shadows. Cupping his hands to his mouth, he called out to Ecgfrith, now watching from within a knot of his companions.

'Farewell Ecgfrith, shield-brother. Keep the edge on your blade keen. We will fight the king's enemies together again soon.'

THE GUDA DOUSED the brand with a hiss, and the troop drew close about their eorle as the shadows crept closer. Away to the east the first tinge of light, steel grey against the starry sky above, drew a line on the horizon as Shining Mane hauled the sun back towards the land of the English.

Eofer moved forward with the men of his duguth, kneeling on the board that the stag-priest had thoughtfully provided for them. Cold dark water seeped over the edge to soak the knees of their trews anyway. But the thought had been there, and the eorle appreciated the gesture as his eyes flicked between the guda and the distant horizon, as they awaited the moment. The sky was lightening quickly now as the horse approached, and Eofer studied the holy man as the shadowy figure from the night before hardened by the moment. Crowned by a magnificent set of antlers, the hide from a stag fell in folds about the priest's body. Beneath the cowl of the beast's head, the man's face was marked by the runic spells that told all, god or man alike, that he was a leading exponent of his craft. Despite his appearance, the guda smiled warmly and gave the briefest of nods as the first spark of light told them that the sun had returned after the long night of the northern autumn.

Giant statues of the gods, deep carved and rune spattered, ringed the sacred space. Thunor, Ing, Woden the Allfather himself, their stern faces glowering over the worshippers below as the first glimmers of the dawn painted them pink.

The men of Eofer's troop placed their foreheads onto the offerings and closed their eyes as the priest's voice floated across the barren waste, dedicating them to the gods and asking for their favour in return. Opening his eyes again, Eofer leaned forward and lowered the sword blade beneath the blackened surface of the mere. As the waters closed about the weapon, and it began to grow indistinct, the light played on the Christian cross that had been fixed into its hilt. The memory of the Briton who had owned it flashed into his mind. A chieftain of his people, he had been a fool to place his faith in such a weak god. Not even a mail shirt and helm of the finest quality had saved him from the Englishman's fury, and Eofer hoped that the gift of such a fine blade would cause the true gods to smile upon the adventure they were about to embark upon.

As the blade passed away from the realm of men, Eofer stood and placed his sword hand onto his brow, washing it with the sacred waters of the mere. As he stepped back, the youth moved forward from their places and made their offerings to the gods. Less impressive than those sacrificed by their lord and the more senior members of the hearth troop—a wolf tooth charm, a treasured comb made from the antler of a hart—the items were nevertheless cherished belongings, and the gods would recognise their oblation for what it was.

The sky above was changing by the moment as the horse

galloped on. A hard magenta marbled pink to the east, the stars had been chased away there, leaving the sole point of light that men called the morning star to wrestle for supremacy with the returning sun. Eofer sniffed. The tussle would soon be over, the day was upon them. A glance to the south as he imagined the Heathobeards pulling at their benches as their king led them north to war.

13

The serpent prow tasted the air as it emerged from the fog bank and sought its prey. A moment of anxiety as his hand moved instinctively to the hilt of Blood-Worm was followed by a whistle and a smile as the white dragon of Engeln followed at the masthead.

Sæward spoke. 'Is that her?'

'Let's hope so,' Eofer murmured in reply. 'If a ship thegn can find a scegth in this, he can find anything.'

Coming about, the big snaca turned her bows towards the *Fælcen*, and Eofer watched as a crewman hauled himself onto the prow and shielded his eyes against the glare.

'Who are you?'

'Eofer, king's bane.'

'Where bound?'

'On the king's business.'

The air between them shone like mail as the moisture held suspended within it reflected the sun's rays. Eofer watched as messages passed back and forth along the big ship. At his rear Sæward was ordering the sail shortened and Bassa and Beornwulf jumped to the task, hauling at the braces and spilling the wind from the sheet. On the snake ship, two crewmen rushed forward to fit the beiti-ass to the lower edge of the sail, tautening the sheet as the ship tacked and beat to windward. The man in the bows called out again. 'We are coming across, lord.'

Eofer raised his hand in acknowledgement as the stern of the longship finally emerged and begun its swing to steerbord. The steersman was visible now, and Eofer and Sæward watched as he worked the big paddle blade and brought the great ship onto its new heading. They exchanged a look as the snaca overhauled them, and the eorle chuckled as his steersman mumbled a few grudging words of praise for the work of his opposite number. With a nod to Bassa and Beornwulf, the lads squared the spar, shook out the sail and sheeted it home. The *Fælcen* leapt forward again, and they laughed for the joy of it as the fanged head bobbed up on the bæcbord beam.

Sæward spoke as the crews came abreast of each other, and ribald shouts flew between them. 'She's a fine ship. The *Fælcen* is no slouch, but I think that they have the legs of us.'

The steering platforms came abreast and the *scipthegn* gripped the wale and hailed them.

'My name is Eadward, welcome to Harrow. Are you heading in?'

'Not until we reach Wodensburh, Eadward. How far north does this fog stretch?'

The ship-thegn glanced up and pulled a face. Square jawed and russet haired, Eadward's weatherworn features told the tale of a lifetime at sea. Clad in a red leather battle-shirt and tawny cloak, the man looked every inch the tough guardian that the English coast needed during these troubled times.

'It's patchy, Eofer,' he said. 'This wind is getting up and

will drive it away soon, but the passage here winds about like a drunken sailor. My steersman knows these waters better than any man alive. If you have no objection, we will shadow you until you leave the Belt.' He shot them a grin. 'The Jutes would love you to pitch up on their shore opposite. It's easily done in weather like this, even if you know these waters well.'

Eofer nodded, and the snake ship's steersman widened the distance between them with a flick of the paddle blade. Within the hour the mist had left them and the English ships were shaving the crests as the wind drove them on. Clear of the Belt, they dipped their flags in farewell as the bigger ship bore away, spear points glinting in the pale light of the sun as the crews cheered their countrymen and wished gods-speed.

Sæward spoke again as the *Fælcen* came about and pointed her bow to the east. 'I take it all that about Wodensburh being our destination was a load of guff.'

Eofer's mind came back as images of men tumbling from ships onto the strand, forming up and moving inland as lines of smoke stained the sky, faded. Two days' sail to the south, the first men had died. Chaos would reign in Heorot as Hrothgar summoned his jarls and struck out to face the invader. He tried to force a smile, but none would come, the fire of battle was already kindling in his blood. Wulf, his only brother, was awaiting the Dane's blade in that famous hall, but they were in for a surprise. The axe would fall on them.

A VEILED LIGHTENING over their distant homeland in the west was all that could be seen of the sun as the little *Fælcen* put the island of Hesselo behind her and headed south into the bight that carried its name. The first Danes had died there, put to sword and spear despite their brave stand against numbers, but they had something that the English raiders needed, and their lives were the price. Thrush Hemming spat over the side as he shaped the feelings of the crew into words. 'Tangles my guts to see that at the mast top of the old girl.'

Eofer looked up at the white boar flag of Daneland as it whipped out to the east in the gusting wind and felt a tinge of shame, almost as if he had dishonoured an old friend. The scegth had been a gift from his father, the day he had danced the dance and become a wolf-warrior. She had carried him far and wide across the sail-road through wind and storm, always emerging unscathed when bigger ships, grander ships, had been reduced to driftwood. The men of his duguth clustered around their eorle as they reminisced on old times, sharing memories of raids into the heart of Frankland and Britannia. The shallow draught of the ship taking her to places where no English raider had a right to be and bringing them safely away, rich in plunder and reputation. His fingertips lovingly caressed the wale as they began their final voyage together, and the banter swirled around him.

The weather had turned as the wind had shifted and serried ranks of cloud, dolphin grey, pressed about the mast-head. Suddenly, a spear of light stabbed through the murk to paint the distant coast of their enemy as the little ship drove on, and a passage from the work of a scop came into his mind.

> Then a light shone from Logafell, and from
>   that radiance came bolts of lightning.
> Wearing helmets at Himinvangi came the
>   Wælcyrge.
> Their byrnies were drenched in blood, and
>   rays shone from their spears.

The fighting in Daneland had already begun. Tonight he would stab at its heart.

SÆWARD CHEWED his lip as his eyes flicked from left to right and back again. Pumping the big wooden handle of the steer bord, he almost whimpered in his anxiety. 'It's going to be tight.'

The thin white line had rapidly grown to fill their vision as the breakers dashed the shore with a noise like thunder. Pushed south and west by the unfamiliar currents, the steersman had had to use all of his skill to even wrestle a chance of life. They were the gods' plaything and Eofer watched as Spearhafoc, braced in the bows, sent a silvered object spinning into the darkness. The *Fælcen* shuddered as her keel scraped the bottom, but the next wave lifted her off and she slid over the rocky finger of land as she shot the point and entered the bay.

Sæward exchanged a look with his eorle as the blood-drained faces of the crew showed white in the gloom. 'Never in doubt.'

Eofer laughed and clapped his duguth on the shoulder as the shallow hulled scegth gave them their lives and put the headland behind her.

The last tack to the west, although almost fatal, had carried them clear of the fortress that crowned the promontory opposite. Lights flickered beyond a grove of masts, and Eofer's gaze picked out the figure of Spearhafoc as the youth settled back into her place by the mast step. The gods could not have brought them safely through the Danish defences any better if Wade himself had been steersman, and he called across to her. The girl pushed herself to her feet and skipped the thwarts to the steering platform.

'Yes, lord?'

'What did you sacrifice?'

Spearhavoc pulled a wry face. 'My seax, lord.'

'The one I gave you?'

She shrugged her shoulders. 'I bend my knee at no other gift-stool but your own, lord. Besides,' she offered with an impish smile, 'whether Wade took it from my dead body or as a willing sacrifice, he seemed set to own the blade anyway.'

Eofer snorted at the youth's black humour. Unbuckling the scabbard from his belt, he handed his own seax across to the wide-eyed girl. 'Here, strap this on. You may need it tonight.' She made to protest, but he held up a hand as the men of the duguth looked on in admiration. 'I will take one from a dead Dane. It is in my mind that the friendship of the gods is far more important than any blade, and you deserve it. Well done.'

As the youth proudly buckled on her new blade and returned to her friends, Eofer caught the eye of Thrush Hemming and saw his thoughts reflected there. The young woman promised much, he would make a point of watching her actions in Daneland and decide then. If she survived.

The fortress was well astern now, and no challenge had carried to them across the calmer waters of the bay. Points of light showed along each shoreline as the fjord opened out to its full extent, and Eofer marvelled at the width of the inland sea. He turned to Sæward, but the steersman anticipated his question as his eyes strained to pierce the darkness.

'About ten miles at its widest, lord,' he said. 'It will narrow down in about an hour to a big, low-lying island. Skirt that, and we are into the run in.'

Eofer nodded. 'I am going to run through things with the youth. When we pass this island, I will relieve your boys at the lookout and braces and let them know that they will be walking home.' He flashed a mischievous smile. 'That should please them.'

Eofer walked to the lip of the steering platform and called the men to him. Desperate now for an inkling of the task that lay ahead of them, the youth crowded forward as the men of the duguth, already privy to the details of the raid, hung back. Their eorle clenched his fist as he spat out the words he had ached to say openly since the day at the hunting lodge. 'My brother Wulf still lives!' As the youth exchanged looks of excitement, he continued. 'All of you have heard the story of how he disappeared from the strand near Godmey, fighting against overwhelming numbers of Danish raiders. As you know, he was forced to launch an attack with the men of his hearth troop before help could come up. His men died bravely on the beach, but Wulf was observed from the cliffs to board the ship and take the fight to the enemy there.' The corners of his mouth turned up into a smile, as he could finally reveal Starkad's information to them. All but Spearhafoc knew Wulf and the men of his troop well. Despite the deaths, they would be almost as keen to snatch his brother away and avenge their fallen friends. 'He is being kept at Hrothgar's hall until the time of the winter blod. The Danes mean to sacrifice him to the honour of the gods, but we are going to replace that offering with fire and steel.' He grinned as an animated chatter rolled through the group. At the margins, the men of the duguth beamed. 'King Ingeld of the Heathobeards launched an attack on the southern coast of Daneland two days' hence. That is enough time for Hrothgar to have summoned his jarls and rushed south to meet the threat. Our task is to rescue Wulf and cause as much chaos and mayhem in the Danish rear as we can.' Eofer's eyes shone bright as the youth craned their necks and awaited the details of his plan. 'Listen carefully, this is what we are going to do.'

. . .

FREE OF THE CHANNEL, the *Fælcen* drove south.

'Bassa, get that rag down and run up the White Dragon!'

Wide grins spread across the faces of the crew as they paused at their preparations, relishing the moment that the hel-black flag of the Danes was lowered and the scarlet war flag of the English shot to the mast top. Spear tips stabbed out as the dark banner was passed around, and soon the white boar at its centre was a shredded mess.

'Toss that thing overboard,' Eofer snarled as the war-fire coursed through his veins. 'You know your places, go to them now.' He turned to Spearhafoc and clapped her on the shoulder. 'Get yourself up into the prow, and remember,' he said. 'Keep your eyes away from any lights as well as you are able. We must get ashore with as little opposition as possible.' The youth rolled her eyes, and he snorted as she bent the stave to the bowstring and scampered away into the gloom. She was an experienced hunter, a night stalker, and the advice had been unnecessary, but it amused him to give it anyway.

The whole success of the raid could very well depend on the initial landing. If they could fire the ships and buildings on the waterfront and make their escape, they would be well on the way to fulfilling their aims. If the little scegth with its distinctive red banner was spotted on its approach by an alert guard and the alarm raised, they may have to fight their way ashore. The Danes, although reduced in number, would be on edge as they awaited news of the fighting in the south. The War-Beards' actions were a double-edged sword. They could die, there and then.

Eofer glanced up at the war flag and considered lowering it again, but the pride that filled him forbade it. Rippling forward, its white dragon glimmering in the steel-like sliver of the new moon, the great arms of the beast seemed to be reaching out to grasp its enemies. He could not deny the trusty old *Fælcen* such a glorious death after all they had been through together. Dismissing the thought as unworthy, he put the fear out of his mind. If the Danes came, they would kill them; on the waterfront or in the streets, it made little difference.

The course set, the wind blowing steadily abaft, Sæward was in a huddle on the steering platform with his lads. Eofer shot them all what he hoped was a wink of encouragement as they rushed to don mail and helm, their shipborne duties all but done as far as the little *Fælcen* was concerned.

The smattering of lights on each beam were rapidly drawing in on the ship, as the waterway funnelled them down to the landing place. They had been told to expect to find a dozen or so small craft moored there for the winter. As the *Fælcen* cleared the final headland and swept down on the anchorage, Eofer clenched his fist with joy as the brazier of a distant watchman revealed the dark shapes herded together at the quayside. He turned to Sæward and, gripping forearms, they exchanged a look that required no words before Eofer went for'ard. The men of his hearth troop held their spear and sword points forward as he passed, and their eorle drew Blood-Worm with a flourish, touching blades together in an act the English called *bindung*, the binding.

Ducking under the sail, Eofer was pleased to see that the dark twins, Crawa and his brother Hræfen, were already set in the bows, their helmeted heads dipped below the level of the wale lest any light reflect and alert those ashore that this small boat that had suddenly appeared from the gloom contained anything other than a Danish latecomer.

Spearhafoc alone wore a cap of sealskin in the fashion of a seaman as she stood, foot braced against the prow, her head moving methodically from side to side as the youth marked her targets. Any Danes watching their approach would expect to see crewmen working the ship, not least a man in the bow to guide her to her berth. Eofer's lips stretched into a smile of admiration as he crouched and watched the young woman curl and uncurl the fingers of her right hand around the bowstring, the only outward sign of the nerves he knew must be plucking at her insides at the weight of responsibility that weighed on her young shoulders. Her longbow was held low in the shadow of the prow, an arrow nocked and ready to loose, as she waited for the moment that was coming closer with every heartbeat.

Eofer stole a look behind. The men were crouched in the lee of their lord, almost panting with excitement like wolfhounds at the slips. He took a last look up at the sail, full and taut in the following wind, as it billowed like a summer cloud in the light from the shore. At its head the blood-red flag of Engeln whipped forward, now in plain sight, and Eofer's head snapped back for'ard as he realised that their identity must be revealed to the sleepy guards within the next few moments.

They were close enough now to make out details on the shore, and Eofer looked on with mounting excitement as the dark shape of a watchman rose from his place beside a brazier and moved towards them. Leaning forward, he was squinting into the gloom as he attempted to understand the actions of the strange ship that came on with no sign of the crew spilling the wind from its sail. Suddenly, they saw the man start as he recognised the pennant that flew proudly above the little scegth and, within a heartbeat, Spearhafoc's bow came up, and a shaft sped away into the darkness. The youth fitted another and swung to the left, the arrow whickering away as the bow swung back, and she nocked and loosed again.

The spell broken, Eofer stood and watched as the first arrow found its mark, the watchman shooting backwards as if tugged by the hand of a giant. The metallic chinking of mail and arms to his rear told him that the men of his troop were rising from the scuppers and forming on their duguth. Each man, his weorthman Thrush Hemming, Imma Gold, Osbeorn, Octa, knew their task, and the men gathered the youth assigned to them like hens with their brood as they waited for the *Fælcen* to strike home.

The fat bellied hulls of the cargo ships were now a line across their bows, rotten teeth jutting up from the cold mouth of the sound. Sæward peered around the sheet, and aimed her elegant prow between two of the fattest.

Another arrow found its mark, and a dark shape tumbled into the waters from the stern of a nearby hull. Eofer placed a hand on the shoulder of the girl, and she nodded that she understood without a backwards glance. The Danish hulls were now a rampart before them. They braced as the scegth passed into the shadows and shouldered them aside, the prow rising in challenge to her enemies ashore as she wedged her narrow body tightly between her victims. With a leap, they were over the sides, pouring forward along the decks of the neighbouring ships and searching for their first opponents. The high-pitched twang of a bowstring sounded at his elbow, and another shaft sped away. Eofer watched the flight of the arrow as, a silvered dart in the glow of the dead watchman's fire, it flew to send another Dane tumbling down into the arms of Hel. Reaching the bows, the eorle vaulted the gap and braced, the first to place his feet on the soil of Daneland. Swinging his shield forward, he hunched behind the board as he hurried across the open quay towards the road that led inland. A glance down, and he smiled despite the tension of the moment as he saw the body of Spearhafoc's first victim sprawled on its back, the gory shaft of the arrow that had taken his life placed perfectly between his unseeing eyes.

A flash of light appeared to his left as a door was thrown open. But a glance told him that Octa and Oswin were there, and the shadowy outline of the figure it contained crumpled as the spear thrust found its mark and the English pushed their way inside the building.

Thrush Hemming came up. 'How far, lord?'

Eofer scanned the shadows for any sign of a threat as he replied. 'Not far, the stud farm should be on the outskirts.' He indicated a twin storied building at the head of the track. 'Just past that barn.'

They fanned out into a broad front as they jogged up the road to their goal. Eofer with Crawa and Hræfen proudly flanking their lord, Thrush Hemming to the right with Rand and Finn, Imma Gold to the left with his youth, Cæd and Æsc as Spearhafoc brought up the rear, her bow taut and ready to loose as she covered their backs.

The sound of crashing doors to the rear was replaced by that of splintering wood, as any opposition from the houses lining the waterfront waned. Sæward and his boys hacked at the ships, preparing them for the flames to follow. Eofer passed from light back into darkness as he led the charge out of town, and the flames from the watchman's brazier were left behind. The clouds were ragged now as they cleared away to the east, and they caught their breath as an owl, huge and white in the light of the new moon, swept across their path with a lazy beat of its great wings. The bird foretold a death, and Eofer seized the moment to round on his men with a grin. 'The gods are watching us, lads. Let's give them something to remember us by.' Without waiting for a reply, Eofer rounded the barn but slowed to a halt, horror-stricken at the sight that met his eyes.

14

Eofer glowered from beneath his battle helm. Cunningly worked, the four silvered plates depicted his moment of victory in war over the king of Swedes, beating down the old battle-boar Ongentheow, as his brother Wulf lay prone and helpless at their feet; Woden riding down a foeman as the eagle and raven circled overhead. On the left-hand side spearmen marched, shields held high to war and, above the left eye, danced the wolf warriors, marking the Engle as a member of the warrior elite. Blood-Worm, the finest of blades, killer of kings, hung suspended from a magnificent baldric of fine red leather and gold, his spear, the finest in the company, pierced the sky. He looked, he was, an English eorle in his war glory. He turned to Thrush Hemming, his right-hand man in the clash of shields, the dance of spears, and spoke. 'I feel an utter cock.'

He glanced across to his weorthman as he shot into the air for what seemed like the thousandth time, and his black mood cleared like autumn smoke. They had travelled more than a mile now, and his duguth had clearly not yet mastered the rise and fall of the ass's movements. His arse was still hitting the rump of the beast each time it rose with a crash like Thunor's hammer. To add to the hilarity, Hemming's helm had worked loose under the strain and now bobbled about his head like an egg in boiling water, falling to cover first one eye and then the other as the animal trotted on. Hemming attempted to answer his lord, but the pounding on his rump defeated him: 'I—I—I—I…'

Eofer managed to gasp out a retort as he finally succumbed to the ridiculousness of the situation. 'We haven't got time for singing, you arse. We are in the shit!' Both men laughed liked idiots, and the tension of the night evaporated as the laughter trailed away.

Eofer reined in and slid from the threadbare blanket that served as a saddle, massaging his rump and flexing his battered legs. He realised that Hemming's ass was still trotting on and called after him. 'Thrush, I have stopped.' He watched as his duguth's arm moved up to push his helm away from his eyes; the man made a hasty grab for the reins as, already unbalanced, he crashed down into the animal's back again. 'Stopped what?'

'I have stopped. I am standing on the roadway. I am not moving.'

Hemming leapt from the animal and gave it a vicious kick. 'Thank the gods!'

He walked back towards his lord as he loosened his helm and drew it from his head. Running a hand through his hair, his teeth flashed in the moonlight. 'We must be almost there, the woman said it was only a mile. Women have a habit of telling the truth when men with bloodstained spears are bouncing their bairns upon their knee.'

A shallow fold in the ground lay ahead, and the men exchanged a glance. Both men knew that if the stud did not lay, as promised, on the other side of the rise, they would have to retrace their steps and rejoin the men of the troop. The moon was transiting the sky and, although the dawn was still some way off, they were rapidly running out of time. The sky to the west was a crimson blush as the ships and buildings there met their fiery end, and Eofer felt a pang of remorse as his imagination threw up a picture of the harsh fate of the *Fælcen,* the scegth little more than a hulk, burned to the waterline.

Hobbling the animals, the pair trotted up the grassy slope. Reaching the top, they exchanged a look that combined triumph and relief in equal measure as the moonlight revealed their goal. Before them lay King Hrothgar's stud, the unmistakable paraphernalia of a horse farm, tack, and bridles resting on the fence tops of the half dozen neatly demarcated fields. Nestling at the northern end of the pasture a small hall had been built to accommodate the king and his men when they visited, with a larger, more workaday building set to one side to house the men who worked the farm daily. Barns, stables and an exercise paddock completed the scene.

'There are no horses,' Hemming said with a hint of despair.

Eofer nodded towards the stables. 'No, but the dung looks fresh. Come on, let's get down there.'

Angling across the back slope, the pair regained the track and jogged across. The fold petered out as it approached the entrance to the estate, and the Englishmen lowered their spears and searched the shadows as they passed through a gate and into the compound. Unable to bring their shields with them on the backs of the bouncing asses, each man swept their gar before them as they searched out their first victim. Heavier than the *daroth*, the slim shafted javelin used for hurling at the enemy, the gar was perfect for use in constricted places, shield walls and buildings, where there was little space to swing a sword or axe.

As the pair drew up before the hall, a Danish voice caused them to spin around anxiously as it hailed them from the stable entrance. 'Are you looking for a horse, lord?'

Eofer had expected to find someone awake, even during the hours of darkness. The king's horses were valuable objects, they would be under guard constantly. 'A shipload of Heathobeards have fired the docks. Our horses were killed under us, so we made our way here. We must ride to Hroar's Kilde—an attack could be imminent at the docks there also.'

A look of unease flashed across the face of the Dane before he managed to suppress it, and Eofer felt Hemming tense at his side.

'I will go and wake a few of the lads, lord,' the Dane said. 'They will have you mounted and on your way in no time.'

Eofer moved to block his path as he smiled disarmingly. 'There's no need, we can saddle a horse. Time is important, an attack could come at any time.'

The guard lowered his spear and shuffled back into the shadows, drawing a breath as he prepared to shout for help. Eofer and Hemming started to make a desperate lunge to silence the Dane. But they froze in surprise as a look of shock and horror crossed the man's face, and the bloody point of a spear emerged from his throat. His spear clattered to the ground as, tottering and wheezing, the Dane's hands went to his neck as the air that would have carried his cry for salvation bubbled from the wound in a darkening froth. The spear point slid from sight as a hand clasped itself around the Dane's mouth, and he was tugged bodily back into the shadows. As Eofer and Hemming exchanged a look of surprise, the spear man finally emerged into the light.

'Your accent is shocking, lord, but you might have got

away with it.' He turned and spat at the body of the Dane. 'This one's not too bright, that's why he is guarding horses while the better warriors are in the south.' He tapped at Eofer's shoulder. 'He noticed this, though—you may as well have spoken in English. Danes don't wear square headed brooches, theirs are always round.'

Eofer finally found his tongue. 'You are English?'

The man nodded. 'Yes, lord. My name is Grimwulf.' A look of savage delight came upon him as he aimed a kick at the Dane's body. 'I was a thræl here until a few moments ago.'

'Are there any more guards here, Grimwulf?'

'One out the back. I will take care of him, he won't suspect anything until it's too late.' Grimwulf indicated the halls with a flick of his head. 'There are only a dozen thræls left in the hall, lord. No English, mostly Saxons. Good with horses, the Saxons. The warriors left the day before yesterday.'

'Will these Saxons fight?'

He nodded eagerly. 'Ooh yes, lord.'

Eofer began to relax. The wheel of fortune was beginning to turn his way again after the shock at the first farm. To round a barn and come face-to-face with a field of turnips, when you had staked the life of yourself and every man with you on finding a stock of fine Hunters, had been a low point in his many years of raiding—around the rim of the German Sea, and beyond. 'Take care of the guard and then round up your friends, Grimwulf. We will make a start saddling up the horses.'

They walked forward into the stable as Grimwulf stooped to slide the dead Dane's dagger from its scabbard before melting into the darkness. Hemming let out a low whistle of appreciation. 'If this is where he keeps his horses, I can't wait to see Heorot.' The central passageway was lined by dozens of stalls, the sweet equine smell adding a pleasant air to the place. The tack room led off to one side of the big double doors, and Hemming threw a saddle across each shoulder as Eofer examined the mounts. Most were awake now, and they lowered their heads as the eorle passed by with a gentle stroke of their muzzles. He made a quick calculation: 'Thirty.'

Hemming came up and shifted the weight of the saddles he carried on each shoulder. 'We'll need them all, lord, if we have just doubled the size of our war-band. Wait until Grimwulf returns, and he can show us the king's two horses.' He shot his eorle a smile. 'Hrothgar's bound to have a remount, and we did do all the hard work.'

THEY WERE AWAY AS SOON as the horses were ready. The men who had come from the hall, despite the bemusement at the sudden change in their fortunes that had stolen upon them in the night, looked a tough bunch. Eofer was elated as they thundered back through the gateway and took the road towards the smear of red that marked the death of the dockyard. Pausing only to let a gleeful Hemming stop to give his previous mount a parting kick, they were back with the men of Eofer's troop in no time. The unexpected arrival of a dozen mounted men caused a moment of panic among them, but Eofer looked on with pride as Imma Gold formed a bordhedge with a clatter of shields and roared out a challenge. Imma beamed as the brawl of riders cantered into the light, and he recognised the men at their head. He strode proud of the line. 'Welcome back, lord.' He ran a questioning gaze across the new additions to their ranks and looked back to Eofer.

'More spears for our wall,' he explained as he ran a calming hand along the neck of his mount. 'Saxons mostly, but Saxons with a score to settle. Dangerous men if you are Dane.' He called out to Grimwulf and the man urged his mount forward with a practised squeeze of his thighs. 'Yes, lord?'

'Grimwulf, This is Imma Gold, my duguth. How disciplined are your Saxon friends?'

'Many of them have fought in the south, in Frankland and Britannia. They were all free men, so they are experienced spearmen. But they are all first-rate horsemen too, lord.' He pulled a lupine smile. 'You can count on them—they are good lads.'

'And you?'

'I grew up on a horse farm among the Mercians, but got bored and ran away to sea when I was a youth.' He screwed up his face in embarrassment as he finished his tale. 'A big storm, and we were wrecked on the shore here. So, I ended up back with the horses after all. Except now, I get to sleep on the floor and eat leftovers.' He gave an ironic chuckle. 'You can't cheat your wyrd, lord. I was meant to look after horses, and that's that.'

Eofer nodded, satisfied, and walked his mount back to the Saxons, stifling a smile at the look of wonder that still painted their features. They had gone to sleep a few short hours ago as thræls, the lowest of the low. Now they were saddled on the Danish king's horses and free men once again.

'I can use your spears. Are you with me?'

The men roared their acceptance as one, and Eofer pointed out Imma as he mounted his stallion.

'That man is Imma Gold. He will lead you tonight against our common enemy. Mark him now, you will follow his every instruction.'

Eofer turned back to Grimwulf. 'Do you know the fastest road to Hleidre?'

Grimwulf flashed a smile. 'Fastest or quietest, lord?'

Eofer pursed his lips and looked at the moon. It was a good way across the star scattered vault, but the sky horse, Frost Mane, still had a way to go before it had finished its work for the night and hauled it beyond the Earth's rim. A quick glance to the east confirmed that no light yet fell from the shining one's mane to colour the horizon there. Imma Gold had barked out his instructions and he led the Saxons away with a noise like thunder. The flash of a grin, and a cry for gods-luck swallowed by the din.

Eofer regarded his troop, now set in their saddles awaiting his word, and his heart swelled with pride. He touched the hilt of Blood-Worm and swore that he could sense the eagerness in the blade as it awaited the night's work to come. His eyes narrowed as he caught the mood. 'Let's go the quick way.'

15

The pair crabbed up the grassy slope made slick with frost. The air had stilled as they rode east, almost as if the gods were holding their breath at the audacity of the tiny band of warriors below them. Eofer moved into a crouch and dipped his head as they came up to the crest of the barrow.

'Wonder of the North?' Hemming rolled his tongue and sent a gobbet of phlegm spinning into the darkness. 'It's not even as big as Eorthdraca.'

Eofer was oblivious to his man's judgement, running the pads of his thumb and forefinger up and down the bridge of his nose as he thought. The moon was low in the west now as the hours of darkness slipped away, and the eorle cast an anxious look to the north for a sign that the dragon had awoken there.

Suddenly, it came, and he clasped his weorthman's sleeve. 'Look! Imma and his boys have set to work.' He flashed a grin as the line of red blossomed and waited for the cry of alarm to carry from the compound opposite. Eofer dug Hemming in the ribs and gave a soft chuckle of delight. 'There he goes.'

As they watched, a figure detached itself from the shadows of the great hall on the mound and hurried down to the buildings below. Others were gathering at the northern corner of Heorot, spear points glistening in the soft light of the moon as they pointed and gesticulated. Within moments, a heavy-set figure bounded up the steps two at a time as he raced to see the conflagration that had appeared above the fleet anchorage at Hroar's Kilde.

Hemming turned his head to the side. 'What if they don't go?'

Eofer cocked a brow. 'Then I hope that you are feeling fighting-fit because all we would have achieved, is alert them to our presence.' He looked back as the Danish lord hurried back down the steps, a comet-tail of warriors streaking in his wake, and smiled. 'They're going. What would he tell Hrothgar when he returned from seeing off the War-Beards, only to find that his ships had been reduced to charcoal, and they had stood by and watched? Besides,' he sniffed, 'the men here will already be disappointed that they were left when the army marched south. This will be like a gift sent from Woden himself, they won't even stop to think before their arses hit the saddle.'

As if to confirm the Englishman's thinking, the heavy timber doors to the stockade swung inward to reveal a scene of chaos as Danish warriors tumbled from halls and dishevelled thræls led horses forward from the stables. Eofer took a final look and clapped Hemming on the shoulder. 'Thrush, wait until the first of them begin to leave and then hurry down.' The duguth nodded, his eyes flicking from side to side as he watched the mayhem within the palisade begin to take on a sense of order, and he recognised that the first riders would soon appear.

Eofer held his scabbard to one side as he gambolled down

the back slope of the ancient burial mound and replaced his helm.

'The dragon's awake and the Danes are about to take the bait,' he beamed as he fastened his chinstrap. A quick glance at the men of his duguth confirmed that they all now sported a Danish brooch at their shoulder, and he adjusted his own and gave it a huff and a shine with the sleeve of his tunic. Its original owner had died before he was even aware that they were enemy raiders, his body now lying in a bloody heap alongside those of his men on the roadway to the west. He rolled his shoulders and looked at the youth, their breath feathering in the chill air. 'You all know what to do. When we are inside, reform on your duguth. Move quickly, and we will all live to see the sunrise.'

As Eofer swung himself back into the saddle, Thrush Hemming came bounding down the slope and threw himself onto his mount. 'The big bastard's not waiting, he is already out and on the road north,' he said. 'All the others are strung out along the track, trying to catch up as each horse is saddled and brought forward.'

Eofer threw a last look around the burial ground, and edged his mount forward. Every barrow glistened beneath a frosty cap as the moonlight clipped the crests. He glanced upward as an image of the ghosts of these kings of yore looking down from the benches in Valhall flashed into his mind, and shot them a cheeky wink. Breaking cover, Eofer sawed at the reins and, kicking in, guided his mount towards the gate. It was half a mile from the burial ground of the ancient kings to the royal compound of the present-day lord of the Danes, and Eofer put the spur to his horse as he led the men of his troop onward.

Away to the north, the last of the Danish warriors had gained the road, the distinctive blue cloaks of the Danish hall guard billowing in their wake as they galloped away. Ahead, the gates to the compound were drawing into view as unseen hands pushed them to, and Eofer sat tall and cried above the sound of the hooves; 'Hold the gate!'

The white oval of a face appeared around the door's edge, and Eofer waved and galloped on. The Dane slipped through the gap and watched as they approached. Eofer reined in and brought his stallion to a halt a few paces shy of the guard as the man raised an arm and pointed off to the north. Eofer cut him short. 'Open the gate, man!' The Dane persisted. 'Hroar's Kilde is under attack, lord. My orders are to keep the gates closed until the men of the hall guard return.' Eofer drew Blood-Worm with a swish and glared down at the man. 'I am on the king's business. Open the gate or lose your head.' As the Dane dithered, Eofer seized his chance and urged his mount forward, knocking the guard aside. Barging the big gates open, he led the men of his hearth troop beneath the gatehouse and into the royal compound of their king's greatest enemy.

His men burst through behind him and the Dane from the roadway rushed across as the few men left in the burh stopped and stared at the newcomers. 'I will have your saddles transferred to fresh mounts, lord. You'll be wanting to follow Lord Ubba.'

Eofer shook his head as his men began to dismount and fan out across the clearing. 'No, I will take them as remounts when I leave.' As the confused Dane looked about him and the English began to draw their weapons and move towards the buildings, the eorle gazed down at the man and sighed. 'What is your name?'

The Dane flinched with shock as the first of his men was cut down by Osbeorn and Porta, but his reply was already half-formed, and it came out anyway. 'Haldor…lord…'

'Haldor, I was going to kill you, but I am of a mind that I would do more useful service to my king by letting you live.'

The Dane still looked nonplussed. '*Your* king?'

Eofer gasped in frustration. The dirty grey smear that marked the onset of the pre-dawn was tainting the eastern horizon. Soon the golden horse would return, they needed to be away. 'King Eomær, you fool. Now, tell me where the English prisoner Wulf is being held.'

Haldor screwed up his face, his mind working to unravel the weft and weave of the threads that the gods had brought together in his compound that night. But his eyes flicked up to the hall on its mount above, and the thegn knew that he had his answer. Eofer jerked his head, and Spearhafoc and the dark twins hurried to their eorle's side as he spurred his mount towards the steps.

As they swept by, Haldor finally began to understand the identity of the men in his midst, but the snarl that twisted his features lasted less than a heartbeat as Octa's blade emerged from it to send the top half of his skull spinning through the air in a spray of gore. Oswin word-poor kicked the bloody bowl casually aside as he trotted after the duguth, and Octa threw a comment over his shoulder as he began to take the stairs. 'Start working on a stanza for that, Oswin. I will want to hear it later.'

Eofer gripped the reins tightly, urging his mount on as they reached the foot of the staircase. The horse baulked as it came face-to-face with the steep incline. But a cry and a spur from its rider drove it forward, and its Hunter's blood began to quicken as the stallion clattered up the wood lined shelves like the pure-blood he was. Up ahead, shadowy figures raced in from the sides and began to gather at the head of the steps, shields clacking as a wall began to form there. Eofer thought of his shield, safely strapped to the horse's flank, and wondered for a moment whether he had time to slip it on. It had been an important part of the initial deception at the gatehouse that their shields remain covered and stowed, and it had done its job, they were in. He discounted the idea as he looked up and saw that they were almost upon the enemy. He would have to rely on Imma Gold's gods-luck and his own war-fury to see him through.

The Danish shields had come together now, but the glint of steel was absent, and Eofer yelled his mount on, closing the gap between the foes as quickly as he could. The horse reached a wide platform and slithered as he lost his footing. Eofer's heart leapt as he thought that he was going down. But the stallion gathered itself, hauling its great bulk up the final rise to the Danish shield wall above. Eofer had the momentary glimpse of gigantic sun-bleached antlers, the spreading wings of a mighty bird of prey capping the gable of Heorot, as the horse reared before the line of snarling faces and turned side on.

Seizing their chance to kill the enemy leader, the Danish wall broke apart, and Eofer laughed at their stupidity as they moved to surround him. His men would be rushing to support their lord. Spearhafoc and the twins must be almost up with him already, and he had seen Octa and Oswin not far behind them. The Danes had thrown away the best chance that they had by breaking their wall, attacking him instead of retreating to the safety of the great entryway to the hall at their rear. He knew them to be inexperienced, and wretchedly led. Heartened at the realisation, Eofer turned away the first spear strike with the flat of his sword and swept the blade in a great arc as he yelled his battle cry. Another lanced in towards his chest and the eorle rolled it away and down as he brought the blade of Blood-Worm back across to bite deeply into the Dane's shoulder.

Eofer squirmed in his saddle, dodging the wicked points as the steel tipped ash darted this way and that and his world shrunk down to little more than the reach of his sword. A face, crazy-eyed and spittle-flecked, hardened into focus ahead of him and Blood-Worm flicked out to pierce the owner's throat. The point was already free as the man began to fall, and Eofer backhanded another as the pommel punched out to pulverise a nose. The crush of Danes was working against them, as they jostled for the space to bring their unwieldy shafts to bear upon this madman in their midst. Eofer hacked down into a shoulder, shouting with joy as leather and steel was driven deep into muscle and bone.

Bred for the chase, the press of men told as the nerves of the horse finally snapped, and it careered off to one side, cutting a swathe through Eofer's attackers there. The eorle leapt from the saddle as the horse, nostrils flaring, eyes wildly staring balls of fear, cantered along the slope of the mound, its flank and mane blushed by the first glimpses of the dawn.

The Danes were still in disarray, and Eofer grasped the opportunity to snatch a look down the hillside. Angry red petals were beginning to blossom among the smaller halls there as Sæward, Osbeorn and their youth mopped up any remaining opposition and touched flame to thatch. Thrush Hemming was surging up the staircase, Rand and Finn hurrying in his wake. Closer to hand, sunlight lanced across, flashing from raised blades as Octa prepared to lead Oswin and his youth into the disorganised knot of Danes. The fight was over, and the Danes broke and ran, fleeing for their lives down the slope as fast as the greasy grass allowed.

Eofer dragged down great gulps of air as the danger receded, and he realised that a sharp pain nagged at his side. Reaching across, he winced and stared at the blood smeared palm in disbelief. Carefully kneading the slash with his fingertips, he was relieved to find that it was no more than a surface wound, and he wondered that he had not felt the spear stab home when it had occurred. A quick check of the remainder of his body reassured him that his snaking movement during the fight had saved him from serious injury once again, and he sent a thought of thanks to far away Imma for his gods-luck.

Octa and the youth had come up, and a brief look told Eofer that Hemming was now across the wooden platform and beginning to take the final staircase. He cupped his hand and called down to his weorthman. 'Thrush!' The big man paused and looked up, raising his chin in acknowledgement. Pointing with the bloodied tip of his sword, Eofer called again. 'Get the doors!'

Octa cast a look of concern at the blood staining his lord's side and back up in question, and Eofer moved to reassure his duguth that all was well. Patting his flank with the palm of his hand, he smiled encouragement. 'Sore, but I will live. A spear blade must have grazed my side during the fight, I didn't even notice it at the time.'

He looked beyond them to the great doorway that led into the hall of the Danish king, the very heart of the kingdom. Thrush Hemming had overturned an iron weapons stand that stood beside the end wall, the magnificent silvered stag heads that crowned the piece now laying in the dirt. Heavy oak benches lined the wall there, a place for visitors to rest while they awaited admittance to the king, and Eofer watched as Hemming, Rand and Finn struggled to drag the nearest one to the doorway. Octa noticed also, and Eofer nodded as his duguth threw him a questioning look before hurrying across with the youth to help, as Eofer took a moment to drink in his surroundings.

The sun lay on the horizon now in a smear of orange

shading into yellow, the sky above a deep blue, as hard as an anvil. Below him smoke and flame curled up from the smaller halls and huts as Sæward and Osbeorn, their works of destruction complete, gathered in their youth and moved across to guard the gateway. In the settlement that crowded about the road leading to Hroar's Kilde several groups had congregated, but even at this distance it was obvious by their demeanour that they were lowly ceorls, dragged from their beds by the mayhem that had appeared so suddenly on their doorsteps. The barrow field where they had waited for the moment to attack lay to the south, looking for all the world like a basket of eggs, as the sunlight clipped the brows of the mounds and cast the valleys between into the darkest shadow. Away to the north billowed a cloud, oily grey, its eastern flank painted pink in the dawn light. Imma Gold and his Saxons had done better than he could ever have hoped when he saw them on their way.

The Danes had disappeared, and Eofer relaxed his guard slightly as he wondered at the detail revealed on the great hall by the returning light. Serpents, dragons and otherworldly monsters writhed about the eves and walls while, moving his eyes towards the doorway itself, he noticed for the first time that they were flanked by twin figures of great height. Nearest to him, beneath a waxy sheen of the reddest gold, the recumbent figure of Sceaf nestled among great stands of barley. The foundling had washed ashore to found many of the northern folk, the English included, and he hoped that the old king would understand his action to come. On the far side of the doorway glowered the figure of a great warrior, his oversized shield held resolutely before him. It was obviously a representation of the founder of the Danish clan of the Scyldings, Scyld himself. Eofer was under no illusion that Scyld would be so understanding about what was to follow. Capping it all, beyond the great golden antlers, the roof of Heorot shone a dazzling bronze as the returning sun lit the tiles there with its glow. Hemming was wrong, he reflected. Heorot really was a wonder of the North.

A horse left the shadow of the northern palisade and galloped away towards the fires of distant Hroar's Kilde sending the knots of town folk scattering away from its path, and his mind snapped back. One of the Danes had obviously been sent to recall the guard, and he cursed. They must have missed a gateway in the night. A saying of the Allfather came to him, and he recognised the truth of the warning, as he sent two of the youth to make a fast circuit of the hall:

All the entrances, before you walk forward, you should look at, you should spy out;

For you can't know for certain where enemies are sitting ahead in the hall.

Eofer hurried across as the men of his troop manhandled the great oak bench into position before the doors. Thrush Hemming looked over as he came up; 'Cunning bastards, the Danes.' He spat on his palms as he prepared to heft the bench and begin the assault on the great doors. 'They have made the benches so long that there is no room to take a run at the doors without having to go down the steps.' He indicated the massive iron hinges set into the oak door posts with a jerk of his head. 'You can still see where the monster smashed them open, though, look.' Great wedges of newer oak—butter-yellow, streaked a muddy brown by the tannin that leached from the wood—had been scarfed in to the weathered posts to replace those torn asunder by the inhuman strength of the Grendel troll several years before. Hemming set-to, gripping the bench as Octa and the remaining youth braced to lift the great weight. His broad shoulders rose and fell as he dragged down great breaths, preparing for the lift and swing. Eofer ran his eyes across the great doors and took a pace forwards. Octa and the youth, still poised at their places, watched him go.

'Right, you lot,' Hemming snorted like a bull. 'After three!'

Eofer placed the tip of Blood-Worm onto the leaf of the door and gave a push. The door swung silently inward on its greased hinges, and all but Hemming slowly straightened, their mouths agape. Oblivious, the duguth reached three and hauled his end into the air, the muscles on his neck and shoulders standing proud like a tangle of knotted ropes at his single-handed effort. He managed to spit out an exhortation through gritted teeth as his face came up, *'come on—come on...'* before he too opened his eyes and a look of disbelief and embarrassment swept his features.

Eofer quickly checked the shadows and, reassured that no Danes lurked immediately within, his mouth widened into a grin. Hemming recovered quickly as he let the bench drop with a boom that echoed through the empty hall. The duguth's expression became deadpan, sweeping the happily smiling faces of his companions with a look as the tension of the morning found an outlet. 'What?' he said, his tone innocence itself. 'I knew.'

Eofer gave his weorthman's shoulder an affectionate squeeze and passed beneath the lintel and into the hall itself. His men hurried in his wake and fanned out protectively as their shields came together with a clatter of lime wood. Spearhafoc, her bow strung, an arrow nocked and ready to loose, scurried across to the flank and quartered the gloom with deliberate movements of her head. Eofer stood at the point that the English called *ord*, the very tip of the boar snout, as he searched out the benches for any signs of opposition. Ahead of him, twin lines of pillars bestrode the long central hearth, marching away to the king's dais at the head of the room and the golden gift-stool of the Danes that crowned it. To its rear a lighter patch on the wall, square shaped and pale, showed where the war flag of King Hrothgar had rested before it had been taken down to accompany its owner south. A small knot of thræls knelt in the brightest part of the hall, their hands splayed out on the floor before them to show that they were unarmed and offered no threat to the invaders.

Eofer called out, his voice booming in the great space. 'Wulf? Wulf Wonreding?'

One of the slaves slowly raised an arm and pointed towards a curtained off area tucked away in the corner of Heorot, and a grin of anticipation illuminated Eofer's face as he rushed across and threw back the covering. 'Wulf, you are free!'

His brother looked up and smirked as he gripped the young woman by the hips and thrust again, the curving whiteness of her cheeks rippling as their bodies came together with a wet slap. Eofer's mouth opened in surprise as Wulf threw him a wink. 'Help yourself to Hrothgar's ale. I will be with you soon, I am nearly finished.'

16

The boy shifted to one side, peering past the bough as he looked down from the treetop. 'Yes, lord, I can see them. About a mile away, coming up fast.'

Eofer squinted up against the harsh winter light. 'You are convinced that it is Imma and his Saxon friends?'

Bassa made a face, and a twinkle of amusement came into his eyes as a peal of laughter rolled around the group.

The eorle's mouth broadened into a smile. 'I know. You are not a wizard, but you do have keen eyesight.'

The boy grinned as Thrush Hemming explained to his lord's mystified brother about their previous exchange at the masthead following the storm in the German Sea. All eyes now strained to see through the pockets of mist that clung to the hollows and groves, as the sound of hooves on cold earth began to carry to them. The sun had cleared the eastern horizon now and, even in the frigid air of the northern winter, its warmth was beginning to burn off the milky veil that had covered the land in the night. Bassa shinned down the trunk and swung himself back into the saddle.

Wulf urged his mount forward and came abreast of his

brother and Thrush Hemming as they stared to the west. 'It's a burning land. We had better not let them catch us.' Eofer was about to reply that he would never give the Danes the chance of taking him alive when he caught his tongue. Wulf had been taken of course, it was the reason that they had made this dangerous journey. His brother had not told the tale of his capture, that would come soon, hopefully this day.

Eofer inhaled deeply and fancied that he could catch a whiff of the smoke that clouded the western skies. Ahead of them, the pall of smoke that drifted slowly northwards from the anchorage at Hroar's Kilde was lessening now as the Danes fought the fires with the water to hand. He smiled as an image of lines of men and women snaking up from the waters of the fjord came to him, icy water spilling from hastily swung pails as the grim faced inhabitants began to wilt after their nightlong effort.

Further west, a grey smudge on the horizon marked the death of Hrothgar's stud and the little port where they had stormed ashore at the beginning of the night. The *Fælcen* would be little more than another skeleton of charred timber now at the base of the column, but he smiled again with pride as he recalled the final moments he had spent on the little scegth. She had borne down on their fiend like her namesake, her battle flag snaking forward proudly in the following wind, unstoppable. It had been a fitting end, the death of a hero, an eorle's ship, and he felt a warm sense of pride that he had saved her from the end that awaited so many vessels; broken up to feed the flames, another anonymous wreck on the strand. Past glories forgotten as the men who had sailed her slowly lost their struggle with the passage of time.

Eofer turned his head to the south-west as the sound of hooves grew louder and the men of his troop fingered their sword hilts. The thegn saw their preparedness and was pleased. Bassa had the eyes of a hawk, but it still paid to be certain. The pyre that had been Heorot, the hall of the Hart, still burned brightly on its mound. A turgid column of thick black smoke billowed up from the noble structure, angry yellow tongues of flame dancing at its base, and he thought on their actions with more than a tinge of regret. Hundreds of men had laboured for thousands of hours to construct the great building. Trees had been chosen, cut, trimmed and chased. Wealhtheow, Hrothgar's cwen, must have bent her back with her ladies as, needle in hand, she had crafted the magnificent tapestries that had festooned the walls. The statue of Scyld was already in flames when they had taken a final look and turned their mounts to the gatehouse. He was a Scylding, he deserved his fate, but what of Sceaf? He resolved to offer sacrifice to the ancestor of the English kings as soon as he was able.

Wulf prodded his arm, he seemed to have been reading his mind. 'What do you think that our kinsman would have made of our work here this day?'

Eofer snorted as he watched the spreading cloud. 'He forged his reputation in the place, but it was just a shell. Woden himself told Beowulf that cattle and kinsman die, as he shall himself, but glory never dies for the man who can achieve it in his lifetime.' He shrugged. 'I think that you are right to talk of him as a shade. It's been months since he was last seen, a warrior of his fame and renown must be in Valhall.' He threw his brother a sidelong look. 'Now we have added to ours, for good or ill.'

Shadowy shapes appeared on the road, hardening in moments into the forms of their friends. Bassa's eyesight had triumphed again, and Eofer instinctively totted the heads as the men were reunited after the trials and worries of the night before and found them to be light.

Imma Gold walked his mount across, his eyes rimmed scarlet by smoky air. 'You were successful then, lord,' he said as he nodded a greeting to Wulf. 'I am glad.' Eofer's expression told of his concern, and Imma nodded grimly. 'Three of the Saxon lads, and Æsc.' The duguth held the brothers with an impassive stare. 'He may have been a youth, but he died like a man.'

Imma and his men hauled at their reins, turning the heads of their mounts back to the west. The group, reunited for the first time since they had left the landing place, gazed in awe at their night's work as Oswin's words floated over them:

> 'This is not the eastern dawn, no dragon flies
>   there, the antlered one towered, golden
>   backed.
> Its gables shone 'till the bane of the battle-boar
>   set pride to ash.
> Fed the Hart to the destroyer of wood…'

Eofer twisted in the saddle and looked at his youth in astonishment. 'Oswin, that was wordcræft.' The lad basked in the judgement of his eorle as the remainder of the troop gaped. Wulf nodded as Eofer urged his mount forward, 'That's a fine talent you have there, boy.' Slipping a gold ring from his finger, Eofer handed it to the delighted youth. 'That was well said, you do me honour.' Oswin beamed with pride, and Eofer exchanged a glance with Octa and saw the pride reflected there as he led the riders eastwards. He was proud of them both. Octa's careful tuition was turning the young man into a valuable member of the war-band, and he was pleased to see the new-found respect for their companion illuminate the faces of the youth.

The road before them passed away through a small settlement before leading, arrow straight, across a heathland and becoming lost among the tree covered slopes of a shallow ridge. Eofer put a spur to the horse and led them away. 'Let's go,' he cried, as the men exchanged grins and funnelled in his wake, 'before Oswin silk-tongue has to make a stanza describing Hrothgar's revenge.'

Clattering through the settlement, Eofer was only dimly aware of the frightened faces that peered out from the doorways before they were through and crossing the heathland beyond. Gulls called above as they neared the coast and, clearing the ridge, Eofer reined in and waited for the rest to come up and take in the welcome sight. A wide beach, its sandy crescent arcing away to the north and south, lay spread out before the battle-troop and Eofer smiled with pride and relief as the men looked upon their salve.

A magnificent snake ship rode at anchor just offshore, the great curve of her prow wallowing in the swell; the familiar beast that capped it seeming to nod in recognition with the rise and fall of the sea. Eofer led the riders down onto the strand as the anchor was hauled and oars were slipped into thole-pins. Eadward grinned and waved from the prow as the snaca drew close to the shore and, their charges safely in sight, the white dragon of Engeln unfurled at the mast-head.

The eorle dismounted and moved forward with a heavy heart to tease his horse's ears as his subdued men gathered their war gear and said their goodbyes to their mounts. The pale autumnal sunlight glinted from polished steel as the blade was withdrawn and slipped upwards. As the horse's eyes went wide, and its nostrils flared with surprise and shock, the blade was drawn across and a hot jet of blood pulsed out to darken the sand.

17

The riders walked their mounts along the track and turned off at the brook. As one of the men ran ahead to slip the rope and swing the gate open, they clicked their tongues and came into the field. 'Here she is, lord.' Osric sucked in his breath in admiration. 'She's a real beauty, she is. I have been saving her for a special occasion.'

Eofer pulled his horse to one side and ran his eyes over the tree as the shipwright pointed out the oak to his gang of artisans. 'There, that's the one. Get yourself across and get everything ready. We'll be along soon.' Osric rejoined Eofer and Sæward as the goad flicked out above the oxen, and the heavy wagon began to lurch across the field on its big, solid wheels. Iron rimmed, they would need their strength if they were to carry the roughly hewn timbers back to the yard for final trimming. Osric turned back with a smile. 'When the king sent word that he wanted a fine ship built, with no expense spared, I knew straight away where I would be heading.'

It was the week before Yule, and the ground beneath them

was as hard as any stone. A cold snap had descended on the land as soon as Eadward and his crew had carried them safely back to the English coast and on down the waters of the Sley to Sleyswic itself. King Eomær had feasted the brothers' triumphant return that evening, and the aged timbers of Eorthdraca had resounded to the sound of hundreds of warriors celebrating the burning of their fiend's hall of Heorot. It had gone some way to lessening the loss of their Heathobeard allies, who had been soundly defeated by King Hrothgar's army even as Hleidra and Hroar's Kilde burned.

Eadward's snake ship had cut through the disordered remnants of the War-Beard fleet as they had fled back to their southern coast in defeat but, to Eofer's surprise, the news of King Ingeld's death at the hands of the Danes had received little more than a shrug of indifference from the English king. Shorn now of allies, he had explained, he had no need to share his plans or aims with others. The English had always been at their best standing alone with their backs to the wall. King Offa had dealt their rivals, the Myrgings, such a blow at Monster Gate that they had never ventured near to the southern bank of the River Egedore ever again. Within a generation, their lands had been added to those of the English. He would smite the Danes in the spring as the people left for the new lands across the German Sea, before the army embarked and followed on.

Osric spoke again, cutting into his thoughts. 'It's all prepared for you, lord.'

Eofer dismounted and walked across. The ground rose gently as it approached the outliers of the Wolds, and the eorle saw to his astonishment that Osric's men had already cut back a barrel shaped area where the tree would fall.

'Lucky for you, lord,' Osric added as they approached the

base of the tree, 'this is the best time of the year to fell.' He scratched at several days' growth that stubbled his chin as he spoke. 'It's always best when the leaves are off the tree and the undergrowth has died back. The sap in the tree withdraws into the trunk as the cold weather begins to bite. Drier wood is always easier to cut than sappy.' Several of the artisans had dug out and hacked away smaller trees and saplings that had grown in the shadow of the oak, and one of them grinned and gave the thumbs up as the pair approached. 'They are working like dæmons today, lord,' the shipwright chuckled, 'there's not much daylight at this time of the year and there's Yule ale to sample back at the yard.' Osric took up an axe that had been placed against the trunk in readiness and tested the edge with a brush of his thumb. Satisfied that the blade was keen, he pointed to a small knot roughly waist high on the uphill side of the trunk. 'Cut the first notch, what we call a kerf, there. Remember what we discussed, lord,' he said. 'Keep the bottom cut perfectly horizontal and cut down to it when you are about a third of the way into the trunk.'

Eofer spat on his hands and gripped the haft, flashing Osric's men a grin as goodnatured laughter rolled around the group. He worked his shoulders, warming muscles against the chill, and cut the air with the axe. The axe head sank deeply into the stem, and he worked it loose and swung again, the first chips flying as the new ship was birthed. Under the watchful eye of Osric and his men the kerf was soon cut and Eofer stood, glistening with sweat, his body steaming like a bull in the coldness of the day. The sky was a deep indigo above them as he handed the axe across to Sæward who would be cutting the second kerf on the opposite side of the trunk. A clamour of rooks finally seemed to accept the inevitable, reluctantly giving up their chosen roost in the canopy of the great oak. In a thunderhead of beating wings, the dark birds rose cawing into the chill air, circling noisily overhead as the ship master swung and swung again.

Osric's men had made a pyre of the raked up undergrowth and wind fallen branches that had littered the floor, and Eofer went across as Sæward worked. One of the artisans handed him a cup of ale, and he sank it in one. 'Thirsty work!' he grinned as he held out the cup for a refill, the chorus of agreement from the experienced woodcutters cut off as Osric called across to Eofer's man. 'That's deep enough, Sæward, or you will be wearing your new ship on your head.' The men laughed as the ship master began to cut down to form the wedge, and Eofer tore at a hunk of bread and cheese as he watched. The simple fare and hard physical toil were invigorating, and the thegn found to his surprise that he was enjoying the work immensely.

'Do you want to bring her down or shall I, lord?'

Eofer nodded and mumbled through a mouthful. 'I will share the honour with Sæward.'

'Right you are. When he is finished there, both go back to the first kerf and cut upwards towards the base of the second. It's only a foot higher, so be ready to move back over here when I shout a warning. The tree will fall into the first notch and land up slope.' He rubbed his hands vigorously together as the cold began to bite. The sun was low on the southern horizon, its weak light casting long shadows across the field. 'We always fell up slope if the wind direction permits. You'd be surprised just how far a bucking tree can bounce once she gets going.' He held up a finger and listened, but no sound came from his companions. 'Not even a snigger!' he exclaimed with a look of surprise. 'They must be keen to be away, lord!' The dull sound of iron biting wood stopped suddenly, and Osric nodded. 'Here, he's ready.'

The pair walked across to the oak, and Osric watched as Eofer and his duguth took up position on either side of the lower notch. 'Remember,' he said as he backed away, 'when I say so, get yourself back across to me and the lads as quick as you can. Roots can flick up out of the ground without much warning as she goes down.' He clutched at his groin and grimaced. 'Be a shame to look on as your balls sail off over the Wolds without you!'

Eofer and Sæward exchanged a look and spat on their palms as the shipwright inclined his head and moved to a safer distance. 'After you, lord.'

Eofer heft the axe and swung, angling the head upwards as wood chips filled the air. Soon they were finding the rhythm, alternating strokes as the great bole of the tree groaned ominously. The sharp tang of tannin and sap hung in the air as they worked, and Eofer risked a glance across to the bellicose seabird he had brought for the blooding. They had discussed the name of the new ship for weeks. Eofer had all but decided that the name Fælcen had served them as well as any other, and that he was of a mind to retain it for the new ship. But a voice had piped up at the back, and a smile had slowly formed upon Eofer's lips as he thought on Osric's suggestion. They had all seen the bird harrying much larger gulls, inches above the waves, and coming away with their catch. It was the perfect name for an English scegth, and the answering smiles on the faces of the men of his troop had confirmed the choice. Now, the new *Skua* was in the process of being hatched.

Unexpected, the axehead stuck as the body of the trunk pinched tightly around it, and Osric's voice cut across the pasture. 'That will do you, there. Work your axe out and get yourselves back over here, sharpish.' Eofer and Sæward hurried across, glancing back as the great bulk of the oak began its death plunge. The tree moved slowly at first, but as its weight moved past the centreline, a great crack rent the air, and it crashed to the ground in a blast of dead wood and leaves.

As soon as the tree was still, Osric's men were swarming forward to begin their work. Eofer wiped the sweat from his brow as he took a cup of ale and sank it in one. To his surprise, he saw that a look of sadness had come to the face of the shipwright. Osric noticed Eofer's questioning look, and he gave a snort and smiled sheepishly. 'Sorry, lord,' he said. 'I always feel a pang of regret when a tree falls. When you work with wood day-in day-out, you get to appreciate what magnificent things trees are.' The men were already teeming over the great trunk, axes rising and falling as they trimmed the boughs of their smaller side branches. 'This one in particular,' he explained as they walked across. 'To a shipwright's eye it is almost a ship already. Because it stood alone, isolated from other trees, the lower branches had the room to push outwards as they grew before they started to grow upwards. See the curve that results?' he explained as he followed the graceful outline of the bough with his finger. 'Spot on for fashioning into the ribs of a ship. Those big ones, right at the bottom, they will be the prow and stern of the *Skua,* and we'll scarf them to a single run from the trunk itself to form the keel plate. With a tree like this one, lord,' he smiled in admiration, 'even the side strakes will be formed from one continuous piece of timber. In a heavy sea, she'll flex and twist like a sausage on a griddle,' he chuckled, 'but snap back into shape in the blink of an eye.' Osric looked at the pair, and they saw the pride shining in his eyes as he held their gaze. 'This will be the finest ship that I will ever build, lord, the culmination of a lifetime spent in the yards. She'll be ready to take her first dip within the month, you can count on it.'

FIRE & STEEL

. . .

THE SUN HAD LABOURED to its zenith as Grimwulf slipped out of his tunic and kicked his shoes under the bench. Twisting his upper body and rolling his neck and shoulders, he proceeded to flex and stretch his wiry frame.

'What's he doing?'

Eofer took another pull from his cup and shifted on the log. Wherever he sat, the knot seemed to follow him regardless. 'Ritual is important. It concentrates your thoughts on the task ahead, you should know that, Thrush.'

'Do you think he will do it?'

'He better had,' Eofer replied. 'I have wagered a gold ring with Coelwulf that he will. If he loses, he could find himself back shovelling horse muck all day.'

With Æsc's death on the Hleidra raid and a new ship to crew, Imma Gold had persuaded Eofer to offer the lad a place at the hearth. Despite Grimwulf's lack of experience fighting with a war-band, the duguth had told his eorle that he had acted with bravery and aggression during the fighting at the anchorage. Grimwulf had leapt at the chance and, as his Saxon friends had trudged away to home and freedom down The Oxen Way, he had accompanied his new brothers north. Now he was set to become a highlight of the Yule Day celebrations, and Eofer hoped for all their sakes that the boy knew what he was doing. He had never witnessed a man race a horse before, and he was as intrigued as anyone to see the result.

After the windblown chaos of the previous night, Yule Day had dawned gull grey, strips of clouds, ragged edged, clearing away to the north-east in a gusting wind. The good folk of Engeln had sat out the night as King Herla led his Wild Hunt through the skies, as he had every Yule Eve as far back as the tales of the scops could tell. Herla was one of the many names that Woden had taken as he passed through Middle-earth on his wanderings, and the violence of the ride foretold the year ahead. This year, the people had cowered in their huts and halls as the spectral horses and hounds had howled through the sky. The thegns and ealdormen who had been present at the king's great symbel in Eorthdraca in the presence of the god had smiled with pleasure. War was coming, and soon. They would repay the Danes tenfold for the humiliations heaped upon them before they left for the new land.

The people had risen before the dawn and travelled with their families to the meadow near to the sacred grove at Thunorsleah. It was the place where the people of the western Wolds gathered on the shortest and longest days of the year to feast and show honour to the gods. Strong Yule ale would be sunk, games played and old friendships and alliances reaffirmed. It was a day of fun and laughter as the people came together with their gods to welcome the return of the sun at the dawn of the new year.

The stallion that was to race Eofer's youth was already set in position, a helper struggling to hold the bit as the horse, excited by the hubbub that surrounded it, snorted and tossed its head, pawing at the turf. Its owner was already set in the saddle waiting for the off, and they watched as he craned forward and attempted to calm the steed with soft words.

Thrush Hemming pulled a face as they watched, jutting his ale sodden chin towards the skittish animal. 'He's a bit spunky, that one. Looks like you are going to be a ring light tonight, lord.' He nudged his eorle with his elbow and shot him a smile as he pointed to the heavy band on Eofer's finger. 'Shall I have a quick whip around the lads, see if anyone has something smaller?'

Eofer nodded earnestly to Grimwulf as he flashed the thumbs up and trotted across to the start line. 'No, but you can refill this for me and then bring it over. I am going across to watch this wonder of speed for myself. Our boy is going to win, I am sure of it.' Eofer hauled himself from the log and walked across to the place where the men of his troop had gathered to cheer on their new member.

Sæward looked sceptical. 'Can't be done.'

Eofer nodded and replied with a confidence that was growing within him by the moment. 'You'll see.'

Hemming returned with the cups as Eofer's father, Wonred, came forward and a silence slowly descended on the gathering. The ealdorman's voice boomed out across the clearing as he explained the unusual event.

'To the glory of Woden and all the gods,' he paused theatrically as he swept his arms wide, 'we have a race!' The crowd cheered and Wonred waited, his face a ruddy bloom of ale-fuelled joy, until the noise lessened. 'Once around Thunor's shard and back,' he explained. 'The first one to pass the old oak wins.'

Wonred raised his arm and looked at the contestants. As the crowd quietened and all eyes turned to the ealdorman, Eofer's father brought his arm chopping down and the race was on. The multitude roared with delight, jostling for the best positions as Eofer caught Coelwulf's eye and walked across.

Glancing down the slope, Eofer could see that his new youth was already nearing the turning point, and the crowd let out a gasp as his hand shot out to steady himself as he made the turn. The priests told that the shard had lain there ever since the thunder god had fought a duel with an *eoten* named Brawler. Thunor had hurled his hammer at the giant, striking a whetstone that had been aimed his way in return. The missiles had met mid-air and the stone had shattered and fallen to earth, scattering the shards across the northern lands. It was a crime punishable by death to touch a thing that had come into contact with the hammer of the god. Eofer joined the rest of the onlookers, laughing with relief as Grimwulf drew back his hand at the last moment.

Less agile, the horse went wide, and Eofer drew a laugh from his friend as he held out a hand and wriggled a finger ring as Grimwulf closed in on the oak. The race had been won, and Imma Gold led a raucous group across to congratulate their new brother as Coelwulf shook his head in disbelief. The thegn slipped a heavy ring from his finger and tossed it across. 'I would never have believed such a thing, but that was well-earned Eofer. Where did you find him?'

Eofer gave the ring a swift shine on his sleeve and slipped it on to his finger. 'In a barn in Daneland.'

Coelwulf glanced around him. Satisfied that the few people within earshot were still caught up in the acclamation of the runner, he leaned in and lowered his voice. 'I shall see if I can find one for myself soon enough.' He plucked at Eofer's sleeve, and the thegns wandered across to the ale barrel and refilled their cups. The vicinity was free of folk for the first time that day as they flocked to look upon the man who could outrun a horse as Coelwulf continued. 'I was with the king not five days ago. The plans are made. The war-sword has been sent to Anglia, and the first ships should arrive at the east coast before Eostre. Before the great war against the Danes commences, there is one further raid that the king intends to make.' He glanced about them and, satisfied that they were alone, a proud smile spread across his features. 'He has asked me to gather an army from the western Wolds and join them to a force led by the king's son, Icel. The ætheling is to lead an attack against the Jutes and return with as many prisoners as we can manage.' He saw the mask of disappointment on Eofer's face and chuckled. 'King Eomær mentioned you in our conversation, and he described the face you would pull to perfection. He holds you in the highest regard, as I am sure you are aware, mighty king's bane,' he teased, 'but he thought that you should spend time with your family before you go to war again.' Coelwulf leaned in, and his nostrils flared as the thegn gave an exaggerated sniff. 'I am sure that I can still smell the smoke from old Hrothgar's hall in your hair!'

A cry drew their attention, and both men chuckled as they watched Astrid and her old thyften, Editha, chasing young Weohstan across the meadow. 'She looks like she could do with some help,' Coelwulf quipped as Astrid scooped up the lad and threw him across her shoulder.

Eofer looked back to his friend and the smile drained from his face. 'The king forgets that my wife is the daughter of King Hygelac, not some scatty milk maid squeezing a teat and daydreaming of her cock. Her father just died in battle and her brother is King of Geats, she knows the duties of a peace-weaver.'

Coelwulf brought their cups together with a chink. 'The king said that you would say that too. Not quite in those words,' he admitted with a chuckle, 'but they carried the gist!' He gripped Eofer by the sleeve and excitement shone in his eyes. 'The new moon is in twenty days' time. Bring your men to Wihtlæg's Stone, and we ride.'

THE SHADOWS WERE LENGTHENING by the moment as the group split and went their separate ways with waves and happy smiles. Ealdorman Wonred paused the armed warriors on the road as the men bent low and kissed wives and children before hurrying across to rejoin them.

Eofer embraced Astrid and tousled Weohstan's hair affectionately as they made to follow the guda towards the sacred place. With the setting of the sun on the first day of the new year, the people would leave offerings to the weather god at the great oak. Thunorsleah, Thunor's holy grove, stood deep within the shadows of the Wolds and each adult carried a flaming brand to help draw the attention of the thunderer to the place and to aid in their homeward journey.

Astrid drew back from Eofer's embrace, as Weohstan hefted his small shield at her side and looked on proudly.

'How long?'

Eofer looked at her, confused. 'We will be back in the hall before breakfast, as ever.'

She smiled sweetly and laid a hand lightly on his chest as she looked into his eyes. 'No, how long until you leave again?' she said. 'I saw you talking with Coelwulf. Eorles and thegns don't ignore horse fights unless the prospect of fighting and plunder draws them away.'

He chuckled and bent to kiss her again. 'Twenty days, it will be a short raid—no ships.'

She nodded and turned to go before pausing and shooting him a coy look. Laying the hand on her belly, she moved it slowly in a circle. 'Good, I should be certain by then.'

THE MIGHTY WAR horse tossed its head and whinnied, its nostrils flaring as the warriors formed a circle and raised their brands aloft. The holt was dense in this part of the Wolds, and the light that sawed and danced from the torches barely penetrated the deep shadow of Hangman's Wood that surrounded them. From their lofty position, the warriors watched as the sun sank to the westward until it was an ochre blush on the horizon, the dying rays reaching up to paint the undersides of the clouds a fiery red.

The ash stood hard on the crossroads, the dying light painting its great trunk a ruddy gold as the rope was tossed over a sturdy bough and the slack taken up.

Eofer stood, surrounded by his duguth, and he exchanged a look with the only member of the youth he had invited along. Pride shone in the young woman's eyes as Spearhafoc stood among the warriors who towered all around her, and although there had been a few looks from the men in other troops, his had accepted her into their ranks without a murmur. The memory of the youth's arrows speeding away into the dark as the *Fælcen* had neared the Danish shore was still fresh, and every man there knew that her sharpshooting that night had made the difference between surprise and a hard fight.

Eofer marked the wounds of the animal and nodded to himself. It would please the Allfather to receive such a gift, and he would send them victory in the coming time that men were already beginning to call the year of fire and steel. He had, as Astrid had noticed, missed the great fight between the steeds. The men of his troop had returned from the corral thrilled by the savagery, their faces reflecting the amount of silver that they had won or lost in the contest. The neck and flanks of the stallion were bloodied and torn by hooves and teeth, but its eyes shone bright with victory and its spirit remained undimmed. Each man there knew the thrill that came with outthinking and overpowering a tough opponent, and they swelled with pride as their ealdorman walked into the circle and called on their god to witness the act.

'Woden, fury, lord of battle, witness our devotion and

accept this offering to you, bring victory in the great battles that lie ahead.

Hold your spear over our people as they wrest a new land from the followers of a lesser god, a new Engeln, unyielding in its fervour for the true gods...'

Wonred raised his shield and spear high as the sliver of the sun finally slipped below the distant horizon. The timing was perfect and the men of his hearth troop hauled on the rope and drew the horse on to its hind quarters. As the rope bit and the animal thrashed the air with its bloodied hoofs, an unearthly yowl split the air as the noose tightened. The blood drained from the faces of the English warriors with the power of the moment as they beat spear shafts against the rims of their shields and chanted the god's name. Wonred walked across to the steed as the men of his troop strained against the rope and finally managed to lift the war horse clear of the ground. Raising his face to the quickly darkening sky, the ealdorman spoke again.

'An ash I know there stands. Terror Horse is its name, the bane of the hanged, a rare fruit;

As the horse fought to free itself, the hanging tree shook and creaked as the grim faced men dug in their heels and took up the strain. As the struggles of the terrified horse began to abate and its kicks grew increasingly spasmodic, the great bulk broached and its tongue lolled from its mouth as Wonred approached.

'Terror Horse shivers, the ash as it stands, the old tree groans...

He raised his spear and plunged it deep into the horse's flank, making the dedication as the light from the brands flickered and played about the mail and weapons that ringed them.

'You hung on a windy tree nine long nights, wounded with

a spear, dedicated to Woden, yourself to yourself, on that tree of which no man knows from where its roots run...'

Wonred thrust the spear upwards and the horse kicked out a final time as the blade divided its great heart. As the blood from the sacrifice ran the length of the spear shaft to gush from its base, the warriors came forward to anoint their weapons as they readied themselves for war.

18

'Here she is, lord, our masterpiece.'

Osric pulled open the rickety door and ducked inside. Eofer and Sæward followed on, eager to take the first glimpse of their new scegth. Both men inhaled deeply as the distinctive smells of the boat shed washed around them, tar, pitch, the sharp tang of oak and pine. The pair exchanged a look, and Eofer's ship master was the first to break the silence. 'It's a masterpiece, all right,' he breathed. 'What a beauty!'

Osric led them forward, the pride in the work of his team obvious to all. He ran a hand lovingly along the curve of her sheer strake as he described the ship to the wonderstruck men. 'Six strakes each side, same as before. I have asked one of the lads to bring his brother down to the sheds, lord. The man can carve a scene that's so lifelike you'd think that it was real.' Osric flashed them a smile. 'May as well have the best when the king is paying for it, eh?' He hopped up onto a bench. Shuffling to the end as Eofer and his duguth joined him, he rested his arms on the wale and peered inside. 'As you ordered, lord, the same dimensions as the *Fælcen*.

Twelve thwarts with twenty-four thole-pins, a dozen a side. No through-deck and,' he pointed to the bow and stern, 'a steering platform at either end with a complete rudder assembly at each, just like you wanted.' Sæward's features broke into a smile as the shipwright described the extra fitting. 'There's not much you can see now that the planking is in place, but it's all there. You can see the strengthening block where it emerges from the deck, the rudder rib and the withy are hidden, but the boss and rudder band remain in place at all times. You'll have the rudder where you need it in no time.' Osric rubbed his chin as he looked sidelong at the pair. 'If you don't mind me asking, lord, why do you want to be able to mount the rudder at either end?'

Sæward exchanged a look with his eorle and Eofer nodded that he should explain. 'We will use the ship to follow the rivers, deep into the lands of the Franks and the Britons. The shallow drought of the scegth allows us to raid almost up to the headwaters of the rivers there, large and small, places which never thought to see an English ship. But,' he shrugged, 'there is never enough room to turn the ship when the time comes to beat a hasty retreat.'

'Sometimes very hasty!' Eofer added with a snort of amusement. Looking up, he noticed that Osric's artisans had paused at their work and were listening to the tale. He beckoned them over with a jerk of his head. 'Come across and hear the importance of your work. We often owe our lives to your craftsmanship, you deserve to know how much it means to us.'

The men downed tools and sauntered across. A pair of them had been hammering in what looked to be the final nails as they fixed the thwarts to the side strakes. Unlike the heavier ships they had seen in the South, the English shipyards always constructed the hulls from the outside in. The keel was scarfed into the bow and stern posts and then the side strakes added until the shell of the hull was complete. The frames known as the thwarts were then added to brace the hull, iron nails driven through from the outside and cleated over a small square piece of iron known as a rove. Strong and flexible, the ships were ideal for use in the shallow waters of the German Sea and the rivers that ran into it.

Eofer ran his eyes along his new ship for the first time as the men assembled, admiring her sleek lines, comparing her to the *Fælcen* and finding nothing to fault.

Sæward asked a question of his own. 'What about tholepins? If we swap the rudder around, the hook of the thorn will be pointing back the wrong way. We won't be able to row.'

The shipwright clapped him on the shoulder. 'We have included a few mallets in the tool chest, amidships. Pop the tree nails out the same as you would any belaying pin and switch them around when needs be. It should take you no time, you'll be leaving these wealas shouting at your wake.'

Eofer nodded, satisfied. 'When can she be launched?'

Osric exchanged a look with his leading artisan, who pursed his lips and nodded. Obviously, the matter had already been discussed between the two. Now he was confirming the shipwright's own assessment. 'Tomorrow morning, if we stay late tonight, lord. There is a bit of tarring to touch up and the pine fittings need to be added, the oars and such like. They come from stock, we always have a supply to hand. We can step the mast and get a team of riggers in to finish her off tonight. It shouldn't be hard to drag them away from their ale this once, they all know we do the king's work. Fit her a sail, and she's done—the design on the sheer strake can be added later. I'll fit her with a wind vane for now, no doubt you will want to replace it with something grander when you get the chance.'

Sæward's triumphant smile told them all that he had been waiting a long time for just this moment. Slipping a bag from his shoulder, he undid the ties that bound it and brought out a large object wrapped securely in a red cloth. Carefully unfolding the leaves of the bundle, Sæward revealed the old bronze weathervane from the *Fælcen* wrapped in the storm weathered flag of Engeln. He turned to Eofer and smiled proudly at the look of surprise on his lord's face. 'I had Bassa and Beornwulf shimmy up the mast before the flames engulfed them, lord. Never seen them move so fast,' he added with a chuckle. 'It seemed like the right thing to do.'

19

Astrid paused and listened. 'There it is again.'

Eofer concentrated on his hearing, but there was nothing beyond the baleful sounds of midwinter. The soft sweep of the treetops as they sawed back and forth in the wind that blew up from the Muddy Sea, the harsh call of a rook. Somewhere in the Wolds, a badger screeched.

Astrid looked at her husband askance. 'You must hear it?' Eofer listened again and pulled a face as Astrid shook her head and chided him. 'Your hearing is going, you'll end up like your father. We shall all have to repeat ourselves three times before you pretend to know what we are saying.'

Armed and dressed in a hastily thrown on mail shirt, Thrush came from the hall and handed him his sword and shield as the breeze finally carried a trace of the sound to Eofer's ears. 'Oh, you mean the hunting horn,' he bluffed. 'Have you just heard it?' The rest of the troop tumbled from the doorway and formed a wall across the entrance as Astrid threw Eofer a knowing look, smiling to herself as she went to check on the whereabouts of Weohstan. Men were approaching, openly, it was true—but it always paid to be certain.

Eofer gave the shield wall a quick glance and smiled his thanks as Imma handed him his battle helm. Slipping it on, he adjusted the fastening as the mounted party finally broke free from the tree line. Searching out the banners that would announce the identity of the unexpected visitor, Eofer smiled with delight as he recognised the Raven banner of the ætheling, Icel, alongside the dragon of Engeln. Unfastening his helm, he tossed it back to Imma and bade them keep their weapons sheathed before striding forward to welcome his lord.

The mounted column shone like glass in the weak sun of the northern winter as it snaked its way down to the hall of the thegn. Eofer smiled a greeting as the outriders passed the paddock and clattered into the courtyard. Fanning out to the left and right, the men of Icel's hearth troop turned the heads of their mounts inward and drew up facing one another as the ætheling followed his war banners into the open space.

Without his helm, Icel was unmistakable among the leading men of the English. Almost alone among the warrior class, the ætheling kept his straw blond hair cropped short in the fashion of the ceorls and fishermen. Naturally unruly, the tufts crowned a body made broad and muscular in the service of his father the king, and had been responsible for the nickname 'haystack' that the people had affectionately bestowed upon their popular prince.

Leaping from the back of his horse, Icel laughed and threw his arms around the eorle. 'Eofer! It's good to see you, old friend.' The ætheling took a pace back and grinned happily. 'The Britons sent me home to get you,' he quipped. 'They said that life is a little too predictable now that they know that they can go to their rest each night, safe in the knowledge that they will not be awoken by the smell of smoke and the sound of clashing steel.' He glanced across to the shield wall and nodded in recognition. 'Thrush, Imma, Octa, Osbeorn. I understand that you boys have been upsetting our neighbours.' They grinned in return, and Icel clapped Eofer on the arm. 'I learned most of the tale from your brother, Wulf, in Gippeswic before we left. You can tell me all the details as you fill me with ale this evening.' He laughed again and a look of pride and respect came into his eyes. 'Burning Heorot. The tale has swept Anglia like a heath blaze.'

Satisfied that it was safe to do so, Astrid had led Weohstan into the courtyard, and the boy waited patiently to be introduced to his lord. The ætheling noticed them, and Eofer caught the boy's eye and beckoned him across.

Weohstan held Icel's gaze and his voice was strong and firm as he greeted his father's guest.

'My name is Weohstan Eofering. Welcome to my father's hall, lord.'

Icel smiled again. 'I am happy to be here, Weohstan. It would please me to bestow a gift on you. This thing has powerful spell-work, it has been searching for a man with a trim heart and a fearsome countenance such as yourself. What do you say, are you up to the task?'

The boy raised his chin and answered the prince as his proud parents looked on. 'I am a kinsman to kings, folctoga and eorles—I have dragon fire for blood, lord.'

Icel's face lit up at the reply, and he fished inside the purse that hung at his belt. Taking out a pebble, he knelt beside the lad. 'This is an elf-stone, have you seen one before?'

Weohstan shook his head.

'They are powerful things. They can protect the wearer from elf-shot and witchery.' He held it up for the boy to peer through. 'If you close one eye and look through the hole with the other, you can see if there are elves, goblins, or orcs nearby.' Icel slowly moved the stone in an arc as the boy peered through. 'Can you see any?'

Weohstan shook his head again. 'No, lord.'

Icel nodded. 'Good, we are safe. Woden himself turned into a snake and crawled through a hole in a mountain to gain the mead of poetry. As a reward for its help, the Allfather hallowed all holey stones. Guard it well, Weohstan dragon-blood, and it will take good care of you. It will help to keep you safe from *deofols*.'

Icel rose again as the boy proudly examined his gift, and his gaze grew sombre. 'I am afraid that I also have a far less pleasant duty.'

The smile fled from Astrid's face, and her hand went to her mouth. 'My cousin has fallen.'

Icel pulled a face. 'It would appear so. The king heard the tale from a Frisian merchant, a man who has always proved to be reliable in the past.'

To the ætheling's astonishment, Eofer and Astrid shared a smile. Astrid was the first to reply. 'If Beowulf *is* dead, he sups in a far greater hall than we will this night. Did this merchant know the details of his death?'

As relief flooded through him, Icel found that he too was grinning. 'We were told that he marched with just a few of his duguth into the midst of the victorious Frankish army and tore the heart from the man who killed your father, the king. The Franks were so impressed by his valour that they allowed him to leave unmolested. But he was later overtaken by a vengeful Frisian force, and slain after a savage fight with the hearth troop of a warlord who calls himself the Dragon.'

Eofer fixed Icel with a stare. 'It would seem that I have a duty of honour to perform in Frisia.' To his surprise, the ætheling shook his head. 'A far greater thing awaits us, Eofer. Besides,' he added with a glance towards Astrid, 'I am confident that King Heardred will be making plans to avenge both his father, and his cousin, as we speak. I rather suspect that this Dragon will soon feel the heat of an avenging Geatish flame.'

Brecc, the senior thræl, had ushered the ætheling's horses into the corral and the men of his troop were shouldering their shields and weapons as they sauntered across the yard. Icel unhooked his baldric and tossed it and the sword it contained to one of his men as he sought to lighten the mood. 'Coelwulf tells me that you have a fast runner here, Eofer—a horse chaser no-less.'

Eofer nodded across to the shield wall. Relaxed and smiling happily now, his men perked up as they began to suspect that another race might be in the offing. 'Grimwulf outpaced a horse at the midwinter festival,' he replied proudly.

Icel smiled. 'You relieved Coelwulf of a gold ring, I understand.' He looked at Eofer with a twinkle in his eye. 'How would you like to win another? Let me see if I can pick out this thunderbolt from the ranks of your motley crew of cut-throats.' His eyes scanned the ranks of Eofer's youth as he searched for the most likely suspect. Suddenly, his gaze alighted on Grimwulf, and he smiled in triumph. 'There he is!' The ætheling called across. 'Harefoot, dress for war. Let's see how fast you are bearing arms. You can leave your sword off if you have one, but arm yourself with shield, spear, mail, and helm.' He slipped a pair of gold arm rings from his forearm and tossed them to the ground. Gasps of admiration escaped the watching men as they realised the significance of the action. The rings were a work of wonder. Worked from a single rod of gold, each twist of the rings was highlighted with the delicate beading the smiths called filigree. 'One for you and one for your lord.' Grimwulf was clearly overcome at the thought of owning such a thing. As his new companions cheered him on, the youth managed to drag his gaze away from the treasure in the dust. 'What if I lose, lord?' he asked with a smile of innocence.

Icel looked confused for a moment, before answering. 'Your lord gets to keep both rings, of course, as compensation for your life.'

ICEL LEANED back from the bench and gently kneaded his belly with the tips of his fingers. 'That was great pork.' He made a fist and pushed it firmly into his stomach until a belch eased the pressure. 'I know that it is not as tender as deer or lamb, but it is my favourite.' He scooped up the last piece of meat and popped it into his mouth with relish. 'Lamb is nice and fatty, but you can only get it at Eostre, what good is that? That race did wonders for my appetite, I should try it more often.' He looked across to the place where Grimwulf was proudly showing off his arm ring. 'Coelwulf was right, you have a sight hound there, he left me floundering in his wake. Not many men can do that, it could be useful to you Eofer,' he said distantly. The ætheling's mind was clearly on other things, and Eofer waited until his lord ordered his thoughts.

Icel, finally satisfied that the contents of his stomach were under control, leaned across and came to the point of his visit. 'Everything has been moved forward, this attack on the Jutes will herald the start of the year of battles.' Eofer couldn't contain his surprise and the ætheling went on. 'All the Heathobeard have accomplished with their hopeless attack on Daneland is to wake the monster from its winter slumber. King Ingeld is dead along with half of his warriors, and Hrothgar is running around like a stallion with a hard on.' He chuckled softly, and a smirk came to his face. 'If it wasn't for you and your lads, he would have had Ingeld's king helm sitting atop the pile of plunder at the great victory feast in Heorot.' A glint came into his eye as he continued. 'I would have loved to see his face, when he returned to Hleidre and saw a pile of ash where his lovely hall had stood. Ten years sleeping in the women's bower; as soon as the monster is slain, and he can use it again, some English bastard burns it down.' They shared a laugh, and Eofer managed to splutter a reply. 'I was glad that I was *not* around when Hrothgar returned. It was the happiest sight that has ever greeted my eyes, when I crested that last rise and saw Eadward and his snake ship.'

The sound of the wind outside grew as the door opened, causing the pair to glance up from their cups. Eofer was pleased to see Rand and Finn take up their gar from the spear rack and disappear into the darkness. Within moments, the chilled and windswept figures of Porta and Edwin quickly entered the hall, grinning their thanks as cups of warmed mead were thrust upon them. It was, Eofer reflected, a sign of the times that an Englishman could not feel completely safe within the walls of his hall, even in the heart of the kingdom.

Icel noticed the thegn's look, and his face grew more sober. 'What you did in Daneland was a great deed. The rescue of your brother, visiting fire and destruction on the enemy of your king and people, has thrilled the English at this difficult time. However,' he added, 'it now means that the thirst for revenge among the Danes can only be quenched by an attack on us, and soon. Hrothgar has lost face, and his attentions will turn from an attack on the War-Beard homeland to those lands that he covets most of all. As you know, I have just returned from Anglia. Your brother Wulf and others are carrying the war-sword to the thegns there, they will be here as soon as they can refit their ships. The first to arrive will shadow the army as we march north into Juteland, capturing as many ships as they can on the West Coast. These will be sent south to the Muddy Sea, and the first farmers and their families will set off for the new lands immediately.'

He noticed Eofer's look of surprise, and he took a sip from his ale before explaining. 'The king is sure that the Danes will attack us when the campaigning season starts after Eostre. We cannot let that happen, we must strike first. If heavy fighting breaks out in our lands as we are trying to move the people across the German Sea, it could end in disaster. We cannot wait until the harvest is in as we had planned, so we have to go as early as possible to enable the ceorls to sow their seed in the soil of Anglia. The next harvest gathered by English hands will be the first in the new land, my friend.' Icel reached across and charged their cups. Handing one to Eofer, he set his features into a look of determination and brought the cups together with a heavy clunk. 'The king wishes to reward your loyalty and fighting spirit with a new command, Eofer. Let's drink to our success.'

20

The early morning sky was a deep indigo, as hard and cold as ice. Away to the west, the darkness still held sway. But Shining Mane was clearing the horizon and the stars had dimmed, leaving only the brilliance of the morning star, and the ruddy point of light that men called the blood star to share the vault with the sun.

Sure now that any wandering spirits would be back in the earth, Wonred nodded, and brands were thrust deep inside the woodpiles. Fingers of smoke curled up at once from the brushwood tinder, and within moments the first daggers of flame were stabbing upwards from the stacks.

Eofer rested his hand on the hilt of Blood-Worm as his father called across to the waiting men, his voice muffled by the plates of the full faced grim-helm of an English folctoga. 'Start your work.'

The ceorls, tenant farmers who owed allegiance to the family as their fathers had before them, took up their picks and swung at the side of the mound and the first earth of the morning tumbled away. The night had been windless and a hoar frost, crisp and white, had thickened the grass and bushes all around.

'At least this frost will keep the mud down.' Wonred said to his son. 'It had rained for weeks when we placed your grandfather in there, and the place was slick with mud.' He shook his head at the memory. 'What a mess.'

The pair had dressed for battle, honouring the spirit of their ancestors with their finery. The men of their hearth troop, mailed and helmed, shone like torches in the reflected light of the fires as they ringed the scene while, further back, the wives and children of the men looked on respectfully.

Wonred spoke again. 'Your brother should be here, but I couldn't afford to wait until he returns.' He stared ahead at the ceorls as the picks rose and fell. 'I never thought that I would live to see the day when we left our land for good.' He looked at Eofer, and his son could sense the conflicting emotions tearing at the old man. 'Are they that much better, these new lands?'

'Britannia is huge, father,' Eofer replied. 'No longer will we be squeezed between Grim's Dyke and the River Egedore, the Jutes and the Saxons, the Muddy Sea and the Beltic. The land is fertile, with great woods and rivers teeming with fish and fowl.' He touched the blade of his spear to his father's, and the corner of his mouth turned up into a smile. 'Arthur is dead, and the Britons are divided among themselves, the land is there for the taking. I witnessed their disunity with my own eyes this summer. Christians fight against those who still honour the old gods, and the Saxons are encroaching everywhere in the south.' He gave his father a stern look, eager to impress on the older man the importance of the moment despite the nearness of their ancestors' shades. 'Even the Jutes are well established, both in the lands they call Cent and now on a great island that Cerdic called

Vectis. Both places are perfectly placed to control trade between Britannia and the new kingdoms emerging in Gaul. If we do not take our future into our hands, our enemies will grow stronger.'

He paused again to add emphasis to his words as Wonred stared into the distance. A stillness lay on the land, broken only by the mournful howl of a wolf in the distance and the rhythmic sound of pick on earth. 'I believe that if we remain in this land of Engeln while our young men carry their spears across the sea to Anglia, that the day is not so far off that our enemies here will grow too strong.' Shame caused Eofer to lower his voice, aware as he was that he was only yards from the burial mounds of his ancestors, but the point needed to be made nevertheless. 'If we don't leave Engeln of our own free will, it will fall to Jutish sword or Danish axe. It is the will of the gods that we leave, father, the Allfather himself guided us at the symbol. We are still the gods' chosen people.'

The sun had fully risen now and fires were beginning to be lit to prepare food. Ale and mead were plentiful and the mood of the crowd was beginning to take on the air of a festival, despite the early start and the biting cold. The pair stood, deep in thought, watching dispassionately as an ox hauled a flat-backed wagon onto the crest, a misting of vapour rising from its back, sweet smelling in the crisp air. Halting at the barrow, the ceorls set to, shovelling the spoil onto its wide platform.

Eofer sought to lighten the mood that had descended upon them. 'Where are they taking it?'

'It will be scattered across the old fields,' Wonred replied, distantly. He indicated beyond the gathering with his head. A team of oxen stood there patiently, the heavy wooden crescents of their yolks already in place. 'Once we have removed Gleaming, the entire field will be ploughed flat. It will look like any other, and the bones of our kinsmen can rest in peace until the end of days, whoever occupies these lands when we are gone.' Wonred turned his head, and Eofer was pleased to see a smile form there.

Eofer returned the gesture. 'A similar scene is being enacted all across Engeln, father. Once we attack the Jutes, the year of battles will have begun. There will be no going back.'

They were interrupted as a worker hurried across and dipped his head respectfully. 'We have reached the chamber wall, lord.'

Wonred nodded. His last lingering doubts removed, he was back to himself, a folctoga of the English, and his voice was firm. 'Clear away the last of the earth Coela, and we will be across.' He threw the man a smile. 'Once you have removed the planking, you can take a break. The meats look like they are ready—I have no doubt that the lads will make short work of them.'

The ceorl smiled and dipped his head once again, before doubling across to spread the news among his companions. Hemming crossed to his lord with Wonred's own weorthman, Penda. At the mound, Coela stood tall and looked in their direction as the wagon was hauled to one side.

'Time to go,' Wonred sniffed. 'Let's get this done.'

Hemming and Penda took up positions flanking their lords as the group strode purposefully towards the opening. The workmen stood to one side as the warriors moved into the shadow of the mound and approached the burial chamber. Coela stood ready, a mattock poised to begin the task of levering away the heavy oak planking. Wonred nodded to the man, and he worked the chisel edge of the blade into the join between two of the boards. A robin appeared at the top of the mound and the men smiled despite the solemnity of the occasion as the red breasted bird watched the goings-on with undisguised interest. The first board suddenly gave with a crack as Coela levered it way and moved on.

The stale air, decades beneath the earth, washed over the group as the boards came away and Eofer fought against the urge to crane his neck to catch the first glimpse of the treasures within. The earth had been cleared from the top of the mound and a few of the oak beams that lay there were flicked up to allow the pale light of winter to illuminate the chamber. Coela looked across to Wonred for a sign that he had done enough, and the folctoga gave a curt nod. As the ceorl cleared away, Wonred led them in.

A latticework of sunbeams patterned the space, and Eofer paused as his eyes became accustomed to the light. The skeleton of a horse lay at his feet, the curved bones of the ribcage brown with age, remnants of skin still clinging to them like a badly raised tent. His gaze ran on, past the skull to the figure at the head of the chamber. Raised on a shallow dais above the level of the earthen floor, Eofer's grandfather, Ælfgar, sat upon his gift-stool.

More familiar with the layout of the tomb, Wonred had already crossed to the figure, and they watched as he bent his knee and laid his forehead upon the withered hand of his long dead father.

Rising again, Wonred turned and motioned to Penda. 'Bring it in. I want there to be no trace left here before sundown.' Eofer crossed to his father's side as their duguth left the chamber and reappeared moments later leading a pair of men shouldering a heavy oak coffin. Eofer straddled the great bones of the war horse with a heavy iron trestle, and the pair placed the casket down with a grunt of effort. Wonred indicated to Eofer that he help him to remove the lid of the coffin, and the pair propped it against the side wall of the chamber and returned to the figure of Ælfgar. Eofer studied his ancestor as they to prepared to transfer his remains.

Dressed in a tunic of fine red cloth edged with gold braiding, the ealdorman was still dressed in blue trews bound at the calf by delicately woven *winingas*, the golden strips of cloth crisscrossing to the knee. Gleaming, the ancestral sword of their clan, lay across the lap of the long dead ealdorman and Wonred spoke as he moved forward to lift it with reverence from the lap of his father.

'Father, this is your grandson, Eofer, called king's bane. Slayer of Ongentheow, King of Swedes, hall burner of the king of Danes. My other son, Wulf, has been shown great honour for his battle-fury and carries the war-spear to the king's thegns as we speak. When he returns, he will go to join the king's own hearth troop, become a trusted gesith. Our king, Eomær of the Engle, has ordered that his people will leave these lands. The Allfather has guided us to another land, a better land, a land where the people can grow, prosper and bring the worship of the real gods to the people there. Before we leave these Wolds, we will move to smite our enemies. Your grandson Eofer will carry Gleaming to Anglia so that it will remain in the clan always, but first he will carry it to war against our greatest foes as you did in your time.'

Wonred turned and handed the ancestral blade to Eofer, who took it with pride as the duguth looked on. The blade was untarnished, despite the passage of decades as it lay beneath the ground, and it shone brightly in the light filtering down from above. Eofer's heart raced as he looked at the golden hilt for the first time, and felt the perfect balance of the blade as it rested in his hands.

He had always held that his sword, Blood-Worm, was a thing of great beauty. With a handle of pale horn capped by an intricately worked silver pommel, the blade that had taken the life of King Ongentheow had always been his proudest possession. It was, he now knew, a pale imitation of the sword that his ancestors had carried into battle, the blade he would soon carry against his king's foemen. He had always assumed that the sword had earned its name from the quality of its blade, but he could see now that he had been mistaken. His blood quickened as he ran his eyes along the length of the fuller, a whirling mass of stars edged by razor-sharp strips of shining steel, to the hilt. The hand grip was a series of alternating hoops, wide bands of horn and lighter, almost white, whalebone or walrus tusk. Gold guards terminated the grip at each end, and the whole was capped by a magnificent pommel of garnet and gold. Eofer had seen such a cap on the swords of royalty, both King Eomær and his son Icel had such a pommel on their own weapons, and the golden backed cells that held the garnets gleamed like stars within the gloom in the mound.

Eofer handed the sword to Hemming for safekeeping, before exchanging a look of pride with his father as they both moved forward to lift the remains of their ancestor from his stool. Wonred gripped the sleeve of his father's tunic and prepared to lift, but a thought came to his son, who held up a hand to stop him. 'If we try to lift Ælfgar like this, we are inviting disaster. Either the clothing will turn to dust in our hands, or the bones will come apart. Either way,' Eofer said, 'we shall have to scoop the remains of my grandfather off the floor.'

Wonred blew out and nodded in agreement. 'Grip the back and handles of the gift-stool, and we'll carry him across. If the lads remove the chair at the last moment, hopefully we can just lower him down into the casket.' Wonred laughed suddenly and grinned at the dried husk that he had known so well in life. 'I know that you are enjoying this, watching from the ale bench in Valhall.' He flicked Eofer a look as they took the weight. 'He had a wicked sense of humour. You and Wulf would have liked the old goat.'

They carried the chair across and lowered it to the level of the coffin. As Hemming and Penda moved to replace them, Wonred and Eofer cradled the body in their arms and lowered it to its final resting place. Hewn from a solid piece of oak, the silk lined casket had been left deliberately free from decoration, in contrast to the opulence of the grave goods that had been placed there decades before.

Alone with their thoughts, both men took a final look at the face of their forefather as the lid slid across to remove it from the gaze of men for all time.

EOFER WAS reflective as he rode the final mile to the hall. Thrush Hemming recognised his lord's mood and remained silent, his presence being all the support the man would need. His grandfather would be closed up again by now, and the very thought of that dark, airless space was enough to move the eorle's hand instinctively to the hammer charm that hung at his neck.

Once the grave goods had been taken down from their pegs and redistributed around the body of the old ealdorman, the workmen had returned and lowered the roof beams to little more than waist height. Now several feet below the ground level above, the grave would disappear into the landscape completely once the field had been ploughed over and the extra soil scattered elsewhere.

Across the length and breadth of Engeln, men were doing the same for their ancestors. Soon the English would move away from their ancestral lands, and the memories of such places would be lost forever. But the shades of the men would remain, and Eofer smiled at the thought of the old battle-lords haunting their fields and woods until the end of days.

Gleaming lay across his lap as he rode, and he gave the old blade a pat as he thought back to the final acts in the tomb. They had placed the grave goods at the head and feet of the chamber. On the far end, towards the ealdorman's head, they had laid his war gear and treasure. Eofer recalled his grandfather's wealth with pride as he rode. A shirt of mail was carefully folded and laid alongside a heavy spear and several of the lighter daroth. The horse's bridle lay alongside a magnificent saddle, its leather work cut and chased, inlaid with gold. At his grandfather's feet rested a bowl of hazelnuts and a bag of lamb joints, shrivelled and desiccated with age. A distant smile had washed across Wonred's face as he had explained to his son that they had been a few of his grandfather's favourite foods. A lyre in a beaver skin bag was placed to one side along with a gaming board, its pieces arranged in lines, ready for the gamers to take their places.

Wonred had placed his father's grim-helm at the head of the coffin lid, and together they had lifted the man's great war-shield onto the case. Across this lay a pair of drinking horns as long as a man's arm. Made from the great horn of the aurochs, the lip of each vessel was encircled by a deep band of silver, delicately cast, while each horn terminated in the silver head of an eagle, its curving beak and gem studded eyes glittering in the gloom of the grave.

As they had turned to go, Eofer had delighted his father with a final gesture. Removing the scabbard containing Blood-Worm from his baldric, he had placed it and the sword it contained alongside the shield and described their history to the old man's shade. He had used it to take the life of a king in battle, and he had wielded the same blade outside Heorot as they fought to free their kinsman and bring fire and destruction to the king's enemies. It was a fitting replacement for Gleaming, and Eofer had asked Ælfgar to show Ongentheow honour on his behalf until they met again in Valhall, for he had faced his death like a king.

IMMA GOLD POPPED his head inside and squinted into the gloom. Seeing Eofer by the hearth, he broke into a smile, 'Sæward's here, lord.' Eofer nodded that he understood and sent Weohstan to find his mother. The lad scampered away, and Eofer stepped across the threshold of his hall and into the yard. The air was still, overhead a thick drugget of clouds, grey and soft edged, was shifting slowly to the east. Eofer smiled as the duguth hauled on the reins and brought the wagon to a halt.

'Good journey?'

Sæward jumped to the ground, kneading his buttocks as he flexed his legs. 'If I ever give up on the sea, lord, remind me never to become a carter.' He made a circle of his lips and exhaled, 'I felt every bump in the road. Whatever you do,' he grimaced, 'don't move for a moment so that I can focus on you. My eyes are still joggling up and down.'

They shared a laugh and Eofer pushed a cup onto the man. Sæward's face lit up as he noticed what the vessel contained.

'Cider!'

Eofer grinned. 'Astrid's best. We can't take it all with us, it's got to go.'

The steersman swilled the drink before swallowing it with a look of relish. 'That was worth a sore arse. Got any more?' The eorle clapped him on the shoulder and indicated the door to the hall with a jerk of his head. 'Inside, help yourself to anything you find, there's food and drink piled high. Yuletide has come again.'

Sæward hurried inside, and Eofer looked back to the wagon. The youth from the ship, Bassa, Beornwulf and Edwin were loading the hangings and tapestries onto the back of the wagon and Eofer strolled across. 'Leave that and get yourself inside, lads. Eat and drink as much as you want, the rest is going to the gods.'

The thræl, Brecc, was busy preparing the horses for their journey, and Eofer called him across to give him a hand with the loading. Eofer watched the man as they worked. He was not home enough to really know the man's worth, but Astrid had spoken well of him. He had noticed that she had even trusted the slave with a spear the night he had returned from Britannia, and she had assured him that he was dependable when he had questioned her judgement. The slave was solidly built and bore the scars on his forearm that were typical, if not of a warrior, at least of a man who had fought in the levy and was no stranger to the shield wall. Eofer decided to find out more about the man's past. 'Tell me about yourself, Brecc,' he said. 'How did you come into thrældom?'

The man looked up from his work, and Eofer could see the surprise and wariness writ on his features. Great events were happening in Engeln, and Eofer realised that the man was right to be cautious. In times of trouble, famine, or war, thræls would be the first to pay the price if there were suddenly too many mouths to feed, or there was any question as to their trustworthiness. He smiled what he hoped was a reassuring smile. 'You are in no danger. You have my word.'

A guarded look washed across the man's features, and Eofer saw that he was weighing his words carefully until he was sure of his position. It showed an intelligence and self-confidence that was uncommon in those born to his position, qualities that would likely go some way to explaining his usefulness.

The last of the goods were on the wagon, and Eofer whistled as Spearhafoc walked by with a jug of ale and a pair of cups for Octa and Osbeorn. The young woman stifled a sigh as Eofer took the tray from her, and he laughed as his duguth tried to hide their disappointment as the girl trudged back towards the hall to fetch replacements.

He smiled again as he handed Brecc a cup of drink. 'Here, this will help loosen your tongue.'

Thræls were forbidden to drink anything but water on pain of death, and Eofer recognised the look of bliss that swept his features as he sank his first mouthful. Brecc drained the remainder in one, and Eofer's eyes sparkled with amusement as he noticed the man decide to chance his luck, throwing caution to the wind as he held his cup out for a refill. Brecc drank again, wiping the froth from his beard with the back of his hand as the ale worked its magic, and he began to relax.

'I come from a land called Dumnonia, lord, although you would call us all Britons. It's a long way from the part of Britannia where your settlements are, but we do get quite a few Saxon ships in our waters.' Eofer kept topping up the thræl's cup as he drank, and soon he had shed his inhibitions and was in full flow. 'I used to work the fish, lord, you know, from a boat. One day, the owner got carried away and chased a shoal of mackerel out to sea.' Brecc's gaze misted over, and Eofer could see that the man was back at sea in his mind. He smiled to himself, he knew the feeling well. 'What happened then Brecc, a storm?' The man snorted. 'As I said, lord. The sea is full of Saxon pirates. We turned for home when we saw them, but the wind died on us and that was that, there's no way that a boat with four oars is going to outrun one shipping two score or more. I guess that I am lucky to be here at all.' The ale had worked quickly on a mind that had been denied it for so long, and Brecc shot Eofer a smile. 'Bastards took our fish and us with them.' He laughed. 'Sold us to a slaver in Gaul.'

Eofer drained his cup as he reached a decision. There was no place for the man where his family were going, and the alternative was unthinkable. The Briton had stood shoulder to shoulder with Astrid and Weohstan the night he had arrived back from Britannia, unflinching as the war-band thundered into the yard before them. The man was loyal, dependable, and reliable, despite the cruel twist in his life-thread that the norns had woven for him. Besides, he reflected as he watched Brecc chuckle happily as he finished another tale, he was just too likeable. He charged the cups again. 'Have you a family at home?' Brecc's smile fell from his features and he shifted uncomfortably on the tail gate of the wagon. 'A *gwr* called Bleddyn and a boy, Arwel.' He looked wistfully into his cup and swilled the drink in a circle as he remembered. 'He will be ten winters old now, lord,' he said wistfully. 'All grown up.'

THE CART PAUSED at the exit to the yard, and Eofer looked up as the horses carrying the men of his hearth troop gathered in its wake. The riders turned back, and their lord reached out to his wife and pulled her close. 'It's a shame that the hall will never echo to the sound of a bairn again.'

Eofer dropped a hand and caressed her belly. The new life that was growing there was obvious now, and he rested his hand on the swelling as she nuzzled in to his chest. 'We will build a better hall in the new country,' he said. 'With woods to hunt in, dark soil to sow crops and a brook to fish.'

She looked up at him and there was a twinkle in her eye. 'So, you are going to hang up your shield and spear and become a farmer?' She moved her hand down to cup his balls, rolling them between her thumb and fingers as Weohstan shook his head and moved away in disgust. She smiled and shook her head. 'No, I thought not, king's bane. I can't see you wading through mud and shit all day when there is a reputation to build upon. Not with plums like those.' They shared a kiss, giggling as the men on the road whistled and catcalled. 'Thank you,' she murmured as they parted. 'It was a good thing, that which you did—worthy of an eorle.' Eofer thought back to the great white cliffs, the cry of the gulls, the salty bite in the air, and shrugged. 'I sailed those waters this summer past with Cerdic. I could not deny the man his freedom. Brecc should be there to guide his boy to manhood.'

Crossing to the fire, each took up a brand, Weohstan following their example as the family moved towards the hall. Ducking inside for the last time, they made their way across to the great mound of timber that had been stacked there. Benches and tables, their broken joints ragged and white against the darker surface wood, shards of pottery and bolts of yarn awaiting the hunger of the flames.

Astrid thrust her torch deep inside the pile, jamming it into its heart where the pyre had been packed with old thatch. The flames crackled into life, and she turned to go as her husband and son followed her example. 'It's no longer a home,' she said with a shrug of indifference. 'Without the people, it is just another room.'

21

Thrush Hemming gave a low whistle. 'Looks like we're last.'

Eofer tugged at his reins, bringing them all to a halt at the edge of the tree line as his eyes scanned the gathering.

An army swirled within the bowl of land ahead as men crossed to and fro, renewing friendships from earlier campaigns and greeting distant kinsmen. The *hildbeacn*, the war-banners of the thegns, snapped and writhed in a freshening wind, their colours, reds, golds and blues, shimmering against the paler hues of an English winter. At its centre, standing proudly beside the stone of Wihtlæg the ætheling had planted the royal standard, white on scarlet, a sight to chill the most valiant Jutish heart.

'Let's get down there,' Eofer said at last. He shot his duguth a wolfish smile. 'In case they go without us.'

Putting spur to horse they broke free of the shadows and his own hildbeacn went forward to mingle among the men of the fyrd for the first time. Faces turned outwards, war horns sounded, and voices rose in acclamation as Eofer led his hearth troop into the heart of them, exchanging smiles and hailing old friends as they approached the dragon flag.

Icel stood by the stone itself, and he grinned in welcome as they slowed and dismounted. Eofer handed the reins to Thrush and returned the grin as he took the cup that the ætheling thrust his way.

'The king's bane has arrived. We can start the war!'

Icel swept the gathering with a look of mirth as they all beamed at their lord's good humour. He crossed and placed a friendly arm around Eofer's shoulder and guided him to one side as Coelwulf flashed him a wink.

'Are you all set?'

'Yes, lord.'

'Good, you are the last group to arrive. We will leave here and move north.'

Icel squinted up at the sun. The orb had just moved beyond its highest point as it tracked to the west. Ragged clouds raced by, pale grey shot through with white, but the day was mild for the time of year and the fact was reflected in the faces of the surrounding men. 'We will move from here as soon as this barrel is dry, which should be just long enough for us to mount up now that Osbeorn has arrived,' he said with a snort. 'The king told me about your duguth and the pickled eggs; the Barley Mow?' Eofer nodded and Icel pulled a knowing smile in return. 'He's not the first, and he won't be the last.'

The ætheling grabbed a pair of pork ribs from the table and handed one across. As Eofer tore a strip of flesh from the bone, Icel went on. 'It will be as I outlined at your hall. We will leave here separately, you move up The Oxen Way and I will lead the army along the tracks to the west of the Wolds. We will camp near the border for a day to give you time to launch your attack and allow the enemy time to respond before we cross the river.' He glanced across, and the usual relaxed features of the prince had taken on a harder edge. 'Have you any last questions?'

Eofer shook his head. 'No, lord.'

Icel nodded, satisfied. 'We shall have riders out keeping an eye on you. Even if you don't see them, they will see you —count on it.'

Icel's expression cleared, and he was back to his usual jocular self. 'I like your new hildbeacn, the burning hart. I will wager that you can't wait to carry it against the Danes next month.' He caught the look of surprise that crossed Eofer's face at the news and nodded. 'Yes, it will be as soon as that. The first men from Britannia have reached Sleyswic, and others are making their way along the Trene to the Old Ford. By the time we return, the town will be a forest of spears. Add the fyrd of Engeln to their numbers, and we will have an overwhelming force with which to repay the Danes for their arrogance.' He took a bite from the rib and waved it in the direction of the coast. 'Are your family safely away?'

'Yes, lord.'

'To Geatland?'

Eofer nodded. 'Yes, lord. My duguth, Sæward, is carrying them there in the scegth that your father had built for me as we speak.'

It was Icel's turn to look surprised. 'Already? Doesn't the oak need to season first?'

'It will be some time before the hull needs any attention,' Eofer replied, 'it can season just as well in Geatland. Osric, the master shipwright at Strand, has sent his eldest son with them to take care of any minor adjustments that crop up. Sæward knows his way around a ship, and he has been sailing her every day since she was launched. She is as fine a vessel as ever skimmed the waves, there will be no problem with her seaworthiness if he says so. He assures me that she is even faster than the *Fælcen*. They are moving north along the coast with the fleet that will attack the Jutish settlements there, before one of my father's snake ships shepherds them the rest of the way.'

Icel inhaled deeply as a breeze swept up the ridge, bringing with it the brackish tang of the Muddy Sea. He took a last nibble from the pork rib and sent the bone spinning through the air. 'Then we are set.'

Away to the west the island of Silt lay like a dark stone set in a pewter sea as the pale light of the sun reflected from the surface. 'The gods are with us, Eofer,' he said distantly. 'What else could explain the mildness of the weather at this time of year?'

EOFER BURIED his chin deeper into his cloak and shook another droplet from the tip of his nose. Dropping free of the trees, he led the long, sodden column out of the Wolds and onto the flooded plain. High above, a dark mass of cloud lay over the eastern half of the kingdom, its serrated edge a giant's saw as it pointed to the north. To the west, the sky was the pale blue of winter. But the sun shone brightly, and the land beneath it shimmered like a sheet of beaten silver as the rainstorm moved away.

'What was it that Haystack said, lord?'

Eofer pinched his nose and flicked the droplets away as he turned to the man to his left. 'Something about the gods being with us due to the weather?'

Hemming added his voice from the right. 'Maybe they are.' He glanced away to the north. The great ragged edge of the storm lay almost directly above The Oxen Way and the land beneath lay deep in shadow. Darker patches showed where showers were falling. 'It will keep them all at home. No man ventures far from a warm hearth and a horn of ale in weather like this unless there is good reason, especially at this time of the year.'

At his side, Penda nodded in agreement. 'Thrush could have the right of it.' He ran his hand down his face and tousled the moisture from his beard. 'That's where I would be if I had nothing better to do.' The edge of the storm finally reached the eastern foothills of the Wolds and the rain stopped as suddenly as it had begun, the column watching in wonder and delight as the line of sunlight raced across the meadow towards them. Moments later they were within its embrace, and Eofer glanced back along the long line of riders and chuckled to himself as he saw the mood lift. Smiles appeared on rain-lashed faces, as the standard-bearers shook the moisture from their banners and the breeze teased them out once more.

Ahead of them the dark stain that was The Oxen Way snaked across the countryside, its boundary ditches brim-full from the deluge that had gone before, and Eofer led them across and turned the head of his mount north.

The road was seldom travelled during the darker months. Trade between the Jutish kingdom to the north and those of the Saxons and others far to the south fell away, and barely a cart was seen, the drivers staring in wonder at the steel-clad magnificence of the warriors as they passed with a smile and a nod to labouring countrymen.

Within the hour the palisade that marked the line of Grim's Dyke hove into view, and soon they were corralling their horses and settling in its shadow. Fires flickered into life as men set to with fire-steel and kindling. Before long, the smell of roasting meat permeated the air as the first stars of the evening speckled the sky to the east.

Eofer called Penda to him, as the men began to gravitate towards the other members of their troop. He made a request as his father's duguth came across. 'Stand alongside me, will you? I want to go over the details of the attack, and it might help a few of the older men to see us together.' Penda made to protest, but Eofer held up a finger and continued. 'I know that they will follow me as an eorle and a man of reputation, but more than a few of my father's fighters knew me as a boy. It's natural that some may still see me that way without even realising that they are. There are a hundred ways in which this raid can turn out badly for us. I want them to see that we are all in this together.'

The pair scaled the stairway that had been cut into the bank by hands long ago and came out onto the crest of the fortification. As the sound of Penda's war horn carried across the heads of the gathering and faces turned towards them, Eofer ran his eyes along the line of the earthworks as the sun sank in the west. Twin ramparts, the southern higher than that on the northern side, snaked away across country towards the distant line of willow that marked the course of Grim's Brook. The brook ran west to the distant Muddy Sea, and he instinctively searched the horizon for any sign of light reflecting from the polished mail and helms of the ætheling's army that would be encamping there. The old timbers of the palisade were weathered and cracked by their exposure to a century of cold winters, and the hot summer sun. Peering across, Eofer could see the remains of the dyke that had guarded the old frontier for so many years. The sharpened stakes that had lined the rampart had long fallen into the bottom of the ditch, and brambles and hawthorn now grew where men had once clawed and died.

The eorle suddenly realised that the voices had stilled, and he came back from his musings to see that Penda was waiting for him to begin his address. Below them a sea of upturned faces turned towards him, and he felt a sudden wave of affection for these men who were sworn to serve his family unto death. They were, he had to admit to himself, an uncouth bunch. Some were already happily chewing at hunks of meat, their beards glistening with the fat that ran to coat it. But all seemed to be drinking, and every face reflected a grim determination that the war would be won, and the part they would play in it would be glorious. He pulled a smile and began as the daylight finally left the west, and the firelight cast long shadows all around.

'I know that most of you already have a good idea of what we are doing here, but I will outline what is expected of us this night and assign men to their tasks.' He glanced towards the west and turned back with a smile. 'I have just been looking at the work of our ancestors, those great men of old who overcame Jutes, Danes, War-Beards and Myrgings, carving out a motherland for our people. It is not by chance that I chose to rest at this place before our attack.' Eofer swept a hand across the place where the men had congregated. 'This is the very place where King Wihtlæg turned back the invasion of our land by the tyrant, Amleth. For three days the Jute attacks broke upon these walls like storm-driven waves against a rocky headland until, judging the moment to perfection, the king of the English fell upon them. Pouring through the breach before you, the great king harried the Jutes as far as their horses would carry them, hewing them from behind so that as far as a man could ride in a day the road was littered with the corpses of the slain. For four generations, our forefathers have defended those lands until the gods showed them a better land as a reward for their vigour.'

He paused as the men settled, turning his gaze to the men of the fyrd. 'You men will relish the work we do more than most. King Eomær has discovered that a Jutish jarl named Wictgils invited the Danes to his hall at a place known simply as The Crossing, there to launch the raid that caused so much misery last autumn. This Wictgils,' he went on as the ceorls exchanged looks of excitement and determination, 'thought it a good bargain to exchange horses and English lives for gold and silver. *I* know that, despite what he thought he had done at the time, he had made a bargain that would cost him his life.' Eofer paused again and lowered his voice for effect. 'The faces I see before me now are not the faces of a cowed and beaten people. The heart of a bear beats within the breast of every Englishman, be he king or ceorl. The time has come to take your vengeance for the nights and days you men spent chasing this wolf pack of Danes that had been flung into your midst; ever watchful of the sky, lest a line of smoke tell the tale of another hall burned—another family slaughtered. Each man guiltily asking the gods to drive the raiders towards another man's family, sparing his own from their violence while he was away serving his lord and unable to protect them.' He looked at the faces of the fyrdmen and saw that most had lowered their gaze and knew it to be true. Judging the moment to be right, he slipped down the bank and walked among them. 'I will not blame you if you did. But now you have the chance to repay the Jutes for their greed.' They followed him with their eyes, and Eofer could see that the raid had taken on a more profound meaning. No longer were they riding merely out of a duty owed to king and ealdorman; a chance for plunder.

The young thegn took up a cup of ale from the ground and sank the contents. Wiping his mouth with the back of his hand, he spoke again as the short, sharp bark of a badger call drifted across to them from a nearby grove. 'When Shining Mane returns to the east two days hence, we take the blood-price for their treachery. Bring to mind the faces of the dead you buried, and give thanks to the gods that they saw fit to make you spearmen.'

22

Osbeorn pulled the heavy woollen cloak tighter and spoke in an undertone to the fyrdman. 'Here, friend, loan me that travelling hat for a while and I promise that you will have a tale to tell your grand bairns when you are old and grey.' Despite his confusion, the farmer whipped off his tatty old leather headpiece and held it forward. The duguth smiled his thanks and forced it onto his head. 'A bit tight,' he said, 'but it will do nicely.' His features now deep in the shadow cast by the wide brim, the ceorls caught the merest hint of a smile on the big warrior's face before he turned and was swallowed by the night.

Spearhafoc was waiting for him near the tree line, and she hauled her tunic over her head at his approach and draped it across a bush. Her upper body shone pale in the iron grey light of the predawn, and Osbeorn pulled a face and tossed her a spear. 'A bit scrawny, but you'll have to do, battle-maiden. Your tits are pert at least,' he smirked. 'Like little puppies.' Rolling her eyes, the youth slipped the bow over her head and rearranged the tawny feathers of the sparrowhawk fixed in her hair. 'Can we get this over with?' she sighed wearily. 'There are a hundred and fifty men ogling me at the moment, and my little puppies are freezing.'

The pair slipped from cover and set off along the road that led past the hall to the causeway. Osbeorn used the heavy gar as a staff, placing the heel deliberately as he went. He had borrowed the showy spear from his lord and, failing the timely arrival of a raven or two, it was the final piece of his hoped-for deception.

Eofer and Imma Gold had scouted the area as the warband waited patiently on the reverse slope of the hill, readying weapons and nerves for the coming fight. Their thegn had returned with the encouraging news that it appeared that the Jutes felt safe enough in their lands to leave a solitary warrior to guard the important crossing place. Nevertheless, Osbeorn's eyes flicked out to the left and right as he closed on the warrior, now fully in view by the light of a brazier, as he rose to challenge them. A gust of wind blew down the valley from the fjord away to the east, and Osbeorn's stomach churned as he felt the farmer's hat shift and lift from his head as the breeze got under the wide brim. Burying his chin to avert disaster, the English pair were past the dark outline of the hall and moving into the full light of the watchman's fire, and Osbeorn flicked his eyes up in time to see the moment when the lone Jute recognised the pair who had appeared suddenly from the shadows. He kept his voice low as he hailed the man, and fought to stifle a snigger as the warrior's jaw gaped, and the blood drained from his features.

'The norns stand poised to snip your life-thread, War-Jute. Grip your sword hilt and my battle-maiden will guide you to my hall.'

Eofer's duguth fought against the overwhelming desire to increase his pace as the Jute did as the god bade him. The man must recover from his surprise soon, he knew, and he must not be allowed the chance to alert those in the nearby hall to the danger that was stealthily encircling them.

Osbeorn fixed his stare on the Jute's expression and the very instant that the man began to doubt the evidence of his eyes the gar shot forward to pierce his throat.

'IsN'T this the bit where an owl glides across the clearing, and we all kiss our hammers and wonder at the portent?' Penda gripped Hemming's sleeve and gasped. 'Thrush, you fool. There it is, look what you have done!' Hemming's smile fled as he dropped his eyes to scan the clearing beneath the hill. The others glanced away as they stifled a laugh at the fear that showed in his face. 'Where? I can't see it.' Hemming turned back to be confronted with a circle of smirking warriors. 'Oh, funny, you lot are,' he sniffed. 'Let's see how hard you laugh when Woden really does stride across the battlefield and taps you on the shoulder with his spear.'

Eofer returned from the tree line and took in the scene with a glance. 'When you lads have finished having fun, I will start the war.'

'It's the right place then, lord?'

'Unless you know another hall that sits beside a half mile long causeway?' Eofer snapped irritably. 'In which case, lead on Penda.'

The eorle's comment drew the humour from the moment, as had been intended, and Eofer threw them an icy stare. 'You men are the best of the best. Just because you have the experience and ability to fight your way out of almost any situation, it does not follow that every man who rode with us to this place has the same,' he hissed. 'We have a hundred fyrdmen with us who have just discovered that they are to abandon their farms and move their families across the sea on the king's say-so.' He exhaled in a conscious attempt to calm his temper as the duguth grew shamefaced. 'Let's keep on our toes,' he said as the anger left him. 'The ætheling has chosen us from all the men of the northern Wolds to spearhead this attack. Let's show him that he was not mistaken in his choice.'

Hemming broke the ice as the others shifted uncomfortably. 'Are there any more guards, lord?'

He shook his head. 'None that we could see. But there is at least one dog in the courtyard. I have told the Allfather to stay by the causeway,' he joked as his mood began to lighten, 'and returned the grateful battle-maiden's shirt. I sent her to silence the hound. She'll kill it from distance with a single shot.'

Eofer untied the bindings known as peace bands from the hilt of Gleaming, and the demeanour of the warriors changed instantly as they followed suit. The action had driven any thoughts of humour from the men and concentrated their minds on the fighting to come.

Penda spoke again. 'It's to be a burning then, lord?'

Eofer nodded. 'It may not be very honourable, but it is what this Wictgils and his Jutes deserve.' He glanced back into the shadows and saw that the leading men of the fyrd had come forward, waiting silently in groups to take their revenge. He spoke to the duguth again. 'You heard these men describe the results of the Danish raid. The fire-blackened bodies of women reduced to the size of children by the heat of the flames, children shrivelled to little more than the size of bairns.' Eofer indicated the fyrdmen with a flick of his head. 'Go and gather your chicks and take up the positions you have been assigned.'

He peered to the east, where the faintest line of light lay on the earth's rim. The timing was perfect, and he looked back to the hall in the clearing below, checking the deep shadows for any movement that could indicate that the English war-band had been seen. As he watched, the shaft of an arrow cut the air. But no noise came, and Eofer raised his eyes to take in his surroundings before the mayhem began. This would be the final time that an English *here* would fight in these lands.

The hall of Wictgils stood on a spur raised above the level of the water meadow. The roadway traced this firmer land, leading past the hall to the marsh and river beyond. A series of wooden causeways had been constructed to carry travellers to the nearby town, the shabby collection of huts, and the nearby dark outlines of fishing boats drawn up on the strand telling the tale of the settlement's main reason for existence. Wictgils' hall was the only building of any note in sight, and it was plain to the English eorle that the stranglehold that his opponent had on The Crossing was absolute. The wide river valley snaked away inland, its floor a mishmash of water meadows, swamps and ponds, studded with stands of alder and goat willow. Away to the north, the jagged edge of the tree covered hills was hardening by the moment as Shining Mane hauled her charge from the east. It was time to strike.

Eofer turned and raised his spear. Already slick and bloodstained from Osbeorn's attack on the lone guard, the leaf-shaped blade glimmered as the first of the day's light crept along the valley sides to penetrate the canopy. Within moments the first men appeared over the crest of the ridge, flaming brands held low in a final effort at concealment. Hemming came up and handed a torch to his lord as the lights cascaded down through the shadows like a meteor shower.

Emerging from the tree line, the duguth led the youth and their allotted ceorls to the left and right as they doubled across the track to encircle the hall.

Eofer glanced across to Osbeorn, still holding his position at the head of the causeway, and was pleased to see that the youth, Porta and Edwin, were hurrying across with a dozen of the fyrd to buttress the position there. Spearhafoc appeared from the rear of the hall, an arrow nocked and ready to loose, and despite the urgency of the moment Eofer took the time to nod to her in thanks. No yelp of pain, nor warning bark, had broken the stillness of the dawn air to send the inhabitants within the hall reaching for their weapons. He saw the body of the animal in the dust—a single shaft passing through its head, with a dark stain pooling beneath it.

The hall was much like his own had been before he had reduced it to a pile of ash and blackened beams. Its north-south orientation was sensible in its exposed position, helping to reduce the effects of the harsh winter winds and hot summer sun. Wisps of vapour rose into the chill morning air from the great ridge line of the roof, as the returning sun lanced down the fjord to warm the age-blackened thatch.

Eofer pointed with his spear as eager faces turned his way. 'There.'

Hemming and Penda drew up facing the heavy oak door and the hearth troop formed up to either side, raising their shields to form a wall as scores of the fyrdmen gathered to their rear. Secure in the knowledge that Wictgils' hall held only the single entrance, Eofer strode around the perimeter of the hall, placing knots of his youth backed up by a dozen men of the fyrd at intervals around the walls. Returning to the long front wall, he nodded to himself in satisfaction as he saw the mass of English warriors assembled there and the look of determination on their faces. Exchanging a look of determination of his own with the men of the combined hearth troops, he hefted his shield and took up the position of ord, the very tip of the formation. The sun had cleared the horizon to the east and its steely light had moved down to paint the door as he motioned with his spear. Several fyrdmen had been tasked with removing the thatch from a small boathouse that squatted near the causeway, and they hurried forward to pile the tinder against the door as the first signs of movement inside came to their ears. Transferring his spear to his shield hand, Eofer took the brand from Hemming and tossed it into the kindling. Fronds of flame appeared as the fire took hold, and Eofer moved forward to call on the owner of the hall.

'Wictgils!'

At the sound of their leader's summons, those men brandishing torches moved around the hall, touching flame to the eves before tossing the brands high up on to the thatch. As the fire took hold and dirty black smoke began to billow into the rapidly lightening sky, the sound of frenzied movement came from within the hall as the Jutish warriors there rushed to their arms. Within moments the door was pulled inward by an unseen hand and a voice answered from the gloom.

'I am Wictgils. Who seeks to burn me in my hall?'

Eofer stepped forward and swung his shield up. It was not unknown for an arrow to fly from the shadows in such a situation, and he was aware of Spearhafoc moving into position to cover him, a shaft nocked and ready to loose in a heartbeat. Despite the smoke that was being drawn into the building through the open door, Eofer could see the glint of mail and arms within as the warriors there clustered about their lord. The sun was directly behind the English, their long shadows stretching to fill the space before them, and Eofer felt a stab of satisfaction, confident now that the low orb must be blinding to those within.

'I am Eofer Wonreding, known as king's bane, an English thegn. I have been sent by King Eomær to repay a debt.'

The muffled sound of choking came from those within the

doorway as the smoke thickened, but Wictgils answered clearly. 'Your king owed me nothing before you burned my hall. Let us come out and defend ourselves or promise to build me another, and I will let you go, king's bane.'

Eofer snorted at the man's bluster. 'You are in no position to make demands, Jute. You brought this fate upon yourself when you sold English lives for Danish silver. My king has learnt of the part that you played in the raids last autumn, and I have been sent as the instrument of his vengeance.'

The sound of urgent muttering carried from the hall despite the increasing roar of the flames there. Eofer risked a quick glance at the roof. The fire had taken a firm grip now, and flames and smoke were cleaving the ridge line like the bow wave of a ship.

'Let my people come out, king's bane, and I will accept my wyrd is to die here.'

A low growl came from the fyrdmen, and Eofer recognised that the men there were in no mood to take pity on the inhabitants of the hall, be they women, bairn or thræl.

'The men at my back spent blood-month chasing a murderous band of Danes about the Wolds. Hall burning Danes; Danes who were moving too fast to take captives.' He hawked and spat in disgust. 'These men spent the time of sacrifices raking through embers to retrieve the little that the flames had not consumed of their loved ones and neighbours. I sense no desire within them to forgive the man who sold their lives for a casket of silver, nor his people. I doubt that they refused the profit from your deal, they can share the cost.'

Eofer narrowed his eyes as he saw a flicker of movement within the hall, and he braced as the door was suddenly wrenched inwards. Drawing Gleaming from its scabbard with a sweep of his arm, he cried out a command to the men behind as he realised what was about to happen.

'Daroth!'

A heartbeat later a huge warrior burst through the smoke and flames screaming his war-cry. As Eofer moved forward, a shadow passed across the pair as the throwing spears he had ordered released arced across, inches from his head. The darts fell in a concentrated pattern within the doorway just as Wictgils' hearth-warriors emerged into the light. With the rising sun full in their faces and the thick smoke curling about them, the Jutes failed to see the danger. Within moments their charge had faltered as the doorway was blocked by a bloodied heap and burning thatch. Eofer swung at the Jute, hoping to catch him before he settled, but the warrior parried the blow with his shield and stabbed back with his sword. The strike was well-made and Eofer twisted his neck to one side as the blade slid by only inches away. Both men had failed to connect in the opening moves, and they withdrew as if by mutual consent and began to circle warily. The eorle spoke as he sought to confirm that the man he faced was the jarl, and unnerve him at the same time. 'Wictgils?' The man gave a curt nod, never taking his eye from the Englishman's sword, and Eofer immediately knew that the Jute would be a tough opponent. He sailed a different tack as he sought an advantage. 'I think that I can hear your woman calling you.'

The terror filled screams of women and girls were coming from the hall as those trapped within realised that there was to be no escape for them. Above the doomed occupants, the roofline sagged as the flames ate into the structure, and a sudden whoo-mph told both men that part had collapsed inward in a gout of flames and wildly spinning sparks.

A look of anguish lasted barely an eye-blink, as a flash of cold hatred swept Wictgils' face. The jarl lunged forward instinctively, but Eofer skipped aside as an animal bellowed in fear and the heat intensified.

He cocked an ear. 'Yes, I think that I can hear her,' he smiled with a savagery that, in truth, he did not really feel. It was a necessary act of war that he could not deny those who had suffered a similar fate at the hands if the Danes. Had it not been for the greed of the man who now stood before him, there were fyrdmen present who would still have families of their own. Eofer knew that no feelings of pity would cloud his thoughts if Astrid and Weohstan had suffered such a fate.

The Jute's eyes flared, and a snarl swept across his features as he made the wild lunge that Eofer hoped his goading would produce. Twisting past the blade, Eofer rolled his wrist, pulling Gleaming low with a backhanded sweep that bit deeply into Wictgils' calf. The man let out a roar of pain and frustration that he had allowed Eofer's provocation to draw him into a rash attack, and he settled back into a fighting stance as Eofer risked a quick glance at the results of his handiwork.

A long ragged tear had been cut into the rear of Wictgils' trews, and the bindings that gathered them were hanging loose where they too had been cut, dragging on the ground and threatening to trip the Jute at every step. Below the slash, Eofer could see that the cloth was blood-soaked, and both men knew that the strike would soon prove debilitating as the muscle stiffened, and the blood loss began to tell. Experience gained on the battlefields of the North told both men that time was now against the Jute, and Eofer withdrew a pace and let his opponent come on.

Seeing his lord injured spurred a warrior to brave the furnace-like flames that gripped the doorway. The blazing form caught Eofer's eye as it emerged, bellowing its death cry, but two arrows flew in quick succession and Eofer discounted the threat, confident in his youth's prowess with her chosen weapon. As several spears flew overhead to finish the job, Wictgils made his move. Certain now that he was to die here, alone in the shadow of his burning hall, the Jute suddenly launched his shield at the Engle. Taken unawares, Eofer was too late to dodge aside, and the iron rim of the board slammed into his midriff. In a heartbeat, Wictgils was upon him, gripping his sword in both hands and bringing it down in a mighty sweep. Winded by the shield strike, Eofer instinctively pulled his blade across, deflecting the blow. As the heavy blade glanced off the side of his helm to bury its tip in the dust, the energy of the attack carried Wictgils onward and Eofer seized his chance. Flicking Gleaming upright, he gripped the hilt tightly, bracing the blade as the Jute's unstoppable momentum delivered the jarl's death wound. Eofer watched as Wictgils' eyes widened in horror as he saw what must follow, but he was powerless to avoid his fate as the sword tip met his chest. A moment of resistance, and Eofer felt the links of Wictgils' mail shirt buckle and give way as the man's great size told against him. The ancestral blade slipped easily into his the jarl's chest, and Eofer rolled away as the man fell to the ground and a tortured rattle escaped his throat.

The eorle sprang to his feet as the watching warriors roared their acclaim at his victory over the Jutish giant. But the shouts of triumph began to peter out, and Eofer saw to his surprise that Wictgils had raised himself to his knees. The jarl spat a giant gobbet of blood at the English shield wall in a last act of defiance as Eofer walked across. With a final scowl at the cause of so much pain and loss in his homeland, he placed his foot on the man's shoulder, and the jarl gritted his teeth against the pain as the eorle reclaimed the bloody blade. Eofer's eyes moved up to Wictgils' helm, and he saw the dancing warriors who marked the man as a member of the wolf brotherhood. Their eyes met, and the Englishman indicated the Jute's sword with a flick of his eyes. Relief swept the jarl's features as he reached forward with the last of his strength and his bloody fingers curled around the hilt. It was the final act of a dying man. Eofer took a pace back as a crimson flow gushed from Wictgils' lips, and a pink froth bubbled from his wound as the air from his punctured lung mixed with his lifeblood.

As the jarl slumped at his feet, Eofer turned to the men of the fyrd and called out above the roaring of the flames. 'Any man who suffered loss in the autumn raids. Now is the moment to wet your spears with the blood of the man who caused your grief.'

23

Imma feinted left with his spear and the Jute whipped his shield across to cover his flank. As quick as a lash, the spear came back to sink into the man's groin. He fell with a scream, and Imma withdrew the blade and jabbed again. Watching from the riverbank, his lord pursed his lips and nodded. It was good work. The latest attack was faltering, and the English jeered as their fiend moved their shields to the sides and backed warily away from the spear-hedge. A momentarily exposed knee was instantly punished, as an arrow flew across the gap to add to the injured. But even as his friends moved to cover the warrior and help him hobble back to the safety of the town, Eofer knew that it was unlikely that any other shafts would follow.

The day had been long, and he knew that the supply of arrows left available to the bowmen was dwindling fast. He squinted up at the sun as it rolled across the sky to the south. It was now late afternoon and the English force had watched as men came from the north to fill the bank opposite ever since word had spread of their attack. Alerted by the great column of greasy black smoke that had boiled up from the hall and its doomed inhabitants, the Jutes had been gathering in numbers since mid-morning.

Eofer turned to Octa as they swigged from their water skins. 'How many do you think there are?'

His duguth puffed out his cheeks as he gazed across the river from his place on the log. 'A hundred? Could be more,' he volunteered. 'They are only the ones we can see. There could be as many again, hidden by the shacks over there. What I want to know,' he continued with a sidelong glance, 'is what they are hoping to gain by making these half-arsed attacks.'

Eofer reached forward and picked up a short stick from the ground. Smoothing a patch of dust with his foot, he marked out a long straight line. 'This is the river before us, and here we are,' he said as he stabbed the centre of the line. 'Over here,' he said, reaching across to his left, 'there is another causeway across the marshland. It's about a dozen miles inland, but its even longer than the one in front of us. It's the only good crossing place for miles around, so of course it carries The Oxen Way. That's where Penda led the dozen riders you saw leave earlier.'

Octa nodded that he understood. 'The very road that we need to use to return home,' he muttered. 'They are keeping us busy here, so they can throw an army across and cut us off.' He pulled a pained expression. 'That doesn't sound too healthy, lord. If I didn't know better, I might have suggested that we make tracks while we still can. But of course,' he grinned, 'there is a loki-cunning scheme that I am as yet unaware of.'

Eofer laughed at his friend's description. If all went well, Haystack's plan was worthy of the trickster god. He looked up and whistled as Imma Gold walked back from the causeway and one of Wonred's duguth replaced him as ord.

Imma skirted the old guards' shelter and jogged across. 'I was about to explain to Octa what, I hope, will come next,' Eofer said as he came up, 'now that we have repaid Wictgils for his part in the Danish raids.'

He looked across to the men of the fyrd. Driven by a steady breeze that blew in from the nearby fjord, the majority of Wictgils' hall had quickly become an angry blaze, the flames licking at the nearby tree line as they were driven to the west. By mid-morning all that remained had been the heavier oak beams of the frame itself, and the fyrdmen had delighted in attaching ropes to their horses and bringing them down in a cloud of ash. Ever since then they had been raking through the debris, and the pile of silver and gold, twisted and molten into unrecognisable shapes by the heat, that had steadily grown had surprised even Eofer. Obviously, he had mused, the Danes paid well, and he had promised to share out the spoils equally among the men of the fyrd like any worthy lord. Now that the silver had been collected and retribution visited on the Jutish jarl, the ceorls were looking increasingly eager to be away. He threw the stick to the ground and pulled himself to his feet.

'It will be dark in what, two hours?'

The pair glanced across to the west and nodded in agreement.

'I'll let them think that they have succeeded in holding us here, but as soon as it is fully dark we leave. We have given the thegns a full day to muster their fyrdmen,' he said. 'We will let them believe that they are chasing us south.'

'I'll remain as a rearguard with a few men,' Octa volunteered. 'Otherwise, they will be across the causeway and on our tails before we know it. It's a long ride home, lord, and we have no remounts.' Eofer nodded his agreement. 'Imma, I want you to take a couple of men and ride to Penda. Double back to The Oxen Way and head north, you'll be there within the hour. Stay with him and leave this other causeway at dusk. Meet us at the place where you joined the road, and we'll head back south together.'

A flurry of activity drew their attention across to the smoking pile that was all that remained of Wictgils' hall. The fyrdmen there had stopped raking through the last of the ashes and were peering back along the road. Within moments the reason for their interest hove into view and Eofer exchanged a look with his men. 'It looks like our plans may be about to change,' he muttered.

They walked across to the roadway and waited for the rider to clatter to a halt. The horse's flanks glistened with a fine sheen of sweat, and the flaring of its nostrils told the men that it had been ridden hard. Eofer waited patiently as the rider slipped from his saddle and came up.

'There is a large force of Jutes approaching down The Oxen Way, lord. We couldn't see the end of the column, but judging by the number of banners at its head, it must be a large one.'

Eofer nodded that he understood. 'Could you see what the banners were? Did you get an idea of the composition of this army, Frithgar?'

'The White Horse, hildbeacn of the Jutes flies at its head.'

Eofer's eyes widened in surprise. 'King Osea is here?'

'And at least two of their jarls, lord,' Frithgar added. 'We saw the war-banners of Hrethmund and Heorogar tucked in behind that of the king.'

'And Penda?' Eofer probed. 'What are his plans?'

Frithgar licked his lips as he struggled to reply. The mad dash and the dust of the road had robbed his mouth of moisture, and he smiled gratefully as Octa handed him his water skin. Taking a mouthful, he swilled it gratefully and swallowed. 'Penda is out of sight in a grove of alder. He said that he would remain there until the Jutes began to move across the causeway and then return here unless he receives word that we have already left for the South.'

A great roar made them look across to the town, and the Englishmen could see the Jutish warriors there waving spears; beating their shields as they stared away to the west. The road that led away to link up with The Oxen Way followed the line of higher, dryer ground there and was visible from the northern bank. It could only mean one thing, and Eofer's fears were confirmed a moment later as Penda led his band from the cover of the trees and into the clearing.

Eofer's mind raced as he scanned the meadow for a place to draw up his troop. Like any good war leader, the eorle had already scouted out a sound defensive position to fall back upon if a hostile force came against them in numbers. A mile or so to the east of the meadow, the land began to rise in a series of gentle hills. One of them was steeper than the others and, hemmed in on either side by dense woodland, the crest of the hill was perfect for his needs. As he was about to give the order to mount up, Penda reached him, and Eofer's heart sank at the concern he saw there.

'Scouts are right behind me and the king not far behind them, riding hard.'

'How long do we have?'

Penda slipped from the saddle and unhooked his shield. 'Just time for a piss if you are quick.' Slipping his hand into the grip, he slapped his horse on the rump and the animal trotted away. Turning back, the duguth rolled his shoulders, warming muscles as he prepared himself for war. 'Where do you want me, lord?'

Knowing now that he would never reach the ridge line he had hoped to defend, Eofer's eyes were already scouring the meadow for any sign of a feature that would give him the edge in a fight. He had to admit to himself, the search looked to have been in vain. The roadway crossed from the town opposite and came straight on for a hundred yards or so before arcing away where it reached the tree line and following the line of the valley to the west. The land rose in a gentle gradient as it approached the wood, so a shield wall anywhere on the meadow would face an enemy charging downhill. He considered forming a barrier using the charred timbers from the hall as a bulwark, but quickly discounted it. They were out of time, and he made the only sensible choice available.

'Fall back on the causeway.' He turned to his duguth. 'Gather the best of the youth and take them onto the bridge like you said. Octa,' he continued as he held the man's gaze, 'hold that position, whatever they throw against you. I will try to send you further help when we know what we are facing, but you *must* keep those in the town from attacking our rear.'

Octa nodded and rushed off to round up his chosen companions, as Eofer anxiously flicked a look at the place where the Jutes would emerge from the tree cover. A brace of culvers rose into the air with a clatter and coasted away to the north. Any man who had hunted knew that wood pigeons were easily spooked, and the sight caused a look of alarm to spread among the group. Eofer knew the enemy were upon them, and he hurried across to retrieve his shield as he called to the duguth. 'Arm yourselves, quickly. Form yourselves into a screen about the entrance to the causeway.'

Looking across to the remains of the hall, he saw to his horror that the fyrdmen were still standing in groups, discussing the goings-on as if they were at a summer fair. He cupped his hand to his mouth as he ran and bellowed an order. 'Fyrd! Grab your weapons and fall back on the bridge, now!'

As he did so the first of the enemy burst into view at the head of the meadow and, seeing the men spread out before them, kicked in their heels and came on at a gallop. Screaming their war cries, the Jutes were lowering their spears before most of the men had realised that their enemy had arrived, and within a heartbeat the Jutes were among them. Stabbing out to the left and right, the horsemen wheeled and turned as the terrified ceorls scattered like startled deer towards the river. Eofer drew Gleaming and shouted across to Hemming as he pounded towards the fight. *'Thrush!'* He saw his duguth begin to draw his sword and call to others before he turned his attention back to the fight.

Despite the ferocity of the Jutish attack the fyrdmen had begun to recover, and dozens were now fighting back as the riders dropped their spears, pulling swords from scabbards as they slashed down at shoulders and heads. Very few ceorls wore anything more than a toughened leather cap for protection; a shirt of mail was far beyond the means of even the wealthiest. Once the enemy swords had cut through the shaft of their spears, the men would be helpless, and Eofer discarded his shield to close with the fighting as quickly as he could.

A horseman broke free from the crush and wheeled his mount, swinging his blade above his head as he prepared to re-enter the fray. Eofer was upon him before he could strike again, Gleaming taking the man in the small of the back as the eorle gripped the blade with both hands and brought it across in a powerful sweep. Like all scouts, the man wore no mail or heavy armour and Eofer felt his spine snap as Gleaming bit deeply.

Before the Jute had fallen from his saddle, Eofer was past

him. Another was there, the horse wide-eyed in the din, and he drove his sword into its great chest and withdrew the bloody blade and ducked away. As the horse screamed in terror and staggered, Eofer parried a powerful downward strike from its rider as the man began to tumble from its back. He became aware that bodies were clustering around him and the thegn raised his sword to strike out before he froze as he saw that it was the men of the fyrd rallying to his side. He had become an island in the fighting, a focal point within the chaos as the men of the fyrd rushed to form a spear burh about their lord.

The attack began to falter as the resistance stiffened, and Eofer looked across as Hemming arrived with more seasoned warriors to bolster their position. He watched in admiration as the big man feinted a strike on a rider only to duck beneath the belly of his mount. Light flashed on steel as Hemming struck, rolling away on the far side as ropes of blueish entrails slipped to the grass in a steaming mess.

The leader of the scouts had seen enough, and Eofer watched as he pulled a horn from his battle-shirt and sounded a long, shrill note. Immediately, the remaining riders spurred their mounts away, revealing a battleground littered with the bloodied bodies of men and horses.

As the Jutes reformed at the head of the meadow, Eofer looked about him. A quick tally told him that seven of the fyrd had paid for their bravery with their lives, while at least a further three were carrying wounds of varying severity. Four of the scouts lay dead, three beside the bodies of their mounts, and Eofer nodded in grim satisfaction, it could have been a lot worse. If all the ceorls had broken and run, they would have been cut down from behind before the warriors could come to their aid. The meadow would have become a killing ground, robbing him of a good part of his force before the fighting had even begun.

The fyrdmen were looking to him for direction, and he gave them a smile of encouragement. 'Well fought, lads. We gave them a bloody nose.' The faces surrounding him brightened immediately at the praise from their leader, and he indicated the causeway with a jerk of his head. 'Quickly, gather any weapons and take yourselves across to the bridge. Penda is forming a shield wall there.'

As they moved away, Hemming came across, wiping the blood from his blade on a fistful of grass. The pensive look on his weorthman's features told the eorle that it would take far more than a few words of comfort to reassure the grizzled veteran that all would be well.

'We've already lost the horses,' he sniffed. 'We should have brought them down here sooner.'

Eofer's face twisted into a grimace at the warrior's thinly veiled criticism. He was right, of course. The horses had been left at the top of the meadow while the hall blazed to destruction. No animal is comfortable around flames, and Wictgils' hall had roared like a dragon in the steady breeze that had blown in from the sea. Later, he had allowed himself to become distracted by the fighting at the causeway, and he had forgotten to order their mounts brought down to them. It was a simple mistake, but one that could easily now cost them their lives, and he acknowledged the fact with a nod. 'You're right. The error was mine, but it is done now and cannot be undone, however much I wish it.'

The Jutish scouts suddenly cried out in acclaim, raising their bloodied weapons aloft as the first of their main force emerged from the forest edge and trotted across their front. Moments later, Eofer and Hemming watched as King Osea broke cover and moved to the centre of the slope beneath the white horse hildbeacn of Juteland. The jarls, Hrethmund and Heorogar moved to either flank of their king as horsemen held their own banners at their side, and the group walked their mounts down the slope as the trees to the west spewed forth a tide of mailed warriors.

'Time to go, lord,' Hemming muttered as the first of the Jutes chased the English horse guards away into the trees, moving across to deny them any chance of reaching their mounts. Eofer failed to respond, and Hemming plucked at his sleeve as he sought to remove his lord from harms way. 'Eofer—lord. It's time to rejoin the others.'

An insolent smile curled at the corners of his mouth, and the thegn shot his duguth a wink. 'Let's go and ask for our horses back, Thrush.'

Hemming's mouth fell open before a smile crept across his features, and the deep rumble of a laugh came from the man at the insanity of his lord's words.

Eofer led the way past the body of the scout he had unhorsed with his second attack. Thrown by his fatally wounded mount, the scout had been stabbed into meat as the fyrdmen had crowded around like a wolf pack at the kill, and the grass there was slick with the man's blood. Hemming skipped around it as Eofer started to angle across the slope. King Osea was already within hailing distance, and Hemming watched out the corner of his eye as the royal party looked on with mounting bemusement. Eofer led them across the face of the Jute battle line and pushed his way between the mounted warriors lined up there before speaking in a tone that he hoped would sound far more confident than he felt.

'Where is your horse, Thrush?'

Hemming grabbed the reins of the nearest animal and slipped it from the line.

'Don't push them too hard, lord,' he murmured. 'They can't stay shocked forever.'

Eofer had slipped the reins of his mount and stood glaring up at the nearest Jute riders. They looked for direction from their king, and Eofer was relieved to see Osea give a slight nod to let him through. Back in the open, the pair mounted and guided the horses across towards King Osea and the jarls.

Eofer reined in before the king and inclined his head.

'Health, and happiness, to King Osea. I am Eofer Wonreding. I come to ask you for the return of our horses so that we may be on our way.'

The king's mouth slowly creased into a smile, and he shook his head as the jarls glowered at his side.

'Eofer Wonreding, the aptly named bane of kings,' he said as he lifted his chin and ran his eyes across the blackened scar that was all that remained of his jarl's hall. 'You seem to have developed an unhealthy liking for hall burning. If you had lived long enough,' he added with malice, 'perhaps you might have become Eofer hall burner after your exploits here and in Daneland.'

Eofer inclined his head. 'Thank you, but I like king's bane. I think that I will keep it. As for the length of my life-thread,' he shrugged, 'that is in the hands of the three old ladies, as are all. We need not trouble the old girls here, their work can cease if that is our wish. Jarl Wictgils sold English lives for silver, I was sent here by King Eomær to pay the balance owed to him and his kin.' Eofer glanced back down to the ruin of the building. 'As you can see, the debt has been paid in full.'

The king raised his brow and Eofer could see Heorogar bristle at his side.

'The women and children?'

'Are being welcomed below by their English sisters,

burned and slaughtered by the Danes who came to this place to be supplied with horses and hospitality in exchange for that silver.'

Jarl Heorogar suddenly urged his mount forward and came abreast of Eofer. Leaning forward, he shook with hatred as he spat the words. 'You talk of blood price and kinship. Know that my sister was wife to Wictgils and that I hold you responsible for her death.'

Eofer copied Heorogar's action and spoke evenly as hands moved to sword hilts and the men stared at each other with ill-disguised loathing. 'Then I think that you will agree that she made a poor choice of husband,' he replied, his eyes as cold and hard as flint. Before the man could respond, Eofer sawed at his reins and turned into Heorogar's horse, making it skitter sideways. As the Jarl fought to bring it back under control, Eofer turned back to the king. 'It would seem that we are to fight after all, just when we were starting to get along. I wonder,' he said as the horse moved away. 'How many men have killed two kings in battle?'

24

A distant rumble of laughter split the night air and Eofer came awake instantly. Bleary-eyed from the sleep that he had never expected to have, he knuckled them and blinked as he attempted to focus.

'There are no threatening movements, lord,' Octa spoke softly. 'They are still drinking.'

Eofer settled back and rubbed his face as vigorously as he could without waking the others. He glanced across to the east and was surprised to see the first signs of the dawn as his mind began to replay the events of the previous evening. The grey tinge to the horizon could very well be his last, and Eofer watched with newfound interest as the light there slowly widened into a band of iron.

Despite the presence of the Jutish Royal Army mere paces away, Eofer and Hemming had walked the horses unhurriedly back down the meadow to the English position. Slipping from the saddle near the scene of the skirmish with the scouts, he had retrieved his shield and driven the horse away with a slap of its rump.

The confrontation with King Osea and his jarls had eaten

up valuable time, as he had hoped that it would. The sun had been low in the west and, confident in his numbers, the old king had clearly decided to delay the attack until the following day. Every moment that he had snatched from the situation had helped. Sharing out the remaining food, he had posted guards as Jutish campfires had flickered into life like a hundred suns, and they had caroused into the night with all the vigour of men on the cusp of a crushing victory.

Osbeorn shifted and yawned as the first whiff of cooking drifted down to them from the head of the clearing. Raising his head, he sniffed the air, like a hound catching the scent. 'Bacon,' he sighed, 'the bastards. I can face a charging boar snout, no problem, but that's just cruel.'

Eofer chuckled. 'I have got some dried pork left if you feel up to a good chew.'

Their backs swayed gently in time as his duguth shook his head and replied.

'No, thanks, lord. I will wait until we take their camp and help myself.'

A round of sniggers rolled around the group and Eofer realised that they were all awake. Sat in a circle, resting against each other back-to-back, every movement was felt by the others; it was a rare night that anyone could slumber on once his friends began to stir. It was a trick that they had learned together while raiding in the depths of Britannia. With one duguth always on guard, Eofer and the remaining four could face in every direction, supporting each other as they dozed. The slightest movement would be felt by their hearth companions and any sudden movement would have the group instantly awake and reaching for their weapons.

Eofer looked over his shoulder and recognised the familiar outline of Imma Gold at the causeway, flanked by the dark figures of Crawa and his brother Hræfen. An untidy knot of fyrdmen made up a solid wall there. Satisfied that all was well, the eorle settled back.

'What would you eat if you could choose anything, Ozzy?' he spoke into the gloom.

'Anything?'

'Yes, if you could have anything to eat, now, what would it be?'

Osbeorn sighed as he thought, but Eofer could sense the amusement of his hearth troop through their backs as they imagined the torment that the question would be causing their friend. Finally, he said the word that they all knew that he would.

'Bacon…' As a rumble of laughter came from the others, Osbeorn went on. 'Bacon and pork are big things in my family. My cousin,' he continued as they all listened in amusement, 'puts bacon in bread.'

They all chuckled and a patter of laughter came from those in the fyrd nearest to them. It would seem that most were awake now that the sun had risen to light the edge of the fjord, its pale light dancing on the wave tops and throwing the troughs between into a jet-like blackness. Above them the first gulls glided and called, their raucous cries harsh in the chill air as the creatures of Middle-earth came back from their slumber.

Hemming sighed as he finally gave up any hope that he may have harboured of sleep. Once the men started to discuss food, he knew that only an enemy charge could stop them. 'Why does he do that?' he asked. 'That's daft.'

'He doesn't like his fingers getting greasy, Thrush,' Osbeorn offered as they all laughed again, 'or too hot.' Osbeorn's voice trailed away as the image came into his mind. 'Come to think of it,' he decided finally, 'he is a bit daft.'

Folk were beginning to rise now and make their way to

the riverbank to take the first piss of the day, but there was a tangible feeling of anticipation hanging in the air as Osbeorn defended his kinsman. 'It makes sense when you think about it, though, daft or not. Bacon can get really hot, especially the rind. Moreover, you can cram lots of rashers in if you use both hands to hold the bread. You get more that way.'

A great sigh went up as the real reason for his cousin's inventiveness was revealed.

'Your whole family are *swelgend*. You eat anything as long as there is plenty of it,' Hemming said. 'I am almost afraid to ask, but is there anything else this kinsman of yours sticks into a loaf?'

'Egg,' Osbeorn replied, 'sometimes with bacon too! Now that,' he conceded with a shrug, 'is definitely a bit daft.'

The first war horns sounded from the opposite end of the field, and they began to rise and reach for their weapons as an answering blast from the town drifted across. Eofer stretched and walked across to empty his bladder into the bulrushes as spearmen appeared at the head of the causeway opposite. Loosening his clothing, he relaxed as the flow arced away, and he threw a look across to Imma on the causeway. 'Early start, Goldy. Has it been quiet?'

Imma nodded. 'They have been moving about all night, but there has only ever been a few guards visible at the end of the causeway. They tried to lob a few arrows into us during the night, but they all fell well short, so I left everyone sleeping.'

Eofer finished and adjusted his clothing, walking across to his duguth as the men of his war-band rose and began to gather in their divisions. Every man knew his place, and the thegn was encouraged to see that their spirits seemed high, despite their desperate situation and lack of bacon. 'It's a trap,' he said as he pulled himself up onto the planking.

Imma raised his brow in mock surprise and threw his eorle a look of beatific innocence. 'Really, lord?' he gasped. 'The cunning bastards!'

Eofer snorted at his man's humour. 'If we had charged across there, we would have found the whole town waiting for us in arms. Trap a raiding force and leave it with an apparently lightly defended escape route.' He shook his head in disappointment at the obvious transparency of the Jutish plan. Only a fool would fall for such a ruse, and the Engle found that he was offended that they had even attempted to entice him across and onto the points of the waiting spears.

'But,' Imma countered as he correctly read his eorle's thoughts, 'if they are willing to underestimate us all day, we may yet live to see our beards turn grey.'

Eofer clapped him on the shoulder. 'You are right, this is going to be a great day, a day to test the scops' skill with words. Tell Ozzy to round up some men and relieve you here. Get your lads to grab something to eat before it's all gone. We have already given King Hrothgar and his Danes a Yule gift to remember. Today we strike the first blow in the year of fire and steel.'

The thegn unhooked his battle helm and settled it onto his head, fastening the leather bindings securely as he looked across to the northern bank. The war horns had done their work and the strand was teeming with warriors, all crowding down to the causeway. He gave a knowing snort as he thought of their night spent waiting for the panicked flight that never came as Osbeorn clattered on to the walkway with his party of men.

Eofer threw them a welcoming smile. 'How do I look?'

Osbeorn ran his eyes over him and shook his head. 'A bit grubby for a lord, but you'll have to do.'

Eofer chuckled to himself as Osbeorn set about placing

the men where they would be most useful to him. The position was vital for their defence, and Eofer decided to replace them as soon as he had made his battle speech with a party taken from his father's hearth troop.

Osbeorn's comment caused him to examine his war gear and, to his disappointment, he found that his duguth had been right, he *had* looked better. Spots of dried mud and blood still clung to his mail shirt from the fights against Wictgils and King Osea's scouts. The red quilted battle shirt that he wore beneath his mail was marked by smuts from the hall burning, and the legs of his trews were stained by the blood of the Jutish jarl. He had seen to his weapons, of course, and Gleaming was once again living up to its name and honed to a razor sharp edge. But the lining on the face of his shield had taken a glancing blow, and a small strip of leather hung loose, exposing the pale wood beneath. Looking up, he saw that Oswin was nearby, and he called the youth across.

'Oswin, check me over, will you? Remove the worst of the grime before I address the men.'

Eofer stood and regarded his forces as the youth scrubbed furiously at the worst of the grime. Penda had led the core of his men to the centre of the roadway, and was already set as ord. The remainder of the ealdorman's hearth troop had fanned out to either side, curving back to anchor themselves against the wetlands that backed up their position. The men of the fyrd were still organising themselves with their friends and kinsmen in the rear. Eofer estimated that there were enough men to form at least three ranks, with a stiffening to the centre and flanks, where the main thrust of the Jutish attacks could be expected. The roadway on which he was standing rose slightly as it approached the causeway, its edges canted to the east and west. It was the perfect position to set up his hildbeacn—with a commanding view of both the main battlefield on the meadow, and the fighting that would be taking place on the causeway itself as the men from the town attempted to fall upon their rear. While the youth of his troop fought to earn a reputation within the shield wall, the men of his duguth could cluster around him there, fulfilling the oath they had made to their lord, and acting as a flying reserve if any part of the wall came under intolerable pressure. At the head of the meadow, the Jutes appeared to have finished their breakfast and horses were being led forward as the warriors began to organise themselves for the attack that must come soon.

'That will have to do, Oswin,' he said. 'Give me a quick stanza for luck and I will address the men.'

Oswin stood back. 'A poem fit for an eorle in his war glory, lord,' he smiled as his mind worked on the rhyme. Soon the beginning came to him, and he set his face and began:

> 'Battle-play befits a thegn;
> bravery belongs to an eorle.
> Heft Gleaming, bear your shield forward,
> under steep helms in the press of enemies;
> slayer of warlords, doomed leaders…'

Eofer looked at him in amazement. 'Oswin, you have really come on.' The youth beamed happily. 'One of your father's youth, Edgar, has some training in wordcræft, lord. I have been pestering him to teach me all he knows ever since I found out. It's a sort of code,' he went on. 'Once you understand the structure, what scops call the metre of the wordplay, it becomes much easier. It's like another language, but once you grasp the basics, the rest follows on quickly.' Out of the corner of his eye, Eofer saw Hemming and Imma waiting for their orders. A brief look up at the top of the meadow confirmed that time was pressing.

'Oswin,' he said. 'Your father was a great warrior, but I think that your strength is a rarer quality. You will never have the strength of Thunor, but you can develop Woden's sharpness of mind. I want you to be my banner man today.' He fixed the youth with a stare as he explained the importance of the duty. 'Stand at my side and follow me wherever I go. You will be a key target for their bravest warriors, so you must promise to place the safety of the hildbeacn above that of your life, it is the beating heart of our war-band. Keep it upright at all times or the heart will go out of our men. Watch all that goes on in the battle, and you will have the floor of Eorthdraca to yourself when you recount the great deeds of this day before the king and his gesithas.'

Eofer left the shocked youth and paced across to the high point of the roadway as he looked to his men. 'Right, here. This is our position,' he declared as he stamped the earth. 'Oswin will be banner man and the five of us will form around him as a reserve. My father's men far outnumber us, so they will bear the brunt of the attack.'

Leaving Hemming to organise them, Eofer hefted his shield and spear as he pushed his way through to the front of the wall and out into the dead land before them. As he turned to face the shield wall the white dragon was raised at the high point, and his heart leapt as the breeze gently unfurled it, the ruddy field a blaze in the early morning light. He paused as the front rank parted to allow Oswin to join his lord, the burning hart battle flag held proudly aloft.

The sun had fully risen now, and the light raked the meadow as a light wind plucked at the treetops. Above them, mackerel grey clouds pushed slowly to the west on a fitful breeze, their tails painted pink by the returning light.

Eofer ran his gaze along the line of brightly coloured shields: wolf heads, axes and dragons, as the familiar pre-battle thrill gripped him. He walked the line and the hubbub subsided as all heads turned his way.

'The day has dawned at last,' he smiled as he walked, locking eyes with each man as he came up, 'the very beginning of the day that you will remember for the rest of your lives.' Taunts drifted down to them from the Jutish battle line as he spoke, and he cocked his head to listen. One cry rose above the rest and a roar of laughter followed, but it was just too far away to hear, although the mocking tone to it was clear. He sniffed and shrugged. 'They think that they have already won, but they are mistaken. They have spent the night sinking ale and gambling away the fortunes that they expect to take from our bodies.' He paused to add weight to his words before setting his face and repeating his conclusion. 'But they are mistaken.'

Eofer searched the second rank and found a familiar face peering from beneath a dome of hardened leather. Stabbing out a finger, he called a question to his ceorl. 'Dægwulf, did I ever make you a promise?' The man smiled cheerfully, honoured to be chosen from among the sea of faces by his lord. 'Yes, lord. I came to you for help when an old wolf was taking my lambs. You promised that the wolf would die, and I had its pelt within the week.'

His finger moved on and he called out another. 'Beada, how about you?' The man stood taller as faces turned his way and he answered proudly. 'You promised to come to my daughter's wedding, lord. You showed me honour by bringing your wife and son along with fine gifts.' Eofer snorted at the memory. 'It was a good day,' he chuckled. 'It was the day that Osbeorn fell in the piss trench, and we had to form a chain and haul him out, as I recall.' The men of the war-band laughed and Osbeorn took a bow as faces turned his way.

'How is Æda?' Eofer asked.

'With bairn, lord,' Beada beamed as those around him slapped his back and wished them well.

'Then your grandson and my son will fight together when we are grey beards and warming our old bones beside the hearth, carving out a land for the Engle in Britain and keeping us old folk safe from Welsh spears.'

Eofer called out as he swept the gathering with his spear. 'Ask any man here who knows me, and they will tell you that I am a man of my word. My word, today, says that we will still hold this place of slaughter when Shining Mane gallops down in the west. These men,' he called as he pointed to the front rank, 'are not known as doughty men for nothing. They are the wall upon which the enemy tide will dash itself to pieces. Men of the fyrd, keep your shield straight and your head up. Mark your foe as he comes within range and strike firmly with your spear. Remember how we practised at the muster, feet anchored to the earth and shoulder to shoulder. Remain steadfast and we will take the day.'

A chorus of war horns split the air, and Eofer looked back to see that the Jutish horsemen had finally clustered into some semblance of order. Beyond, the gaudy banners and draco battle-standards of the enemy hung limp in the shelter of the trees that surrounded them as the warriors there clashed spears against shields and their chants filled the air.

As the flags were dipped to herald the attack and the horses moved forward, Eofer exchanged a nod with Penda and took his place beneath the white dragon.

25

'How many do you have left?'

Spearhafoc tipped the rim of her quiver forward and pulled a face. 'Five, lord.'

Eofer plucked at her sleeve and led her to the highest point of the rise. 'One will be enough, eagle eye.'

The youth allowed herself a small smile at the compliment, as the eorle placed his hand on her shoulder and turned her bodily towards the horsemen. As the only woman in the raiding force, she was always on her guard against what she knew were unjust taunts or ridicule. But she also knew that her lord valued her abilities and fighting spirit, and a word of praise from the king slayer was always enough to scrub the scowl from her face.

'You see the big man on the dun coloured gelding? The one with the axe head painted on his shield?'

Spearhafoc ran her eyes across the circling horses until she had him. 'Yes, lord.'

Eofer lowered his head to her level and raised his voice above the din of battle. 'Watch as he comes around again.'

The attack had begun as soon as he had regained his position on the high ground. Sweeping down on the beleaguered English force, the riders had drawn up just beyond spear throw and cried their challenges. As the main army echoed their cries at the head of the clearing, the horsemen had turned to canter along the front of the English shield wall, releasing their own daroth before looping back in a great circle. As the riders came back around, they prepared the next throwing spear, the impetus of their ride and the raised position of the riders adding greatly to the distance and power of the throw. Although the darts had only found a home in English wood, the constant need to throw the big boards in the way of each missile was wearing on the man and damaging to the shield, the barbed heads often puncturing the boards and proving difficult to dislodge. With the main attackers already moving down the field, they may not have enough time to chop the shafts from the board face before the final charge crashed into them. Eofer knew that the inability to strike back at their tormentors would sap the spirit of the men of the fyrd, he had to find a way to take a small victory from the situation. The pair watched as the Jute reached the end of the line and tugged at his reins to bring the horse back around for another attack. Eofer stabbed out a finger. 'There!'

The youth gave a grim smile as she understood immediately what her lord wanted from her. Lulled into a sense of complacency by the lack of opposition, this rider had become slapdash with his defence. It would cost him his life.

Fitting an arrow to her bow, the Briton watched as the warrior lowered his shield once again, thundering along the front line as he marked his target and released. She flicked a look and gave a slight nod as Eofer moved away to give her room to take the shot. Curling her fingers around the bowstring, she held the yew stave low as her eyes remained fixed on the target. The warrior released, and his shield snapped back up as he cantered along the English line and arced back to the west. Spearhafoc calmed her breathing and raised the bow as the Jute reached the turning point. Bringing the sinew up to crease her lips, the youth tracked the man's head as he swept back around. At the same spot as before, the shield slipped down once again as he searched for a target for his next missile. Spearhavoc released the string with a soft grunt, and the arrow sped away. Eofer stepped back in, and together the pair watched as the dart dipped below the level of the rider's helm to punch into the gap beside the nasal, the point bursting from the back of the Jute's head a heartbeat later.

Eofer and the duguth cried out as the Jute's hand flew to his face and the horse, no longer under control, bolted across the front of the English position. Despite his terrible wound, it was clear that the man was still alive as he tumbled from the horse's back and jounced along the grass at the feet of the delighted English.

As the men of both sides looked on a salient appeared in the English shield wall, reaching forward like a great steel hand to envelop the agonised victim, and the *here* roared their defiance as spear butts rose and fell, and the man was sent to the gods.

Whether it was responding to witnessing their hearth companion stuck like a boar or not, the death of the rider seemed to be the signal for the horsemen to disengage and wheel away. The army of the Jutes, led by their king, were approaching the dark scab that only hours before had been the magnificent hall of one of his leading jarls, the blackened timbers littering the ground like the bones of a long-dead giant. The meadow shelved gently at that point, and Eofer and his men watched as the Jutes dressed their ranks and prepared for their charge. Free from the confines of the trees, the enemy battle banners unfurled in the breeze, and the sunlight slanted in to pick out the cold glint of shield bosses and the freshly honed blades of spears and axes. Flags and draco of red, gold, and green streamed away to the west as the great white horse hildbeacn of Juteland flew proudly at the centre.

The pause had allowed the men of the English front line to hack at shafts and tease out the spearheads from their shields, and Eofer watched as they reformed and brought their boards together with a clatter. Englishmen began to answer their tormentors. Singly at first—but soon the surrounding air resounded to their own war cries, curses, and insults as they checked their stance, their weapons, or wiped the war-sweat from their palms for the hundredth time that morning.

A brief look towards the north told him that, although the men there were still not in contact with the enemy from the town, large numbers of them had crowded onto the causeway, headed by a knot of seasoned warriors. It was obvious that they were awaiting the main attack to launch their own, and Eofer ordered the nearest men of the fyrd onto the causeway to support Penda's men there. If nothing else they would be able to lend solidity to the position if, as he suspected, it did turn into a savage pushing match. Should the men break or be overwhelmed, the Jutes would fall on their unprotected rear, pouring into the position in an unstoppable tide.

From the high point of the roadway, Eofer ran an experienced eye over his dispositions as the clamour opposite rose to a crescendo and the Jutes, confident in their numbers, prepared to reap a grim harvest of English bodies.

The entire *here* was set and waiting to receive the charge. Penda stood tall beneath the plumes of his boar helm at the centre, flanked by his chosen men, an armoured fist itching to strike. Other men of his father's hearth troop shone like newly driven nails among the russet colours of the fyrdmen as they sought to stiffen the more useful looking or experienced ceorls who made up the remainder of the front rank. Each man there, grim faced and resolute beneath a helm of steel or leather cap, gripping his spear and taking comfort from the press of his neighbour. More fyrdmen backed these up, the line thickening at the points that could be expected to come under the most sustained and ferocious attack, the centre, and flanks.

With a further force filling the first fifty yards of the causeway to their rear, a gap had opened up between both fronts that would enable the eorle to lead the men of his troop quickly across—hopefully snuffing out any signs of an enemy breakthrough before things became critical.

Satisfied he had done all that he could, Eofer glanced back to the front just as a great roar rent the air and the Jutes came on.

THE CHARGE quickly developed into all that Eofer hoped it would be. Made overconfident by their weight of numbers and a night spent at their ale, the Jutes had worked themselves into a frenzy of retribution when they had paused alongside the charred remains of Jarl Wictgils' hall. The bodies of the scouts and their horses remained where they lay from the fighting of the previous evening, and Eofer had watched as Jarl Heorogar led his men across to witness the lacerated remains of his kinsman. Wictgils had been finished off by those within the English ranks who had most reason to hate the man—those ceorls who had lost property and kin in the Danish raids of the previous autumn. Eofer was sure that the man could only have been recognised by the quality of those clothes that remained, after the mail and weapons had been stripped from him by eager hands.

All sense of order quickly dissipated as the Jutes came on at their best pace, and within a few steps the order of the shield wall, so carefully aligned and ordered only moments before, had degenerated into a ragged mass of individuals as the fastest and keenest pulled ahead. At the front of the English position a hundred shafts of ash, their silvered tips flaming as they caught the morning light, pushed proud of the wall as Penda as his men prepared to meet the onslaught. As the first of the enemy reached the foot of the slope and began to scale the camber towards them, Eofer watched as Penda raised his spear and let it drop back into position. It was the sign to those in the rear ranks to let go their daroth, and the eorle watched with satisfaction as the fyrdmen launched the slender javelins over the heads of their companions. The darts arced over and fell among the charging men just as the bottoming out of the slope robbed them of some of their momentum, and a score of them fell to litter the path of those who followed close behind.

The Jutes pushed on and the dark mass of men surged up to the English wall, sweeping out to either flank in a silver flecked tide as the defenders braced and stabbed.

Hemming began to throw his lord anxious glances as he itched to get among the fighting, but, despite the chaotic scrum of the Jute attack, Eofer hesitated. Chewing his lip as he thought, he gave his weorthman a slight shake of his head as his eyes scanned the battlefield.

King Osea had planted his banner opposite the English dragon and surrounded himself with the men of his bodyguard. The gesithas had formed a wall of lime and steel around their lord, and Eofer watched as the war banners of the jarls moved out to the flanks. But it was becoming clearer by the moment, that the best of the Jutish warriors were being held back from the fighting. Suddenly, the flag of Jarl Heorogar peeled away and hurried off towards the river, and Eofer drew Gleaming as the main thrust of the attack revealed itself.

'Oswin,' he snapped out as the men followed his example. 'Stand at my shoulder, but don't get in our way.' He flashed the youth a wink of encouragement. 'We may be busy.' The attack developed at lightning speed and Eofer addressed the men, his voice a snarl, as he prepared to counter-attack. 'Isolate the jarl. I want him!'

As they rushed down from the roadway, Eofer could see that the Jutes had already slammed into the flank of the English shield wall, pushing it back as the warriors there desperately threw themselves bodily into their shields and their feet scrabbled at the turf. There was no time to call the English battle-cry, *out…out…out*, and the men of Eofer's troop tumbled down the slope bellowing the first cries that came into their heads.

Eofer threw his shoulder into his shield as Hemming and Imma Gold moved to his flanks, and within a heartbeat, they had come up to the rear of the English line. A young lad turned and ran past them, his face little more than a gaping maw where his lower jaw had been only moments before, the horror of his plight screaming in his eyes.

The leading enemy warrior was only moments away from breaking the wall, and the thegn fixed his gaze upon him as he threw his shoulder into the boards of his shield and crashed into the rear ranks of the defenders. The men there, unaware of his approach and already desperately trying to push back the attack that threatened to overwhelm their position, were shoved aside as Eofer, sword raised, shield braced, pushed towards the blood-crazed Jute. The giant, made even larger by the pelt of a brown bear that hung at his shoulders, was scything his blade in a deadly arc—cutting a path through the English flank. Other Jutes hugged the riverbank, as they sought to end the battle quickly by rolling up the position from the west.

Within the wedge, the Jutes fought with all the fury of Woden himself, slashing and hacking as Penda's hearth men and farmers were pushed back in a muddle. The line buckled inwards and Eofer saw to his horror that it was a heartbeat away from bursting open like an overripe fruit, spilling death and defeat into the heart of the position. As he reached the fighting and threw himself bodily into the breach, fyrdmen scattered before him as the eorle powered Gleaming down with all of his might, driving his helm into the face of the bear-warrior with a sickening crunch. As his ancestral blade bit deeply into unseen flesh, the eorle dug in his heels and drove the stunned ord back. He stole a look as a gap appeared between them, and was gratified to see the man's face had been transformed into a mash of blood and broken teeth by his strike. Before the big Jute could recover his balance, the English thegn was upon him. Lifting the point of the sword, he drove the blade upwards towards the face of the reeling Jute. To his astonishment, the man saw the strike coming, twisting his head away as the blade skimmed his face and carried on up. But Hemming was there to thrust his sword into the warrior's groin, before shoulder-barging him aside and stepping up with a yell. The bear-man clutched at Eofer's mail as he fell, but he kneed him aside and moved on in the knowledge that Octa, a heartbeat behind him, would finish him off.

Eofer saw a face bob into his vision and he hacked down with his blade, but the press of bodies was growing, and the power was squeezed from the blow. Gleaming bit down into the Jute's shoulder, but the mail held, and the next moment the enemy warrior had whipped up his shield in defence. Eofer winced in pain as the steel bound rim of the board struck his wrist with a sickening crack, knocking Gleaming from his grip. Unable to draw his seax in the mad scrum, the eorle reached out and clutched desperately at his opponent as his sword hand fished desperately for the hilt. As the fingers of his left hand clawed at the snotty wetness of the Jute's face and stabbed at his eyes, his right inched down the lanyard that led from his wrist to the hilt, and his heart leapt as his fingers closed around it. His nails had done their work, and a gap opened up as the Jute took a pace back. Eofer moved forward, driving the hilt of his sword up into the man's jaw again and again as the bone splintered and teeth showered the air.

Imma and Hemming had moved to his side as the enemy began to wilt under the fury of their onslaught, and Eofer looked up to see that Heorogar's fiercest warriors had abandoned the attack and now clustered protectively about their lord. Both sides knew that it was the turning point in the struggle, and the jarl threw the eorle a last long look of loathing before accepting the inevitable, sounding a long falling note on his war horn, abandoning the assault.

As the Jutes backed away, Eofer and his men were left staring at a tree lined riverbank, and he blinked at the sight of a group of swans as they rode the waters of the fjord with a majestic air, watching the madness with casual interest as it unfolded before them.

Oswin was at his side and he threw him a nod of recognition as the fyrdmen began to pour back into the breach and rebuild their wall. His youth, Porta and Rand were nearby and Eofer looked across as men, English and Jute, roared in pain, exultation, or fear. 'You two!' he called. 'Stand here, in the front row.'

The pair hurried across as Eofer's duguth closed protectively about him, and they strode together back to the roadway. A quick headcount told him that all were there, miraculously unscathed, and Imma reached across to pluck something from Eofer's hair, holding it aloft with a look of incomprehension. 'A tooth?'

26

'What do you think, Thrush?'

Hemming blinked the grit from his eyes and stared to the west. 'I think that it is.' He exchanged a look with his eorle, and the first smile that morning began to tug at the corners of his mouth. 'It's still a fair distance away, but it looks like smoke to me.'

Eofer dug his weorthman excitedly in the ribs as his eyes moved back to check on the enemy. 'It looks as if they have noticed, too!'

As they watched, a horseman spurred his mount across to the eastern side of the clearing and sat tall in the saddle as he scanned the distant horizon. The land rose gently towards the tree line there, and the Jute shielded his eyes as he peered west. All at once, he tugged at his reins and cantered across to the place where the white horse banner snapped in the breeze. Eofer gave a low chuckle as he went. 'It looks as though our friend over there agrees with us.'

Men in the Jutish shield wall were beginning to crane their necks as the news spread through their ranks, and moments later a pair of riders galloped away from the rear of the army and disappeared back along the path that led toward The Oxen Way.

As word spread among the exhausted men in the English burh, and they began to understand the situation, Eofer watched as their faces turned and broke into smiles as the electrifying idea that the day might not be their last on Middle-earth began to take root.

As indecision gripped their leaders, the men in the leading ranks of the enemy shuffled away beyond the reach of English spears and awaited their king's response to the new threat.

Eofer's mind raced. He knew that the attacks in the west could very well be the salvation of his force, but equally he knew that he had drawn King Osea and his household warriors to an ideal killing ground. He knew that he must act to keep the king and his finest men away from the army in the west. Every moment that he could hold some of the finest fighting men in the kingdom on this insignificant field would be of inestimable value to Icel and his ravaging army. He turned to his duguth as ceorls moved between the men in the wall with well-earned skins of ale.

'We need to keep them here as long as possible. I am going to challenge their champion to a fight between the armies.'

The men of his hearth troop turned their faces to him in shock. Thrush Hemming was the first to find his tongue. 'No, you're not.' He pointed down at Eofer's swollen wrist. 'How can you fight such a man when you can barely wield a weapon?' Eofer winced as Thrush suddenly shot out a finger and prodded the red and purple swelling. Spearhafoc knew a few of the cunning arts, and she had managed to reduce the worst results of the earlier shield strike by using a poultice of spit-sodden leaves.

It would be enough to enable her lord to continue to swing a sword and handle a spear, but they all knew that the limitations would soon show in a prolonged struggle against a bear shirt.

Eofer determined to overcome their protests as he hefted his spear and exchanged a look with Oswin. 'You remain here with the hildbeacn. Plant it firmly in the soil of our enemies. If they break through, use your spear and keep the flag flying for as long as you can. Remember,' he smiled grimly. 'If you die well, you may get the chance to learn from the word master himself in Valhall.' Oswin nodded wearily, but his eyes were bright. 'I can recite my poem in the hall of heroes just as well as Eorthdraca, lord.'

Imma Gold suddenly cut in. 'I'll do it.' Eofer and Hemming both protested, but the duguth was adamant. He shrugged. 'Only a fool would fight between the lines with that injury, lord, and you have never been a fool before. Your wrist will hold up in the shield wall against regular warriors, but you know as well as I do that a warrior of reputation would spot any weakness in a heartbeat and exploit it mercilessly. The men are in a hard enough place as it is,' he said, 'without watching their eorle being diced up before them.' As Eofer sucked his teeth at the admonishment, Imma turned to Hemming. 'You are weorthman, your place is at your lord's side, especially in a situation like this. Besides,' he winked mischievously at his friend, 'we all know that I am the better man in a fight.'

The wail of a war horn pierced the air, and they looked across at the Jutish host as their leaders began to dress the ranks for another attack.

'It looks as if they have made their decision,' Imma said, 'they want to finish us quickly and be away. If we give them time to think, they will realise that they have enough men to leave a force to pin us here and ride west at the same time. I need to go now.'

Before Eofer could protest, his duguth had hefted his shield and spear and shouldered his way into the ranks of the fyrdmen. 'Come on, Oswin,' he called over his shoulder, 'come and watch a hero fight. You can craft a verse and make me an eorle.'

The youth looked at Eofer and the thegn nodded. 'Take the dragon flag, but leave my banner with Spearhafoc,' he said with a jerk of his head. 'Hurry.'

As Oswin frantically searched out Spearhafoc, Eofer called Grimwulf across.

'Feeling sprightly?'

'Never better, lord,' he said with a wry smile. 'I never thought that I would look back with fondness to the night that I was shipwrecked, but it just might happen today.'

Despite the bone-aching weariness he felt, Eofer gave a snort and pointed to the west. 'You see the tree line there? Do you think that you could make it into the woods before the horses ride you down?'

'Easy, lord.'

'Good, when Imma and Oswin have their attention, I want you to make a break for it. Follow the river to the west and find the ætheling. Tell him what is happening here.'

Imma had already left the safety of the shield wall, and they watched as their friend began to pace the blood-slick grass between the rival hosts as Grimwulf made his way to the western end of the position. An excited buzz came from both sides as the men realised that a challenge was about to be made, and Eofer watched with pride as Imma crossed to the Jutes and stalked the line. The Jutes remained steadfast behind their shields as Imma strode along, pushing against the boards with the point of his spear and clattering the leaf-like blade against the helm of any man who averted his gaze. It was one of the most provocative acts that Eofer had ever witnessed on the battlefield, and within moments one of the enemy had taken the bait.

As Imma shoved against the man's shield, he returned the push with a snarl, and the English watched with mounting excitement as Imma paused and backtracked. As he did so he brought his spear shaft across to strike the man smartly across the side of his helm, and within a heartbeat, they were facing one another, toe-to-toe. With the men of both hosts filling the air with raucous cries of support and encouragement, Eofer watched with pride as his duguth exchanged insults with his foe.

Hemming leaned close, a pensive look on his features. 'I don't like the look of that, something is happening, lord,' he said. 'I have a bad feeling about this. Bring the boys back.'

Eofer raised his brow. 'What's wrong?'

'They don't look as if they are coming down to discuss the rules of the fight,' he said, pointing out a group of men pushing their way through the ranks opposite. 'That looks like Jarl Heorogar and his hearth men.'

Eofer looked and narrowed his eyes in suspicion. Hemming was right, it *was* Heorogar, and despite the distance and the sea of faces that swam between them, their determined movements reeked of aggression.

Hemming spoke again, his voice heavy with concern. 'Call Imma and Oswin back, lord.'

Eofer's gaze took in the rival armies. Both hosts were a seething broth of stabbing spears and snarling faces as they sought to support their respective champion; it would take a clap of thunder to drown them out. Heorogar and his men were close now, there was no way that Eofer could bring support to their brothers in time. He flashed a look at Spearhafoc. 'How many arrows?'

She dragged her gaze away from the confrontation opposite and looked at him in surprise.

He snapped out again. 'How many? Quickly!'

The youth's mouth gaped, but she swung the opening of her quiver forward. 'Just one, lord,' she finally blurted out. 'I was saving it in case I got the chance of a shot at their king.'

Eofer snatched the hildbeacn from the girl and pointed with his sword hand. 'Put it into Imma's shield, now!'

She hesitated, unsure if she had heard him correctly, but he snapped out again and his expression left no room for doubt. *'Now!'*

As Spearhafoc slipped the bow from her shoulder and nocked the arrow, Eofer looked back. The Jutes in the front ranks were beginning to turn as they became aware of the pushing and shoving behind them, but Imma's shield was still facing the English position, and they had a chance. A moment later a rush of air caressed the thegn's ear as the shaft sped away, and he watched anxiously as it cleared the heads of Penda and his men by a hand's breadth and thudded into Imma's board.

The big man took a sideways step at the unexpected jolt to his shield arm, glancing down at the shaft that had appeared there before looking back towards his lord. Even at distance, Eofer could see the look of incomprehension written on his friend's features as he desperately pointed towards the oncoming threat with the shaft of his spear.

At last, Eofer saw the moment when Imma noticed the jostling at his shoulder as Heorogar and his men approached, and he reacted instantly as he understood the danger. With one sweep of his arm, he brought his spear crashing up into the unprotected neck of his adversary. As the man staggered and his hands went instinctively to his throat, Imma danced back and drew his sword with a graceful sweep as a shocked hush descended on both armies. Oswin had yet to develop the instinctive reactions of a warrior faced by sudden, unexpected danger, and Eofer looked on helplessly as his youth stared about him. A moment later, Heorogar burst from the ranks of the Jutes and the English found their voices again as the jarl plunged his spear into the undefended side of the boy. Oswin spun around to face the English wall, and a dark gout of blood spewed forth as his mouth fell open in a rictus of pain and horror. As the spears stabbed out and the youth slumped to the turf, the English looked on helplessly as Oswin bared his teeth in his agony. Despite the pain and fear, the boy recalled his lord's instructions, thrusting the banner high until, with a silvered slash, a sword chopped down to sever his arm at the elbow.

A great roar issued from the watching Engle as their war flag was beaten down into the mud and trampled, as the Jutes advanced over the gore-slick lad and came upon Imma. Penda's voice came above the indignant cries of the men in the shield burh, and despite the desperation that he felt at the sight that was unfolding before him, Eofer recognised the value of the man as he roared an instruction to keep their formation. Penda knew as well as Eofer that the next few moments would determine whether they survived the day or not. If the English broke and chased the killers, abandoning the relative safety of the burh for a fight in the open, they would be quickly surrounded and cut to pieces. For a heartbeat, the front rank of the English wall bowed and splintered as the less disciplined men of the fyrd surged forward—eager to avenge the killing, and snatch back the banner of their nation from the hands of its enemies.

As the war dragon was gathered up and tossed from

spearpoint to spearpoint over the heads of the jeering Jutes, Eofer watched in dread as Heorogar and his men moved to surround his duguth. The way was still open for his friend to beat a hasty retreat back to the safety of the burh, and he recognised the torment between self-preservation and reputation that must be fighting for control. Suddenly, Imma glanced his way, and a knot of emotion came to Eofer's throat as he recognised the warrior's eyes fix upon the burning hart hildbeacn, and follow its staff down to the place where his lord stood with his friends.

Imma and Eofer locked eyes, and the duguth flashed a fatalistic smile as his mind accepted the only honourable decision available to it. A tangible sense of expectation fell upon the men of both armies as they too came to realise they were about to witness the death of an eorle, a hero.

Imma was the first to strike. Throwing his shoulder into the boards of his great shield, he charged into the Jutes who had gathered to his left, barging them aside as he brought his blade swinging down to take the leading warrior just above the knee. As a bloody arc sprayed from the wound, the man went down, his sprawling form adding to the chaos all around. As fast as a snake, Imma had reversed his sword. Now it was scything out to his right as Heorogar led his hearth troop in to the attack. Surprised by the speed of his lone opponent, the jarl barely had time to swing his shield across to deflect the strike aside as, stirred by their man's courage and already inflamed by the fate of the war flag and the youth who had held it, the English host roared their support.

Eofer looked on with a stomach-churning mixture of pride and shame as his duguth fought his final battle. At his side, Hemming sensed his lord's humour, and he leaned in and spoke above the din. 'You share no part of Heorogar's shame, lord. We needed to keep the king here while our lads burned their lands to the west.' Eofer went to reply, but his weorthman anticipated his words and cut him short. 'If you had gone down there, it would have been you now fighting your last battle. If this Heorogar is so blinded by the need to take the blood-price for his kin that he is willing to lay aside his honour and reputation to kill a duguth, what chance would you have had? If you had fallen,' he added sternly, 'either our shield wall would have broken as the men surged forward to take their revenge or the fighting spirit would have deserted them. We've seen that happen before, and you know it to be true.'

The fevered yells that had engulfed the pair suddenly trailed away, and their heads snapped back, already certain of the cause. Imma had taken his first wound, a spear thrust to the back of his thigh and, as the Jute tore the blade free, Imma staggered as the strength deserted his limb. One of his attackers grew overconfident and Imma's blade shot out to take the man in the throat, but the strike had laid him open to a counterattack, and it quickly came. The English fell silent as Heorogar's sword stabbed forward to take the Englishman in the shoulder, and as the strength left his shield arm and the great board dropped to his side, Imma called on the last of his strength to make one final attack. His sword blade flashed silver in the morning light as the eorle struck at the jarl's helm, but his duguth raised their shields to deflect the blow as Heorogar stabbed forward to pierce the Engle's gut. As the swords and spears of the enemy began to rain down on his helpless friend, Eofer searched again for a sign that Icel was near. If Grimwulf hadn't made it through, Imma and Oswin may be merely the first of his band to die that day.

27

Eofer sighed and pushed Hemming away with his shoulder. 'For the gods' sake, Thrush,' he pleaded, 'will you keep still?' His duguth looked sheepish, but his shoulders still dipped, and his spear arm stabbed out at imaginary enemies. 'Sorry, lord,' he replied. 'I can't help it.'

Osbeorn added his voice. 'We are going to have to split up, lord. Give the remaining men a strong point to fall back on.' He held the eorle with his gaze. 'We can't carry on as we have been. While we are fighting desperately to shore up one part of the wall, another will collapse.'

Eofer remained silent as he cast an anxious look across his shoulder to the west. The smoke there was thickening, more and more columns rising into the sky until they merged into a seal grey wall. He muttered under his breath and his men looked away, conscious of the weight of responsibility on the young thegn's shoulders. 'They *must* give way soon.' As the noise of battle roared about them, Eofer spoke again. 'How far away do you think the ravaging is taking place?'

Octa grimaced as he worried his beard; 'a dozen miles or

thereabouts.' He pulled a face as he made a suggestion. 'Jelling?'

Eofer nodded. 'It would make sense. Send men to draw off the wasps and burn the main hive while the defenders are away.' The fear that he had tried to push down deep all day returned with a vengeance. What if the ætheling had always planned to sacrifice them here? Eofer was experienced enough in the ways of war to know that his little band were expendable; it was a real possibility. He suppressed the fear with difficulty. The men looked to him for leadership. If the old hags were hovering about his life thread with their shears, he would go to Woden with his head held high. 'Unfortunately for us,' he joked, 'we were the stick that they used to strike the nest.'

A rumble of grim laughter rolled around the group as the men there reached the same conclusion as their lord. If the ætheling and his army were still that far away, there was little hope that relief would arrive before the desperate knot of defenders were overwhelmed. The Jutes could see the smoke as well as they, and they had attacked with renewed ferocity as they struck back at the only English force within reach, hoping to crush it quickly and move west to confront this new threat that had appeared in their midst.

Osbeorn spoke again. 'Eofer, we can't wait. If we don't go to the fight, the fight will come to us—and soon.'

A last look of regret over his shoulder and Eofer came to his decision. 'No, we stick together. If I am going to Valhall, I am taking you ugly bastards with me,' he smiled. 'I have an idea that may sow some confusion in their ranks and win us a little more time. At the moment it is too easy for them. A short burst of spear-play at the place of slaughter, and then back for a drink and a rest.' The eorle bared his war grin and his men took heart as he pointed deep into the Jutish host with the point of his spear. 'We have yet to avenge our hearth friend. You see that bastard, Heorogar?' he snarled. 'Let's see if we can send him on ahead. He can tell Woden to tap another barrel so that it is ready and waiting for us when we arrive.'

The Jutes had pulled back as they exchanged places with the next wave to batter the English cliff, and the thegn inhaled deeply and took the half dozen paces required to reach the rear of the shield wall. As Osbeorn and Hemming moved to his sides, Octa tucked in behind as the fyrdmen moved aside.

Eofer came abreast of Penda and laid a hand on his shoulder. 'I shall soon be supping ale with my grandfather,' he quipped as his father's weorthman glanced his way in surprise. 'Hold out as long as you can, Haystack must be here soon. See if you can give them a fight to keep the scops busy until the end of days.'

As the big man gave a grim nod, Eofer's eyes searched out Heorogar's banner from among the rest, and his heart leapt as he saw that the tides of battle had swept it closer still. The Jutish line was still in the throes of change as those at the front pulled back, comparing their wounds and turning their backs, confident that no attack would come from the ever shrinking ranks of the English. A line of dead lay between the hosts like wrack on a shore, the stink of blood and shit filling the air there; Grim's tide line awaiting the gulls and crows that circled and called hungrily above.

Eofer picked out the easiest route through the heap of corpses before him and threw his companions a fatalistic smile. 'What's the best way to get into the cold sea?' he said, recalling one of Imma Gold's favourite sayings.

Osbeorn and Hemming answered together, and he could

sense the men returning the smile as they did so. 'Straight in, you bastards!'

As their laughter faded, Eofer burst forth from the shield wall. Five paces, six and then a seventh, and he crashed into the stunned Jutes beneath the rise. His shield slammed into the backs of men as they shrank away from the sudden onslaught, opening up a gap as he brought Gleaming over in a crashing blow on to the shoulder of a panic-stricken warrior. The Jutes parted like ripe barley, and he scythed to the left and right as he reaped the bloody harvest. Within a heartbeat Eofer was deep within the enemy lines, and he sensed Osbeorn and Hemming at his sides, driving them away and moving onward.

He snatched a look and was heartened to see that Heorogar and his men were only a dozen paces away, but they were quicker to recover than most, and tougher too. Already two of the jarl's men were locking shields before their lord as others shoved their countrymen brutally aside, rushing to bolster the defence as the strident blare of war horns floated down from further up the meadow.

All around him, the Jutes were recovering fast. Osbeorn and Thrush Hemming kept to Eofer's side as they began to hack a path through to the jarl, swinging their bloody blades down upon heads and shoulders, driving their foemen before them like geese. Another quick look and the jarl was almost within reach. The pale sunlight glimmered from his boar-crested helm, polished silver against the dun sky. Their eyes met for an instant and Eofer saw fear there, the first he imagined that the man had ever felt, and it gave him heart for the final push. A voice cried out above the noise, loud and close by, and he was confused for a moment before he realised that it was his own. 'There he is! Kill him!'

A warrior came forward, hunched behind a shield, his spear raised as he prepared to stab down at this mad Englishman. Eofer knocked it aside with Gleaming, as a blood reddened spear tip shot past his ear and Octa lunged forward to run the Jute through. It was an attack they had used again and again across the battlefields of the North: Eofer as ord, flanked by the swords of Imma and Hemming with Octa and Osbeorn completing the deadly knot of warriors, keeping the flanks clear with their spears. Even with Imma now supping with the Allfather in Valhall, the formation proved its worth once more. The Jute fell as the spear was ripped clear, twisting in his agony as Osbeorn chopped down with his sword to leave the arm swinging uselessly by a belt of skin and a livid tongue of red flesh.

The mass of bodies at last began to tell, blunting the attack, slowing the advance. As the momentum drained away from the charge, the Engle were brought to a halt, but they stabbed and slashed and the Jutes took a pace back. It was enough. Throwing their shoulders into their shields, they inched forward again, boots slipping and sliding on grass made slick with blood as they battered their way towards the jarl like men wading through the surf.

Seeing the eorle's attack falter and stall, Heorogar seized his chance. Scattering his shield men before him, he came on, raising his own great blade as Eofer, trapped within the whirling mass, hunkered into his shield and braced to receive the blow. As the blade swept down, Eofer threw his shoulder into his board and drove upwards, inside the killing arc. The heavy steel point of his shield boss slammed into the jarl's chest, driving the air from his lungs in an explosive rush and sending the man staggering backwards. Heorogar had seen the threat and tried to pull his sword strike, but both men knew that it was too late, he was committed. Robbed of much of its force by Eofer's counter punch, the jarl's blade glanced off Eofer's helm, hissing past his shoulder and on down his side as the eorle dragged the steel lined rim of his shield up and into the Jute's chin. As Heorogar's head snapped back, Eofer heard the sickening crack as the board splintered teeth and bone. A heartbeat later, his sword had jabbed upwards, aiming to slide beneath the hem of the jarl's war shirt and take him in the belly. But the crush was too great, and the blade was forced down to take the jarl in the thigh. The sword tip dipped beneath the skirt of his byrnie and across, gauging bone as the razor-sharp edge ploughed muscle and sinew and the jarl's screams filled the air. Eofer stood poised for the killing blow as Heorogar clutched at his side and went down. But an instant later his world exploded in light and pain, as the jarl's hearth warriors leapt across the sprawling figure of their lord and slammed him backwards with their shields.

The power of the surge had unseated his helm, and it was Eofer's turn to feel the cold hand of fear clutch at his guts as he blindly raised his shield and braced for the strike that must be a heartbeat away. Twin blows slammed into his shoulder blades and a spark of hope returned as he knew that Octa and Osbeorn had thrown their shields into his back to bolster him. As his composure began to return, he realised that he could still sense the presence of Hemming at his side, and he dragged the rim of his shield across his face and levered the helm away. Crouched behind the board, he shook away the mugginess from his brain as he braced for a follow-up strike but, to his astonishment, the blow never came. Risking a glance to his side, he saw that Hemming was looking away to the west, his mouth working in silent despair as a knot of horsemen broke free from the tree line, couching their spears as they came on.

Ignoring this new threat to their flank, Eofer gripped his friend's sleeve and urged him forward, desperate to take the blood price for their friend Imma before the man who had led his cold-blooded killers escaped once again. A bloody line in the grass led unerringly to the stricken form of Heorogar as his hearth men dragged him towards safety. A river the colour of lead was pulsing from the jarl's thigh to darken the surrounding ground, and a long line of a paler hue hinted at the bone beneath the open flesh. It was a death wound, he was certain, but Eofer wanted more. He had watched the man lead a cowardly attack on a lifelong friend, and he would have his vengeance. 'Come on, Thrush,' he yelled. 'We have him!'

Hemming responded to his lord's words instantly, his head snapping back, and they surged forward together in their death charge. Howling their war cries the pair crashed into the Jutes, shield on shield, bludgeoning them aside, cutting them down as their jarl looked on impotently from the turf. Hemming was joined by Osbeorn and Octa and, as the trio made short work of the remaining Jutes, Eofer glowered at his enemy. As their eyes locked, Heorogar moved his hand across to the hilt of his sword. Eofer aimed a savage kick, and a look of despair crossed his foe's features as the blade spun away, and the jarl realised that the Englishman would deny him a place in Valhall.

Eofer looked down as his duguth backed around him, their weapons ready to stab out at any who came near. He had seen the wolf dancers above the jarl's eye, but it was not enough. 'Wolf brother or not,' he snarled as a look of disgust crossed his features. 'I doubt that Imma wants to drink with you on his death day.' Pinning the jarl's sword arm to the ground with his boot, the eorle snarled again. 'You are not worthy of a place in the hall of the Allfather, go to Hel!' Heorogar's eyes went wide as Eofer's sword point found the soft flesh of his throat and the eorle pushed down. As Gleaming's wide blade slid through tendon and muscle and on into the ground beneath, Hemming spoke at his side, his voice joyful. 'Thank the gods!'

As the last spasms of life left Heorogar, Eofer dragged his eyes away from the twitching figure at his feet as his duguth began to laugh and point. A line of horses galloped across his line of sight, and Eofer instinctively looked back towards the safety of the English shield wall to their rear. Caught in the open by horse warriors in their exhausted state, their lives could be measured in moments. But the eorle blinked again as he saw that the men there were also cheering and laughing, their spears and swords stabbing the air. His duguth were calling out to the riders, throwing their arms around each other and lowering their shields to their sides. Eofer looked back in bewilderment as a horseman reined in and slipped from the saddle before him.

'What's this? No hug for the man who saved your hide?'

A smile began to tug at the corners of Eofer's mouth as his befuddled mind finally recognised that it was Wulf who stood before him, and they threw their arms around each other and laughed like fools as riders thundered around the tiny group.

The brothers watched as the English horsemen rode down the Jutish stragglers before wheeling about to form a protective screen before the weary shield burh at the bridge.

'I have to get back there,' he said. 'They are still fighting on the causeway, they will need help.'

Wulf laughed. 'You still don't realise what is happening here, do you? This is more than just a rescue column. Here,' he said, 'climb on my horse and watch the fun.'

Eofer hauled himself into his brother's saddle and looked across the heads of his old shield hedge. Out beyond the place where Spearhafoc stood resolutely beneath the standard, his burning hart hildbeacn, the last of the Jute attackers were streaming back towards the town as the defenders dropped to the floor in exhaustion.

Switching his gaze to the south, a lone rider sat outlined against the tree line, dazzling in armour and grim helm that shone like winter ice. Sat astride a magnificent war horse, the warrior's own raven war flag writhed in the fitful breeze and Eofer recognised the horseman immediately, watching as the ætheling raised a war horn and blew again. Shining Mane had pulled the sun to its zenith, the shadows of that interminable morning had been chased away, and the eorle looked on with a rising sense of excitement as the tree line too began to shimmer with light. Within moments the spectral glimmer slowly hardened into the figures of hundreds of steel-clad warriors, thegns, men of the shires, as they strode purposefully forward in battle array to form their ranks in the lee of their leader.

As the new English shield wall formed at the head of the field with a clash of lime on lime, the Jutes clustered protectively about their king and hurried forward to throw their line across the narrowest part of the clearing.

Before they were set in their defences, an English champion strode free of the host and shook his spear at the enemy. The sun chose that moment to break free of the clouds, bathing the warrior in its glow, as Eofer looked on in admiration. As the silvered plates of the man's helm shone in the light, the figure of a boar, a ruddy flash of bristles sprouting from its back like a hedge of spears, stood out boldly above. Thrown over a shirt of mail, a heavy cloak of bearskin lay on the warrior's shoulders, the gold, and garnet pin that fastened it sparkling like a dagger against the tawny pelt. As the Jutes shuffled into line, the hero beat his chest, raising his spear and shield as the haunting cry of his challenge washed across his fiend.

As the hail bled away, the English line moved forward, throwing their shields before them as they began to call the barritus, the war challenge of the northern folk. Like the distant roll of thunder that heralded a summer storm, the cry slowly rose with each step taken until, reflected and amplified by the wall of shields raised before them, the war cry boomed across the field.

'Unnsh...aaah...ooosh!'

The Jutes set up their cry in response, but their numbers were fewer and, although their hearts were trim, a half day of battle play had sapped at their strength. Faced now with a new foe confident in their arms and numbers, the Jutish reply petered out as the English bear-man stalked the ground before them, calling and pointing out to individuals in their ranks in challenge.

Eofer's eyes widened, the battle thrill coursing his veins again as the ætheling's champion spun and danced, throwing his head back with a growl as he called on the Allfather to send the bear spirit that would render him invincible. As other eorles came forward, wolf-men and boar-men, to spin and dance, Eofer was thrilled to hear the barritus echoed by those to his rear. Despite the trials of the day his men, be they hearth warrior or fyrdman, ceorl, farmer, bowyer, woodsman, all gripped their spears tightly and prepared to go again.

The English battle line moved forward once again and, as the barritus trailed away, the massed ranks beat spear shaft on shield and thundered out the age-old chant.

'Ut!... Ut!... Ut!'

As the cry was taken up by the men at the bridge, Eofer noticed the shadowy shapes of riders moving among the woods that flanked the clearing. Wulf noticed the look of concern that swept across his brother's face and leaned close as the pre battle noises roared around them like an autumn gale. 'Have no fear, brother, the horsemen are ours. King Eomær wants a ghost army,' he explained as he indicated the Jutes with a flick of his head. 'The only choice they have, is whether they try to earn a place at the benches of Valhall today or live awhile longer and go to await the end of days in Hel's chill hall.'

Eofer raised his brow in surprise. The songs told of the last time that a ghost army had been arrayed to watch over the border lands along the River Egedore, in the time of King Offa. It was powerful spell-work, and the eorle found that he was thrilled and unnerved in equal measure that he would get to witness such a thing in his time.

At the head of the field the war horn sounded its note a last time and the flags of the English dipped in response. A heartbeat later, a roar split the air as the massed ranks surged forward and cascaded down the slope.

28

Ena placed the pitchers of ale on the table with a clack and threw them a smile. 'Pickled eggs, boys? They are nice and fresh.'

The group turned and looked at Osbeorn to a man, their expressions bright with anticipation. He looked up and grimaced.

'No, not for me thanks, Ena,' he answered. 'I doubt that my arse would thank me.'

The ale wyf narrowed her eyes and pulled a face, before deciding that she didn't really want to discover the answer to the question that was forming in her mind. The momentary image that had appeared there had been more than enough. 'Suit yourself,' she said after a pause, 'although I tend to find that most people prefer to eat them. Mind you,' she added, glancing across the packed room with a look of disdain, 'you can always go and join them if you like *that* sort of thing.'

As the men of Eofer's troop laughed into their ale, they looked across to the source of Ena's ire. A group of warriors had formed a circle, arms entwined as they belted out another verse. The accent placed their origin in the south of the country, and Eofer called across to his newest youth as the song rolled around the room. 'Grimwulf, you are from their part of Engeln. What are they singing about?'

The youth was chuckling at his countrymen's antics, and he replied with a sidelong glance at Spearhafoc. 'It's an old favourite of the men who work the River Egedore, lord,' he cried above the din. 'It's about a woodsman who keeps putting his finger in a woodpecker's hole. It can go on for quite some time,' he said with a smirk.

Ena shook her head and sighed. 'Mercians, bloody southerners. No wonder they are kept down on the border, away from decent folk.' She threw a parting comment over her shoulder as she forced her way through the throng. 'There's too much Saxon in them if you ask me.'

They laughed again, but Eofer quietened as the sound washed around him, and he decided that the time was right. They had been at their cups since early afternoon as they celebrated both the victorious campaign in Juteland and their part in it. The marches had been put to fire and sword, their army destroyed. King Osea himself was held captive in Eorthdraca, not half a mile from where he sat. The fleet had harried the ports and towns all along the western coast, and his family were safely away. His father's ship master had returned with the news that he had escorted the *Skua* to within sight of the Geatish coast. A guard ship had set out from Marstrand at their approach, and the English snaca had dipped its flag in recognition and bore away. Great events were afoot, and the Geats would be anxious for news, but they would have to await events. Sailor's mouths flapped like sails in a gale and the stakes were just too high for English plans to leak out, even unwittingly, from the mouths of friends. No, he knew. With Astrid and Weohstan safe under the protection of her brother, King Heardred, he could concentrate on the war that would start within days.

As the laughter died away, Eofer rapped the tabletop with his knuckles and waited for quiet. They hushed immediately and turned their eyes to their lord. As another roar of laughter carried across from the fireside, he ran his eyes across the men of his hearth troop and began.

'We have won a great victory, but the war has just begun. Soon we will move to smite our greatest fiend, Hrothgar's Spear-Danes. They have already discovered that to attack the English is to invite fire and steel into your own land.' The warriors nodded earnestly as they thought back on the sight of Heorot in flames on its high mound, the hall guard slain or fleeing before their swords. Eofer lowered his voice. 'We have already lost friends, and we shall lose more before this thing is done.' He swept them with his gaze, and they firmed their jawline, resolute. 'Fill your cups now and drink to our friends in Valhall, for they will be in no other place. Recall their faces as I say their names and honour their memory.'

As an eorle and a man of reputation, Ena had served his drink in a horn, and he raised it now as he began.

'Æsc—wæs hæl!'

The men of the troop brought their cups together and thundered the reply.

'Æsc—drinc hæl!'

'Oswin silk-tongue—wæs hæl!'

'Oswin silk-tongue—drinc hæl!'

The noise trailed away and Eofer paused as he refilled his horn. As he glanced up, he saw for the first time that the men who had crowded the ale hus had quietened and turned his way, charging their cups as they awaited the name to come. The tale of Imma's death on the field beside The Crossing had swept the

English army as they had driven their captives back across the border into Engeln. All knew that the duguth had ample time to escape the treacherous assault by Jarl Heorogar and his men, but had chosen to stay and die with the honour that his opponents had lacked. His sacrifice had restored the will to resist in a flagging English defence and allowed Grimwulf the chance to escape and link up with the ætheling's army, bringing swift retribution down on the Jutish king and sealing his fate.

Eofer choked back a knot of emotion as he raised the horn, and a calm descended on the room as the action was mirrored by scores of hands.

'Imma Gold... Goldy,' he cried as he fought to keep a tremor from his voice. 'Breaker of shield walls and women's hearts. My friend. *Wæs hæl!*'

Tight smiles came as he said the words, and the men attempted to lift the roof from its rafters as they belted out the reply.

'Imma Gold—*drinc hæl!*'

Eofer threw back his head and drained the horn as the men in the room stamped out a beat on the floor with their boots and chanted the English war cry.

'Ut!... Ut!... Ut!...'

Wiping his beard on his sleeve, the eorle began to feel overcome by the emotion of the moment. Swinging his legs from the ale bench, he hauled himself to his feet and made his excuses. 'I am going to get some air,' he said. Slipping the purse from his belt, he caught Ena's eye and tossed it across. 'I pay for the ale and food under this roof tonight. Give the men anything they want.'

As a deafening cheer rent the air, Hemming rose and followed his lord through the sea of smiling faces and out into the dusk. They paused on the road outside and hungrily sucked in the cool air, their minds clearing slowly as the heady fog of ale fumes and men left them.

Eofer indicated the great hog-backed silhouette of Eorthdraca glowering over the town with a jerk of his head. 'Come on, Thrush,' he said. 'Let's take a walk.'

Hemming had picked up a gallon of ale as he moved through the Barley Mow, and they took turns to gulp from the tap as they walked. The air was crisp, but it had already lost the savage bite of the northern winter, and the first green shoots had appeared in the hedgerows and swards around Sleyswic. The guards at the gate smiled in welcome as they came up, their smiles broadening as Hemming passed the barrel around and shared a joke. Eofer walked through as the men wished each other good cheer, pausing before the Jutish captives as he contemplated their fate. Corralled in a vast open pen, their wyrd, he knew, was upon them. Their fate was grim, and to his surprise he found that he pitied the men who had tried so hard to kill them all on the meadow beside the wreck of Wictgils' hall.

Hemming came through the gateway and Eofer called across. 'Here, Thrush. Toss me the ale.' A guard sensed what he was about to do, and he took half a pace forwards before he realised the identity of the man who had appeared from the gloom. As the sentinel turned and walked slowly away, Eofer called the nearest Jute to him. 'Here,' he said, 'share this with your friends.'

The man unwound his arms and reached forward, hesitant, fearing a trick, but his eyes widened as he felt the weight of the thing. 'Thank you, lord,' he said, 'for your kindness.' Eofer shrugged and moved away. Another voice came from the gloom. 'What's to become of us, lord?' He answered without breaking his stride as the sight of the hate filled faces that had cheered on the death of his friends came back to him.

'Enjoy the ale,' he said before lowering his voice to a murmur, 'it will be your last.'

Passing through the palisade, they mounted the steps of King Eomær's hall and paused at the doorway. Hemming gave a soft chuckle and plucked at his lord's sleeve. 'Come on Eofer,' he said with a smile, 'we don't need to hear this one. We were there.'

Broad smiles illuminated the faces of the king's gesithas as they realised the identity of the man before them, and one of the guards motioned towards the great doorway with his spear. 'You should be inside, lord. The scop is the best that you will hear.'

Eofer nodded. 'I know. I heard him tell this tale before, in the hall of another king.'

The pair paused for a moment as the words of the poet echoed around the hall and their minds drifted back to that fateful fight.

> 'Before he could move, the lord of the Shylfings was upon him.
> Geat and Engle alike marvelled that they could witness such a thing as the old grey-hair, gory from his wound, fought back all the harder.
> He did not withhold the blow. The wælcyrge could wait awhile yet!
> The blade flashed down, a thunderbolt worthy of the red bearded one.
> Wulf fell, his helm divided, blooded and gory, his head bowed.
> But it was not his doom!'
> 'For, seeing his brother down, his kith and kin lying among the slain, Eofer stepped up.

> He did not care for his life, but thrust forward
>> where the fight was hardest.
> Astride his brother, one blood and one bone,
>> he stood, shielding him from the death
>> blow.
> Ongentheow faltered, and Eofer seized his
>> chance.
> Advancing furiously, he brought blood-worm,
>> that ancient blade, slashing down,
>> smashing murderously at the royal helm,
>> cleaving it asunder.
> There fell the king, at the head of his troop.
> No-man can say that the shepherd of the
>> shylfings turned from the strife and
>> sought the wildwood, looking to save his
>> life.
> Thaet waes god cyning!'

Two kings had fallen in battle that day, and the man who had plucked the king helm of the Geats from the mud—the same man who had given him his wife—now too lay hacked into gore down in Frankland. Eofer walked away, voicing a lament as the poet carried on. 'It's a pity that Oswin missed his chance to learn from the king's scop.'

A voice answered from the shadows, and Eofer smiled as he recognised it at once.

'From what I hear of his death, Oswin is likely to be learning his craft from the word master himself in Valhall.'

'Maybe he is supping from the mead of poetry itself,' Hemming suggested as they walked across.

The three stood in silence for a moment as they looked out across the waters of the Sley. The moon had risen to paint the surface of the waters with its silver glow, and Icel shook his head. 'Such a sight,' he breathed. 'That we should live at such a time!'

Below them, the masts and hulls of the English fleet slid back into shadow as high-torn clouds drove from the west.

'You know,' the ætheling said. 'I heard that a man wagered that he could cross the Sley from bank to bank by leaping from one deck to another. That's how many ships have already answered the war-sword.'

Eofer looked at Icel in astonishment. 'A man crossed from bank to bank without getting wet?'

Icel looked at him with a twinkle in his eye. 'Don't be silly. They managed to fish the fool out just before he went under for the final time, but that's not the point,' he said with a smile. 'He thought that he could, even if his judgement may have been slightly impaired by the amount of ale he had supped.'

The three warriors shared a laugh as Icel passed around the cups. Points of light began to spark into life in the fields below Eorthdraca as the men of the army settled in for the night. Within a short time, the land surrounding Sleyswic mirrored the star speckled sky above.

Icel moved between Eofer and Hemming as they drank in the sight and clapped a palm on each man's shoulder. 'The army are set, the wind is in the west.'

A thunderclap of sound carried through from the great hall doors as warriors bellowed their war cries and beat the tables with their fists. Icel's eyes flashed in the night, and a chill ran down Eofer's spine as he thought he caught the savage glare of the wolf there.

'My father has risen to speak. Whet your blades and gather your men about you,' he growled. 'We have Danes to hunt.'

AFTERWORD

As far as we can tell, at this distance in time, the decade that began in 520 AD appears to have been a crucial point in the birth of the nation that later came to be called England. The later kings of Wessex certainly took the arrival of Cerdic and his son Cynric as the beginning of their dynasty, but the dates given in the Anglo-Saxon Chronicle, which began to be compiled during the time of Ælfred in the later ninth century, give us a confusing picture at best. Cerdic's landing appears twice within the narrative, once in 493 and again in 514, and both descriptions are very similar. Some scholars have taken the latter to be a duplication by a later scribe, but I decided to use this discrepancy to my advantage. By making Cerdic, a Briton driven from his land in the civil war that followed the death of Arthur, I could easily explain this possible double entry. Cerdicsford, the name of the battle site, lies at a strategically important junction on the River Avon, and it seemed perfectly possible that more than one battle could be fought here. What's more, many historians believe that the return of Cerdic happened later than the dates in the Chronicle, even as late as the early 520's. Many also believe that King Eomær of

Afterword

the Engles led his people to Britain during this decade. Modern scholarship is beginning to chip away at the traditional view of Anglo-Saxon conquerors replacing and driving out indigenous Romano-Britons with a far more complex and, I think, likely scenario.

Because of these discrepancies in the dating of even major events, I thought that it would be helpful to provide the timeline here within which I have set both this new series and my earlier series, Sword of Woden.

470's: The 'king' of British Dumnonia, Riothamus, extends his control overseas to include the territory of Armorica, an area of Gaul with long-standing trade and cultural links to that part of Britain, dividing the region into Domnonee and Cornouaille to reflect the divisions found within British Dumnonia. Large numbers of settlers and troops cross the channel, either to defend the area against the turmoil within Gaul or take advantage of the chaos and extend the borders of their new land of Bro Gwereg.

500: The Battle of Mons Badonicus/Mount Badon. The Britons under Arthur defeat the Anglo-Saxons in a decisive battle that, according to the British writer Gildas who claims to have been born in the same year as the great battle, ushered in a period of peace that lasted 'a generation'.

520: The death of Arthur at the Battle of Camlann. Arthurian forces under Cerdic and others are defeated and driven into exile to Bro Gwereg. Hythcyn becomes King of Geats following a coup in Geatland. The Swedes sensing weakness invade, but are repulsed at the Battle of Sorrow Hill.

521: A combined Geatish/English army defeats the Swedes in the fighting at Ravenswood. The English thegn, Eofer, kills the Swedish King Ongentheow and Hygelac becomes King of Geats following the death of his brother, Hythcyn.

523: Cerdic and his son Cynric return to Britain and defeat a rival force at Cerdicsford. On the continent, the Geats under King Hygelac raid the lands of the Frisians and Francs. Following a successful summer raiding they are overtaken by a powerful Frankish army and in the ensuing battle Hygelac is killed and their fleet driven off.

524: The migration of the English from their continental homeland of Engeln to what we now call East Anglia under the leadership of King Eomær and his son Icel.

If not a 'Dark Age' exactly, the various histories, mostly written hundreds of years after the events themselves, are nothing if not a confused mishmash of semi-legendary figures and battles. The above timeline at least gives a coherent and logical order of events within which to base my narrative, and if I am wildly out then at least it will be difficult to prove!

In many ways, the area that began as the civitas of the Belgae, and later became the kingdom of Wessex, appears central to this process. This was the area after all that appears to have been crucially important during the earlier Roman invasion and occupation of the isles. As the most 'Romanised' part of the British Isles, it would have been natural for this area to employ Germanic troops, both as læti, armed war bands, and foederati, the settlement of family groups in border areas in order to bolster their defences. This was common practice in the later years of the Empire, so its use by the British authorities would be seen as 'business as usual',

Afterword

both by themselves and the incoming settlers. In this novel, the Gewisse are an example of læti, a powerful armed force placed by the British Atrebates tribe to protect their northern border and control the important trade routes of the Icknield Way and River Thames. Further south Cerdic's enemy, Natan, settled Jutes, a seafaring people, as foederati to control the area of the Solent, the southern border of their lands.

It's becoming increasingly difficult to see the creation of Wessex as the work of Germanic settlers alone. Later kings of Wessex claimed their descent and right to rule from their relationship to Cerdic, right up to Edgar the Ætheling in 1066, and the lists of the early kings of Wessex are strewn with what can only be described as British names. Cerdic itself is a later form of the British name Caratacus, the name of the great leader of the British resistance to Rome following the invasion in the first century, and the following kings in the Wessex king list, Cynric, Ceawlin and Coel all bear British names. Cerdic Strongarm was a historical figure known within the British settlements of Bro Gwereg, and it was a nice fit with my desire to show him as a Belgic leader who was returning home to re fight a civil war at home.

I decided to have King Eomær of Engeln leading the Engles across the North Sea from their continental homeland on present day Jutland in the year 524. This seemed to be about the midpoint of the various estimates made by later historians, and fitted in well with my timeline. The Venerable Bede, a Northumbrian cleric writing in the eighth century, stated that the area that was still called Engeln in his day was emptied by the migration, and through my research for this book I have come to the conclusion that this was no exaggeration. Almost any attempt to discover the history of place names on the Jutland peninsula gets no further than the later Viking Age. This allowed me a licence to import names from

Afterword

Anglo-Saxon England. Harrow is the ancient English name for a temple, *Hearg*, and it seemed the perfect name to use for the island that contained the famous votive site at Gudme, which I Anglicised to Godmey. On the same island the modern town of Odense takes its name from the Norse god Odin, so it was natural to change this to Wodensburh to reflect the earlier English name for the god. Like many early peoples, the English raised earthworks to mark the borders of their territory if no obvious physical feature existed or, more commonly, to link those that did. The feature that I have called Grim's Dyke in Engeln is such an earthwork, known today as the Olgerdiget. Dendrochronological dating of the oak timbers used in its construction place its origin as far back as the first century, and it is commonly held to mark the earliest border between the continental Angles and the Jutes. Likewise, the earthworks known as Fleama and Miceldic in Anglia are known today as Fleam Dyke and Devil's Dyke and mark an early border of the East Anglian kingdom, stretching between the wetlands of the fens to the west and the heavily forested belt to the east.

If anything illustrates the difficulties faced by the historian in piecing together a cohesive narrative for this time, the events surrounding the conflict between the Danes and the Heathobeards is as good as any. In this tale, I have largely followed the progression of events as laid out in the old English epic, Beowulf, to tie in neatly with the narrative in my earlier books. The possibly older English poem Widsith contains the passage that I quoted on the frontispiece to this book, with Ingeld and his War-Beards being repulsed in the hall of the Danish King Hrothgar itself. The Gesta Danorum, the 'Deeds of the Danes' written in the twelfth century, contains no less than three accounts of the events and all differ to a greater or lesser degree, and there are others. The

Afterword

difficulties of the historian are of course a novelist's opportunity, and I grabbed at the chance for Eofer to rescue his brother and fire Heorot, the Danish hall at Hleidre of Beowulf fame, the spark that would soon flare into the war of Fire & Steel.

Those who have read my earlier books will have already come across the exploits of Eofer and his family. Eofer first appears at his betrothal to Hygelac's daughter, Astrid, and later, along with his father Wonred and brother Wulf, he is part of a joint English/Geat expedition to Swede Land in which he kills the Swedish king, Ongentheow, the deed that leads to his nickname of king's bane. This book, Fire & Steel, is in many ways a continuation of that earlier series. In it, Beowulf kills Grendel in 521 and the series ends with the historically attested raid by the Geats to Frisia in 523. All the dates dove-tailed nicely together, allowing Eofer's rescue of his brother-in-law to follow on from the ending of the last tale in that series, Dayraven. Changing the main character from Beowulf to the Englishman, Eofer, allowed me to move the main focus of the new series from events in sixth century Scandinavia, across the North Sea to Britain at the time when the first English kingdoms were beginning to form. Eofer's kinship with the Geatish royal family will enable me to involve him and his war band in events throughout the North. There is a wealth of information contained within the Beowulf poem and the Scandinavian sagas and histories that can be brought into the story that will enable me to widen the scope of the books as they progress to encompass the whole of the northern world. Although it is unlikely that Beowulf himself actually existed, the other principal characters contained within these books certainly did. Hygelac and Heardred were kings of Geats in the early sixth century and the burial mound of King Ongentheow, the king of Swedes

Afterword

killed in battle by Eofer, can still be seen in Uppsala today. Another book written in England and dated to the later years of the sixth century known as the *Liber Monstrorum*, tells us that Hygelac's bones were 'of wondrous size' and that they were still to that day 'preserved on an island in the Rhine, where it flows into the sea, and they are exhibited as a marvel to travellers coming from afar.' Whether these bones were the remains of King Hygelac or Beowulf, it certainly illustrates the sheer physical size of the Geat ruling class. The wars and alliances contained within the Beowulf poem were very real, and removing the character Beowulf from the storyline will remove any fantasy element, grounding this later series in what facts we do know of that far-off time.

I will address the hoary old question of ships with sails for the last time here. Again, those who have read my earlier books will know that I, along with an increasing number of experts, believe that the ships that carried the Engles, Saxons and others southwards to raid and settle must have carried sails. Sails had been in use in the Mediterranean for thousands of years, and it seems beyond ridiculous that seafaring peoples would not use a means of propulsion that they must have been aware of. Greek and Phoenician traders were visiting Northern Europe in ships with sails at least one thousand years before the events in this book, and the Roman fleets that plied the North Sea certainly carried sail. It seems too fantastic to imagine that the Roman and post Roman forces that were stationed at the forts that lined both sides of the North Sea and English Channel, the so-called Saxon Shore forts, would have been unable to sweep the seas clear of raiders whose ships were crewed by exhausted men sweating over banks of oars for days on end.

In the following book, Gods of War, the full might of King Eomær's army makes a pre-emptive strike against the

Danes as the English people begin to move west across the sea.

Cliff May
East Anglia
January 2016

CHARACTERS

Anwyl—Cerdic's helmsman.

Astrid—Daughter of King Hygelac of Geatland, wife of Eofer.

Bassa—A youth.

Beornwulf—A youth.

Beowulf—Ealdorman of Wægmundings, kinsman of King Heardred of Geatland and Eofer king's bane.

Brecca—Eofer's British *thræl*.

Cerdic strongarm—Belgic exile, a Briton.

Coelwulf—An English thegn.

Crawa—A youth, twin to Hræfen.

Characters

Cynric—Son of the British leader, Cerdic strongarm.

Eahlswith—King Eomær's cwen.

Eofer Wonreding, king's bane—Son of Wonred, brother of Wulf.

Eomær Engeltheowing—King of the English.

Finn—A youth.

Freawaru—Daughter of King Hrothgar of the Danes, betrothed to King Ingeld of the War-Beards.

Frithgar—Ealdorman Wonred's duguth.

Grimma—Leader of the English bowmen.

Grimwulf—An English *thræl*, freed in Daneland. Joins Eofer's youth.

Heardred Hygelacson—Son of King Hygelac of Geatland. Inherits the throne on his father's death in Frisland. Eofer's brother-in-law.

Hræfen—A youth, brother of Crawa.

Heorogar—A Jutish jarl.

Hrethmund—A Jutish jarl.

Hrothgar Halfdanson—King of Daneland.

Characters

Hrothwulf Halgason—Nephew of King Hrothgar.

Icel Eomæring—English ætheling, son of King Eomær.

Imma Gold—Eofer's duguth.

Ingeld Frodason—King of the Heathobeards – the War-Beards.

Octa—Eofer's duguth.

Osbeorn—Eofer's duguth.

Osea—King of Jutes.

Osric—A shipwright at Strand.

Osgar—The chief guda at Sleyswic.

Oswin word-poor—A youth.

Penda—A duguth, Wonred's *weorthman.*

Porta—A youth.

Rand—A youth.

Sæward—Eofer's steersman. A duguth.

Spearhafoc/Dwynwyn—Sparrowhawk, Eofer's British shield-maiden.

Starkad Storvirkson—A Heathobeard warrior.

Thrush Hemming—Eofer's *weorthman*, his senior duguth.

Ubba Silk-beard—A Danish war lord.

Weohstan—Young son of Eofer and Astrid.

Wictgils—A Jutish jarl.

Withergeld—A Heathobeard warrior.

Wonred—Folctoga and father of Eofer and Wulf.

Wulf Wonreding—Son of Wonred, brother of Eofer.

PLACES/LOCATIONS

The River Afen—The River Avon, Wessex, England.

The River Aldu—The River Alde, Suffolk, England.

The Bight—Flensburg Firth.

The River Blithe—The River Blyth, Suffolk, England.

Gwened—Vannes, Brittany, France.

Bro Gwereg—A British kingdom in present day Brittany, France.

Bunoncga-haye—Bungay, Suffolk, England.

Cerdicsford—Charford, Hampshire, England.

Clausentum—A Roman fort at the head of Southampton Water, England.

Places/Locations

Cnobheresburg—The Roman Saxon shore fort of Garianonum, now known as Burgh castle, Norfolk, England.

The Crossing—Vejle, Jutland, Denmark.

The River Egedore—River Eider, Schleswig-Holstein, Germany.

Fleama—Fleam dyke, Cambridgeshire, England.

The River Gipping—The River Orwell, Suffolk, England.

Godmey—Gudme, Fyn, Denmark.

Grantebrycge—Cambridge, Cambridgeshire, England.

Grim's Brook—River Vida, Jutland, Denmark.

Grim's Dyke—Olgerdiget, near Aabenraa, Jutland, Denmark.

Great Belt—The channel between Fyn and Zeeland.

Harrow—*Hearg*/temple, now the Danish island of Fyn.

Hereford—Rendsburg, Schleswig-Holstein, Germany.

Hesselo—A small island north of Zeeland, Denmark.

Hleidre—Lejre, Zeeland, Denmark.

Hroar's Kilde—Roskilde, Zeeland, Denmark.

Places/Locations

Hwælness—Whale Ness—Sankt Peter-Ording, Schleswig-Holstein, Germany.

Iceni Hill Way/Great South Road—Icknield Way, southern England.

King's River—Kongeaen River, Jutland, Denmark.

Little Belt—The channel between Jutland and Fyn in present day Denmark.

Miceldic—The Great Dyke — Devils Dyke, Cambridgeshire, England.

The Muddy Sea—Nordfriesisches Wattenmeer, Schleswig-Holstein, Germany.

Needham—Nydam Mose archaeological site, near Sonderborg, Jutland, Denmark.

North Strand—Nordstrand—Wattenmeer, Nordfriesland, Germany.

Old Ford—Hollingstedt, Schleswig-Flensburg, Germany.

The Oxen Way—An ancient roadway, still known today as the Ochsenweg, running approximately north-south the length of the Jutland peninsula.

Porta's Mutha—Portsmouth, now Friedrichstadt, Nordfriesland, Germany.

Silt—Sylt, Nordfriesland, Germany.

Places/Locations

The Sley—Schlei, Schleswig-Flensburg, Germany.

Sleyswic—Schleswig, Schleswig-Flensburg, Germany.

Sorbiodunum—Old Sarum, Wiltshire, England.

Strand—Suderhafen, Nordstrand, Germany.

Suthworthig—Eckernforde, Schleswig-Holstein, Germany.

The Ringing Stones—Stonehenge, Wiltshire, England.

Theodford (1)—Kappeln, Schleswig-Flensburg, Germany.

Theodford (2)—Thetford, Breckland, Norfolk, England.

Thunor's Leah—Thorsberger Moor, near Suderbrarup, Schleswig-Flensburg, Germany.

The River Trene—River Treene, Schleswig-Holstein, Germany.

The River Udsos—The River Ouse, East Anglia, England.

Vectis/Ictis—The Isle Of Wight, England.

Venta Belgarum/Cair Guinntguic—Winchester, Hampshire, England.

The River Wahenhe—The River Waveney, Suffolk, England.

Wodensburh—Odense, Fyn, Denmark.

ALSO BY C.R.MAY

GODS OF WAR

THE SCATHING

BLOODAXE

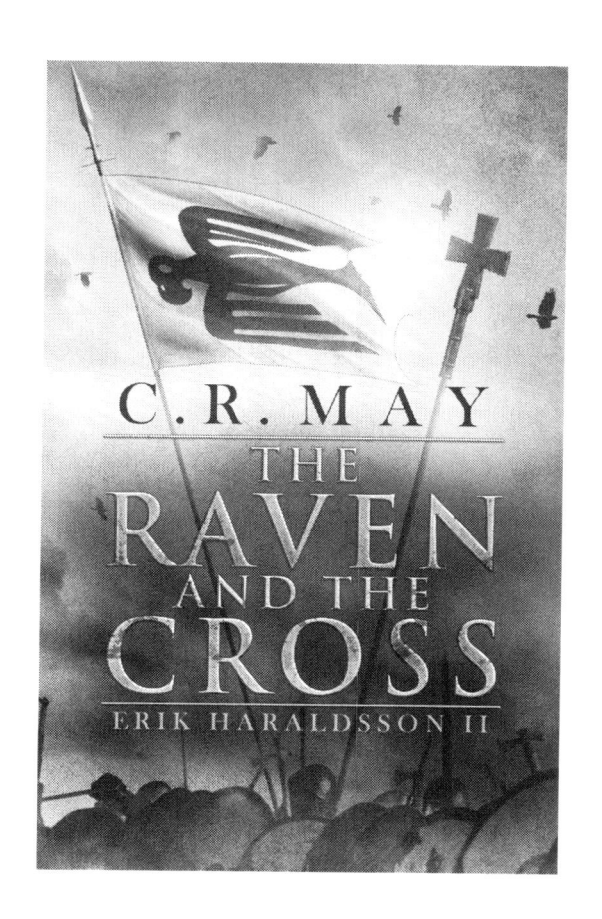

THE RAVEN AND THE CROSS

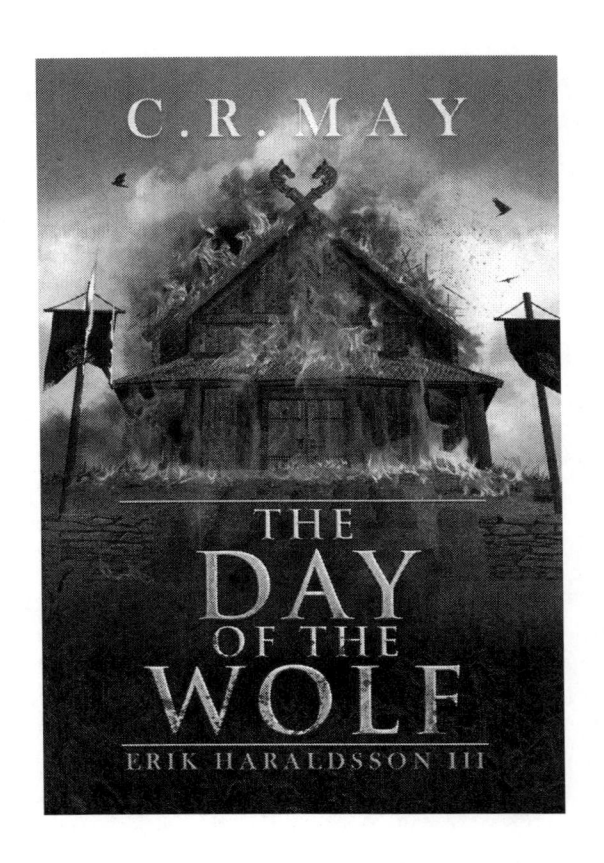

THE DAY OF THE WOLF

SPEAR HAVOC

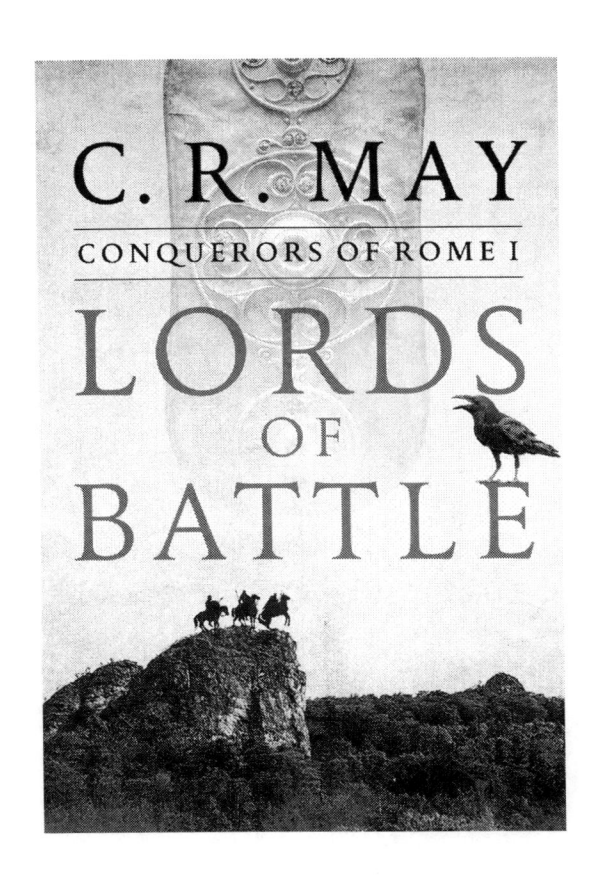

LORDS OF BATTLE

NEMESIS

SORROW HILL

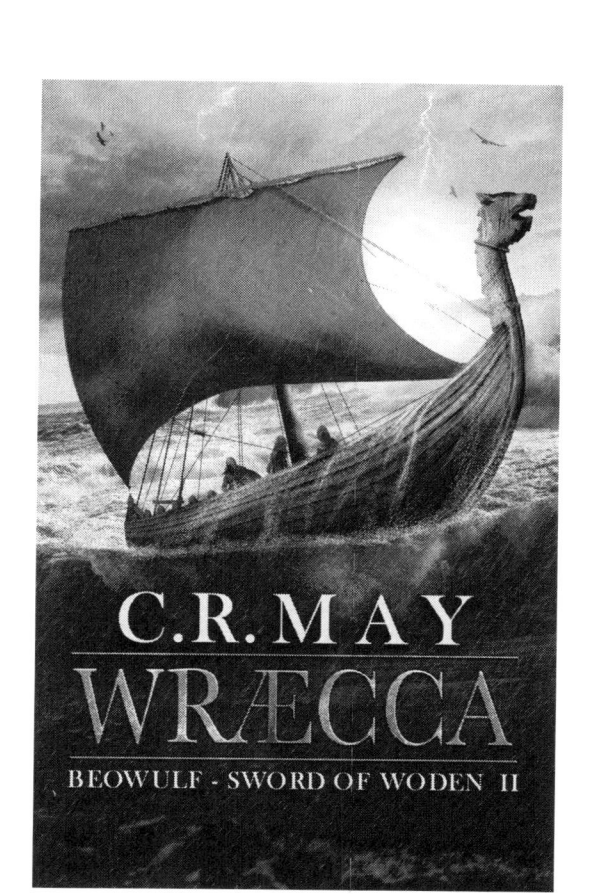

WRÆCCA

MONSTERS

DAYRAVEN